hummingbirds

A Novel

hummingbirds

JOSHUA GAYLORD

HARPER

An Imprint of HarperCollinsPublishers
www.harpercollins.com

HarperCollins books may be purchased for educational, business, or sales promotional use. For information, please write: Special Markets Department, HarperCollins Publishers, 10 East 53rd Street, New York, NY 10022.

FIRST EDITION

Excerpt from "A Modest Proposal" from *Collected Poems* by Ted Hughes. Copyright © 2003 by The Estate of Ted Hughes. Reprinted by permission of Farrar, Straus and Giroux, LLC, and Faber and Faber Ltd.

Designed by William Ruoto

Library of Congress Cataloging-in-Publication Data
    Gaylord, Joshua A. (Joshua Alden)
    Hummingbirds : a novel / by Joshua Gaylord.—1st ed.
        p.   cm.
    ISBN: 978-0-06-176901-6
    1. Preparatory school students—Fiction. 2. Teacher-student relationships—Fiction. 3. Preparatory schools—Fiction. I. Title.
PS3607.A9859H86   2009
813'.6—dc22

2008055456

09 10 11 12 13   ID/RRD   10 9 8 7 6 5 4 3 2 1

for megan.

hummingbirds

chapter I

September means pressed white shirts. New socks. School shoes. Rigidly pleated skirts. "Those pleats. That's what morality looks like," one of the history teachers said once in class. He was young and exciting, and he was talking about the Inquisition, which seemed to give him a particular thrill. "That pleat right there," he said with an arch smile, pointing to one of the girls' freshly pressed skirts. "That's morality for you." No one knew exactly what he meant. But all of the girls laughed and shifted a little sideways in their seats.

They had brothers and uncles and fathers of friends.

They knew the feeling of watering, avuncular eyes getting under your clothes. *Squidgy* might be a word for it.

But for the girls of the Carmine-Casey School, September, when it comes, feels like waking up to an overcast morning—that diluted and deceptive quality of light that seems to die on the windowsill. Not night nor morning nor even dawn, but rather the approximation of daylight—the best effort in bad circumstances. The weather has gotten sick. It languishes there in the corner by your unread books, circled by a cloud of dust motes. Clammy ambiguity. That's what September is like.

On the first day of school, everything feels old and new at the same time. The exchange of summer stories. The smell of laundered uniforms. The comparison of anklets bought either by out-of-town uncles (which is good) or by out-of-town boyfriends (which risks unbelievability). The walk to school with its familiar byways, the doormen in their tasseled coats, the widestaired stoops of buildings where you can sit and watch the other girls go by. That girl has goose pimples on her arms—the wind this morning is chilly, but she isn't sure if she really likes her new sweater, which is currently bunched up in the bottom of her bag.

Still, as familiar as these things are, they also seem to imply possibility and promise. Each girl thinks, in terms large or small, Perhaps this will finally be the year that I have been waiting for. Maybe this is the year for me.

So when September comes, the girls of Carmine-Casey—CC girls, as they are sometimes known among the community of Manhattan prep schools—are already flush with minor-key dramas of hope and apprehension.

The building itself—whose side windows overlook Fifth Avenue and Central Park—houses a venerable institution dating back to 1895, since which time its marble staircases have been worn into arcs so subtle and soft that new adhesive traction strips have to be added at the beginning of each year. In fact, the girls are no longer allowed to wear open-backed shoes ever since, two years ago, a freshman girl tripped on the stairs and sprained her knee. It could have been worse, said the administration, evoking images of skulls cracking against the yellowing marble. It could have been much worse.

The facade of the building is stark white, and the only thing that identifies it as a school is a small brass plaque, the size of a sheet of notebook paper, mounted to the left of the main entrance. There are four stories above the ground and two below, and the building is shaped like a U, with the bottom of the U facing the street and the center containing a private courtyard where the girls can take their lunch trays when the weather permits. There is also an old sugar maple, which at this time of year still has bright green leaves, and from a branch of which, it is rumored, a girl once hanged herself to death after a particularly difficult calculus final.

It is near the base of this same tree that two girls can now be seen malingering in poses of boredom or irritation on one of the picnic tables set up around the yard. They are seniors, and they take it as an obligation to be constantly gazing with disinterest in directions that nobody else is gazing.

One of them, Dixie Doyle, a pretty girl with ironic pig-tails, takes a lollipop from her mouth and says, "So I think my formative years are over."

"Really?" says the other. This is Andie. She is tall and never quite knows what to do with her shoulders.

"Over the summer I marked on the calendar every day that something formative happened. I looked back at it yesterday—four formatives and seventy-two blank squares."

"Well, maybe something formative will happen today."

"It seems unlikely," Dixie sighs. "It's September. Formative things happen in June and July mostly. August at the latest."

Andie nods at the irrefutability of Dixie's logic. Andie is the daughter of Mrs. Abramson, one of the English teachers at Carmine-Casey, and everyone suspects her of having an intellect that towers over that of her friends.

Dixie takes the lollipop out of her mouth and looks at it with one eye squeezed closed—as if measuring it against some-thing in the distance. "Did I tell you," she says, "that I slept in the hall for two weeks?"

"The hall?" Andie says. "What hall?"

"In the hall, while my folks were gone. They went to Rome for two weeks."

"What for?"

"They wanted to see a pita."

"The round bread?"

"No," Dixie says. "Not the bread, don't be silly."

"Pisa? You mean Pisa, Dix? The Leaning Tower of Pisa?"

"No," Dixie says again, shaking her head. "A pita. It's a sculpture. It's a marble sculpture of Mary Magdalene or some-thing."

"Oh. The Pietà," Andie says. "Michelangelo."

"Right."

Of Dixie Doyle it is said that she could convince grown men

of anything. While she is only a mediocre student and a wholly untalented tennis player, she possesses a quality of performed girl-ishness that turns sex into a ragged paradox for men beyond the age of thirty. She speaks with the hint of a babyish lisp, the pink end of her tongue frequently peeking out from between her teeth, but her eyes are implacable fields of gray that at any moment could conceal everything you imagine—or nothing at all. She might be an X-ray registering the skeleton of your soul, or, like Oscar Wilde's women, she might be a sphinx without a secret.

But when her friends look at her, especially Andie, who now rubs her eyes open as though her mother were waking her up from bed, what they see is a violence of feminine spirit—their own desire for which they can only begin to articulate.

"So anyway," Dixie continues, "after they left I realized I couldn't stand my room anymore. You know—I was just *done* with everything in it. I wanted a new perspective. I wanted a non-bedroom perspective. And I saw this thing on TV where in old mansions in England some of the servants used to sleep in the hall. So I got Brady to come upstairs one day, and he moved my bed into the hall. All I know is that hallways in England must be bigger, because it just barely fit."

"Brady moved your bed?" Andie asks with a half smile. Brady is a boy from the Bardolph Boys' Academy. He lives in Dixie's building on Park Avenue.

"He just *moved* it. And it's just Brady. Anyway, when the folks came home, they made me put it back. My mom kept asking why I was sleeping in the hall. 'How come you weren't sleeping in your room? Why do you want to scratch up the wainscoting?' She just about went crazy over it. I think she wants to send me back to the therapist now."

"God," Andie says.

"Oh, Donald's okay. That's the therapist. He knows a lot about TV. For a therapist."

"Hmm." Andie looks up at the sky again, and then at her watch. "I guess we better get inside. Everybody's going to want to be on time today."

Dixie and Andie rise from the picnic table and straighten the skirts of their blue and gray uniforms. Then the two girls march side by side toward the rear doors of the building.

"I once slept in the garage, in the back seat of our car," Andie says, almost wistful. The Abramsons live in an upscale New Jersey suburb. "But I never slept in the hall."

Through the windows, Dixie spots a figure she recognizes— a tall shadow of movement whose pale face and racing eyes are visible only briefly behind the panes of glass. Feeling suddenly agitated, she takes the lollipop and looks for a trash can to toss it into, then reconsiders and puts it back in her mouth, wondering with deep concern if it has made her lips purple. She removes the lollipop again and runs her pinky fingernail along the corners of her mouth; she hates it when she sees girls who have sticky stuff in the corners of their mouths.

She thinks about her father—how he didn't say anything when he took her bed apart and moved it back into her room. There was a gaunt stoicism in his movements, as though it were the prerogative of every daughter to move her bed into the hall and the obligation of every father to move it back.

"Was that Binhammer who just went by?" Andie asks. She must have seen the same figure.

Dixie doesn't say anything.

"I think that was Binhammer," Andie says again. "Did you see him?" No answer. "At least I have Binhammer again this year for English. That's something. You got Binhammer again too, didn't you, Dix?"

"Yeah," she says.

"Thank god. I don't know what I would have done. . . . At least there's Binhammer."

Yes, Dixie thinks, at least there's Binhammer.

chapter 2

The girls move up the stairs in anxious and gaudy pageants, each one of them a carnival pier at midnight, brightly lit, intricately mechanistic, with an electrical heartbeat that turns the dark air around them a color of white that is like the negative of dark—but not light, not quite light, never just light. Each one of them is a flash along a black shoreline, and there is something laughingly obscene in the display, something decadent in the strings of teardrop bulbs that resist encroachment by the landscape around them. This one has Ferris wheels dangling from her ears. That one has a carousel in her eyes.

They brush by him with their awkward broad gestures and their attitudes of coy instability, saying Good morning to him and How was your summer? and Guess what, Mr. Binhammer, I'm in your class this year. Aren't you excited?

He smiles and gives a distant, all-encompassing nod that serves as a response to all of them at once. He learned a long time ago that they do not expect much—that they are insectlike in their ability to pollinate an entire building with their gushing affections by alighting on each individual for only a second or two at a time. All that is required of him is a nod. To do more is to risk the embarrassment of a sudden and baseless intimacy. So he does not meet their eyes, keeping focused on the backs of the knees of the girls in front of him on the stairs, trying to wedge himself between the clots of bodies pushing their way up on the right and the steady trickle of the ones tiptoeing down on the left.

And he thinks, What is that smell? Is that lilac? It must be shampoo. I smelled something else like that once. . . . Or some girl has lilacs in her hair. I wonder what boy might be burrowing his face into her neck later. . . . I don't like to look at the backs of their knees. Sometimes there are little accumulations of dirt in the creases. They look unclean. . . .

But now one of the girls coming down on his left, a sophomore with an armful of books, trips on her own shoes and begins a slow-motion tumbling dance down the stairs, twisting her body this way and that, beginning to run despite herself in order to keep her legs underneath her as the gravity of the fall presses her downward, the panic evident in her eyes and in her hands that clasp tightly to the books. She shrieks quietly.

Fortunately, Binhammer sees it coming and sticks his left arm out to stop her fall, bracing himself for the weight of her small body. When they collide, his arm cuts across the upper part of her stomach, pulling the shirt out of her skirt and exposing a little white strip of belly. Not only that, but, as one of her books goes flying forward to strike another girl in the back of the head, he finds that his forearm is wedged up underneath her breasts—

Oh god.

—and that her whole weight is on him now, so he can't let go. The only thing he can do is lift his arm even more and push her back upright where she can regain her balance.

"Sorry, Mr. Binhammer," she says as she sets down her books on one of the steps while the other girls maneuver around them. She seems unbothered by the recent commerce between her breasts and his arm. Her hands fly up to fix her hair, clicking and unclicking barrettes.

So many fasteners they have! So many little metallic snaps and zippers. These girls are held together with clips and buttons.

"It's okay," he says. "Just be careful."

He continues up the stairs to the third floor, where the teachers' lounge is. When the door closes behind him, the noise of the hallway grows distant and muffled. The only other person in the lounge is Walter, who has been a history teacher at the school for twenty years. He's knocking straight a stack of copies on the table in the middle of the room.

"I just saved somebody's life," Binhammer says.

"Good for you."

"Good for me."

"Anyone I know?"

"One of the girls."

"Hm." Walter doesn't like him. He thinks Binhammer isn't a serious teacher, that teachers don't reach their prime until at least age fifty.

The bell rings.

Walter gathers his things and heads for the door. He looks back. "Aren't you teaching first period?"

Binhammer is now standing by the window, looking out over the tops of the Central Park trees across the street. "I'm just letting them get settled."

As Walter goes out, Lonnie Abramson, another English teacher, comes in looking splendid.

"Well, well," she says. "Binhammer. How was your summer?"

"I just saved somebody's life."

"I don't doubt it." She comes over and gives him a kiss on each cheek, putting her hands on his shoulders to lift herself up. "You've saved my life lots of times."

She throws herself down on the couch dramatically and lets out a sigh.

"Can you believe the summer's over already? Can you believe it? I can't even tell you how unprepared I am to teach this year. It seems like every year I get a little more unraveled. So what did you do over the summer? Anything interesting? Oh—have you seen Pepper? What about Sibyl? They were looking for you this morning." She lowers her voice and winks. "I think Sibyl wants to tell you about her marriage situation. You didn't hear it from me, but I think things have taken a turn. If you follow me."

"How's George?" he asks to divert her attention, sitting down next to her on the couch.

"Oh, George. Well, you know. Husbands." She rolls her eyes back. Then she catches her breath as if reminded suddenly of something. "Oh, do I have a story to tell you. You should see this character Andie brought home over the summer. I don't know where she found him. I mean, he's a cute boy—charming, and bright, I think—but there's something about him. Something a little off. I want to ask your advice about it when you have time for the whole story."

"Sure. Sure. I have a class now, but—"

"You know how the girls adore you," she says, leaning forward and putting her hand on his knee. Her breath smells faintly of peppermint. "And I just can't talk about it with her father. You know George—he can only think in the extremes. Either he wants to cut off their you-know-whats or he wants to make them junior partners in his firm. My husband lives in the 1950s. No subtlety."

The hall outside has gone quiet. The clock on the wall reads five minutes after the hour. He points to the clock and stands, and she stands too—stretching her whole body with a feline fluidity, as though she has been lounging for hours.

"I can't wait to hear about it," he says. "Maybe at lunch?"

"That would be great," she says, giving him a hug that lingers. "It's good to see you again. And I'm dying to hear about your summer. I want all the details."

"I've written them down," he says, extracting himself from her embrace and crossing the room to the door. "Just for you."

She giggles. Then, as he steps into the hall, she calls out, "Oh, Binhammer! Don't forget the department meeting after school. Mrs. Mayhew will kill you."

Down the hall he peeks into his room and sees the girls of his senior class sitting in packs on the tops of their desks, giddily reacquainting themselves.

They're fine.

So he goes around the corner and into the nurse's office—

where she says, "Already? It's only the first day"—then into the faculty men's room a few doors down, where he swallows the two aspirin the nurse gave him, scooping a handful of water from the sink into his mouth. From outside in the hall, he hears a girl whistling—or trying to whistle, her breath getting in the way of her tune.

He leans with his hands on the edges of the sink and looks into the mirror. The face looking back at him is still young and dark, gaunt in a way that would be unsettling if it weren't for the soft features that give the blurred impression of movement. The eyes contain something: a gaze that weighs a ton and requires a crane to move it from one place to the other, a sackful of crumbled concrete attention that pins you to the ground. Sometimes people ask him what he thinks he's staring at—who does he think he is? Other times people, frequently women, seem to warm themselves under his gaze, as though the weight of boulders makes them feel safe and assured.

He looks at himself with lazy interest and thinks, That's the face that used to get me called a boy by the other teachers, that used to make the girls wonder how someone so young could actually be teaching literature. And what now? All their chirping girlvoices. What do they want from me next? What can they be asking of me now that I will have no strength to refuse them?

In the classroom the girls are picking at the hems of their skirts, putting their hands in each other's hair, lifting it into various configurations, saying, "Look, what about this? Here, give me a clip." When Binhammer finally comes through the door, they drop everything and swarm to him. Almost all of them have been in a class of his before, and now they surround him as though he were a mysterious but favorite relative they haven't seen in years.

"Aren't you glad I'm in your class, Mr. Binhammer?"

"What did you do over the summer, Mr. Binhammer?"

"Mr. Binhammer, do you want to see pictures of me in Saint-Tropez? But you can't look at all of them, because over there you're not supposed to wear a top on the beach."

"How is your wife, Mr. Binhammer?"

He likes the attention—this flurry of femininity stirred up solely because of his entrance into the room. And the fact that it takes so little to appease them—a simple smile, a raised eyebrow, an obligatory chuckle. He is reminded of hummingbirds, their delicate, overheated bodies fretting in short, angled bursts of movement around a bottle of red sugar water.

Once they are quiet, their voices running down like little wind-up toys, he passes out to each girl two pages of text—explaining to them that they are the opening passages of two different books. Then he sits at the desk in front of the room and leans back in the chair to watch them read. Miriam likes to pinch her lower lip when she concentrates. She has to reapply her lipstick after every class. Judy twirls a strand of hair between two fingers. Sometimes she draws the strand across her upper lip as though it were a moustache.

"Here's what I want you to do," he says after a few minutes. "I want you to figure out if you can tell which one was written by a woman and which by a man."

He wonders if they appreciate the irony of the situation, that the Women in Literature senior seminar is being taught by the only man on the faculty of the English department. In truth, they seem to take it in stride, as though it were perfectly natural—if you want to learn about women, you have to ask a man.

They have too much faith in men, he thinks. They believe too easily.

The class is one of six themed English seminars offered to the Carmine-Casey seniors in preparation for their college courses. Each class is taught by a different English teacher and is built around that teacher's individual interests. When he came on the faculty seven years ago, Binhammer suggested that some-one should teach a course on gender theory—deferring, as he imagined was only right, to the other members of the depart-ment, who were all both senior and female. But none of them wanted to do it. Pepper was too deeply entrenched in her Other

America course, which focused on minority writers, and Sibyl said simply, "I'm tired of women." So it fell to him.

"I think this one is the one by the man, Mr. Binhammer," says one of the girls, holding up a sheet. "I mean, who cares about fishing?"

He says something to make them laugh. They are a willing audience; they are ready to be amused. They sit and listen to his voice and watch his hand gestures. At one point a girl yawns inadvertently and makes a silent gesture to him that it's not his fault—she's just not used to getting up early. They are nice girls.

Except for Liz Warren. She's sitting in the back of the room, and about halfway through the class period it becomes apparent that she's not going to let herself laugh at any of his jokes. Realizing this, Binhammer finds it more and more difficult to distract himself from her sullen, hunched shape. She's paying attention, there's no question about that. But she stares at him from under eyelids drooping with apathy.

She was in his class before, last year, carrying with her the same dour indifference, and he was sure she would never elect to take a class with him again. But now there she sits, like a dead battery. Worse still is that she is a bright girl, one of the true intellects in the school, a fulminating insight stirring behind that severe, immutable expression, and it was with a begrudging antagonism that he had labeled the top of each of her papers with an A.

He can feel himself getting nervous, jittery. He wonders what it is she wants. Does she want him to get down to business? Does she think he isn't serious enough? Does she believe her time is being wasted? He can feel her intractable presence pricking behind his eyes like a burr or a stinging bee.

When the bell rings at the end of class, he watches her gather her things silently and walk to the door, her limbs seeming to resent any superfluous movement.

"Great class, Mr. Binhammer," says a voice at his side.

It's Dixie Doyle. She's gotten up from her seat in the front row and is now standing over him, leaning her hip against his desk.

"Really. It was really interesting."

"Thanks, Dixie. It seems like a good group, doesn't it? With Mary and Judy. And Liz—did you see Liz over the summer?"

"Liz?" She lowers her voice confidentially. "You think I hang out with Liz?"

Dixie and Liz despise each other, he knows that. But he also knows that Dixie is a rich soil in which to dowse for information. She rarely suspects her resources are being tapped.

"I always wondered about that," he says, leaning in toward her. "How come you and Liz aren't closer friends?"

Her face coils up in distaste. "I don't know," she says. "She's just . . . I don't know. She just thinks she's so *smart*."

What she's thinking about as she says this is that Binhammer's tie is a little crooked. She feels her hands wanting to reach out and straighten it for him. She would straighten the tie and then smooth her hands down the front of his jacket, as though he were her mannequin husband.

Then she wonders why he thinks she and Liz should be friends. Does he really think she is the kind of person who would be friends with Liz? She doesn't like the way he kept glancing at Liz in the back of the room while he was talking to the class. She followed his eyeline and found the girl sitting there like a patch of weeds. This is the girl he thinks she should be having lunch with?

She used to like to imagine that Binhammer had really figured her out—that he knew her even better than she knew herself. Now she just feels frustrated. As she leaves for her next class, she looks behind her and sees him staring at the back of the room as though Liz Warren were still there.

What she'll do, she decides, is stop him in the hall later to say something casual. She'll say, "Oh, Mr. Binhammer, I wanted to ask you when the first paper is due." A little thing. She'll put herself in front of him so he'll have to look at her. And then he'll walk away having had two encounters with Dixie Doyle that day, while all the other girls will have only been able to claim him for one.

Later, during lunch, she finds Andie Abramson sitting at the same picnic table under the sugar maple where the two convened earlier in the morning. After a while they are joined by Caroline Cox and Beth Barber. There are only a few other groups of girls scattered about the yard—which is not a popular place because of the chilly air and because of the dingy squirrels that scurry down from the trees.

Caroline stuffs a cream cheese and jelly sandwich into her mouth, but the others seem reluctant to eat. Beth climbs on top of the table and lies down.

Everything seems fanciful.

Dixie looks straight up in the air and makes herself dizzy looking at the deep blue sky. Then she says, "In September for a while, I will ride a crocodile, down the chicken soupy Nile."

"What's that from?" Caroline says. But nobody answers her. Caroline is the kind of girl who does not always require a response.

"Oh god," Beth moans. "Don't remind me it's September. I can't think about September. I almost didn't wake up this morning at all."

"Wait, what's that from?" Caroline says again. "That crocodile line?"

"It feels like I've been here my whole life," says Beth, who now lies flat out on the tabletop with her hands folded on her stomach as though entombed in a sarcophagus. Then she puts her palms together over her chest and closes her eyes in imitation of prayer. "And it's only the first day."

Dixie, in her pigtails, unwraps her second lollipop of the day and begins to suck on it. The crocodile rhyme seems to be her only contribution for the time being.

Andie sits hunched over the table with her shoulders pulled in toward each other, drawing intricate filigrees in ballpoint pen in one corner of her notebook. Without looking up, she says, "Who do you have for biology?"

"I mean it," Caroline goes on, "I've heard that crocodile thing before. But I can't remember from where."

"Meyers," says the praying Beth. "I've got Meyers again. She hates me so much she wanted me two years in a row. She loves to hate people. *Et ne nos inducas in tentationem, sed libera nos a malo—*"

"Stop it, Beth," says Andie. "That's creepy."

"I have Ms. Doone." Caroline has given up on discovering the source of the crocodile poem. She cannot sit still and instead walks in circles around the table, sometimes pretending she's balancing on a beam. She is not as pretty as the other three girls, but she does not seem to know it—which gives her a fumblingly seductive quality. "Was the summer shorter this year?" she asks.

"Oh god, I feel like I was *just here.*" Beth twists her hands out of the palm-together position and does a little trick with her fingers. Then she puts her hands over her face and sighs. "Doesn't it feel like we were *just here?*"

Behind them, a door opens and from inside the school comes the itinerant bustle and chirping of students on their way to and from the cafeteria. Beth raises her head and sees a miniature-looking girl—obviously a freshman—come out into the yard toward them. When the door closes behind her, the relative quiet of the yard reasserts itself.

"Hi," says the freshman cheerily. "Do you know where the cafeteria is? Someone told me I could get to it this way."

The four girls look at each other, trying silently to decide who should be obliged to answer. Finally dark-haired and silly Caroline, still pretending she is balancing on a beam, speaks. "Only if you're coming from that side of the building," she says, pointing. "You have to go back in and down the hall all the way to your right."

"Oh, okay," the girl says, not yet moving. "I don't know *what* I'm doing. I'm new here. My name is Sally."

Caroline nods and smiles faintly.

"Introduce yourself, Caroline," Beth scolds from the table and lays her head back down.

"Oh . . . sure. I'm Caroline. Nice to meet you. That's Beth.

And this is Andie," she says, putting her hand on top of the head of Andie, who is still drawing elaborate curlicues. "And over there is Dixie."

"Ugh," Beth says, after the freshman girl has gone back inside. "Was she a cartoon character? *Sally*."

"*Sally*," Andie says.

"*Sally*," Beth says again.

"I don't know." Caroline reconsiders. "I guess she seemed like a nice girl. Maybe we should make friends with her."

Andie looks up from her notebook. "She was kind of pretty. You can tell she's going to be pretty. Can't you?"

"Ugh," Beth says again, sitting up sleepily. "It's too early in the year even to think. I'm not ready to go back yet. What about you, Dix?"

"I don't know," pigtailed Dixie Doyle says, taking the lollipop out of her mouth with an audible slurp. It is the first she's spoken in a while. "I'm actually kind of glad the summer's over. I was getting tired of *doing* things."

The other girls stop to think about this. The leaves of the sugar maple rustle thoughtfully.

"Everywhere you go there's someone calling you wanting to *do* something. Let's *do* something tonight. Why don't we *do* something tomorrow. How come we always have to be doing something?"

Caroline looks concerned. "But not me, right, Dix? I mean, you never thought that when I called, right?"

"No, of course not, sweetie. Not you. Everyone else."

"You're not kidding, Dix," Beth says. "Every day it was something else. Now that you mention it, I'm glad it's over."

"And my summer clothes," Dixie says. "I can't tell you how tired of them I am. We should just make a big bonfire of our summer clothes."

"And then start fresh next year," Andie says.

"I am *so* tired of my summer clothes," Caroline adds, belatedly.

Beth looks back toward the school, which seems to swell

with a frenzy of girls. "Yeah, I guess it's okay to be back. I mean, I guess it's all right."

"Sure," Dixie says. "Look at it this way. If Carmine-Casey was a boat, like the Jolly Roger or something, then we'd all be pirates. You can't deny it."

And they can't.

chapter 3

Lonnie Abramson is the first person at the English department meeting other than the chair, Mrs. Mayhew, who
already has her plan books spread out on the conference table
before her and is sitting, immobile, with her hands folded in her
lap. For a few minutes the two women just sit on opposite sides
of the table—the older gazing down at her plan books without
moving her head, and the younger delivering sighs and clucks
and chuckles that seem to indicate she has a story to tell if anyone is interested in asking.

"I reminded Binhammer about the meeting," she says finally, as though everyone were his communal mother, sharing
the responsibility of keeping him accountable. "So he should be
here."

Mrs. Mayhew nods.

For three more long minutes the two women sit in silence.
Mrs. Mayhew is one of the matriarchs of the school—not only
the chair of the English department, but also one of the three
headmistresses, one of the triumvirate of broad-shouldered and
hefty women who watch like perched carrion birds over the
school. The three women are of the industrial age, their spines
girded by steel and their faces ferrous with the ash and grime of
harder generations.

No one is comfortable around Mrs. Mayhew, who, indeed, seems like an algebraic counterfunction to the theorem of
comfort. The only exception to this rule is Binhammer. Many
people have said that Binhammer is able to evoke, alchemist-

like, whatever half-smiling affection remains unincinerated in the furnace of her heart.

At this moment, therefore, Lonnie Abramson is beginning to wish she had not been so eager to be on time for this meeting.

"They're quite some students I have this year," she says, fixing her hair. When Mrs. Mayhew doesn't respond, she repeats, as if remembering a distant dream, "Some students . . ."

Finally Pepper Carmichael shows up, and even though the two are not the most intimate of friends, Lonnie wants to get up and hug her. Pepper is the one who, after Lonnie told her about a student who had the nerve to characterize her earrings as "grandmother jewelry," said, "Oh, let the girl vent. The poor thing—already feeling the fingers of age, no doubt. Creeping along her skin, like they do." Pepper's specialty is empathy. She grew up in California. That's the way people are out there. Lonnie can never entirely clear her mind of the image of a young Pepper sitting on a beach at night, in a circle of long-haired boys and bead-wearing girls, passing some narcotic cigarette to the person next to her. For Lonnie, Pepper is one person who represents many—she stands in for hundreds of people whom Lonnie will never meet.

Right away the two fall to talking in hushed tones, as though they themselves are students and Mrs. Mayhew is the teacher waiting to begin class. They pull out their class lists and start comparing students.

"Oh, *her*," Lonnie says. "You're going to have a time with her."

"Needy?"

"If you can call it that." Lonnie herself would call it being a melodramatic little overachiever. But she suspects that Mrs. Mayhew favors the grade-grubbers, that Mrs. Mayhew sees them as industriously pounding away at the door of the American dream—and so she keeps her mouth shut.

Then she puts a finger on another name in Pepper's class list and has begun to frown expressively—as though this one, well, this one needs no comment—when Sibyl appears in the doorway and starts apologizing in a way that makes everyone look at her at once.

"Sorry I'm late," she says. "I wish I could say that it's not my fault. But I'm just such a goddamn mess today. . . ."

"What's the matter, honey?" Pepper says.

"Oh, it's nothing, really." Sibyl lets her handbag drop on the table, and it sounds like it's filled with marbles. Her colleagues imagine that the inside of her purse must look like a cosmetics counter when you bring it all out into the open—even though Sibyl never seems to have a moment to put any of it on. Lonnie has observed her applying lipstick as though it were a timed event. Especially now that Sibyl has been separated for half a year and her divorce is imminent, as her colleagues know, she sometimes looks at the makeup in her purse with a smirk of resentment, as though the rouges and eyeliners themselves are responsible, at least in part, for the elaborate masquerade her marriage has been for ten years. "I'm just being silly. That's all. The first day always sneaks up on me."

"Sure, of course," Pepper says, shifting into demonstrative concern. "But you're okay, right? I mean, it's nothing to do with . . ."

This is the first time that Mrs. Mayhew raises her eyes, setting her hammered gaze upon Sibyl. Everyone, even Mrs. Mayhew, knows that Sibyl's relationship with her husband has been disintegrating for a long time.

"Oh, Christ, no. Bruce is one thing I can count on. He's the most consistent jackass I've ever met."

Mrs. Mayhew hmphs in satisfaction and looks back down at her plan books.

In the pause that follows, Sibyl begins to sift through her bag. She's not looking for anything in particular, but she doesn't want to meet anyone's eyes at the moment. So she stares into the shifting tangle of objects and thinks about the woman in today's newspaper who was shot in the head by a mugger because she wouldn't give up her purse. There must be something important in here, she thinks. There must be some important wedge of my identity that I would be willing to die for. But from here it just looks like so much confusion.

Then she looks around the room and says, "So where's our boy?"

"Not here yet," Lonnie says. "But I reminded him earlier, so he knows about it."

Pepper glances at the three other women, saying, "It seems so much smaller now. I mean without Maureen. Our department is *perishing*."

"How *is* Maureen?" Sibyl asks. "Have you spoken to her?"

Pepper nods. "She called me last week. She seems to be doing fine."

"But she's gotten into the habit," Lonnie adds, "of using her baby and her book as metaphors for each other. She told me the baby's growing a lot faster than the book. And that the baby is producing more dirty diapers than she is producing pages."

"But it *is* an adorable baby," Pepper says. "Did you see the announcement?"

"Oh god yes." Lonnie's hand flutters up and presses itself to her chest as though she has just had the first bite of some sumptuous dessert. "That baby is one in a million."

"Gorgeous," Sibyl agrees, and then she tries to remember what the baby looked like. She is sure she received the announcement, but now she can't recall. Did the baby have a lot of hair? That's something people usually admire in babies.

"And the *size* of that baby!" Lonnie marvels, which brings the conversation around to childbirth—Lonnie and Pepper sounding like the younger CC girls who come back from camp and want to compare their experiences.

Then Lonnie turns to Sibyl and starts to say, "So when—" and realizes too late that it's not the appropriate time to be asking Sibyl about her plans for children, now that her marriage is in the dumps. So she stumbles and checks herself, looking to the door and starting over with, "So when is Binhammer going to show up?"

And it is at that exact moment that he comes around the corner and into the room, looking distracted. For a second he doesn't seem to see anyone, and then he looks at the four women around the table and smiles. "Am I late?"

"No, no," Pepper says automatically, even though he is, in fact, quite late.

"Just your regular," Lonnie says.

Each of the women has left a place open beside her at the conference table, and Binhammer has to decide who to sit next to. He does some quick calculations in his head and picks the seat next to Lonnie, who leans over and confides to him that he just missed a great conversation about childbirth.

"Oh," he says, "my favorite subject." Then to everyone else, "Who doesn't love a good childbirth story?"

Pepper chuckles and makes a swatting gesture at him. "We were talking about *Maureen*."

"Oh, sure," Binhammer says. "How is she doing? Do we have a replacement for her yet?"

"That's one of the things," Mrs. Mayhew says, emerging from her rigid silence, "that we're going to talk about today."

When Maureen left at the end of the previous school year to become a stay-at-home mother and novel writer, it was unclear whether it was just a temporary leave of absence or whether she was going to rely on her husband's considerable income to leave teaching for good. Then, a few weeks before this current year began, she decided that she wouldn't be coming back, leaving Mrs. Mayhew a very short period of time to find not only a temporary substitute but a permanent replacement.

"We have found someone," Mrs. Mayhew says now. "He couldn't start today because we didn't give him very much notice, and he's out of town at a conference. But he'll be here starting next week."

"*He*?" Binhammer says.

"Uh-oh, Binhammer," Sibyl says maliciously. "Looks like you're not the only cock in the henhouse anymore."

Lonnie recoils from the vulgarity. Mrs. Mayhew appears not to have heard.

"I think he'll fit in just fine," Mrs. Mayhew continues. "He hasn't taught high school before, but he's highly qualified. *Highly* qualified. And I think he has the characteristics the school is looking for."

The way Binhammer looks right now—Sibyl wants a picture of it—it's obvious he's looking right through Mrs. Mayhew and into his own future, looking ahead to the next faculty meeting where his won't be the only male voice echoing through the room. Little by little, he's shivering to pieces on the inside, she can see that. It's a serious blow to his identity. If he's not the only man on the faculty of the Carmine-Casey English department, then what is he? Just another teacher.

Yes, this is a picture she wants to keep. Maybe that's what she would like to find at the bottom of her purse, underneath all the confusion. The poor suffering boy. The little soldier, knocked over like the slow-moving king in a game of chess. There's something beautiful about him when he's damaged. Men are like phoenixes: their tragedies are gorgeous because everyone knows how lovely they will be when they rise. When he rises.

She has seen him run his hand through his hair, when he thinks no one is looking. She has seen him lean against the window frame in the teachers' lounge and rub his eyes until they are red and tired-looking—desperate and private. So small, his shoulders hunched against the cold glass of the windowpane. His gaze sunken into himself with the gravity of distant, objective despair. As though he were watching a film reel of his own past. She has seen his hands, knotting themselves together, disclosing things he would not like disclosed.

Times like this, she would watch him until he would notice her gaze and straighten himself up with immediate and smiling rigor. Clicking back into place, click, click, snap, ready again to tell everyone his stories.

"Hey," he would say. "You wouldn't believe what I just saw."

"What? What did you just see?"

"Down on the sidewalk, these students . . ." Then, shrugging, fixing himself, soldering up all the seams. "It wasn't anything, really. Listen, you want to get out of here for a while? I need some coffee." That's what he would say.

Now, she thinks, looking at him across the conference table, now I will watch his hands. What will he tell me with his hands?

He leans back in his chair, putting the weight of his upper body on his left elbow against the arm of the chair. He leaves his right arm extended and resting on the table, his long forefinger casually following a scar in the wooden surface. He never writes on the board in his classroom, so his hands are never dry and chalky like the rest of theirs. Then she sees Lonnie staring down at his hand, and she knows that the other woman wants to reach out and cover it with her own, to pat it softly with maternal affection.

And so Sibyl looks away, hating herself.

But Mrs. Mayhew has said something to her and seems to be awaiting a response.

"I'm sorry," Sibyl says. "What was that again?"

"*Mentor*. I wonder if you could mentor him. It would simply involve your being available if he has any questions."

"Oh, sure. Of course."

"Well," Binhammer says, raising himself to his full seated height and leaning forward across the table. With the look of brave determination in his face, it might appear as though he were going to scale a mountain. "I'm looking forward to meeting him. It'll be nice having another man on the faculty. Maybe we'll go hunting together. Or work on his car."

Lonnie smiles and swats his forearm.

"What's his name, anyway?"

"Well," Mrs. Mayhew says, and her eyes squint as though in distant memory of girlishness. "That's something you're not going to believe."

chapter 4

Ted Hughes. That's the name. Ted Hughes. As in Ted Hughes, the husband of tragic suicidal poetess Sylvia Plath. As in Ted Hughes, husband of not just one but *two* women who took their own lives. Shockingly handsome Ted Hughes—the face to die over. Ted Hughes, the poet laureate of England. Ted Hughes, who is buried in Westminster Abbey and once wrote about the "maggoty deaths which poison our lives." That Ted Hughes. Except for one thing: Ted Hughes the poet is really named Edward, and *this* Ted Hughes is a Theodore.

So who is this person who would use the nickname Ted, knowing, as he must, what literary baggage it carries?

A week after the department meeting, Binhammer still has visions of Ted Hughes reincarnated, strong jaw and dark hair, wandering the halls of Carmine-Casey and teaching the poetry of e. e. cummings to his girls. *His* girls. He imagines Ted Hughes, a scarf draped around his neck and a pipe in the corner of his mouth, standing wistfully in front of the classroom—smugly unselfconscious about his own masculine beauty. Ted Hughes is the smart girl's dream—the vaguely snobbish nonchalance, the inspirational intellect, the hint of despair behind the eyes of clear, electric blue. He will leave a trail of Carmine-Casey girls in his wake—girls writing morbid poetry in their journals at night and feeling suddenly uncomfortable in their starched clothes.

He imagines what will happen.

The place will become a literary powerhouse. The girls'

poems will be published in the *New Yorker* and *Granta*, and people will start talking about the Carmine-Casey phenomenon. How is it that so many vast poetic talents have emerged from a small prep school on the Upper East Side? Interviewers will come to the school and find the girls in the courtyard, practicing their expressions of disdain—one eyebrow raised, but not too much, because there's pain and experience in that eyebrow as well. They will take a picture of the girls, twenty-seven of them, grouped together in grainy black and white, all with deadpan expressions and many of them not even looking at the camera.

None of them will say anything about Ted Hughes, because each one will believe in her heart that her own relationship with the man is secret and supreme. The critics will be mystified. The Carmine-Casey girls will become the cultural renaissance of a literary form thought dead—other girls around the country will start wearing their hair like the CC girls do.

And that's when the suicides will start. Because no girl loves Ted Hughes for long before she has to kill herself from an overdose of passion. And their suicides will be equally literary. They will stick their heads into ovens. They will load their pockets with rocks and walk into the ocean. They will throw themselves beneath trains or have the local pharmacist mix up a suspension of arsenic so they can quaff it.

They will be beautiful and tragic and wasted. And Binhammer won't be a part of it.

Sitting now in front of his classroom, he looks up at the ceiling to continue the scenario and sees tiny cracks emerging in the paint. People at dinner parties will say, "Oh, you teach at Carmine-Casey? Did you know any of those girls who killed themselves? I heard they were all in love with the same teacher. Did you know him?" The cracks in the ceiling. He thinks, This place is falling apart. What do they want from me now?

The students staring at him believe that he is considering a point just made by a girl in the front row. She claimed that Edna Pontellier, heroine of *The Awakening*, is like the mockingbird in the first scene—all she does is parrot back the things she's told by others. The girl looks pleased with herself, but after a few moments it's clear that Binhammer has gotten distracted by something.

"Mr. Binhammer?" Dixie Doyle says.

He looks down from the cracks in the ceiling. Before him is a class full of girls with eyes variously wide and tired.

"Yes, definitely," he responds suddenly. "No, that was a good point. A good point about Edna . . ."

Then he sits and runs his eyes up and down the rows of girls, noticing something.

"Wait," he says. "What's with all the straight hair?"

Today, for some reason, all the girls are wearing their hair in absolutely dead straight locks. They look like swamp vines. An everglade of teenage girls. There is something alien and unnerving about it—twenty straight-haired teenage girls looking at you with silent expressions.

"It's for our yearbook pictures," Dixie explains. "They're being taken today during lunch."

"Yearbook? But it's only the second week of school."

"I know, but when you're a senior . . ." She trails off as though it were self-explanatory.

"Yes?" Binhammer says. "What about seniors?"

"You know," Dixie continues, rolling her eyes. "The senior pictures are in color. And they're bigger. You have to look really good. It's our *senior year*, Mr. Binhammer. Some girls have to have their picture retaken *four times* before it comes out right."

"Oh," Binhammer says, nodding. Then, "But why straight hair? I mean—"

But the bell rings before he can finish his thought, and the girls pop up from their seats as though they were on some mechanical trigger. He watches them march out, Liz Warren sullen as ever and refusing to even glance in his direction, Dixie giving him a wide, toothy smile. At the last minute Dixie seems to remember something and comes back to his desk.

"By the way, Mr. Binhammer, do you think you have time to meet with me some time? About my paper, I mean?"

"What paper?" he says. "There's not a paper due for three weeks."

"I know," she says, "but I had some ideas I was thinking about, and I don't know if they're any good or not."

He stares at her. He wonders how long her hair can stay straight like that. He always liked her hair before: big curls that seemed to hold together like winding ivy on a wall. He could always pick her out of a crowded hallway, even from behind. He could call her name—"Dixie!"—and when she turned around, there would be her face, all lit up and puckered with the redness of girlhood.

"And also," Dixie continues, her voice heavy with implication, "there are some other things I wanted to talk to you about."

He stares at her. He liked her hair the way it was.

"Sure," he says. "Sure. No problem. Why don't you remind me tomorrow in class, and we'll set up a time."

Dixie thanks him and suddenly realizes she's the last student left in the room. It's quiet in here, just the two of them, and she thinks that this is what it must be like in his living room in the evening when he's reading the paper with his wife—he has one, she knows he does, even though he doesn't talk about her much. She pictures him reaching down and scratching the head of a dog that's sitting next to his chair. The dog wags its tail like crazy. That's what she's thinking about as she leaves and heads to her next class. Physics. She wonders what kind of physics are involved in the crazy wagging of a happy dog's tail.

As she moves through the hall, caught up in the thick coursing of student bodies, she passes the door to the teachers' lounge, which opens suddenly to let out Mr. Tanner, the music teacher with bad teeth. He does not smile often, and never at students, perhaps because of his teeth. But when Ms. Carmichael comes around the corner and heads for the teachers' lounge, he smiles politely—though closemouthed—and holds the door open for her as Dixie continues on down the hall.

Pepper Carmichael, having just come from one of those

impossible classes on grammatical clauses, returns Mr. Tanner's smile and gives a respectful nod as she goes through the doorway. She never knows what to say to that man—he always seems angry. But she gives him little thought as soon as she's inside the teachers' lounge with the door closed behind her. She collapses onto the couch and leans back, closing her eyes.

A moment later the din of the hallway rises again as the door opens and someone else comes in.

"Pepper, good morning." It's Walter.

"Good morning, Walter." She doesn't open her eyes. Walter has trouble talking to women, though this doesn't keep him from trying. Around Pepper, he inevitably adopts formal and old-fashioned gestures, the gentleman's code.

"And how are you today?" he asks.

She opens her eye a crack and sees him standing there with his hands behind his back. He looks like a butler.

"I'm great, Walter. How are you?" She likes to imagine what he's like when he's not around women. She pictures him in the men's bathroom, farting and spitting and talking about how these filthy dames are ruining everything. It makes her chuckle.

"I couldn't be better," he says. Every exchange with Walter has to be played out to the very end. He then goes on to hope that she had a pleasant weekend. She did. Then he wonders if the sky, which is darkening, will open up with showers by the afternoon. She hopes not.

Pepper has begun to sit up and rub her eyes when Lonnie Abramson bursts into the room and points to the two computers set up against the wall.

"I *have* to get on that computer. Is anyone on that computer? I just *have* to get on it."

"I don't think—" Walter begins.

"Is there any coffee made?"

Both Pepper and Walter look simultaneously from the empty seats in front of the computers to the full pot of coffee hissing away on the coffeemaker. Lonnie specializes in questions that she could answer herself by simply looking.

Between classes, the teachers' lounge fills up quickly. Sibyl and Binhammer come into the room one right after the other.

Walter looks deflated at the entrance of Binhammer. His gentlemanly performance withers up when another man comes into the picture. He gives the women a quick smile and then sits down at the round table in the corner to work on his lesson plans.

Binhammer goes to the window and glances out over the trees of the park. He taps at the glass as though trying to communicate with something out there.

"So," Sibyl says, leaning her hip against the edge of the table where Walter is working. She looks mischievous. "Has anyone seen the new guy?"

Binhammer looks at her for a second and then goes back to looking out the window.

"I caught a glimpse of him in the hallway this morning," Lonnie says. She seems to have forgotten her immediate need for a computer. "At least, I think it was him. Tall guy? Nice hair? Wide jaw?"

"That's him," Sibyl says. "He's got a nice look. Did you see him, Pepper?"

Pepper is a single mom, and she has accepted the fact that any single man who makes an appearance on the grounds of the school is immediately tested for potential pairing with her.

"Very nice," Pepper admits. She has a fondness for Sibyl— the woman is a bit calculating, but Pepper likes the fact that she doesn't always seem to know why she's doing what she's doing. Pepper frequently has the fleeting desire to put her arm around Sibyl, like an older sister with a sibling who is about to get into trouble. "Is he single?"

Sibyl holds up her hand and wiggles her fingers. "No ring. I checked."

Binhammer gazes out the window with narrowed eyes.

The door opens again and two other teachers come in, so everyone has to shift their positions and recalculate their vectors of conversation.

Outside the sky continues to darken, and the leaves on the ground get panicky in the gusting wind. From some of the classrooms the girls looking out the windows can see the sugar maple in the courtyard bending over and the gray light coming through its branches. The girls closest to the windows can actually lean over and look up into the sky to where the shadows are forming—and these are the girls who first suspect that something is coming.

chapter 5

Later that afternoon, when the clouds come down hard with rain and the gutters in the street begin to fill, the people on the sidewalks hunch themselves beneath umbrellas and look down at their own feet. Everything now is destination: What is the shortest way to get where I have to go? What corners can I cut? What is the quickest way for me to be inside and out of this wetness that gets into my cuffs?

There are no voices in the rain—just footsteps and car horns, and the sounds of the downpour off building ledges and store awnings and aluminum gutters, the slippery squeak of rubber soles on subway grates. The water gets underneath your clothes, like ants in your collar or crawling up your legs. The moisture like insects on your skin. If this is what guilt felt like, Binhammer thinks, the constant awareness of your own itching skin, then ours would be a sinless society.

The store windows along Madison Avenue are lit, dull yellow candles running the length of the street, stubborn little sanctuaries against the harshness outside. In one of these windows three mannequin women stand in postures of haughty defiance, leaning back with their loins pushed forward aggressively, their heads turned lazily to the side so that even if those eyes had pupils they would still be empty, their hands at their hips or, in one case, raised in a careless shrug, as though she were turned to stone at the very moment she was shooing away the fawning kindness of a man infinitely inferior to her. She makes men shrivel up with that white skin, with those white eyes, and those white lips that never smile.

Binhammer stands underneath the awning of the store, staring through the glass at the three women as though they were weaving, measuring, and cutting the paltry string of his fate. He has forgotten to bring an umbrella, and now, about five minutes into his walk home, he's trapped in this tiny shelter while the rain comes down in ferocious sidelong bursts. He jams his hands deeper into the pockets of his coat and, because it will be impossible to catch a cab now, decides to wait it out.

He stares at the pale gorgons in the window. They are women of machinelike beauty and deadly precision. When he was a boy, shopping in the department stores with his mother, he would fantasize about taking one of the mannequins home with him and setting her up in the corner of his room. She would come to life and tell him what to do, stiff-armed and barking orders with military efficiency. She would do this without any clothes on. And now, even as a grown man, he finds himself spellbound by these three snow-pale women with their smart outfits of brown and cream.

These women. These goddamn women. There is always something else behind those blank white non-eyes—another fiber of weakness like a golden thread you will carry for them in your pocket. And when you are carrying it all, all these bushels and bushels of weakness, it's then you discover that it was your weakness all along. That what you're carrying is only the unraveled heap of your own clothing.

Didn't you know? they say, as you stand there naked. I thought you knew. I'm sorry. I'm sorry. I'm sorry.

Repeated three times. Like a curse. Or an incantation.

They are women of chalk, these mannequin women. They are like the chalk that gets all over your fingers at school. The chalk that gets into your fingerprints.

Earlier that day he went looking for Ted Hughes.

These women. These girls and their bodies—all buttons and snaps. And their minds, all zippers and hidden pockets.

He went looking for Ted Hughes after the conversation in the teachers' lounge among the women who had seen the new teacher's wide jaw and his nice hair and his ringless finger. He went from room to room, peeking in through the windowed doors and glancing at his colleagues who variously sat or stood or paced at the front of their classrooms, preaching with dictatorial passion or droning on and on with what they believed to be patience. He hated to see these things. Normally he would avert his gaze, avoid feeling that voyeuristic intrusion into the intimate dynamic between teacher and students, especially with the male faculty. It is the same policy he has in the bathroom. Look straight ahead. What happens between a man and a porcelain bowl is none of his business.

So each time he glanced into a room, he cringed.

But he loved to see the girls, see them all lined up, their faces lit with choreographed grins. These girls, these women white as marble. What will they ask of him now?

And it was at the end of the hall on the fourth floor that he finally found Ted Hughes. There he was, standing at the front of the class. There he—

Now in the window there is a fourth woman, a window dresser, and she begins taking the clothes off one of the mannequins. She's middle-aged, this window dresser—her hands wrinkled, her knuckles like wooden beads. As he watches her, she handles the garments with the efficiency of a doctor, tossing the old ones over the back of a chair and pulling on the new ones over the inhumanly smooth skin. Skin like an eggshell.

Finally she notices him standing there and gives him a compassionate look. She seems to be saying something to him through the glass, but he can't hear her. She tries one more time to communicate and then gives up and settles for a gesture, empathetically rubbing her arms and shivering. Her fingernails are painted red, and her hands are all bone and tendon.

She has the foreign quality that he finds in all women—a violent landscape of warm flesh. And he suddenly feels the impulse to celebrate her as you would the discovery of a new world, to march his fingers in extravagant parades across her stomach.

There he was, Binhammer recalls, Ted Hughes, standing at the front of his class. And he was no scarf-clad, pipe-smoking poet laureate, and he did not ripple the air with his complex aura—and there were no girls already slitting their wrists in the front row. But there was something about this Ted Hughes, and for a moment Binhammer did not know what it was. Something familiar moved in him—a shifting in his guts that he had felt before. A daylight sickness that lingers in the head and the throat and the hands and twists itself into a ball.

Now, on the street behind him, there is the shattering honk of a car horn and then voices—shrill, laughing voices. "Mr. Binhammer! Mr. Binhammer!"

It's Dixie Doyle and her friends—Andie, Beth . . . he doesn't know all of them. Their faces are framed in the windows of a black town car belonging to one of the girls' families. Binhammer can see the driver—a man of stolid patience, like a Great Dane enduring the paws of a litter of playful kittens.

"Mr. Binhammer, do you want a ride?"

"I'm fine," he calls to them. A taxi behind the girls' car begins honking.

"Are you sure? You'll get wet."

"Really," he says, and the taxi issues another loud, angry honk. "I'm fine. Thanks anyway. . . ." But the car full of girls is already pulling away from the curb.

When he turns back the window dresser is gone, and one of the three eyeless witches is dressed in an entirely different outfit.

Before, when he was standing outside the classroom door, there he was, Ted Hughes. And it was a while before Binhammer recognized him—it wasn't until the man smiled, a peculiar kind of half smile that communicated mild amusement but also tremendous distance, the smile of someone watching the unfolding of events from afar. It wasn't until the man smiled at something one of the girls said that Binhammer recognized him—he knew that face, he'd seen the man before—and that was when things began to unravel.

He'd felt it in the past—that feeling that his insides were melting into his toes, his bottom half filling up with the liquefied remains of his heart, his stomach, his lungs. He braced himself against the wall. Then he tried to move, but there was nowhere he could think to go. So he sat down on the floor outside the door of Ted Hughes's classroom and waited until his breath came back.

These women . . . These women with their . . . their eggshell skin.

He has no idea how long he has been standing there under the awning, but the next time he turns around he realizes that the rain has tapered off to a faint drizzle. So he pulls his coat tighter and tucks his hands underneath his arms and walks the rest of the way home sticking close to the sides of buildings. When at last he climbs the stairs of his apartment on East Ninety-fifth Street and comes through the front door, he can hear her typing away in the small room off the kitchen that they use as an office. He does not want to call out to her, but he shuts the front door with enough force that she will hear.

Sarah, I've gotten wet.

When the door slams shut, the typing stops and she comes out of the back room.

The first thing she says is, "You're all wet."

"I know."

She comes over and strips the coat off his shivering body. Then she puts her palm on his wet cheek and puts her lips to his forehead.

"God, you look like a little stray dog. What happened? Why didn't you take a cab?"

"Couldn't get one."

"What about an umbrella? You could have bought one anywhere."

"I don't know. I didn't think of it."

She looks at him, worried. "Are you okay?"

Sarah, there are things I don't want to remember anymore.

"I'm fine," he says. Then he constructs a little smile for her. "Just wet is all."

"Well, let's get you out of these clothes."

Sarah, do you never wonder about us? Never lose faith? Are you really that good?

And he follows her into the bedroom.

chapter 6

When the last bell of the day rings, there is not, as might be expected, the chaotic din of anarchy set loose in the halls. In fact, Carmine-Casey is a much quieter place in the minutes immediately after the end of school than it is, say, during lunch or between classes, when the girls' voices can be heard wailing with banshee raggedness from one end of the hall to the other. For all their day-long chafing against the confines of their uniforms, their desks, and their classrooms, these captive girls are reluctant to vacate the school when it is over, frequently lingering in front of their lockers and staring into the darkened textbook miasma that holds, they know, essential corners of their identities.

Some of them bolt, like horses at a starting gate, only to stumble over their own feet when they hit the afternoon daylight. Standing bewildered on the sidewalk outside, they look about and wonder what they should do now. Then they gaze broodingly back into the antique gloom of the school.

Some of them huddle in small groups on the front steps of the building. One girl says today, "I'm *bored*. Why doesn't anything ever *happen*?"

Inside, down the hall and toward the back of the building, the auditorium echoes like a huge coffin of waxed wood. Here, in particular, it seems as though the final bell never rang, and the voices of twenty girls bounce like tiny rubber balls over the hardwood floors. There are chairs set up in rows near the stage, and some girls have taken these and formed small circles that look like spontaneous séances, all their faces leaned in to the whispering centers. Some girls are in the corner, pretending to pirouette, while others are sitting by themselves, hunched over notebooks spread across their laps and using pencils to twist their hair into stringy buns on the backs of their heads.

"I have things to do," Dixie Doyle says as she sits on the edge of the stage and gazes contemptuously at a group of sophomore girls. Then she looks at her friends, who are lying side by side on the stage beside her, looking up into the transom of stage lighting hung above. Caroline is imagining what it would be like to walk on the ceiling. "Can't we go?" Dixie asks them.

"Dixie, we can't go yet," Caroline says, sitting up. "Don't you want to know if you made the lead or not?"

Dixie always knows exactly what Caroline is going to say. Caroline surprises nobody. She stumbles from place to place with a sloppy grin on her face, and all the boys like her. Right now she scoots over to Beth, who has her eyes closed, and starts pulling her friend's hair into little braids between her fingers, as she often does.

"Andie," Dixie says, "do you want to draw my picture? I'm engrossing today. Don't you think I'm engrossing?"

"Sure, Dix," Andie says, sitting up and pulling from her backpack a wide black book in which she puts all of her drawings. Andie has artistic promise, everyone says so. She's tall and bony and hunches over when she walks—as though she wants to turn herself inside out, starting with her chest—but she knows how to draw. Dixie likes the way Andie draws her; her eyes always come out looking like they are glistening, as if her lashes are wet with dew or tears. "Raise your chin. I'm going to do your profile."

Dixie juts her chin out belligerently.

Earlier that day Dixie was one of fifteen girls who auditioned for various parts in the new school play. Now, in the small room behind the stage, Mr. Pratt and his student director are poring over the finalists. Dixie has had a starring role in many of the school productions over the course of her three years at Carmine-Casey. Among her dramatic talents is the ability to swoon on command.

"I don't even know what the play is," Dixie says. "Does anybody know what the play is?"

"It's an original Liz Warren," Andie says, her eyes unfocused and glancing between her drawing and the features in Dixie's profile.

"Ugh," Dixie says, deflating. "Not Liz. Why doesn't anybody stop her? She can't be the only one writing plays around here."

"Well," Andie says, "she is."

"Why don't we write a play, Dix?" Caroline offers.

Dixie frowns. She has been in two of Liz Warren's plays already. There was a lot of staring in both. As an actress, it isn't very fulfilling to spend all your time staring into corners with "near grief." In one of the productions the crew had to put a little piece of iridescent tape on the wall because the director said Dixie kept staring in the wrong direction.

She practices her staring now. But her attention is distracted by a freshman girl trying to do a cartwheel. She scowls.

"And," Andie continues, "she's *directing* this one, too."

"No," Dixie says, shaking her head resolutely. "Huh-uh. No way. It's bad enough I have to read her words. I'm not going to act the way she tells me, too. Forget the whole thing." But she doesn't make any move to leave. In fact, she glances over at Andie to make sure she's still drawing and raises her chin again, the stick of the lollipop poking up at an angle like a flagless pole.

The four girls are quiet for a while. Then lethargic Beth, who has been napping, finally sits up and rubs her eyes.

"I was having a strange dream," she says, yawning. "Do you want to know what it was? I was dreaming that I was shaving my legs, right? Except that when I got to the tops of my legs I kept shaving because I had hair all over my stomach. Gross, isn't it?"

"You're an animal," Dixie says, taking the lollipop from her mouth and pointing it meaningfully at Beth. "That's what that means. You're like a wolf or something. Now I bet you want to take a big bite out of Caroline."

Caroline laughs and tumbles off the edge of the stage, pretending to run away even though no one is chasing her. She goes a few yards, and then she comes back.

"So anyway, what's this play called?" Dixie asks.

"*Salmonburger*," Andie says.

"Salmon what?"

"*Salmonburger.* It's based on the *Oresteia.*"

"The *what*?"

"It's a Greek tragedy."

"Oh god."

"Something about women. Or birds. I don't remember."

To anyone who might be watching her, Dixie looks as though she's just been asked to hold a stranger's baby—her face is twisted in confusion, her palms facing up, her shoulders frozen in mid-shrug.

"*Salmonburger?*" she says.

"*Salmonburger*," Andie says.

"*Salmonburger*," Beth repeats to the rafters.

"I don't like salmon," Caroline says absently. "My mother makes salmon loaf. It's like meatloaf but with salmon in it instead."

She bends over to fish a pebble out of her shoe. When she does so, you can see the trim of her underwear beneath her skirt. The girl, Dixie thinks, is a disaster full of sexuality.

"What monologue did you do anyway?" Beth asks disinterestedly. "For the audition, I mean."

"I did Cleopatra," Dixie says. Then, closing her eyes and raising the back of her hand to her forehead: "Oh, my oblivion is a very Antony. And I am all forgotten."

Caroline giggles, and Dixie remembers to raise her chin again for Andie's drawing.

"Mr. Pratt said I was engrossing. That's what he said." Then she lowers her voice and crinkles up her face in imitation of the drama teacher. "'Dixie,' he said to me, 'that performance was really quite engrossing.'"

"That's a good sign, isn't it, Dix?" Caroline asks.

At that, all four girls look toward the door of Mr. Pratt's office, which remains stubbornly closed.

The door has been closed for almost an hour now—since well before the last bell of the day. Liz Warren got out of her last class by telling her biology teacher, Ms. Doone, that she had important school play business to attend to. Ms. Doone simply nodded and smiled. Now, in her senior year, her teachers no longer question anything she does—she has gotten straight As in almost every single class at Carmine-Casey. Because her teachers believe that seriousness is a quality built into her basic circuitry, she is above reproach. If she is not in class, there is no doubt that her reasons are entirely valid.

Now she sits opposite Mr. Pratt, hunched over his desk where a list of names lies between them. She has her forefinger planted like a carpenter's nail on one of the names, and she is waiting for him to say something.

"I don't know, Liz," Mr. Pratt says finally. He is a thin wisp of a man, his spectacles sitting low on his nose and his hair, what remains of it, like a feathery circlet from temple to temple around the back of his head. He looks pained much of the time—not so much physically as spiritually, as though he is carrying the grief of some distant history in the creases of his face. The girls have heard from reliable sources that he's never been married, and the popular belief around school is that he's gay.

"I don't know," he says again, looking at the name under Liz's finger. "Martha is a wonderful girl. She *understands* the play, maybe in a way that the others don't. . . ."

"But?" Liz asks.

"But don't you think her performance . . . lacks something?"

"Like what?"

"She's too . . . self-conscious. Too afraid to be dramatic. It's as though she's embarrassed of drama. Too worried that she's going to be . . . *sincere.*"

He looks up at Liz, his face seemingly in pain—suffering in the hope that Liz will agree.

She can't bear to hurt him. Besides, she knows what he's saying is true. This is why none of her friends has ever been able to break into the school productions. They resent having to take the performance seriously.

"Okay," she says, lifting her finger and sitting back in her chair. They look at each other across the table. "Okay. But *Dixie Doyle*? What about Lauren Schaffer?"

"Dixie can do it."

"But all she wants—" She stops herself. When talking to Mr. Pratt, she sometimes forgets she's talking to a teacher. She lowers her voice and starts again. "Don't you think she's just interested in getting attention?"

He smiles. "That's what we used to call charisma. And no matter how scintillating the writing is, you've got to have somebody delivering the lines who can . . ."

He doesn't finish his thought. He doesn't have to.

Liz wants to make him understand. She wants to make sure he knows this isn't just some petty personality clash—that Dixie Doyle really isn't the right person for the lines she's written. She's willing to go over it again and again until he's convinced that she's seeing things straight where this is concerned. But it already feels like she's said too much. She can see herself from the outside, and she looks an awful lot like a whining schoolgirl. So she determines not to argue anymore.

Instead, she says, "Dixie probably won't take it anyway. Does she know I'm directing?"

"Look," Mr. Pratt says, and now he's the one leaning forward—the conciliatory comfort of the modest victor. "I know you two don't get along. But . . ."

She knows what's coming next. She is going to have to learn how to work with people she doesn't always like. The only concern of the director is the production itself. If she wants to be a successful director, she has to figure out how to compromise. Et cetera. She doesn't like to be lectured to. Even more specifically, she doesn't like to be someone who *needs* to be lectured to. She wants to tell him it's okay, she gets it, he doesn't have to continue—but she doesn't know how to stop him without sounding like a poor loser.

Instead her mind abstracts itself. She begins to think about what it will be like to direct a show. She remembers something her older brother once told her before she went off to camp in the eighth grade. There was a trick she could do, something to test her mettle. (The phrase still calls to mind what it did for her back then: a malleable piece of metal being bent until it snaps.) During the sing-alongs, when everybody is clapping, she should clap in the same rhythm but on the offbeat, in the spaces between the clapping of everybody else. If you did it loudly and consistently enough, he explained, everyone else would be thrown off. And then you might hear a smattering of confused rhythms for a second or two while everyone readjusts to *your* clapping. That's the point at which your offbeat becomes the *on* beat. And nobody in the room, he said, would know what happened. Nobody would know that you were the one controlling their clapping.

When she thinks of directing, that's what she thinks of: everyone clapping to her rhythm without even knowing they are doing it.

"You know, Liz," Mr. Pratt is saying, "I'm really looking forward to seeing what you do with this production. I really believe you can accomplish great things with it. That's one hell of a script you wrote. You're a very talented young woman."

"Thanks, Mr. Pratt." She knows that these compliments are meaningless. She has heard them before. They are code for *I recognize you as one of those fragile students who needs a lot of positive reinforcement to stay afloat.* Sometimes the praise from her teachers seems almost sincere. But mostly it makes her cringe. She's smart—okay—but whatever success she may have, she believes it will only lead to higher expectations, expectations that, at some point, she will not be able to fulfill. Then what will she do with all their disappointment? Tote it around in her knapsack? She would prefer if people just wouldn't compliment her at all.

Mr. Pratt takes a ballpoint pen and puts a little arrow by Dixie Doyle's name, and now the cast list is complete.

He rotates in his chair to the computer keyboard and begins typing up the finalized list. While he does so, he can feel Liz's eyes on him. She is sitting there taut as a ball of rubber bands. She has always been a high-strung girl, he thinks to himself, but this process is pushing her to the precipice of her own abysmal anxieties. He knows that she is not used to relying on other people for her success. She hates having to put the fate of her play in the hands of someone like Dixie Doyle. Which is why, deep in his chest, he feels a tingle of joy at forcing the issue. It will be good for her to be relieved of a little control.

He finishes typing the list, prints it out, and then takes a thumbtack from the drawer of his desk.

"Are you staying here?" he asks.

"Is that okay?"

"Sure. I'll be right back." Of course, he knows she doesn't want to face their eyes—the eyes of all the girls in the auditorium who are about to be disappointed. Or even the eyes of those who aren't. He would pay good money to see Liz Warren and Dixie Doyle's first interaction after the final cast list is revealed, but he supposes he will not be privy to that.

When he comes out of the office, he purposefully avoids looking at any of the girls. He marches over to the corkboard on the wall and tacks the list to it. Then he turns and offers a generous smile to everyone and marches back into his office.

"Now we wait," he says to Liz. "We're trapped in here until the screaming stops."

Outside, Caroline rushes up to Dixie and says, "Dixie, look, there's the list!"

Dixie takes the lollipop out of her mouth and glances over to see if Andie is finished drawing her profile. Then, through the open auditorium door, she sees Binhammer walk past. She wonders briefly if he will come to this show. He normally doesn't attend the school plays, but maybe if she told him that it was important to her . . .

"*Dixie,*" Caroline says again. "The list!"

"So go see what it says," Dixie snaps back.

Caroline scurries off to the group of girls huddled around the list and scurries back.

"You did it, Dixie! You did it again!"

Dixie does not change her expression.

"Congratulations, Dix," Beth says. "Do you want to get some coffee now? I'm *starving*."

"Yeah, congratulations," Andie says. Then she hands Dixie her profile. The eyes in the picture are glistening.

chapter 7

The next day, on the back stairs, Binhammer comes across two girls throwing dice in the corner. As soon as they hear him they scramble to attention, all giggly and red, but not before he can see where those dice go. They are wrapped up tight in the palm of the one on the left, a tall senior with bright curls and, suddenly, a look of disenchanted experience. They stand there frozen as he approaches.

He normally doesn't take these stairs, which are in a dingy corner of the building away from everything else. But he has been avoiding Ted Hughes all day. He is anticipating, reluctantly, the formal introductions that he knows must take place at the big department meeting this afternoon, and he's in no mood to hasten the inevitable.

And now on these back stairs, he and the two girls with the dice stare at each other with expressions of obligatory glumness.

They are enthralling, these two glowing daughters of the social elite who have just been crouching like dockworkers at craps. He imagines them in their skirts and expensive shoes, tossing quarters on the sidewalk, rolling their own cigarettes, heckling the passersby.

"Give them to me," he says to the tall one, indicating the dice in her sweaty little palm.

"But Mr. Binhammer—"

"Give them."

He confiscates the dice—even though his impulse is to leave them be—and as soon as the tall girl puts the contraband in his palm, they both go scurrying off with their hands over their mouths as though they are trying to outrun their own bodies.

He stands there for a few minutes, studying what he has sequestered. The dice are actually pink plastic, and they have letters instead of dots on them. On one are the words KISS, LICK, SUCK, STROKE, SQUEEZE, BLOW, and on the other, FINGERS, TOES, GENITALS, CHEST, STOMACH, EAR. He turns them over in his hand, making different combinations and smiling to himself. Then he puts the dice in his pocket and continues to his next class.

His ninth-grade class goes by quickly. It is filled with girls who squirm in their seats and always seem to be trying to get out of their clothes. They tug at their collars and roll up their cuffs, they slip off their shoes and scratch the ankle of one foot with the white-socked toe of the other. Sometimes they even rest their feet on the crossbars of their desks, unconsciously hiking up their skirts and exposing their polka-dotted underwear. Unlike the seniors on the stairs, these younger girls seem to have a mechanical physicality that chugs along without shame. To these girls he is an object, a piece of furniture, a nightstand or a commode that they are obliged to stare at for a certain amount of time every day—like forced meditation. For the freshman class, he is a splinter in the minds of girls who are all body. They pluck at their bras while they are talking to him in the same way that they do standing before their vanities in the morning.

And when they file out of the room today, they leave behind the mild perfume of girl sweat.

Just as the last of them has gone, the door opens again and Lonnie Abramson's head appears.

"Department meeting, darling, after school. Don't forget."

She winks and is gone before he can respond.

Then the classroom is quiet, and it sounds like the inside of his own head.

Next up is his senior class, and he wonders what Dixie Doyle is so cheerful about. She says hello to him as though they were reunited lovers. During class, when Liz Warren is contributing an insight about Emerson and Kate Chopin, he finds himself distracted by Dixie's fingernails, which seem to be painted with purple glitter. When he realizes that Liz is finished talking, he tries to fake his way through an adequate response, but he must not be very convincing because she merely shrugs and turns her attention to the window.

He has lost Liz. Again. And he must fill the minutes until the end of class. As he gets up and stands before the room to read a passage from *The Awakening* that describes the protagonist's suicide, he fingers the dice in his pocket and remembers his first year at the school—recalling how dynamic he was, how he would never sit down as long as class was in session, how the girls with their sharp, pointy voices would poke at him all day and he would hunger for their attention, like an addict in a cloud of fluttering hypodermics.

When the bell rings, he feels like he has made no progress. Forty-five minutes have elapsed, yet he and these girls have gone nowhere. They have all stood still together.

Something, he thinks, has sprung a leak.

Okay, he says to himself. Okay. And the day goes on.

Fifteen minutes after the last bell of the day has rung, glancing cursorily through a pile of papers to avoid the inevitable, he finally decides he should go to the department meeting and finds himself on those dingy back stairs for the second time today. The halls outside the conference room are uncomfortably quiet—like an awkward pause in a conversation—and he can hear Sibyl's laugh even before he gets there. He can tell from the sound of it that she's covering her mouth with her hand—something she does when she's trying to maintain her decorum.

In fact, in the conference room at that moment, what Sibyl finds herself laughing at is something that Ted Hughes has just whispered to her, his voice sudden and confident, as though they were already intimate friends. Sibyl looks at the other women while leaning in closer to him. She is suddenly conscious of the territory her body proscribes.

But everyone is talking to Ted Hughes at once. Pepper Carmichael is giving him advice on the best Vietnamese restaurants in Manhattan, Lonnie Abramson is telling him a story about her daughter, Andie, and Mrs. Mayhew is guiding him through a tax form that she neglected to give him before.

Sibyl has taken the seat facing the door, so she is the first one to see Binhammer enter the room. He comes in already halfway through his usual apology for being late but stops as soon as he realizes no one is listening.

"So I told her," Lonnie's voice dominates, revving up for the punch line, "I said, 'Darling, if he notices that your barrettes don't match your shoes, then you've got much bigger problems!'"

Sibyl feels Lonnie's cackle at the base of her spine, and she stiffens all over. Ted Hughes glances up at Lonnie and smiles distractedly. Then Mrs. Mayhew points to another place on the form where he should put his signature.

"Oh," Pepper says, "here's Leo." Binhammer cringes at the mention of his first name. "Leo Binhammer, this is Ted Hughes."

Ted Hughes stands and shakes hands with Binhammer, who says, even though he promised himself he wouldn't, "Ted Hughes. Like the poet?"

"No," the man says simply and brings his finger up to his lips as though he's trying to remember something. Everyone waits to see what it will be, but after a few seconds he just shrugs and sits back down before his tax form. Binhammer takes a seat at the far end of the table and leans back in his chair. Sibyl sees something in his response—something that looks like the reticence of a misbehaving child about to be exposed.

Ted Hughes is a slight, pretty young man—well groomed almost to the point of slickness, his starched collar coming to two perfect points on either side of the arch knot in his tie. His eyes have more meaning in their movement than their color, darting like a novelist's pen from one thing to another. Sibyl has already noticed that he has a habit of seeming distracted, as though his true destination were just around the corner and current circumstances are preventing him from reaching it. And when he speaks, he seems to want to say three things at once and is disappointed at having to settle for just one. For women like Lonnie Abramson, who believe that attention directed elsewhere is the most valuable attention there is, he represents a challenge, and she does everything possible to force her body into his line of sight. When he turns his eyes on Lonnie, Sibyl can see the pink flush in her cheeks, the squealing delight of having those eyes—those eyes that go everywhere—rest for a second on her.

As for Sibyl herself, she looks at Ted Hughes in the same way she looks at modern poetry: an accumulation of ecstatica that contains within it (she is sure) moments of beautiful and tragic silence.

"So," Sibyl says, trying to catch his eye, "how have your first couple days been?"

"Rumpled," he says, looking up suddenly at the ceiling.

"Rumpled?" Lonnie says. "How do you mean?"

"I was thinking of something," he says, putting two fingers to his lips, "as I was walking through the halls today. Something someone said about girls liking to be rumpled sometimes. A beautiful line."

"I think I know what line you mean," Sibyl says.

"You do?" Binhammer says from the other end of the table, giving her a look.

"But," she continues, ignoring him, "I don't remember where it's from."

"Played with and rumpled," Ted says.

"I don't know," Binhammer interjects, authoritative and doubtful. "I think you might have just—"

"Goldsmith," Mrs. Mayhew declares, stone-faced. " 'Girls like to be played with, and rumpled a little too, sometimes.' Oliver Goldsmith."

"That's it," Ted says, smiling brightly. "A beautiful line, no?"

Sibyl does not want to look over at Binhammer. She can feel his eyes picking away at her—sharp, angry needles.

Indeed, as the curriculum meeting begins, Sibyl finds herself in the middle of a game of gazes. She can see Binhammer shooting vigilant glances at her from across the room—on guard against any attention she might give Ted Hughes. And Binhammer's reaction only makes her want to look at Ted Hughes more, which she does in surreptitious sidelong glances when Binhammer isn't looking. The only one she doesn't have to worry about, it seems, is Ted Hughes himself. He never looks in her direction at all.

Ted Hughes respectfully demurs during most of the conversation. Only once does he make a comment—muttering, almost under his breath, that he's not looking forward to teaching *The Great Gatsby*.

"Why not?" Pepper cries, horrified. "Don't you think it's beautiful?"

"Like diamonds," he says.

"Then . . ."

"It's this school," he says, apologetically. Then he continues, with increasing fervor, "It's just that I don't relish teaching it without boys in the room. Who's going to be embarrassed? Who's going to be sitting in the back of the class all red with boyish frailty? You know what I mean? You need masculinity, the more crumbled the better. Who are the girls going to feel sorry for? With only girls, the book is in danger of becoming all hurt fingers and billowing skirts."

Everyone is quiet for a while, Pepper tilting her head thoughtfully. Then Lonnie pipes up to say that it's funny because she has always wondered herself whether or not *Gatsby* needed some good old sexual tension in the room to work properly.

Sibyl wishes that Lonnie would just shut up. She wants to try to imagine Ted Hughes getting embarrassed as he reads *Gatsby*. She wants to hear him say more things about crumbled masculinity.

Lonnie beams proudly at everyone, and Mrs. Mayhew gives Ted Hughes an unreadable look before continuing with the meeting.

After it's over Binhammer is the first one out of the conference room. He dashes down the stairs to avoid any interactions. But he has to get his coat from the teachers' lounge, and that's where Sibyl catches up with him.

"So what do you think?" she says.

"About what?" he says, being purposefully obtuse.

"The new guy."

"Oh, I think he's great. I love him. How couldn't I love him? All those clever things he says. So real—almost entirely unrehearsed."

"You don't think he's clever? Or is it that you don't *like* that he's clever?"

"Sure," he says, rubbing his face with his palm. "He was fine. Everything is fine."

"Well, I think it's cute that you're jealous."

He is moving books around on the bookshelf, pretending to be busy, but she comes closer and gets in front of his gaze. Their eyes connect for a second before he turns away.

"I'm not jealous," he says. "This guy is small-time. I know him. I knew everything about him the minute I saw him."

She doesn't say anything. She is trying to figure out why she takes such pleasure in his discomfort.

"What do you want to know?" he continues, shaking open his coat. "You want to know why you and Lonnie and everybody are already so schoolgirl giddy over him? It's because he makes everything he says sound like it's the first time anybody's said it. So he's got nice delivery. Big deal."

"Well, I think it's cute. And besides—"

The door opens then and Ted Hughes comes in, looking distracted. Anyone else would feel the sudden awkwardness of intrusion—the leaden silence as big as a wrecking ball—but he does not seem to notice.

"Anyway," Sibyl says. "I've got to get home. I've got a million things to do." She gives Binhammer a hard stare with a cruel laugh behind it. "And I'm warming up a plate of loneliness for dinner." She turns to Ted Hughes. "It was really nice to meet you, Ted."

After she's gone, Ted Hughes looks confusedly at Binhammer, as though he's just registered something.

"Plate of loneliness?"

"She's a funny lady," Binhammer says, buttoning up his coat and trying not to provoke any further interaction.

But just as he gets to the door, Ted Hughes stops him.

"Listen, Binhammer—" He pronounces it as though it rhymes with *bomber.*

"It's Bin*hammer.* Like a hammer."

"Bin*hammer*? Are you sure?"

"Pretty sure."

"That's a funny name."

"You think so, Ted Hughes?"

"Anyway, I just wanted to say . . . I've, um, heard great things about you."

So that's all—that's what he has to say. Binhammer tightens his fist on the doorknob. He thinks about being outside in the hall—leaping down the stairwell and racing out into the street, into the anonymous dark. But he can feel the eyes of the other man on his back. The distracted eyes. The gypsy's eyes. The eyes of the usurper.

Sibyl called it jealousy. But Sibyl doesn't know.

He can feel the texture of the air between them in the room—a palpable presence, like a woman.

He turns around to see Ted Hughes scratching his head, saying, "From what I've heard you're the teacher extraordinaire around here. The way they talk about you, you're a prodigy."

Binhammer takes a tentative step forward, wondering if this is some kind of trick—if the compliment will be followed by a challenge, a slap in the face with a clever white glove.

"Who?" he asks, trying to make his voice as dismissive as possible. "Who's they?"

"It's all I hear from the girls. From what I can tell, Mr. Binhammer looms large in their fevered imaginations. And the faculty talk about you too."

"The faculty?"

"The ones who don't adore you seem to envy you. Didn't you know that?"

He finds, despite himself, that he wants to hear what the other man has to say. Hughes's performative quality seems to have dissipated in the diminished quiet of the room. Like an actor backstage. As though he were turning himself inside out for Binhammer alone.

"I don't know, Hughes," he says, chuckling modestly. "I think you may have the wrong person."

"Maybe. Maybe." His smile is intimate and fraternal. "But I sure hope not. Because I'll tell you something—I think I'm going to need your help. You see, I haven't got a clue what I'm doing."

Binhammer looks at him. Ted Hughes is someone behind whom every background goes gray. Binhammer feels something in his chest that is not quite pity and not quite hate—but thick and clenching nonetheless. I know you, he thinks. I know who you are.

Then he says it. "I know you. . . . I mean—what I mean is that I remember thinking the same thing. Like you. That I didn't have a clue. When I started. Everyone thinks that."

The other man looks at him gratefully, but he has already started to move around the room again—as though something else has just occurred to him. Collecting some books into his satchel, he says, "It goes away, that feeling?"

"Just remember," Binhammer says, "no matter how little you actually know, they know less."

Ted Hughes laughs, and Binhammer feels as though he has accomplished something significant—without knowing what exactly.

"You'll do fine," Binhammer says. "They'll love you."

At this very moment, three blocks east of the Carmine-Casey School, there are four senior girls walking home, and two of them are telling the story of how Mr. Binhammer caught them earlier on the back stairs with the sex dice. The other two are horrified, claiming that they would have died—they would have just died. How could they ever look at him again?

Then one girl says, "What do you think he's going to do with them?"

"Oh god."

And their eyes go unfocused.

chapter 8

Two years before, in San Diego, California, a woman with much to say on many topics sat silently in the lobby of a Spanish-style hotel, waiting for her husband. If she had been looking for attention from anonymous men she might have been immensely gratified at the moment, because she was smartly dressed, nervous, and, judging from the submissive smile on her face, eager to please—which is a combination of qualities that men frequently find alluring, and which in this case, drew the immodest gaze of almost every man who passed through the lobby that afternoon.

But she was not looking for attention. In fact, she might as well have been the only person in the lobby, for she divided her own gaze between the large set of doors leading onto the street and her own hands that tied themselves into knots in her lap, the rest of the world existing behind a scrim—just shadowed shapes passing in slow motion. The reason for her smart attire was that she had told her husband she was going to attend some of the panel discussions scheduled that afternoon as part of the "Twentieth-Century Literary Theory" conference being held at the hotel. The reason for her nervousness was that she had not attended any panels and instead had spent the afternoon in a room on the sixteenth floor having an affair with a man who was five years younger than she and who possessed the most beautiful hands she had ever seen. Finally, the reason for her submissive smile was that she was expecting her husband to come through the lobby doors at any second, and all she could think about was how good he had been to her—how sincerely and honestly and purely good.

The woman, whose name was Sarah Lewis, had kept her name when she married Leo Binhammer six years before. And Lewis was the name he used now as he came in on a rush of dry air through the doors.

"Well, Ms. Lewis, how was your afternoon among the erudite?"

And she dissembled and smiled and wanted to say a hundred different things but could only bring herself to say, "Fine. Boring, the usual." If they weren't in the lobby of a hotel, she would have thrown her arms around him and clung like a barnacle for dear life.

"Well, I had a great time," he said. "There's a used bookstore down the street—we should go there after dinner. Speaking of which, what are you hungry for?"

"Listen," she said. "Why don't you come with me tomorrow. After I give my paper, I mean. We could go to some panels. I know there are a couple you would—"

"No way. Huh-uh. I've said my farewells to higher education. I take my education lower to middling now."

She looked at him desperately.

"But you have fun," he continued. "Don't worry about me—I can entertain myself."

They were attending the four-day conference because she had been chosen to moderate a panel on the first day, and she was delivering her own paper at a morning session on the last day—and four days in San Diego in early October seemed like a pleasant way to begin the academic year. Her husband's only condition—he having settled into teaching at a prestigious girls' school—was that he not be required to attend any of the sessions, which he was convinced were designed to make him feel small and unworthy.

So she was alone at her session on the first day, and it was then that she noticed the younger man looking at her. She sat between the four members of the panel, and as each one delivered a paper on French feminist theory she saw that his gaze kept stumbling back to her—as though she were an obstacle over which his glance tripped in its anxious pacing.

After the session he was waiting for her outside the conference room.

"I read an article you wrote," he said, by way of greeting.

"*An* article? Maybe you mean *the* article." At that point she had had only one article published. It was on Nathalie Sarraute, and it had appeared in a tiny quarterly published out of Wisconsin.

"Didn't you write something on Colette too? No? Maybe I'm thinking of someone else."

Up and down the hall swam a hundred different breeds of academics, as though the two of them were standing in the shallows on the edge of some great intellectual abyss—self-congratulatory minds like colorful fish floating in eddies around their ankles. He put a hand through his hair, seeming not to care what it looked like after he had done it.

He wondered if she would have a drink with him in the hotel bar.

"I'm meeting my husband," she said as a warning.

"When?"

"Not yet, I guess."

They sat at the bar, where the light from the outside didn't get far enough through the windows to reach them. And she liked the way his hands moved, as though orchestrating something large and invisible just behind her. When he covered her wrist with one of those hands to make a point, there was a delicious guilt in her chest, and she could no longer hear what he was saying.

The conversation was intermittently academic, and when she told him about a Nathalie Sarraute book that had just been reissued in English, he took a miniature notebook out of his back pocket and flipped through the pages until he found what he was looking for. It was a list of book titles, some of which had lines drawn through them.

"So I always have something to read next," he explained, adding the Nathalie Sarraute book to the bottom.

She caught a glimpse of the page.

Melville, Pierre
Samuel Pepys, Diary
Little Women
Henry Miller, Rosy Crucifixion or ~~Charles Bukowski~~
Vesma Grinfelds, Right Dwn Yr Alley: The Comp. Bk of
    Bowling
Anne Edwards, Shirley Temple: Am. Princess
Dance to the Music of Time (3rd movement?)
Uzzi Reiss, How to Make a Pregnant Woman Happy (for
    Lola)
John Ashbery, Self-Portrait in a Convex Mirror
Dickens, ~~Martin Chuzzlewit~~

He smiled. "I never know what I should be reading."

"*Martin Chuzzlewit?*"

"I just finished it. I have a copy with marginal notes by El-liot Gould."

"The actor?"

"The man loved Dickens."

"You're joking."

"I have it upstairs, I'll show you."

Because she had never thought of herself as someone vulnerable to temptation, she had never built any defenses to keep herself from it—and so when he asked if she wanted to come up to his room, she assented with the passive acquiescence of a girl who, in the eagerness of the moment, believes that she is simply going along for the ride.

In the elevator she thought of her husband, and thought of him again while she waited for the young man to unlock the door of his room. But as much as she tried to conjure him in concrete form—as much as she tried to imagine the palpable pain she might cause him—she could only think about him in abstract terms, as though her own actions were simply a fiction, a cinematic illusion thrown up on a screen, and he an audience member delightfully enthralled at the drama. She had always suspected her husband of sharing equally in the longings of her childish heart, and now she could not imagine him being upset at such a tiny thing as this. He would laugh, she thought. A young man luring her to his room with *Martin Chuzzlewit*. He would laugh.

What a joke! He would never stop laughing.

It was impossible to tell how she felt. When she tried to look inside of herself, all she saw were tangled things shifting in and out of focus.

Once inside his room, he offered her a glass of water, and she accepted. To grab hold of something might keep her hands steady. She was aware of her own swallowing—suddenly all throat and stinging breath.

He sat next to her on the edge of the bed and leafed through some of the pages of the Dickens book. It struck her at that moment that it was possible, even likely, that his interest in her was purely academic—and so, suddenly embarrassed by her own girlish fancies, she stood up abruptly and dropped the water glass on the edge of the bureau, where it shattered.

"Oh, I'm sorry," she said.

"No problem. Hold still," he said, taking her by the hips and moving her away from the broken glass. Then he was down on his knees, delicately plucking the shards of glittering glass from the carpet and placing them in the upturned palm of his right hand.

An offering. Those fingers, priest-soft and steady. He could cup in his orchestral hand the broken and the treacherous.

When he stood up he was right in front of her—and everything stopped. The look in his eyes said that he had forgotten what he was just doing. Then he spoke.

"There's one thing," he said. "One thing I want to tell you."

"What is it?"

He spoke slowly. "Your article on Nathalie Sarraute. I think you're wrong about her. She's a romantic."

That's when he kissed her. And he was right about her article. And he kissed her. And he was right.

The glass shards he must have put down somewhere, but she could not remember that part of it. It was only afterward that all the proper lenses suddenly clicked into place—and everything came into sharp focus.

"Oh my god," she said. "I don't even know your name."

She was lying in the bed trying to make herself as small as possible under the sheets. He was leaning back in a chair at the foot of the bed, looking at her.

"It's Ted."

"Ted what?"

He told her.

"Oh Jesus. Fine. My name is Anne Sexton."

He squinted his eyes at her. Then he sifted through the clothes that were on the floor and from the pocket of a pair of pants he brought out a conference badge with his name on it. He held it up as proof.

"Great," she said, shaking her head. "That's just great."

He sat back down silently at the foot of the bed.

"Stop looking at me," she said.

Then, later, riding down in the elevator, she said, "You don't understand. I'm not someone who does illicit things."

"Come back tomorrow."

"Did you hear what I said?"

"It's not about being illicit."

"What is it about then?" But immediately upon saying it she realized that she didn't want to know—and was grateful to him for not answering.

"Come back tomorrow."

And he put his hands on her.

She wondered what it would be like to see her husband. She was sure he would be able to see it on her, like a haircut. She tried to think of things she would say in response, but she could only keep saying *I'm sorry I'm sorry I'm sorry* under her breath. Yes, he would know. He knew her better than anyone.

And then she tried to be angry with him. It was partially his fault. She wouldn't have done it if he hadn't left her alone. Or, no, it was because they had argued on the plane ride out here. If they hadn't argued, then . . . Eventually she was angry with herself for trying to blame him. It was a while before she realized her anger was just old-fashioned panic.

By the time her husband was there, right in front of her, she was tied up in miserable knots, and her stomach hurt.

He said, "What's the matter?"

"My stomach hurts."

He put his hand on her cheek. "Why don't you go up to the room and lie down. I'll get you something to take."

"No," she said. "I'll be fine. Really, I'm okay. Let's just go have dinner."

The rest of the night he was concerned about her stomach. She hated how easy it was to lie to him.

So the next day she told him she was going to some sessions, and she met the young man again. Since she had already betrayed her husband once, she wanted to find out what it was exactly that she felt for this Ted Hughes—because she feared that it was *something* rather than *nothing*. And she knew that if she didn't try to articulate that feeling, to expose it and name it, she would always think of it as lost treasure—something that her husband would never know he wasn't offering her. It wasn't fair to him. She would get to the bottom of this feeling. Held up to the light, it would look frail and small and common, she was sure of it.

But after her second day in the young man's room, she was only less sure of everything. He was like a complex, ephemeral thing, a fleeting notion, that abstract quality of beauty marbled with ribbons of masculine menace and hunger.

Standing in his shower, she heard his voice coming from the bathroom doorway. She peeked out from behind the curtain and saw him leaning against the doorjamb with no shirt on, his hands in his pockets and his eyes cast down distractedly.

"So can I ask you," he said, "where it is you're going back to the day after tomorrow?"

"Why?" she asked. But he didn't answer. She let the water pour over her body, and she tried to get inside it. She thought about being wrapped up in an envelope of warm water. "New York," she said finally.

"That's a coincidence."

"Oh no." Tucking herself into the water. "Don't think . . . ," she started, but then she realized she didn't know what she wanted him to think or not to think.

"You know what I like about New York?" he said. "Everywhere you go, it looks like someplace somebody has a memory of. If you think about all the street corners that mean something to you because you met someone there . . ." His voice faltered, as though he were considering something else for a moment. "Or all the stoops of buildings, or the restaurant windows, or the museum steps. And that's just your experience, you're just one of a million people. There are memories everywhere."

She had stopped trying to put herself inside the water and was now leaning against the tiles, listening to his voice. But then he was quiet for a while, and when she pulled the shower curtain aside to see him again, he was no longer there in the doorway.

His voice, his hands—these things stayed with her.

And that was why, afterward, she waited in the lobby for her husband and paid no attention to all the men whose gazes lingered over her.

And when Binhammer came and said, "So, Ms. Lewis, did you enjoy your afternoon among the erudite?" she dissembled.

The next morning, she told her husband to come meet her immediately after her session. She told him that she was tired of listening to papers, that she would rather see San Diego while she could.

So that was it—a failsafe termination was the way she looked at it. Even if Ted Hughes were there at her panel, even if she felt tempted—she had made it impossible for herself to do anything about it.

And, in fact, Ted Hughes was there. The conference room was half full with unsmiling academics waiting for the panel discussion with the weary acknowledgment that they would most likely be disappointed. She said hello to the other members of her panel, keeping her eyes on the door. He came in late, after the session had already started, and sat at the back—his eyes alternating between looking at her and looking at nothing.

After the session he was waiting for her in the hall.

"My husband is meeting me," she said.

"We just can't—" she said.

"I'm not someone who—" she said.

"There's no way this can—" she said.

She had worked out in advance a hundred different logical arguments about why they couldn't see each other anymore. But he didn't fight her. When she was done talking, he simply asked for her phone number in New York, and she gave it to him without thinking.

Before she left, she said, "I like what you said. About New York. That was . . . I liked it."

And he reached out to her with one of those hands, but she was already turning away, and she kept on turning.

At the end of the hall she saw Binhammer walking toward her.

"Who was that?" he asked.

"Who?"

"That guy you were talking to."

"He was just someone who liked my paper."

"The way he was looking at you, I think he liked more than your paper." He smiled. He liked it when other men found her attractive. It was one of their regular jokes. "Good-looking too. Did he ask for your number?"

"Uh-huh," she said, looking up at him. He was such a good man.

"And did you give it to him?"

"Of course."

She wanted to tell him everything, but she didn't know where to start. She didn't like to imagine what look he would give her—and the thought that whatever the look, it would be a part of every look he ever gave her again.

I have done something, she thought. *Oh my god. I have done something.*

"Can we go?" she asked.

"Sure. Does your stomach feel bad again?"

"No, I think I just need to eat."

When they walked out into the San Diego sun, she felt faint and clung to his arm. But she soon recovered, and they walked three blocks to an outdoor café where she picked at her food and sipped iced tea through a straw. He made jokes, and she laughed at them. After lunch, they continued to walk, and he said he wanted to buy some sunglasses so that he could have a pair of sunglasses from San Diego. So they went into several shops until they found a pair he liked—and then they sat on a bench in a small park and watched everyone else walk by. They were impressed, as you are more likely to be when you are in a foreign place, by the masses of anonymity.

Two boys ran by, and one cried, "How come you did it, Marshall? How come?"

When the sun started to go down, they got up from the bench and walked back toward the hotel; they spoke to each other the whole time, never running out of things to say. And pretty soon they became part of the anonymous crowd, and you couldn't tell them apart from anyone else.

chapter 9

Two weeks later, back in New York, Binhammer sat on the couch gazing at the back of his wife, who was in the other room typing—or trying to type—revisions on an article she hoped would be published the following year, and he knew, knew with the fearful instinct that in another place and another time might have driven a man to physical acts of violence or passion, that something was wrong.

It was just past eight o'clock in the morning, and he had opened the blinds so that every corner of the apartment was saturated with light. Outside, the air was infused with the stillness characteristic of weekend mornings in the city—the dormancy of a great machine being shut off for a mandatory period while all its gears are checked for wear.

He looked at his wife, through the doorway, hunched over in front of the computer with a mug of coffee on the desk beside her—and he looked out the window at the tops of trees and tops of buildings and tops of lampposts. And he looked back at his wife.

There she sat, still and cramped, as someone might who was trying to fold herself out of existence—her hands not even on the keyboard but holding her elbows. He could not see her eyes, but he knew that they were focused somewhere beyond the computer screen.

"What's wrong?" he asked, trying to modulate the fear out of his voice. He did not like to see her like this.

"What do you mean?" she said, half turning. Her face was

now in profile, and she bit her lower lip—something she had a habit of doing when she was put on the spot.

He wasn't sure what he meant, so he didn't say anything more.

She, however, seemed to take his silence as more accusatory than perplexed. When he didn't answer, she turned full around to look at him face-to-face. That was when he first saw the small flickers of desperation in her eyes. He recognized them as a plea, but he could not tell what they were a plea for. It was true: she still possessed a great deal of mystery, even after six years of marriage.

He wondered, briefly, how long men remained explorers in the terra incognita of their wives' minds.

Then she turned toward the computer, and he was looking at her back again.

"I think I did something," she said to her screen, her voice like a crystal bowl crazed with hairline fractures and ready to come apart. "I think I did something—"

He suddenly felt queasy. He wanted to go to her, but her breakability made him feel clumsy. In truth, he didn't care about what she might have done—he just wanted that shivering quality in her to be gone.

The story came out in fragments, sharp little splinters:

"There was someone. He. I didn't know what to do. It's not about. I mean, there's nothing. And I couldn't stop thinking about. It was something that happened. I was afraid. And I didn't know how to stop it. And then there was you. You are so good. So good to me. I didn't know what to do—I didn't know what to do."

He looked out the window. Too bright. It felt like there was white everywhere.

"When?" he asked.

"San Diego," she said.

There was white in his chest and in his head. There was cotton in his ears.

"Twice," she said.

He stood, everything inside him bent double, all his clenched purple viscera, and went into the bedroom and shut the door behind him. "Goddamn it," he said, voice rising. "Goddamn it, goddamn it." On the bed was something, and he grabbed it and threw it against the wall. It fluttered to the ground—her copy of *The Woman in White*, and it must have struck at the very edge of the spine because it left behind a half-moon dent in the paint that he would cringe to look at over the years they were to live in that apartment.

Then he froze. The gesture—so mundane, so unworthy of a literary life. He suddenly thought of himself as a character in a book. He imagined discussing this scene in one of his classes, with his girls. "We expect him to be furious here—after all, his wife has just admitted infidelity. But look, look at his response: sympathy, understanding, goodness. See, anger is—it's old-fashioned. It's boring."

He went back into the living room, where his wife had moved to the couch.

She wept openly now, her body shaken with spasms. She tried to look at him, in his direction, but she seemed unable to. He thought about that, about the fact that at this moment his wife was able to look at anything in the world but him.

He remembered being a child, coming into the kitchen where his mother was hunched over in front of the sink, her hands gripping the edge of the counter. When he had come around to the side of her, he could see she was crying. But when she noticed him, she turned her back and swept her palms across her eyes. Then she busied herself in the refrigerator, telling him she had to make dinner now and didn't have time to play—not allowing herself to meet his gaze.

Now, to his wife, he said, "Listen. Stop crying. We'll figure something out. I mean, there has to be something we can . . . Stop crying."

For a while they sat there not talking.

There was anger, yes, a smoldering anger—but there was something else, too. A need to subdue the panic of the moment.

A need to be superior to this scene. An unsettling calm in the face of calamity.

He went to the corner to buy coffee for them. He also bought bagels, but neither of them ate. He kept looking out the window because it was the only action that seemed to let him think properly.

Then they decided to go for a walk in the park.

"Do you want to take a jacket?" she said as they left.

"No, I'm fine," he replied. "Thank you."

They walked a long time along the winding paths, and sometimes they stopped to sit at a bench.

"Just twice?" he asked. "Only twice?"

She bit her lower lip. "Once more. When we got back here. He lives here. Just once more. And that's when I told him we couldn't anymore."

For a while he didn't want to touch her, and then he couldn't bear seeing her sitting there all folded up into herself. He put his hand on top of hers, and she looked grateful.

They walked some more and talked as they went—they could not seem to stop talking now—and when they came to the Metropolitan Museum at the eastern edge of the park, they went in. There was a special exhibition of a French expressionist painter, and they stood in front of one painting depicting a row of houses on the far bank of a river. There were only two human figures in the painting, and they were tiny in the distance. You would have missed them entirely if you hadn't been looking for them.

She said, "It's the most beautiful thing I've ever seen."

"More beautiful than Matisse?"

She looked at him, trying to read his tone.

"More beautiful than Fitzgerald?" He smiled. "More beautiful than Fellini? More beautiful than Stravinsky?"

"Yes," she said and smiled up at him playfully. "More beautiful than all of them."

After the museum, they walked back home and talked about what they had to do the rest of the weekend, what tasks they had to get done before Monday. They felt safe in the particularities of their day-to-day existence. When evening came, they decided to have Chinese food delivered, and they sat on the floor of the living room with their backs against the couch and watched television. He thought about opening up the fortune cookies but then decided not to.

Once, when they hadn't spoken about it for a while, he said, "Who was he, anyway?"

"Just some guy," she said. He wanted more, so she told him it was the one he had seen her talking to in the hallway outside the conference room.

He nodded. "He was good-looking."

She tried to dismiss him with a wave of her hand.

"No, no," he said, smiling, driving the moment back into something that looked like normalcy. "You did okay for yourself."

She swatted him on the chest with the back of her hand.

By the time they went to bed that night, they were exhausted. There seemed to be nothing else left to talk about. They had fit an entire lifetime of talking into a single day. He wondered if he would be able to fall asleep, but when his head was on the pillow he could hear the sound of his own heartbeat, and it lulled him.

His last thought of the night was about the man's name. He suddenly felt he wanted to know it, and he resolved to ask her in the morning. But by the time he woke up, she was already awake and in the shower—and when she came out she looked so happy to see him that he didn't want to bring it up. He thought maybe it wasn't so important after all.

chapter 10

October comes, and there are dry leaves everywhere. Like the girls of the Carmine-Casey school, the leaves collect in corners and chatter away with their brittle, leafy voices.

It should be said that while, prior to Ted Hughes's arrival at the school, Binhammer enjoyed a great popularity among the girls, by no means did he corner the market on their affections. He was generally considered a favorite teacher, but there were some girls who found him off-putting because he did not pay as much attention to them as they would like, and there were others who found him inscrutable—the way he would forget meetings they had set up with him just the day before. And there were some girls, of course, who simply didn't like him because it seemed that everyone else did.

But this year is different. This year when Mrs. Power goes off to have more babies (the girls pay close attention to whether or not she will lose the baby weight, particularly the puffiness under her chin—and she used to be such a skinny slip of a woman), the addition of a second male English teacher occasions no small amount of conversation. There are some girls, the traditionalists, who consider themselves diehard Binhammer girls, and there are others of more experimental stock who now count themselves Hughes girls. And there are some—still the majority perhaps—who are generally fond of both. As fond as they can be of teachers, of course.

As part of their informal course of study in how the interpersonal relationships of adults can mirror their own, the girls are watchful when it comes to the interaction between the two men. In class, Binhammer is frequently asked:

"Mr. Binhammer, are you and Mr. Hughes *friends*?"

One girl, a junior named Karen Randall, tells a story of when she was once using the faculty-only copy machine in the library. When Binhammer caught her in the act, he didn't seem interested in punishing her. Instead, he asked her politely how her year was going as he waited for her to finish her copying. She thought she was off the hook until Hughes came around the corner and the two men locked eyes. For a few seconds, both men just looked back and forth between each other and Karen Randall and the sign over the copy machine that said FACULTY ONLY!!

Then they both started talking to Karen Randall at the same time:

Binhammer: "I guess you shouldn't be—"

Hughes: "I don't think you ought—"

Binhammer: "The sign is right there, and—"

Hughes: "No, certainly not—"

Binhammer: "I suppose you should come to the office—"

Hughes: "Yes, let's let the office handle this—"

And the two men escorted her to the elevator while her gaze went helplessly back and forth between them. Neither of them had been known for being strict adherents to the edicts of the school, so this moment was unprecedented.

But once they were in the elevator, after some awkward silence and the shifting of many feet, Binhammer started talking to Hughes about the author Henry James.

"Have you started *The Americans* yet?"

Hughes made a dramatic gesture of exhaustion. It looked like he was deflating. "Ugh—they hate it."

"Can you believe it's still on the curriculum?" Binhammer commiserated.

"Intolerable!"

"Five years now we've been trying to teach that book!"

"Outrageous!"

By the time they had reached the top floor, the two teachers were so locked into conversation that they seemed to have forgotten entirely about Karen Randall and actually left her standing there in the hall wondering if she should go to the office by herself.

This story is a great favorite among the girls because they still like to imagine that absentmindedness is a reflection of great genius. To them the story is a glorification of both men. Like two handsome Socrateses.

When the story is told to Dixie Doyle, however, she does not like it. The Socrates part. She doesn't like to imagine Binhammer in a toga—it's silly. And Binhammer is not silly.

But now that October is here and the play rehearsals are under way, she has other things to think about. She has the starring role, after all: Clarissa, who is, according to the script, "a tough young woman of twenty-five with a temper and a pet parrot."

"I'm leaving," Dixie reads from the script in her best dramatic voice. "There's nothing more to say. I'll send you a postcard from Prague."

"But Clarissa," says Caroline, who is helping her rehearse. For her, acting is all about sticking your hand out in front of you as though you were Hamlet holding the skull of Yorick. "But Clarissa, I don't understand."

"There are a lot of things you don't understand, Ivan. I'm just one of them."

"Then it says I'm supposed to kiss you helplessly." Caroline flips through the next couple pages of the script. "I don't know what's going on. They don't seem to like each other very much."

Dixie bites her lip. "I know what you mean. But it's nice that she wants to send him a postcard, right?"

Then Beth, who is sitting on the edge of the stage holding her bare foot, says, "Look at this blister." Everyone gathers around. "Did you ever see a blister like that?" Everyone agrees that it's some blister.

Fifteen minutes later, the auditorium undergoes a dramatic change in atmosphere with the arrival of the Bardolph boys. The Bardolph Boys' Academy is the all-boy school five blocks south of Carmine-Casey. The two schools operate in tandem when it comes to dances, plays, and other extracurriculars. There are five boys in Liz Warren's *Salmonburger* script, and when they come through the doors of the auditorium there is a generalized flurry of self-consciousness and girlhood playfulness.

For the most part, Dixie finds the Bardolph boys to be juvenile—they seem so *small*, like kids you would babysit. Sometimes their cheeks are ruddy, white and red, and look as though a grandmother has been pinching them. And sometimes they are even giggly, which is the worst thing a boy can be. So in general Dixie never understands the dizzying excitement that seems to electrify the school when the Bardolph boys come for a visit.

But Jeremy Notion, the boy who was chosen to play Ivan, the other lead, is something different. He seems bored a lot of the time, especially around the girls who try to impress him. He doesn't have any reaction, for example, when Susie Mayer does her thing—the thing where she fixes her barrettes while talking to him about spending the weekend sunbathing on her father's boat. He gazes down at her as though he's only just tolerating her presence. That's what Dixie likes about him.

"Do you think Binhammer will come to the play this time?" she asks the other girls as the boys settle in.

"Maybe," Caroline says. "I bet you can convince him to come, Dix."

"I don't know," Beth says. "I don't think he likes school plays. He says they're not very good."

Dixie considers this. "Is your father coming, Beth?"

"Sure, Dix, I guess."

She likes the idea of performing in front of an audience of men. She finds them, in general, to be more generous toward her. While her friends' mothers are sometimes wary in her presence, their fathers always greet her with a frothy kind of affection. They always want to know how she's doing in school, what kinds of "scrapes" she's getting herself into. The way they talk seems antique in a barbershop kind of way—a bunch of men with lather on their faces talking about horse races. For a minute or two she entertains a daydream of an audience of men throwing roses at her feet and crying out, "Bravo, bravissimo!"

"Well," she says, "I'm getting bored. Are we going to rehearse or what? Where's the *director*?"

Finally Liz Warren shows up and gathers the cast around to begin rehearsal. It's more of a read-through today, actually, and Dixie wants to remain professional in front of Jeremy Notion, so she resists the temptation to make snide remarks about Liz's shirt, which anybody can see is too big for her and looks like a sack. She makes sure, however, that she's sitting next to her leading man so that she can lean over and point to the script when he loses his place. For a while their shoulders are even touching— but she remains casual.

She puts on her most dramatic vocal performance, even at this early stage of the rehearsals, and afterward Beth and Andie and Caroline surround her to tell her what a fabulous job she's done. They've been sitting in the corner watching the entire thing. Andie even drew a picture of it, like a courtroom artist's rendering.

"But you know," Beth says, "you're going to have to kiss that Jeremy boy. He's got funny lips."

"Yeah," Caroline agrees. "He's not a very good Ivan."

"As far as Ivans go," Andie concludes. The thing about Andie is you never know whether she's agreeing with you or making fun of you. The other girls feel suddenly chastened and disregard her comment.

"Well, I like him," Dixie says, holding her chin up. "Did you see how he didn't pay any attention to Pauline when she was practically flashing her boobs at him? He doesn't like trashy things. He possesses *quality*."

"Yeah," Caroline agrees, "I guess he's kind of cute."

The four girls gaze at Jeremy Notion, who is across the auditorium looking on as two other Bardolph boys punch each other in the arm.

Dixie watches for a moment and then says, "Do you think his ears are funny? I think he could be my boyfriend. Watch this."

She pulls herself up to her most dramatic height and walks across the auditorium to where the three boys are. Then she asks Jeremy if she can talk to him for a second.

"I have an idea," she says as he follows her to a gap near the edge of the stage where unused floodlights are stacked. He seems confused but willing. "We're going to practice our lines together."

"Didn't we just do that?"

"I don't mean here. Anyone can rehearse here. We're the *leads*. We have a greater obligation to the play."

"Oh," he says, nodding. "Okay."

"We can do it at my house. Tuesdays. You should meet me here after school. If I'm not here, wait for me—sometimes I'm a little late."

He looks at her blankly. Then a little grin begins to grow on his face.

"Now don't be silly," she says admonishingly. "This is my last play here. I want it to be good. That means you have to be good, too."

"Are your parents going to be there? I mean in the afternoons?"

Dixie rolls her eyes for an answer. "And one more thing. From now on when we talk, I'm going to call you Ivan, and you should call me Clarissa. That's the way they do it."

"Who?"

"Actors. It's called *method*."

"Okay, Dixie. Whatever you say."

She gives him a playful slap on the arm. "Be good, Ivan. There's a lot of things you don't understand. I'm just one of them."

"What? Huh?" He is nonplussed.

"It's from the play, Ivan. The play. You know, the one we just read?"

"Oh. Sure, I remember that." And then he smiles broadly, proud of himself, and Dixie leaves him standing there.

Liz Warren, who is sitting against the wall just around the corner making emendations to the script, overhears the entire conversation and cringes. Closing her eyes as though in deep concentration, she gnaws on the end of her pen.

What distresses her most is that Dixie Doyle is a more effective actress off the stage than on. Second in descending order of distressing things: Dixie seems to get most of her acting cues from bad television. To Liz there is nothing worse than participating without conscious irony in the clichés of teenage girlhood. She is sure that if cornered she could admit to the existence of worse crimes, but some sins are all the more egregious because of their prevalence.

And it exasperates her that Dixie is invariably successful in her tactics with boys. Everything that comes out of Dixie's mouth should, in the moral universe that Liz inhabits, derail any further engagement. By all reason, boys should find Dixie to be a short ride on a broken track. Liz doesn't understand how, after the mundane exchange she just witnessed, a relationship could ever get to the kissing stage. Much less the holding hands in public, the social partnership, the sex. How could Jeremy, in all seriousness, forget about Dixie's hackneyed performance of girlishness long enough to take off her clothes?

She shakes it out of her head. Jeremy Notion doesn't really concern her—not in terms of the play at least. He may be lacking the common sense to stay away from Dixie Doyle, but he certainly does have that quality of organic masculinity that is perfect for the role of Ivan. She pictures the character as a tight lump of flesh, the unnatural extreme of a natural force: a tumor of manhood balled up in the body somewhere and demanding some kind of response, some kind of action. Like the walls of scuffed flesh she observes walking to and from school, the men and boys who, unknowingly, force her to walk in the street to avoid them—or stand in blind doorways until they pass—with their brute strength.

Liz wonders how Dixie does it, willingly putting herself in the way of that moving wall of masculinity. She wonders if this is, in fact, something to be admired.

When she looks at her watch, she realizes how late it's gotten. She hops up and rushes to the lobby of the school, where, as she wraps herself in her coat, she sees Mr. Hughes walking past distractedly.

"Oh," he says, though she knows he doesn't have any interest in talking to her. "Hello, um—"

"Liz," she says. "Liz Warren. I'm in your class." In fact, she is taking two English classes this year, his and Binhammer's. English is her subject.

"Liz, of course. I knew that."

"Well . . ." She has stopped buttoning her coat. She does not want to appear rude. On the other hand, she doesn't know what else to say to him.

"And how come," he says finally, "you're here so late?"

"The play. The school play. It's nothing. I wrote it. It's nothing."

"The play—let me see. . . ." He puts his hand to his forehead as if trying to coax out the memory he needs. "What is the name of it again?"

"It's stupid, really. I don't even like it. It's called *Salmonburger.*"

"Ah! Wait, I think I remember. The one based on the *Oresteia*, right?"

"Not based on. *Patterned* after." She wants him to understand the difference. She can feel it in her chest, the importance of his comprehending the significant difference.

He squints his eyes and nods. "Patterned after the *Oresteia.* Yes."

She waits for him to say more, but when he doesn't, she thinks she should say something.

"Why are you still here? I mean—do you have meetings?"

He looks around the lobby, frowning. He seems not to have heard her.

Then he says, "You know, when I was in college I had a thing for Ezra Pound. All I did was read *The Cantos* over and over. It's all I did. Then one night I fell asleep reading them and I woke up the next morning and discovered that I had rolled over on the book in my sleep. And the pages were all bent and creased." He looks pained. "And then when I tried to read *The Cantos* again, they sounded different to me. Not as good. Even now."

He looks at her. Something coils up in her stomach.

"Silly," he says. "Isn't it?"

Except she doesn't think it's silly at all. She thinks about it later when she's trying to do her homework under the dim light of the desk lamp in her room. It seems like one of those stories whose meaning is always just around the next corner in your head. But she never really gets settled down to dealing with it—and by the next day it is mostly gone, having left that illusory trace of worry behind.

chapter 11

"It's not that they shouldn't go out together," Liz Warren says to Monica Vargas as they sit at the long lunch table picking at plates of baked ziti with plastic utensils. "I just don't understand why they have to be so *demonstrative*."

"I know what you mean. The other night I was coming out of the building and I saw her blowing him a kiss. Can you believe it? I mean, actually blowing him a kiss."

"Oh my god."

"With her whole arm. She almost clobbered a pedestrian."

It is true that Dixie Doyle and Jeremy Notion have been seen together in the neighborhood by a number of credible witnesses. Though what is less clear is how authentic their interactions are to be judged. There are some girls who say that the two are obviously practicing their roles for the play—with a kind of method-acting diligence. There are others who claim that Dixie drags him around the city like a poodle on a leash, doing all the talking while he bites his fingernails and gazes wearily at her chest, waiting for the next time she'll let him do things to her. Still others believe that the boy is just one of Dixie's hobbies—that there is nothing going on apart from Dixie's using him as a portable audience for the flaunting of her self-admitted electrifying personality.

"Admittedly," Dixie has been overheard saying, "I have an electrifying personality."

Liz wonders if Dixie knows what the word *admittedly* means.

"And he is just annoying," Liz continues. "I'm constantly telling him how to read all his lines. I mean, he puts the same exact emphasis on every single syllable. There's no discrimination. I've never heard anyone stress an 'and' so much before. 'I'm getting a whiskey *and* soda.' I had to explain to him that the soda wasn't what was at stake."

"Ugh. I don't know how you do it, Liz."

Monica Vargas is a pointy-looking girl—sharp eyes, black hair, a striking smile with teeth that are slightly crooked so that you can see the edges of them. At the moment, her long fingers have plucked a burned ziti noodle that she knocks against the table for audible proof that the thing is not meant to be eaten. Like Liz, Monica is an excellent student—the kind of student who, according to the teachers, makes a classroom. Your history class may be filthy with dopey, tight-skirted twits, but Monica's presence will cut through the muck. She has a low tolerance for the ridiculous and will stab through the flabby excess of any of her peers who happen to be standing between her and her intellectual ends.

The two girls, Monica and Liz, are as close as their own swelling intellects allow them to be. Wary about proclamations of friendship, they find in each other at the very least a cohort in derision.

Liz, however, likes to think that she is the more sympathetic of the two—possessing, as she does, a humanistic, artistic bent that is complementary to and conveniently not in competition with Monica's flair for cold science.

"Well," Liz says now. "There's still time. The play isn't for another couple months. I think something can be done."

"Ugh," Monica says again, holding up a stringy ball of greasy cheese with a plastic fork. "Can you believe this? This isn't right." She flops it down on her tray. "Why didn't I just have a hardboiled egg? I'm always happy with a hardboiled egg. No surprises."

After school, the two girls walk to Monica's apartment, where they drink orange juice and sit on the kitchen counter eating miniature carrots out of a bag. Then, in Monica's bedroom, which is a chaos of cultural production—books, CDs, photos cut from magazines—they lie on the floor making themselves sick with stories about the moral and aesthetic outrages of the common man. When they discover they have wasted over an hour of their lives gossiping about their peers, they switch to more worthwhile topics and make outlines of upcoming essays for history and English.

Then Monica reads the script revisions Liz has made to accommodate the talents of her actors. Liz watches her read, Monica leaning over her desk, her black hair hanging straight down, her forehead in her hand—the focused concentration of a coiled rattler.

"I like this line you added," she says finally. " 'You broke my heart and my tibia.' Is that for Jeremy?"

"Yeah," Liz says. "I thought I'd give him an 'and' he could emphasize all he wants."

Monica gives her an evil, complicit smile. Then she goes back to the script.

When she's finished, she says, "It's good. But do you think the social criticism is explicit enough? You don't want to turn it up a little?" Monica, Liz knows, is fonder of strength than subtlety. Her mother is a divorce lawyer, and her father is a self-absorbed, misogynistic jackass. At least that's what Mrs. Vargas tells the girls. But to Monica, who only spends a weekend with him a few times a year, he is just a balding man with nice suits.

In the hall outside Monica's bedroom, Paulo the cleaning man vacuums the carpet and gazes at them with weighty man stares—and with a contempt that both girls feel they deserve as privileged members of upper-class Manhattan.

"Maybe I'll bring Paulo to the prom," Monica whispers after he's passed. "What would Dixie Doyle say then?"

"Come on," Liz says, getting down to business. "You have to help me think about this play. The rehearsals are atrocious. What am I going to do about that Jeremy Notion?"

Monica looks out the window thoughtfully. "At least he looks the part. He's kind of attractive, don't you think?"

Liz begins doodling nervously in the margin of her script. "I guess. I don't know. I never really thought about it."

The two girls are silent for a moment. Then Liz adds:

"That's Dixie's bailiwick anyway."

"Did you just say bailiwick? Tell me you didn't just say bailiwick."

"What? Why? It's a perfectly legitimate word."

After the sun sets, Liz walks home, feeling illuminated and refreshed by the mazy headlights of the passing taxicabs. She eats dinner with her parents, two people who do not feel nearly as embarrassed in the world as Liz believes they should.

While she cuts through a bumblebee-striped slab of grilled eggplant, Liz's father delights in posing philosophical questions to his daughter. Meanwhile, her mother shakes her head, mystified at such seriousness over dinner, and tries to change the topic to something more befitting teenage girlhood.

"Lizzie, do you think art is a form of religion?" her father says.

"Honey, don't you want to come shopping with me tomorrow?" her mother says. "I could get you out of school."

"Lizzie," her father says, "I can't wait to see what you come up with for your Hemingway paper."

"I worry about you, honey," her mother says, "always with your nose in a book."

Liz's days go on like this, week after week, with a comfortable sameness. As she navigates herself quietly past all the people who populate her world, there are times, it is true, when Liz suspects herself of being superior to those around her. But these moments are tempered by an equal number in which she fears that something is truly wrong with her—something fundamental and abstract. Or that, perhaps worse, she is simply *average.* Her great fear is that someone she is close to, a parent or a teacher, will one day let it slip that the myth of her excellence has been created simply to make her feel good. After all, she wonders, isn't one of the most despicable crimes of commonness the foolish belief that one is *uncommon?*

And then, one day, she comes home to hear her mother crying softly through the door of her parents' bedroom and her father standing at the counter in the kitchen, staring blankly into the sink.

It takes her a while to figure out what to do. The little girl part of her, which she can feel in her fingers and toes, wants simply to say, "Daddy?" But she knows, maybe for the first time, that she is beyond that age. And, so realizing, the fear transforms itself into self-hatred and anger. It is unjust of anyone to force that awakening on her so suddenly when she was having such a nice day.

"What did you do to her?" she says finally. She can feel her body refusing to move, drilling itself to the spot in the kitchen.

Her father looks up and tries to smile but then seems embarrassed by the artificiality of it. He is a good man—a beautiful, good man. "Oh, Lizzie. You know how things are. Nobody did anything to anybody. Your mother . . ."

She can hear the click and whir of the refrigerator as it comes on.

"Why is she the one crying?" She is surprised at her own protectiveness with respect to her mother. Normally she considers herself her father's daughter.

She waits for the answer, but her father simply shakes his head at this impossible question.

Folding her arms across her chest, she asks provokingly, "Are you getting a divorce?"

"A divorce? Who mentioned divorce? Really, Lizzie. You know better than that. These things are complicated. More complicated than divorce." He chooses his next words deliberately. "You know, your mother and I are very different people. But we knew that going in."

His voice is like warm sand on the beach. You want to dig yourself into it. You wouldn't mind being buried to your neck in it.

"Let me ask you a question," he goes on—though she knows that this is his rhetorical preamble to a philosophical question and not an actual invitation for an answer. "Don't you think that sometimes we are attracted to other people because of all the ways in which they are *not* like us?"

So her parents are not getting a divorce. And later that evening her mother appears in the doorway looking as though nothing has happened. She comes in and sits on the edge of Liz's bed, beamingly coy.

"See," she says, pointing to her own beaming smile. "This is something you still have to learn about cosmetics. They just cover everything up. A little fresh mascara, some blush, and you're a new woman. Why don't you ever let me try it on you? Well, but you're already so beautiful, aren't you?"

Liz has looked up from her textbook, but she doesn't know how to talk to her mother—who, she suspects, always wanted a different kind of daughter. Someone who can talk about fingernails and hemlines, about hair products and wrinkle creams. Her mother is tragic in the way that exquisite childhood things are always tragic: in the profusion of her personality there is always the discordant note of the exhausted and the lost.

"Really though, Lizzie," her mother continues, "there are some lipsticks that are almost invisible. No one even notices you're wearing them."

She picks at her fingernails for a moment and then looks up to the ceiling, sighing dramatically.

"Oh, life is full of a lot of silly things, Lizzie. Silly, silly things."

chapter 12

For the Carmine-Casey girls, the curiously electrified interactions between Mr. Binhammer and Mr. Hughes are something they continue to be fascinated by even as they feel increasingly excluded from them. Everyone in the hallway stops to listen when Binhammer roars at Hughes, "Can you try to focus for two minutes? Can you?" And then everybody laughs because the two men are smiling at each other with that canny, belligerent male affection the girls recognize from their brothers, their fathers, their uncles. The girls know, on some level, that for boys a punch in the eye is as good as a hug—that the animals they have seen ripping into each other's flesh on nature documentaries are actually just playing, vying for territorial dominion and reassuring themselves of their own maleness. But the girls also believe, with the kind of faith that surpasses understanding, that these boy animals know how silly it all is—and that this is just their way of having fun.

What bothers the girls is that there sometimes seems to be no place for them in this dynamic. When Lydia Crane is talking with Mr. Hughes in the hallway, for example, Mr. Binhammer, who is waiting for the elevator, interrupts and says to him, "You teach Lydia?"

"I do."

"She's great."

"I know it. You don't have to—"

"She wrote a great paper for me last year. On Hawthorne and Melville, wasn't it?" Binhammer looks briefly at Lydia but doesn't wait for her response. "Just a beautiful paper. It took her forever to write it. You remember how many times we went over it, Lydia?"

"You know what?" Lydia begins, "I was just thinking about that paper yester—"

"Well," Hughes interrupts. "You should see what she's working on now. It'll knock you over. Kathy Acker and the surrealists."

"Kathy Acker? What are you teaching Kathy Acker for?"

"Hey, let me ask you a question. On another topic. How many of these girls do you think—"

That's when Hughes realizes that Lydia is still standing between them, her gaze springing back and forth.

He shakes his head. "It's not important," he says to Binhammer. "I'll ask you later."

The whole interaction leaves Lydia Crane feeling funny. Later, in telling the other girls, she tries to come up with an approximation of her feelings, and the closest she can come is jealousy. But she doesn't know how to say it without sounding like she has a crush on both teachers, so she finally stops trying.

But each of the girls who hears the story has at one point or another felt the same thing. The girls daydream, while moving creamed corn around on their plates at dinner, about ways to insert themselves between the two men—about what they might say to get their attention and participate in the conversations that seem so sophisticated, thrilling, and just the slightest bit inappropriate.

And in this way the days of October shuffle themselves into November like a deck of playing cards, each day bearing only an accidental relationship to the one before or after it.

For Binhammer, Ted Hughes becomes a spanner in the works, gumming up the progress of his day. A speed bump in the road. He finds himself having to slow down when Hughes is in sight, having to take stock, having to be more careful of his words. He sometimes catches himself buttoning his coat or straightening his collar, as though he were going in for an interview.

For the first few weeks, he simply hates the man with an uncomplicated fury. He avoids him in the halls. He fantasizes about all the ways in which Ted Hughes might fail at the school, might be humiliated, might be all the more disappointing for the promise everyone seems to believe he possesses. He wants to expose him as an impostor, someone who doesn't belong as Binhammer himself does. Ted Hughes cannot be one of the great intellectual knights-errant of the Carmine-Casey School for Girls. Can he?

But as the days go on, Binhammer's fury gets overgrown with other emotions—like a seed giving rise to some complicated plant.

In short, now he's not sure how he feels about Ted Hughes. He knows that anger should be a larger part of the equation, but he just can't seem to muster it any longer. In fact, he has difficulty picturing this man sleeping with his wife. And yet he knows it happened. Sometimes, sure—sometimes an image will flare up, a bright, overexposed picture of the two of them together like a marquee all over the inside of his skull. Not sex, though. The sex seems secondary. In these bright-as-daylight cases, it's little details he imagines. The intimacy of fingers. Sarah, his wife, combing back his hair with her hand. The two of them furtively touching fingertips in the bar, knowing they might get caught. His fingers tracing the architecture of her face.

These images are painful. They are. But the pain peters out after a while because there is no fear to drive it. Sarah loves him. Feels attached to him by an almost biological bond. She doesn't want to leave him. This he knows. And so it's difficult to feel the sort of things he knows he should feel—the grab bag of jealousies, insecurities, vengeances.

In addition to this, there are moments, gorgeously contorted moments of human fickleness, when he can look at Ted Hughes from across the room and see what his wife must have seen in him. Yes, there is a reason the girls like him. There is a reason his wife was drawn to him. Watching him in the teachers' lounge one day, Binhammer thinks, Yes, it's true, the man has something.

"I'm going home," he announces. In addition to Ted Hughes, three other teachers are reclining in various poses around the room, one of whom is Walter, making notes in the margin of a book about World War II.

"Good night," Walter says, without looking up. The older teacher, Binhammer thinks, is religious about his tragedy: he sees moments of calmness as simply hiatuses before the next coup d'état, the next holocaust.

A few moments later, outside in the hall, Ted Hughes catches up with Binhammer before the elevator.

"There are some girls in my class," Hughes says, "who have started an anti-marriage campaign. They say that marriage is just a way for people who have failed at real love to make themselves feel better."

Ted Hughes smiles widely. His smile is like a roulette wheel. It spins in a crazy blur—but when it slows down and falls on you, you feel as though you've won something.

"This is the best part. They want to call themselves the Nuns of Matrimony."

"Does that mean—"

"They don't have anything against sex," Hughes explains. "In fact, there's a pro-sex statement in their bylaws."

"No kidding."

"They're beautiful, aren't they? Such adorable little bundles of outrage."

Binhammer nods his head. He has been surrounded by women for so long that he is not used to these male exchanges, and they give him a small thrill. Because, yes, the girls are beautiful in their outrage—and until this moment he didn't know that was something he could articulate.

He wonders if some gesture of farewell at the end of the day will be required of him. Is this the time when two men shake hands? Clap their palms on each others' shoulders? Hug? He has discovered that male beginnings are accidental, arbitrary—yet he still does not know how men end things. But it looks like Ted Hughes has more to say anyway.

"Listen," he says, inching so close that Binhammer can smell something stiff and leathery, like aftershave or starched collars or maybe just the man's skin. "What do you know about Sibyl?"

"Sibyl? What about her?" Binhammer feels suddenly hot and presses the down button on the elevator panel.

"What I mean is—I know she's been separated from her husband for a while. Not that that means . . . She's just said some things to me that—"

A student walks by behind them, and the two men gaze around the hall until she passes. Binhammer jabs his finger at the elevator button again.

"Is it possible," Ted Hughes continues, "that she's flirting with me?"

The elevator doors open, and Binhammer steps inside. He turns to face his companion, who remains standing in the hall-way.

"She's upset about her divorce," Binhammer says. "I don't think—I mean, from what people have told me—I don't think she wants to start anything."

Ted Hughes looks relieved. Binhammer realizes he was trying to avoid an entanglement, not seek one out. "Probably just looking for some male attention," Ted Hughes speculates as the doors begin to close between them.

Binhammer nods. "Probably just looking for some male attention," he confirms—but the elevator has already started down.

Out on the street he walks quickly, trying to avoid the eyes of the packs of Carmine-Casey girls left over from the day of school. They roam in small giggling herds around the block for as much as an hour or two after the final bell. Sometimes he will find them crouching in alleys, smoking. In these cases, he pretends not to recognize them. And after he has passed, he can hear them erupting in shrieks.

Once he reaches the corner, he looks around and then wedges himself under the gunmetal umbrella of a pay phone.

He dials a number, and when his wife picks up the phone, he tells her that he has a faculty meeting and will be home an hour later than usual.

Then he hails a cab and gives the driver an address.

He likes being in the backseat of a taxicab—it makes him feel sleepy and meditative. In the intimacy of the little vinyl coffin, his thoughts become large, abstract. He recalls Dixie Doyle becoming agitated in his class that morning—rubbing her fingers up and down her calf and complaining that she missed a spot shaving. Then she took her friend Caroline's hand and put it on her leg. "Doesn't it feel gross? Like a mouse or something?"

He thinks about that—those tiny glistening hairs.

He also thinks of Sarah. The woman whose love is an easy assumption. Even now. Especially now. If the marriage were going to end, it would have ended two years ago. It doesn't even require speculation.

Then there's Ted Hughes. He is like a boy, Binhammer thinks. No one else sees that. That face being closed off by the elevator doors. That smile. The tinny music box of his voice.

Sometimes Binhammer finds him in the hall between classes looking around confusedly. And when asked what's going on, Ted Hughes gets shaken out of his reverie and responds, "Oh, I was just thinking of something." And then he wanders off.

The hand through his hair. The click in the back of his throat that sounds like fragility.

When the cab pulls up at the curb, Binhammer is jolted as though waking up from an afternoon nap. He gives the driver some bills and enters one of the five-story buildings that are lined up like dominoes down the block. At the top of four flights of steps, which he takes two at a time—suddenly feeling like a vigorous child—he has to think hard to remember which apartment door is the one he's looking for. He has only been here twice before.

"Hughes thinks you're flirting with him," he says, brushing by her when she opens the door.

"Binhammer?" she says, touching her hair. "What are you doing here? And why would Hughes think that?"

The thing about Sibyl is she never knows how to hide anything.

"I told him you just wanted some male attention."

She frowns, trying to look hurt.

Binhammer looks around at the apartment. "Did you change something in here? It looks different."

"The couch is new. I needed something classier for all my gentlemen callers. By the way, you can't just come up here anytime you want."

Her refusal is exciting because it wants to be countermanded. Desperation, too, is a kind of desire—and hers compels him. The first time he was in her apartment he was invited for cocktails along with a number of other Carmine-Casey faculty. The second time it was just the two of them. They had taken a walk after school and found themselves on the stoop of her building. Upstairs, he kissed her—twice—before stopping himself and fleeing.

This is the apartment that she could afford on her salary after the separation. The main area is just big enough for a couch and a television she has wedged into a hole in the wall that looks like it might once have been a fireplace. On the other side of a thin wall is the kitchen with its cracked tiles and peeling shelf paper. Beyond that you would find a grimy little bathroom and a bedroom that has her oversize marriage bed—taken like a hostage from her husband, wedding linens and all. He likes the color of her solitude. This is a place where femininity is not buffed and powdered perfect—no, here it's smeared on mirrors and gets stuck in dresser drawers.

What Binhammer can't understand is her obsession with plants. There are plants everywhere. On all the windowsills, in pots on top of the television, in ceramic planters on the coffee table and bedside table, hanging in the bathroom. And all different types of greenery: things that have rubbery leaves, or thorns, flowers and buds. Spidery, tendrilly hanging plants with little organic explosions at the end of each stem. And some strange bamboo-looking stalks with a visceral tangle of white roots growing in a nest in the bottom of a clear vase. Binhammer doesn't like to look at this last plant, which reminds him of embalmed corpses, scientific experiments, and pasty genitalia.

"Aren't you his mentor?" he says to her, looking out the window to the street.

"What?"

"Hughes. Didn't Mrs. Mayhew make you his mentor?"

"So?"

"So, are you mentoring him? Showing him the ropes? Explaining how girls work?"

"We've talked. We've had some conversations." She sits on the couch and tugs at the hem of her shirt, examining it.

"And what—" Binhammer realizes he is stacking one biting remark on top of another, so he checks his tone. The next question is sincere. "And what do you think of him?"

"I don't know," she says slowly. "There's something about him. A quality. The students adore him. And he knows his stuff. He spent an hour explaining post-structuralism to me. And for once in my life it actually began to make sense."

Just like her, he thinks. She's got it all wrong. Just like her to confuse showmanship with intellect. Hughes doesn't care about post-structuralism. He was just acting. Trying to dazzle. A lot of explosions, like fireworks. It's all spectacle. A beautiful spectacle.

I would do the same thing, Binhammer thinks.

"He's not your type," he says to her as he takes a stem of green leaves in his hand. Plants everywhere.

"What do you have against him anyway?"

Not him, he thinks, crushing a waxy leaf between his fingers. Not him.

Then he goes over to the couch where she is sitting and stands in front of her. For a few seconds their eyes are locked, their gaze becoming a steel rod between them. It seems impossible that they should ever be able to move closer or farther apart than they are now. He can imagine them just orbiting each other, at this precise distance, their gazes never breaking, for the rest of their lives.

But then she reaches her hand out, tentatively, and lays her palm flat on his stomach. It's a curious touch, visceral, shivery, and intimate. It reminds him of her viny plants. So he takes her wrist and draws her up to him.

The kiss is full of discordant things—shrieking babies, plastic intimacies, arthritic old women holding themselves up at the edges of tables, unrecognized silences.

Then he pulls away, angry at himself—either for kissing her or for ceasing to kiss her, he cannot tell. He doesn't want to look at her.

"I have to go," he says.

She doesn't say anything.

"I have to go," he says again.

"So go." She sits back down on the couch and picks up a magazine from the coffee table, flipping the pages violently.

When he turns to leave, he can hear her coming up behind him. She catches up with him at the front door.

"What did you come here for anyway?" she says. "What do you—what is it you want? Are you going to start doing this all the time now?"

"We're friends," he says, cringing inside. He doesn't even recognize himself at the moment.

"We are not friends," she says. "Friends don't keep almost falling into bed together. Is this funny to you? Do you like doing this to me?"

"I'm not doing—"

"Just because your wife goes out and has an—"

She brings herself up short just then, shaking her head and grinning to herself with embarrassment. When she speaks again her voice is different altogether.

"Listen," she says, "forget it. Don't listen to me. I'm all knotted up. You're right. We're friends."

"If I've made things difficult, I can stay away from you—"

"No, really. Don't do that. Don't punish me. We're all right."

There is a silence.

"My divorce," she says. She shrugs as if the whole thing isn't worth talking about. "My divorce is finalized next week."

She looks down and starts playing with her own fingers.

"Look," he says, as gently as he can. "I'm married, and—"

"I know, I know." She folds her arms over her breasts. "I didn't mean anything by it. I just thought we might celebrate. A girl's first divorce. That's got to count for something."

He smiles and thinks about leaning over to kiss her cheek. Her hair is a mess and he wants to put his hands in it, his fingers up against her scalp. But what he also wants is to be outside away from all these plants.

Part of him would like to be in love with her, just to make sense of his presence here. But love just doesn't work here. It topples over when he tries to build it too high.

"Sure," he says. "We'll celebrate. We'll have streamers."

After the door closes, Sibyl stands in front of it for a while, leaning against the wall. Then she goes into the bedroom and stands in front of the mirror, pulling her skin in various places to see how she would look if she were thinner, less wrinkled.

When she's had enough of that, she undresses and puts on an oversize T-shirt so she won't have to see herself and goes to the kitchen to open the refrigerator. It's always empty. She retrieves a handful of takeout menus from a drawer and begins to leaf through them while thinking about all the men she's known, a lineage descending straight down from her father— their hands on her back, enfolding her, shrinking her, allowing her to drop away all the superfluous pretense and simply be a little gem in their palms. A beautiful little gem.

chapter 13

For Binhammer, the arrival home has the quality of a high mass—a ceremony conducted in a chamber of echoes, a place where words continue to burn like offertory candles long after the supplicant has gone. Speeches hold here; the echoes of conversations bounce from wall to wall without ever really dying. It sometimes surprises him to come upon the remains of an old argument still quibbling with itself in some undusted corner. But this is also a holy place. A beautiful place.

When he opens the door, he can hear the tap-tap-tap of the computer keyboard coming from the back of the apartment. She is in there. The place is dark save for the low-wattage glow emanating with witchy serenity from that back room.

He stops and listens. Does he like that sound, the bony clatter of keys in an empty apartment? He doesn't know. This too seems religious—like tinkling little sins floating up to the ear of God from a confessional.

When he has listened long enough, he shuts the front door loudly and calls out a hello.

"Hi," Sarah calls back from her sanctum. "How was your meeting?"

"Fine."

There is a pause in the tapping, but no more than a hesitation before it starts again in earnest.

He takes off his coat and hangs it on the hook by the door. Then he goes into the bedroom and sits down on the edge of the bed. He thinks about taking his shoes off, but decides against it.

Instead, he just sits for a few minutes inside the rattling sound of his wife's fingers on the keyboard and thinks about dry, weightless things—dead leaves, insect legs, empty aluminum cans rolling down street gutters in hot desert winds.

Then he goes into the living room and sits on the couch where he can see her through the doorway, her back to him, the white screen of the monitor framing her head with an electric halo.

"I just want to finish this thought," she says, still looking at the screen. "Do you mind?"

"No," he says. "Take your time."

That's when she turns her head and gives him a look, her face soft-eyed and delicate, her smile suddenly intimate.

It's the face of an angel, the face of an infant, the face of a cartoon dog, the face of a total stranger, the face of a carnivorous cat, the face of laughing Buddha. He knows that face. He recognizes it because he sees it everywhere. It fixes in his mind like a signal lamp flashing him messages, telling him what she will think about this or what she will say about that.

Like last week when Walter pulled him close in the teachers' lounge and told that joke about the rabbi's wife. There was her face, behind the shoulder of Walter's dusty old coat, a disapproving smirk. That's when he noticed Walter's grimy yellow teeth, and the dried white spittle in the corner of his mouth. And he wanted to escape Walter, wanted to satisfy Sarah's gaze that was on him always—even in the classroom and hallways, sometimes even the eyes of the girls themselves.

Sarah's face—a face like clarity, like decency, like home fronts.

So he doesn't mind sitting and looking at her, hunched over the keyboard and producing line after line of text, her little body collapsing itself boxlike into its own wrenching endeavors.

He leans back and puts his feet up on the coffee table. As he watches, she stops typing and hugs herself a little. She must be cold. Then she extends her hands again to the keyboard and rests them there a moment, poised, before she continues.

He thinks about Sibyl. The fecund, filthy quality of the air in her apartment just half an hour before. And now this scene before him—the dryness of sticks.

Finally Sarah finishes and, with a sigh, comes over to the couch where he's sitting and collapses on top of him, her head in his lap. She curls up and nestles her face in his belly, and his hand goes in habitual response to her hair.

"Listen," she says. "I'm tired. Why don't you tell me something."

"What do you want me to tell you?"

"It doesn't matter. Tell me anything."

"What goes on with you?" He moves a strand of hair behind her ear. There are a whole lot of nice things about that ear.

"I'm shot for words. I've been at it all day. Just tell me something so my own voice isn't the only one in my head."

He chuckles. "You need a break," he says. "We should go away somewhere."

"That's good," she says. "Tell me more. Where?"

He thinks. "Cancun."

"Come on."

"Switzerland."

"No."

"Spain."

She considers. "That's okay," she decides. "What's there?"

"Um. Wide, dry plains. Plains with white buildings on them."

"What else?"

"Dark-faced men."

"And?"

"Um. Bent, narrow streets. Shops with canopies. Little bars where you can order beer. And when they bring it they set it on nailed aluminum tabletops." She turns his face up to his and closes her eyes. He likes that. And he thinks about Sibyl again, wondering why he continues to see her—trying to feel his way around the dark corners of his own heart for something that might be guilt. Or vengeance. But there's nothing there. The two women don't fit together in any rational way. He tries to picture them side by side, and his mind jams—like looking at an optical illusion that can be a duck or a rabbit but never both at the same time.

"What else?" Sarah asks.

"Bead curtains. Electric fans with rusty blades."

She opens her eyes and squints at him. "You've never been to Spain."

"But I've read books about it. And the books are nice."

She laughs, the tip of her tongue showing pink between her teeth.

He could not hurt her. He is incapable of hurting her. He thinks about Sibyl again, beginning to see her as a tendrilly, organic woman—and he wonders how much of a hazard she could possibly be. He thinks, What could that limp fern do to us?

"Spain," she says. "We'll go there someday. What do you say?"

"Of course. There and lots of places."

"Where else?"

Later, after dinner, he is leaning against the kitchen cabinets and watching as she spoons heaps of instant coffee into a mug and puts some water on to boil. She has a little more work to get done before she can relax.

"You know what Theo said today?" he asks.

Theo. Theodore. Ted. Hughes. When she knew him, she probably assumed his name was Edward. Anyone would. That's what she probably assumed. When she knew him. So Binhammer uses the name Theo instead. It's not a lie, not quite.

The first time he told her about him, he watched her face closely—it seemed an impossibly frail deception he was constructing.

"So there's a new English teacher," he said.

"Oh? To replace Maureen? What's her name?"

"*His* name—"

"His? Uh-oh." She smiled with a teasing self-satisfaction.

"His name is Theo."

"Theo." She scrunched up her face. "Sounds like a children's book character. A mouse with big round glasses."

"He's not. The girls are already in love with him."

"Competition," she said, playfully.

"Competition." He thought about that. Then he shook his head and said, "Actually, he's kind of an asshole. They just can't see it yet."

And now, when she says, "I thought you didn't like him," he shrugs and says, "He's okay. It turns out he's not so bad."

Steam begins to escape in little wisps from the kettle on the stovetop.

"In any case," he goes on, "today he told me that Sibyl is flirting with him."

"Is she?"

"She could be."

"Well, good for them. Does that mean she's done flirting with you?"

"She's not interested in me," he says. "Not really. I just represent something to her."

"What?"

"I don't know. Breakability."

The kettle starts to scream behind her, and she looks at him a moment longer before she turns to take it off the heat.

He doesn't know why he takes these chances, why he is so eager to bring these three people—Sarah, Sibyl, Ted Hughes—into such precarious proximity. Why dangle them together on a cardboard stage? His wife would say that it's because he wants to get caught. She believes that every act of immorality is a cry for correction. She believes in Freud, and in fathers with powerful voices. But that's not it.

"See," he would explain to his girls if he were in class, "We're not talking about *The Scarlet Letter*. We're not even talking about *Dr. Zhivago*. Vengeance? You might as well be reading the Old Testament. Jealousy? That's what prime-time television is for. Look at him—our hero—he's more than just a wronged husband. He's more than just a raging cuckold. Don't make him a stock character. Please, he's *complicated*."

He could imagine their girlheads leaning forward, their imaginations taking flight.

Yes, to play a role in their secret lives, to be the intersection of their most personal vectors, the destination of so many journeys. For all of them: Sarah, Hughes, Sibyl, the girls.

Not drowned by circumstance. Not suffocated like the common dupe. Just so complicated that he becomes the very center of it all, pushing and pulling people like chessmen, tugging them this way and that.

Later, close to midnight, he goes into the room where she is working.

"I'm going to bed," he says.

"I'll be in in a little while. I have to finish this."

"You work too hard."

"Give me a kiss."

He kisses her.

It is after 1:00 a.m. when Sarah finally finishes her work and feels her way into the dark bedroom where her husband is already asleep. She lies down carefully to avoid waking him. He stirs, turns over, but remains asleep.

She can sometimes be difficult, she knows that. Coming to bed late, disrupting his dreamful sleep. Lying in the dark, she thinks about their marriage. They met in graduate school, that intellectual hotbed where she learned to siphon her insecurities into a rhetoric of power and didacticism. She surprised herself at the number of people she knocked down with the simple force of her forensic language. They would tumble off their pedestals and leave her standing, and she would think, How did this happen? Are they simply being nice to me? How can they not see that I am unsure of everything?

And then there was Binhammer, who complimented her on her fingernail polish and poked and prodded at her academic ego.

"You're reading French feminism?" he would condescend. "That's cute."

Which infuriated her, of course. And also excited her.

They would argue for hours about Foucault or Kristeva or Alexander Pope. Pope of all people. He had a thing for Pope, which she found inexplicable. He was arrogant and outrageous and frequently downright mistaken—but he wouldn't be knocked down by her. She couldn't tumble him. And that was the thing.

Now, eight years into their marriage, she looks over at the silhouette of his face while he sleeps beside her. She will never leave him. That is one thing she knows.

But sometimes she wonders if she has finally tumbled him.

chapter 14

"I think I want to kiss your brother," Dixie Doyle says conclusively to her friend Beth as they sit in the front of the classroom awaiting Binhammer's arrival.

"Dixie!" Beth scolds. "That's gross."

"She's right, Beth," Caroline says. Then she holds up her palm as though she were cupping a small, trembling animal. "He's *so cute.*"

"He's just a little kid," Beth says.

"Does he have a girlfriend?" Dixie continues. "Does he want me to be his girlfriend?"

"Dixie just likes the way he looks," Andie interjects lethargically, leaning forward over her desk. "Pocket-sized, hairless. And from what I hear, he can even multiply fractions."

Earlier that morning Beth's mother dropped her off at school with her younger brother Charlie—sixth grade, Bardolph Boys' Academy, voice unbroken—in tow. The presence of the puppyish boy right outside Carmine-Casey caused such a commotion among the students that it took an administrator and a janitor to round them all up and herd them into the building. The crowd was so dense, though, that for a while they misplaced the boy— and eventually found him, blushing, in the middle of three concentric rings of girls who were touching his hair, pinching his cheeks, holding his hands, and asking him about his position on girls vis-à-vis cooties.

To Dixie, he is the most adorable thing she has ever seen. He is little for his age and has long eyelashes, soft round cheeks, and glistening red lips in the shape of a bow. His skin is so smooth that she now hates her own in comparison, and he has the sweetest, softest voice—like something downy and blossomy that you would want to feel against your face. Beth has told them that because of his size he is sometimes picked on in school, and Dixie swears with witnesses present that she will personally castrate any boy who picks on little Charlie.

"Snip, snip," she says. "I'll do it, too."

"Can we not talk about my brother anymore," Beth pleads.

"Come on," Dixie says. "Let me kiss him at least. He doesn't have to be my boyfriend, but at least let me kiss him, *d'accord*?"

Madame Millet-Johnson, the French teacher, complimented Dixie on her accent last week, so Dixie has been peppering her conversation with French phrases ever since.

"Don't be gross."

"I need to practice for the play."

"No."

"Why don't you practice with your costar?" Andie asks. She is now slumped over her entire desk, looking like she wants to fall asleep.

Dixie makes the line of her mouth flat. "Jeremy and I have already practiced. We've practiced enough. I'm tired of practicing with him."

"Really?" says Caroline.

"Already?" Andie mumbles.

"I mean, he can still be my boyfriend. But it's just that—he's everywhere. You know? I think he has four tongues. I swear, at certain points he's had a tongue in my mouth, on my neck, and in both my ears at the same time. It makes me want to throw up. And then I have to go into the bathroom and towel myself down. *Quel dommage!*"

"Too many tongues." Caroline shakes her head as if in experienced commiseration.

"Does he seem to be enjoying himself?" Beth asks.

Dixie considers this and then says, "I guess so. He usually

looks pretty satisfied with himself. He pats his stomach, like he's just eaten a big meal."

"Is that all you've done with him? I mean, you haven't done anything else, right?"

Dixie grimaces. "With *him*? Come on."

When Binhammer comes into the room, Dixie turns to face front and all the girls arrange themselves in their seats. Dixie folds her hands on the desk in front of her in what she imagines to be the posture of eager studenthood.

But before her teacher has a chance to start the class, Dixie states, "Mr. Binhammer, Beth won't let me kiss her brother."

The class laughs. Dixie, the consummate performer, stares straight ahead and ignores her audience.

"Huh," Binhammer says, nodding his head. "Did you ask nicely?"

"*Mais oui.* I did. I'm being a perfect lady about the whole thing."

"He's *twelve*, Mr. Binhammer," Beth says.

"But," Dixie says, "he's wise for his age."

"Twelve, huh?" Binhammer puts on his best Solomon face. "Have you tried candy?"

The class enjoys the exchange. That is, all of them except for Liz Warren, who, like a beacon of sour grievance flashing from the back row, sits there rolling her eyes. Binhammer wonders what's wrong with her—why she has to be so serious all the time. He likes smart girls, but sometimes they're hard to entertain. All she is is correct answers and disapproving looks. Her arms crossed, her face a stony crag, she's like the silent voice of his moral conscience—always telling him that it's time to get down to business. Enough nonsense. Enough playing around.

He wonders, if she's so dissatisfied with the way things work in his class, why she continues to come at all. She's a senior, after all. Most of the senior girls have already earned or bought their way into college and do what they want. But no, that's the other problem with smart girls. They just keep coming to class—long past when they have to—just out of spite.

In the teachers' lounge after class Binhammer finds Ted Hughes bent over a stack of papers and chewing on the end of a ballpoint pen.

"What's wrong?" Ted Hughes asks by way of a greeting. Binhammer has noticed that the man has this uncanny ability to read his emotional state with a single glance. Like some kind of empath. Maybe that's what makes him so attractive to women. There is something appealing about being interpreted by him, your mind a manuscript under his eyes.

"It's nothing. It's this girl in my class. Liz Warren. She—"

"Oh, Liz. She's in my class too. She's wonderful, isn't she?"

She has never mentioned to Binhammer—in the few brief conversations they have had—that she was taking another English class.

"She's smart, I suppose. But don't you find her a bit humorless?"

Ted Hughes thinks about that. "Maybe at first," he concedes. "But she was laughing at something the other day in class—what was it? Oh, sure, it was Chaucer. She was hysterical about it."

"Chaucer? *The Canterbury Tales*?"

"Not *The Canterbury Tales*. She was doing a presentation on one of the minor poems. 'The Book of the Duchess.' She thought it was hilarious."

"Really."

"Sidesplitting." Ted Hughes shakes his head as if sympathizing with Binhammer, but Binhammer doesn't feel like he's being sympathized with. "And then she came up to me afterward and gave me this twenty-minute lecture on how Chaucer was the prefiguration—that's even the word she used—the prefiguration of the TV sitcom."

"Uh-huh. But don't you get tired of the eye-rolling?"

"The eye-rolling?"

"Never mind."

Yes, Binhammer thinks now, it's true. That Liz Warren is a great kid. He has been thinking of her as superior, self-righteous and joyless. But now it seems obvious to him that she is just the opposite. She is a great diviner of joy—dowsing for it among the dead, arid plains of commonness and vulgarity. She is a leader, an aggressive intellect, a bright orbiting light of clarity and reason—for anyone who would bother to look up—and now she is the prize student of the dashing and obviously more insightful Ted Hughes.

Liz Warren. He should have cultivated that seed long ago. Now it's too late. He cannot recover her. She is too used to scowling at him from the back row. And besides, she is now a Hughes girl.

What more can the man take from him? It would be easier if Binhammer could simply hate him. But when he looks at Hughes, he knows why Liz Warren likes him. He understands why his own wife would be attracted to him. The man burns like an ember.

Then he thinks of his own prize student, Dixie Doyle, glowing tepidly from the front row of the class like a low-wattage bulb gathering moths. She and the rest of her alliterative friends: Caroline Cox, Beth Barber, Andie Abramson. Why does he have to have the students with names like cartoon characters? Talking about shaving their legs and kissing each other's brothers. Admiring each other's scented highlighters. Sharing lipstick. Chewing gum.

Instead of laughing at Chaucer, they treat him with misplaced seriousness. Dixie Doyle looks at the woodcut illustration on the cover of the Penguin edition of her *Canterbury Tales* and asks with tremendous gravity, "Was Chaucer fat? He looks fat, *n'est pas?*" And then, "Why is he wearing a dress? Was that the style in Old English?"

"Old English is a language, Dixie. And this isn't it anyway. This is Middle English."

"*Bien sur,*" she says happily, drawing a picture of a sunflower in her notebook.

Now it occurs to him that even this room-temperature quartet of girls may only like him because he lets them get away with things. He doesn't say anything if they come into class late, and he silently tolerates the eating of rice cakes. And the putting on of mascara. He has even been talked into giving them extensions on papers because of the sicknesses of family pets. "Mr. Strawberry was throwing up all night. He's got worms." And he imagines that, if he were ever actually to say no, his little cadre of faithful followers would dissipate in a cloud of outraged harrumphs. There is no loyalty there. There is no permanence.

He spends the rest of the morning in a funk, and later he sits down at a table with Lonnie Abramson, Andie's mother, during lunch.

"Let me ask you a question, Lonnie," he says.

"Someday I'm going to eat real food again," she says, holding up a forkful of dry greens. "This is no way to live." Then she pokes her fork in the direction of his stomach. "You're lucky. Always looking so svelte."

"So—"

"You could even stand to eat more. I'm concerned about your diet."

He looks at his hands in near defeat.

"I'm sorry, honey. What did you want to ask me?"

"About the girls. The students. They talk about other teachers, you've heard them talk."

"Sure."

"What do they say about me?"

She puts down her fork as if astonished. "Are you kidding me? Honestly, are you kidding me? They *adore* you. I swear, my Andie won't listen to a word her father says, but you—you're like a rock star. And the same with her friends. Everyone knows that that Dixie Doyle is in love with you. Where's this coming from anyway?"

"Well. They're nice girls."

She guffaws. "Nice girls, hell! Listen, I'm the mother of a teenage girl. And I was a teenage girl once myself. In the bygone days. I mean, if I had a teacher like you when I was in school, well!" She raises her eyebrows and nods meaningfully. "In fact,

I'm always telling George, that most dull of straight arrows, I'm always telling him, 'There's nothing wrong with a little sex appeal, George.' "

"Anyway, I—"

"I tell him, 'Look at your daughter, George. How do you think she's doing so well in English? She's feeling inspired, if you know what I mean.' That's what I tell him, *inspired*."

"That's nice of you, but I think I have to—"

"In fact, I was going to ask you something. I wanted your advice on this young man Andie has drudged up from the mire of a performing arts school downtown."

"Well, I—"

"The thing is, I think she's . . . going a little too far. You follow me? And even though I've told her she can talk to me about it, she doesn't confide in me the way she confides in you. And what I was wondering—"

The rest of her sentence, much to Binhammer's relief, is cut off by the sound of the period bell. He bolts up from his seat while she's still talking.

"Oh, yes," she continues, "I suppose we'd better get back to it. We'll talk about this some more later. But don't tell Andie I talked to you. She would kill me. This is for your ears only."

And she actually reaches out to pinch the lobe of his left ear.

For the rest of the day, Binhammer moves quickly through the halls trying to avoid entanglements. Some girls call out to him, but he pretends not to hear them and eventually ducks into the teachers' lounge. Walter is in there, but Walter is a fixed quantity. He knows that Walter dislikes him. He understands that. Their rapport has that percentage of dislike built in, a solid bulwark against the possibility of intimacy.

After the last bell of the day rings, he gathers himself into his coat and pushes his way through the swirling mass of girls in the lobby to the sidewalk outside. He is almost to the corner and beginning to feel certain of his escape when he spots Dixie Doyle coming toward him with a huge paper cup from the corner coffee shop.

"*Ou est-ce que vous* going, Mr. Binhammer?"

"Home, Dixie." He tries to keep moving, but she has stationed her silly little body directly in front of him.

"What are you going to have for dinner? Is your wife a good cook? Do you ever cook her dinner? Women like that, you know."

"Thanks for the advice. I'll see you—"

"Where does your wife shop, Mr. Binhammer? For clothes, I mean."

He gives her a look. "Dixie, did you finish reading the Doris Lessing stories?"

"The what?"

"For class."

"Oh, sure. I mean, mostly. Some."

"Dixie, why can't you try to do some work for a change? It's *education* that we're concerned with here."

"Geez! What's wrong? Was some student giving you a hard time? Because I can take care of it, you know. They listen to me around here."

"Forget it. I'll see you tomorrow."

And he leaves her standing there, reaching down to adjust the strap on her shoe, holding her steaming cup high as a torch that heralds something awful, and crying, "*Bon soir*, Mr. Binhammer! *Bon soir!*"

chapter 15

Of all his responsibilities as a teacher of English—the report cards and the faculty meetings, the roll-taking and the conferences with irate parents—there is no duty more objectionable to Binhammer than the grading of papers. The thing about papers is that they accumulate in the most tyrannical of ways. They stack up in unruly piles with torn corners and awkwardly stapled edges hanging out everywhere. They are always too many to carry around as a single quantity, and so it is necessary to break them into smaller piles—knowing as you finish grading each pile that this is only one small part of the whole. And most of them, in Binhammer's experience, offer little more than plagiaristic sentiments by the paragraphful. All in neat little trains of black letters on endless leaves of white.

He always thinks about the plural quantity of papers as a "brick of papers," and uses it in the same way that you might talk about a brace of fowl or a herd of buffalo.

"What have you got there?" Walter asks this morning, leaning over the table in the teachers' lounge where Binhammer is holding a ballpoint pen—in frozen potentiality—over one such brick of papers. He has read the same line five times. He has memorized the words, but he can't seem to make them stick together or make sense in any way—and down they plummet through the gutter of his consciousness.

"Papers," he replies.

"Papers, sure." Then, after a pause: "That's a lot of papers you've got there."

Walter takes a unique pleasure in Binhammer's suffering. If he were an old soldier, he would be the kind to want new recruits hammered and humiliated into shape just as he once was.

Binhammer reads the line again. He underlines it to help him focus. But now he has to write something beside it to justify the underline.

"Are they good?" Walter asks as he sits down in a chair across the table and leans back.

Binhammer looks up. "Not particularly."

"That's a shame." Walter is glowing.

The other thing about this odious task is that it feels like work being dropped down a well. The comments are made, the grade is given—and the student's next paper might as well be a photocopy of the previous assignment with the title of one book whited out and another scrawled in. It seems to make no difference what he writes—whether it is thoughtful, articulated criticism or half-conscious nonsense. Everything, he sometimes thinks, sounds like nonsense to teenage girls. The whole world is nonsense.

He kicks himself awake and, even though his eyes have been concentrating on it for a long time now, looks at the paper before him with renewed vigor. He has managed to get that line lodged securely in his head, now that he has underlined and starred it. The next few lines he reads at a breakneck speed to the end of the paragraph, where he lets out a sigh of relief. Nothing. The girl is saying nothing. Nonsense piled on top of nonsense. He circles a misplaced comma and moves on.

"When were they turned in?" Walter asks pointedly, still quite proud of himself.

"Couple weeks. Three weeks. Four." Binhammer doesn't look up—he's running his fingers through his hair, trying not to express the desperation that the other man obviously wants to evoke.

"Four weeks. Hm."

Walter is about to say something else when, thankfully, the door opens and Ted Hughes comes in. From outside in the hall,

Binhammer can hear the girlvoices, like little chirping birds, calling out "Mr. Hughes! Mr. Hughes!"—but Ted Hughes doesn't seem to hear and lets the door close on them.

He stops in the middle of the room and puts his fingers to his chin, then turns and seems surprised to find Binhammer and Walter sitting there.

"Oh, hi," he says. "There was a girl—I don't know her—painting her nails. Sitting on the ground in the hall painting her nails. She would do one finger and stop and blow on it and then do another."

Ted Hughes has a tendency toward the reverie that Binhammer admires. The absorption into an image, into a moment. The way in which he can seem knotted up in the tendrils of things. Binhammer knows he's the opposite—sufficiently lucky if he can keep his mind on one thing for more than a minute or two.

"And all these other girls were walking by her in the hall, and I kept thinking sooner or later someone's going to trip over her and that nail polish is going to go everywhere. But it never happened. You should have seen it. Like a dance—the way these girls move around each other without looking, as if they were blind. Some of them were even walking backward, but when they came to this girl painting her nails, they knew to step over her. How do they know that? It's like a flock of birds—how the scientists can't figure out why they all know to turn in the air at exactly the same time and avoid colliding with one another."

Finally Ted Hughes looks at Binhammer and Walter. Walter has a deadpan sneer on his face. No one can shut Walter up like Ted Hughes, whose inadvertent poeticism seems to steamroll over Walter's niggling meanness.

Then Ted Hughes shrugs. "Is that a new shirt?" he says to Binhammer.

Binhammer feels suddenly self-conscious. "No," he says, his hand smoothing out the front of it. "I just haven't worn it yet this year."

"It's nice."

"Thanks."

Then Ted Hughes lets fall onto a chair what looks like a very heavy bag from his shoulder and draws out of it a brick of papers even larger than Binhammer's. He brings them over and drops them with a heavy, corpselike thud on the table.

"They got you too, huh?" Binhammer asks.

"What? Oh, the papers. Yeah." He brings out a second brick, the same size as the first. "It made for a rather dull weekend."

Binhammer's stomach sinks. "You already graded all of them?"

Ted Hughes nods. "It took me hours."

"When did you get them? Friday?"

He nods again. "It's the worst thing in the world, isn't it? I can't bear having them around staring at me."

It's another instance when Ted Hughes mistakenly believes he's commiserating with Binhammer. So the man can grade the hell out of a stack of papers. It's a skill, a skill like any other. But it's a skill that Binhammer doesn't have.

"How," he asks with great sincerity, nodding at the stacks of papers in front of Ted Hughes, "how do you do that?"

"I don't know," Ted Hughes responds. "You just start doing it. And when you want to stop, you don't. And then, after a while, you're finished and you feel pure. Think of it like religious penance. I sure like that shirt."

Binhammer shakes his head at the stacks one last time and then looks down at his shirt. "You want it?" he asks. "Is that what you're saying?"

And the two men laugh. Walter, they now realize, is gone, but neither of them can recall when he got up from the table and left the lounge.

But when Ted Hughes has to go to a class the next period, Binhammer is left alone with those two stacks of Hughes papers weighing down the opposite side of the table with the density of supernovas, and he finds himself getting angry. How is he supposed to grade his own papers now—particularly the one he has been trying to focus on for the past hour—with that pile of success across the table?

He gets up and goes to the stacks and begins to thumb through the papers. Sure enough, there are little red marks on each of them. They're authentic. He slows down to read some of the comments. In one margin there's a note that says, "You should try Lacan—let's talk." On another paper: "You know this could be better." On a third, there is a paragraph circled with a single word written in the margin next to it: "Metempsychosis?" This last paper is Liz Warren's. He flips to the last page to see the grade. A-minus.

It takes some nerve to give Liz Warren an A-minus. It's almost admirable. What really gets him: she'll probably respect Hughes even more for it.

He feels spiteful and takes a handful of the neatly ordered papers from each stack and shuffles them into the opposite stack. Then he goes to the window and stares out of it for a while. On the street below a car pulls up and lets out a Carmine-Casey girl, maybe coming late from a dentist appointment. He watches as she adjusts her skirt and her shirt before entering the building.

There's no way he's going back to grading. Not yet at least.

Instead he takes a book of Adrienne Rich poems and walks down the hall to the copy room, where Sam the copy man is bent over his desk with headphones on, doing a crossword puzzle. The copy room is empty, so Binhammer takes the machine in the farthest back corner and opens the book of poems facedown on the glass.

He shuts his eyes as the vertical line of pure bright light sweeps underneath the glass. He can feel the light on his face. Then he turns the page and presses the copy button again.

He'd like to see that Ted Hughes get the wind knocked out of him some time. Ted Hughes and his grotesquely large stacks of corrected papers. It would be nice, just nice, to be there when he stumbled. It would be gratifying to see Mrs. Mayhew thumb through the stacks and say, "Is this what we're calling teaching these days, Mr. Hughes?"

He turns to the next Adrienne Rich poem and slaps the copy button savagely.

The problem is that it seems when Ted Hughes stumbles, he does so into the open arms of adoring fans. Binhammer has never seen someone so *accidental* in his accomplishments.

To hell with him and his lost-looking eyes, his piles of achievement, his gestures of passion and grief. To hell with his sudden camaraderie, his strange moods of intimacy that corner you in silent places, his performances of delicacy. To hell with his seductions. Of the students, of the faculty, of his wife. He is a man who cannot be trusted. A man who will betray you.

When Binhammer slams his palm down on the copy button again the machine gives a quick ratcheting sound and screeches to a halt. On the digital screen flash the words PAPER JAM and a diagram with arrows pointing to the possible location of the problem. Damn.

He looks up briefly at Sam the copy man, but to get Sam involved means a bantering conversation that Binhammer is not in the mood for. Getting down on his knees, he reckons he can fix the problem himself.

Opening the front panel of the machine reveals a complex and disturbingly organic tangle of dials, plates, wheels, cables, and cylinders. He can see the white edge of a page choked up in what he thinks of as the throat of the machine—and he sees that he needs to turn a green plastic dial in order to release the page, but when he grabs hold of the thing it won't turn. He tries again, but his hand slips and his knuckles are driven into the sharp metal edge of the paper drawer.

He is not in the mood for this. Ted Hughes gives meaning-ful criticism to piles and piles of paper, and Binhammer cannot even produce pages with the help of a machine.

That green plastic knob is going to turn.

Gritting his teeth, he grabs hold of the thing and bears down on it until it snaps off, sending him sprawling on the floor. It's not until he looks down at the knob in his hand that he sees an arrow on the face of it—indicating that the knob was only meant to be turned in one direction.

He peeks around the machine at Sam the copy man, but he is still hunched over his crossword puzzle, the earphones emitting a tinny, repetitive music that can be heard even from back here.

So he stands up and brushes off the front of his pants, closes the front panel of the machine, notices that the digital readout now reports that it NEEDS SERVICE, and pockets the green knob surreptitiously.

Everything is coming apart. This is what he thinks as he gathers his Adrienne Rich poems and any other evidence that might implicate him in the malfunction. Everything is coming apart in my hands, he thinks. What do they expect of me now? My pockets are full of pieces of other things.

As he leaves the copy room, he does not look at Sam the copy man, who has squinted his eyes trying to think of a five-letter word for "ordered." He glares at Binhammer's back and chews on the end of his pen.

Sam has never liked Binhammer, who does just as much sulking from place to place as all the little twit girls he teaches. The whole place is going to hell, Sam thinks. If this is what kind of women we're creating, forget it. The snotty rich girls with their doily socks and their arrogant little ponytails.

They think they own the world. And the teachers don't help, like they should. Why don't any of them give these little brats a kick in the ass? They're just as self-involved as the students—like that Binhammer. These girls think they own everything. They think they can have whatever they want. They think everyone is looking at them.

Wait till they find out different.

chapter 16

When the romance between Dixie Doyle and Jeremy Notion peters out before Thanksgiving, no one is really surprised. By the end of November, they seem to have run out of things to say to each other. When he comes to Carmine-Casey for rehearsals, he has been seen to give her a quick, awkward hug and say something inane like, "How's things going?"

To which her only response is, "*Mais oui*," followed by a shrug.

It has been rumored that the beginning of the end came when Jeremy, visiting the Doyle household to practice his lines with Dixie, refused to admire the little bell tied with a red ribbon around the neck of her Lhasa apso, Mr. Strawberry.

"That dog needs a haircut," he said instead.

Which is just about the worst thing he could have said, as anyone could tell you since Dixie's love-me-love-my-Strawberry policy is well documented.

But when it comes to the school play, Dixie prides herself on her professionalism and her ability to commit herself to the greater good of the production.

"Listen, Ivan," she says onstage during one rehearsal. "Forget that war. I should be enough Uncle Sam for you."

"It's not that, Clarissa. You know I have to go."

"I wish you understood me."

"I understand more than you think, baby."

"No, you understand *less* than you think."

"Actually," Liz Warren interrupts, "the word you want to

stress there is *you*. 'You understand less than *you* think.' See, that's what makes it parallel." She stares at her two actors for a second, who look back at her blankly. "But good job in general," she adds. "Try it again."

"I wish you understood me."

"I understand more than you think, baby."

"No, you understand less than *you* think."

"Wrong again, Clarissa. You think more than you understand."

"Ugh," Dixie says, breaking character. "I'm tired of all this thinking and understanding. Can we take a break?"

"Okay," Liz sighs. "But just five minutes."

"Goody," Dixie squeals and leaps off the stage.

Liz has never been so exhausted. It feels like she's towing a school bus with a rope and her bare hands, but it's true that she's got the big lumbering production moving. Not that it's good—she secretly suspects that the whole thing is garbage. She's worried that people will think the dialogue is corny rather than ironic, because, though she will not admit it, she herself has trouble telling the difference sometimes. But it's under way, the wheels are turning, and even if the play crashes into a brick wall, at least she got the thing rolling.

And she has even experienced some moments of affection for her stars—the precociously obnoxious Dixie Doyle who has no embarrassment about acting it all the way up, the slightly dopey Jeremy Notion who lumbers around like a gentle bear. She finds them both to have a wonderfully malleable quality, so eager to impress that they will happily suppress every ounce of their own identities to do so. She thinks it must be just a myth, the idea that actors have big egos. To Liz it seems as though you could measure their authentic selves with teaspoons.

"What are you thinking about?"

Jeremy's voice startles her. He's standing there with his hands in his pockets, a big blank expression on his face. He has trouble looking her in the eyes and looks at her knees instead.

"Nothing," she says.

"Really?" He looks honestly surprised.

"Why?"

"I just didn't think you would say that. From what I've seen you always seem to be thinking *something*."

"Well . . ." He's a strange boy, this Jeremy Notion.

"Hey, listen," he says. "Can I ask you something? How come this Ivan guy always gets beat up so bad?"

"What do you mean?"

"I mean . . . I mean, everything he says, that Clarissa girl has something else to say that beats him down. Makes him look stupid."

"Oh." She is surprised at this. She feels suddenly flustered, put on the spot. For the rest of the rehearsal she thinks about Jeremy's question and wonders why it makes her so uncomfortable. For a while she has difficulty separating the question from the asker. Is he trying to tell her something? Did someone put him up to this? Is Dixie using him as a tool to get back at her? Then the larger implications: Is Jeremy saying that the play is bad? And if even Jeremy thinks the play is bad . . . oh, god.

Sitting in the dark, watching her actors on the stage, she feels her face getting red. Suddenly it's as though everyone watching the action play out on the stage is actually looking into some unswept corner of her own head. Without realizing it, she has cracked open the shell of her own neurosis and is bringing it to school for show-and-tell. How did this happen? And, maybe the bigger question, how is it that Jeremy Notion is the one to tell her about it?

"Actually," she says to him after the rehearsal is over. She has waited until he is by himself, sitting on the edge of the stage and rubbing his eyes tiredly. Trying not to look gawky or ridiculous, she strides up to him as though on official play business. "Actually," she says, "I don't think Ivan is stupid."

"You don't?" He looks pleased.

"No. Think of it like this. Think about Clarissa. I mean, all those comments. Those condescending comments. She's not really happy, is she?"

"Isn't she?"

"Think about—I mean, it's like you said. Who would want to get close to her, right? Don't you think she's making her-self . . . lonely?"

His face brightens suddenly as though he has just made a discovery. And for the first time in her recollection he actually looks her in the eyes.

As she's walking away, he calls out to her.

"Hey, listen."

She turns. He hops off the stage, but seems undecided about whether to approach her or just stand there. He puts his hands in his pockets again.

"I really like your play."

She feels herself getting embarrassed again. "You don't have to say that."

"No, it's really good."

"Well." She shrugs. It feels like someone is laughing at her. She wonders if there is someone watching from behind the cur-tain and laughing at her.

"I don't know how you can write things like that. How you can know what people would say just by thinking about it. I mean, it's nice. I wish I could do it."

She smiles guardedly and shrugs again. She wishes she could stop herself from shrugging, but it seems that her shoul-ders have their own agenda. Autonomic shrugging. The natural defense mechanism of awkward girls in their traditional habitat. She wills her shoulders to remain still.

"I don't know," she says. "You just make it up. It's not a big deal. You could do it. Anyone could do it." Then it occurs to her that she should be complimenting him too. "You're doing a really great job. I mean, the acting. You seem really natural."

"Thanks." But he doesn't seem interested in compliments anyway.

When she starts to walk away again, he calls her back once more.

"So listen," he says, actually approaching her this time. He takes his hands out of his pockets but then doesn't know what to do with them, so they just disappear back into the pockets. "Do you think you would want to go out some time?"

She's not sure what he's asking. She wonders if the point of all this is to embarrass her somehow.

"With me," he adds when she doesn't say anything. "Some time."

She feels, as she usually does, as though the world is setting her up to be the butt of a practical joke. Each reluctant concession brings her one step closer to public humiliation. She ventures a response: "What about Dixie? I thought you two . . ."

"We what?" Only Jeremy Notion would be unable to fill in that blank. Actually, it reassures her that he's not putting her on.

"I thought you two were . . . together."

"I don't know. I think that's finished. She only ever calls me Ivan."

She laughs at this, despite herself, her hand flying up to her mouth. She doesn't like the look of her mouth laughing.

"So what do you say?" he persists, more confident now, looking at her from beneath squinted eyes—as though challenging her to say yes.

And that's when she finds herself saying, "Sure. That would be nice." When in fact, she's not sure at all. But before she has a chance to change her mind or qualify the yes into something else—a maybe or a no—he nods and tugs on his jacket and walks with a swagger out of the auditorium.

A freshman girl who is part of the stage crew overhears the entire conversation and immediately runs to tell her friend. Her friend is the younger sister of a sophisticated sophomore girl who has many friends in the junior class. Then it's just a quick round of whispered exchanges, and in five minutes the story has made its way up through the class ranks and all the way to Dixie Doyle and her friends.

"Can you believe it?" Caroline asks. "I can't believe it. Can you believe it?"

"What does he want with her?" Beth says, outraged. "She's always hunched over. Like a hunchback."

"Hiding her chest," Andie says offhandedly.

"Yeah, what's that about?"

"The bigger question," says Dixie, who has been looking sternly into space, "is what she wants with him. After all, he's got the intellect of an ice cube, *bien sur*?"

"*Bien sur*, Dixie," Andie says with a hint of a smile in the corner of her mouth. The other three girls have the sense that Andie is laughing at them a little.

"Anyway, let's get out of here," Dixie says. "I could use some coffee. I'm feeling brittle all over."

Outside the light is saturated through a gray blanket of clouds, and there are no shadows anywhere. It is still daylight so the streetlamps haven't come on yet, but there is the penetrating quality of evening in the air. It is an in-between time. As the four girls stroll down the sidewalk in the direction of the coffee shop, glazed-eyed men and women push past them in a hurry to get home.

At the intersection, Caroline, who is possessed by the sudden urge to spin herself in circles, spins right into the street and is almost hit by a cab. The driver hammers his fist on the horn—but when Caroline raises her arm to wave apologetically, she nearly topples over again in a mess of girlishness, and the driver's face melts into some slightly sinister version of a paternal smile. He waves back and looks like he might pull over and stop halfway down the street—but then thinks better of it and continues driving.

"What do you think she does," Dixie asks to no one in particular, "when she goes home at night?"

"Who, Dix?"

"Liz Warren. What do you think she does? Do you think she just takes off her little boxy shoes and goes straight to her homework? What do people like her do?"

"She probably reads books," Caroline says, holding out her hand to a nearby wall to balance herself. She has made herself dizzy twirling. "She's really good in English."

"She's good in everything," Beth sneers.

"So where does she read her books?" Dixie says. "I can't picture it. On the couch? Do you think she lays on the couch? She probably eats chips while she's reading. How can anyone eat chips and read all afternoon?"

She really wants to know. It's beginning to bother her. If she wanted to be like Liz Warren, Dixie wonders, could she be? Would she know what to do?

"Also, here's something else," she continues. "How much time do you think she spends thinking about boys?"

"Boys?" Beth says.

"Boys. Do you think she thinks about boys much, or do you think she's too busy reading and eating chips?"

"I'm sure she thinks about boys," Andie says. She's pulling her hair into a ponytail and securing it with a band. A little bit of a wind has risen, and she doesn't like strands of hair blowing in her face.

"Do you think she talks about them with that Monica friend of hers? Do you think," Dixie says, jabbing her right forefinger on her left palm like a judge with a gavel to make sure that everyone understands the gravity of the question. "Do you think they *talk* about *boys*?"

"Why wouldn't they?" Andie says.

"I just can't picture it is all."

"She's not a Martian, you know. She's just like us."

Dixie thinks about this. "Yeah, I guess so." Above them the streetlamp finally comes on, but no one notices. Two blocks away from Carmine-Casey, they have reached the coffee shop where they will wait for a table in the corner—the one they like especially because they can look out the windows in two different directions. One of the Hispanic counter men knows them by name and calls them "*mis ángeles sucios*," which they have figured out has something to do with angels.

"Sure," Dixie says, mostly to herself. "If I wanted to, I could go home and lay on the couch and read and eat chips. I could read a different book every day. I could talk about boys with Monica Vargas. I could say things that would make people confused."

When they open the door to the coffee shop, their counter man is standing there grinning.

"If I wanted to."

But, secretly, she isn't so sure.

chapter 17

"Everything's different now," the girl says. She's got a handful of tissue in a wad that she keeps pressing against her eyes and nose. Her face is all red and wet like the inside of a tomato. Every now and then a little translucent trail of snot crawls down her upper lip, which she takes too long to wipe away. She keeps looking up at the ceiling and shaking her head—a solid but uncreative demonstration of despair. He would give it a B-plus if such performances were available for assessment. Maybe an A-minus if she were to incorporate a story of disillusionment from when she was "young."

"Sure," she continues, "I'm excited about college. I guess. But what about everything here? Everybody's acting weird. Like they're pretending we're all going to stay in touch when everyone knows as soon as we go off to college we'll have new friends, college friends—and who wants to hang out with your high school friends then? And then there's the other people, the ones who are just mean all of a sudden, like they can't wait to get out of here and start disassociating themselves from this place already—and it's like, can't they wait? I mean—"

She puts herself on hold to breathe and rub the tissue ball across her face, which leaves little white tissue crumbles on her cheeks.

Her name is Dorrie Connor, and she opened the conversation with Binhammer like this: "I know I've been out of it for a few days, so can we talk and I'll explain why?"

The truth is that he has barely noticed her all year. She's

one of those students who sits off to the side and kind of blends in with the furniture. *Has* she been out of it? Was she ever *in* it? The only thing he can think of right now is that he'd like to brush those little tissue crumbles off her cheeks. But they would probably stick to his hand.

He grimaces.

"I mean, everything's just weird, you know?" Then she starts crying in earnest—great big gulping sobs, her whole body hunched over so that he can see a little pouch of belly fat sticking out from under her shirt. It looks like a skin-colored balloon. One of those long balloons that circus people use to make animals.

He looks at her as though through the wrong end of a telescope. She looks far away—tiny and insignificant. He thinks about her as being encased in a little glass sphere—one of those ribbons of color inside a marble, and that marble one of fifty knocking together inside some child's chalk circle.

He sniffs. Raises his hand and then lowers it.

What does she want me to do? he wonders. What am I being asked to do now? Who is this girl? Who am I among the characters who populate her life?

"Listen," he says, leaning forward. Then he says some stupid conciliatory thing. Some small self-conscious truism that makes her nod bravely and purse her lips together with newly discovered inner strength.

He thinks, Things are changing in her. She is surprised at how the world does not conform to her maturity. She is disappointed that her epiphany is only her own—that even though she is invited into adulthood, all the outfits remain the same. She thought she would at least get a new pair of shoes.

"Thank you, Mr. Binhammer. Sorry about all this. Look, I went through a whole package of Kleenex." She starts wiping her nose with the back of her hand.

"Here," he says. "I'll get you some more. Be right back." This he can do. He can fetch tissue. He knows how to do that.

It is also around this time—somewhere in this stumbling

stretch of days—that Binhammer has begun to notice Sibyl taking more of an overt interest in Ted Hughes. So when he comes into the teachers' lounge and finds the two of them sitting side by side on the couch, he and Sibyl share a brief glance in which he interprets a palpable sharpness, like a splinter that you can only feel when you brush your finger against it.

He picks up a box of tissue from the table in the middle of the room. "A student," he says. "Crying."

"What is she crying about?" Ted Hughes asks.

But before Binhammer can answer, Sibyl takes Ted Hughes affectionately by the shoulder and gives him a shake.

"But wait," she says. "Finish your story." Then, to Binhammer: "Ted was telling me the strangest story about a summer he spent in Turkey."

"It's not much of a story," he says to Binhammer apologetically.

"Sure it is," Sibyl says. "You're a great storyteller. I bet that's why all the girls love you. Girls love to be told stories."

Binhammer notices that she's got one leg bent up underneath her and the other propped against the coffee table in front of the couch. He determines that he's not going anywhere. So he shuffles around the teachers' lounge, pretending to examine the calendar on the wall, rooting for something in his coat pocket, getting a cup of water from the cooler.

He hears the end of the story. It's a pretty good story.

Then he remembers Dorrie Connor—that little shivering red-faced pup in the room down the hall. It's been a good ten minutes. He takes the box of tissues and rushes out, but the girl is gone by the time he gets back to the room. He sees her at the other end of the hallway talking with two other girls. Their eyes connect and he holds up the box of tissues to show her. She smiles weakly and shrugs.

The bottom falls out of whatever he and Dorrie had together. And she turns and goes down the stairs with the two girls. Leaving him standing in the empty hall, the box of tissues still held high in his hand.

Back in the teachers' lounge, Binhammer and Sibyl listen to Ted Hughes tell stories until a sleepy silence falls over the room. A random air bubble glugs to the top of the water cooler, and then it's time to go home.

Over the course of the next few days, Sibyl, observing the effect it had on Binhammer, decides to make a point of being seen with Ted Hughes in the hallways. Even to the extent that some of her students say to her, "I think Mr. Hughes has a crush on you, Ms. Lockhart." She wonders if these same girls are speculating aloud to Binhammer—"Hughes and Lockhart, Lockhart and Hughes"—and the image of him shriveling up as he hears the talk makes her giddy with delight. She feels cruel and petty, but, honestly, she is through with making assessments all the time—she wants to be careless.

Sibyl thinks the other women in the department, Pepper and Lonnie, are behaving like simpering little girls. Before meetings they can be found, as usual, in the faculty women's room putting on makeup in front of the mirror—which they have always done in the past, but now with Ted Hughes in the picture the practice has an even more acute quality of a girls' dorm room on Saturday night. Two men to garner attention from where before there was only one. They are mothers, both of them, mothers who remember girlhood. As a result, they do not seem to know whether they want to sleep with the two men or feed them grilled cheese sandwiches with the crusts cut off. The affection they lavish is hopelessly confused, desperately flip-flopping back over onto itself with glistening limpness.

When they make room for her in front of the mirror, Sibyl digs through her bag to find a tube of lipstick, which she applies with two quick and decidedly self-confident strokes. The color is a deep, brownish red. She rolls her lips together and draws the fingernail of her pinkie around the corner of her mouth. Then she purses her lips slightly to see how she looks—which is a silly habit because she never purses her lips in real life. Next to her, the other two focus on their cheeks, their eyes. They have foam sponges that they use to pad on powder. They scrape and scour. For them, cosmetics are about disguising imperfection—cleaning up the canvas. For Sibyl they are about accentuating, highlighting, dramatizing. She is not afraid to have men look at her lips. She is not afraid.

And she will go into the faculty meeting and sit next to Ted Hughes and refuse to look at Binhammer. And she will tell Ted Hughes again how much the girls love him, because that's really the only thing these men want to hear. And then she will go home afterward and eat baby carrots from the bag and wonder why she is doing any of it anyway.

Except that on the last day of the week before Veterans Day, Ted Hughes bursts into her class when she's in the middle of teaching Jonathan Swift, and he's got a wild look in his eyes.

"Chalk!" he says. "I need some chalk!"

"What?"

"Chalk. I need to make a"—he gestures with his hand as though he were drawing on a blackboard—"a diagram."

She picks up a broken piece of chalk from the tray along the bottom of her blackboard. Meanwhile, he seems ready to burst—standing there wringing his hands and looking as though he is trying to do a complicated math problem in his head.

"I just thought of something," he says as he takes the chalk from her hand.

Her students are silent, transfixed. They know how to pay attention when they see something *happening*.

"The Wife of Bath," he says, smiling gleefully. "She's a man."

That's when, chalk gripped in his fist, he puts an arm around her waist, seizes her body up against his so only her toes are touching the ground, and plants a big smacking kiss right on her lips.

He's gone before she knows what happened, and the girls in the class are screaming with satisfaction, waving their hands in front of their faces as though they have just taken a bite of something hot.

She knows the whole thing is ridiculous and inappropriate,

but she can't help smiling. And she thinks maybe there is something to this Ted Hughes after all.

Later, when he comes to apologize between classes, his hair is all out of place—like he's been running his hand through it anxiously. She has seen him do this many times. It gives him an unfinished look, as if he were pleased to be jostled about.

"It was inappropriate," she says, aware that she is trying too hard to be chastising. "I mean, the girls—I'll never hear the end of it. How am I supposed to teach Henry James after that?"

"You're right," he says. He's got his hands in his pockets, and he looks downward, even kicks the ground once or twice. "I'm sorry." But he glances up from beneath his tousled, bowed head, and he grins.

He's not sorry.

"You're not sorry at all."

"No," he says, straightening up. "But it would be great if you could forgive me anyway. Listen, here's what we'll do." He seems to have forgotten all about his recent remorse. Now he puts an arm over her shoulder and uses his other hand to gesture toward the horizon, where he indicates a magnificent idea is on the rise. She has been witness to his explosive charm before—but it has never been directed at her with such focus. It is as though all that mercurial charisma is blossoming out, to be laureled all over her. "I'll buy you a drink. No. Even better—I'll buy you dinner. And I'll tell you about the Wife of Bath, and we'll talk about school. Because there are a couple people around here I want to get to the bottom of—and I think you can help me."

"Well—"

"But wait. That's only ten minutes. After ten minutes of that we stop. Because we are young and viable—and ten minutes of work talk is enough. After that, do you know what we talk about then, Sibyl?"

"What?"

"That's when we talk about the *other topics*."

"Other topics?"

"The *other topics*." He says it slowly and with gravity. "Do you know what they are?"

"No."

"No. Neither do I. But you know what? They're there. They're there just waiting to be talked about. It's like Christmas morning, and you and I are little kids sitting on the couch and someone's just come along and plopped down a present between us. Don't you want to open that present? I know I do."

He is becoming more animated by the moment, caught up in his own emerging fantasy.

"But listen," he continues, looking suddenly grave. "It's risky."

"Risky?"

"Sure. You can't tell with the other topics. Might be whole new flashy worlds. Might also be nothing at all. Might be an empty box. Risky."

She looks at him. He is a silly kind of a man. There's something that makes her nervous about the way he climbs the ecstatic precipices of his own craggy words. But he also makes a beautiful picture. His voice is like a rapidly flowing river—white waters of turbid forgetfulness.

"What do you say?" he asks. "Come on. What do you say?"

A man of sheer and breathless heights. She smiles.

And around her the building stirs—girlbodies like a tide of toy motors dictating the ebb and flow before and after class, at the beginning and ending of each day, week after week.

The autumn grows cold at Carmine-Casey, and the radiators clank on in the classrooms. Leaves fall from the trees in the courtyard and are raked away, just as the days pass by imperceptible degrees from tomorrow to yesterday, diminishing the school year period by period and accumulating something else, something with the appearance of weight. Something that the girls like to think of as history. They pick at their forearms and gaze idly out the windows—pretending to get excited, as they did when they were little, at the sight of an ice-cream truck.

But the performance is a weak one, filled with holes and shot through with awkward moments of spontaneous adulthood. And it is during these moments that some of the older girls look at each other and wonder which ones will get married right out of college, which ones will lead the life of the lonely urban sophisticate, and which ones will just disappear.

What will happen to me? they wonder, lagging behind their friends and trying to peek into the windows of the apartment buildings they pass. They say, I am not yet anything. They say, I am becoming something. What am I becoming? I'm tired of becoming. I don't know what clothes to wear. I feel smaller each day. One day I will wake up, and I won't even be there.

Night comes to the city in the same way—spectral and disquieting.

chapter 18

Mr. Pratt, the drama teacher, doesn't understand girls, so he likes to tell them that he has faith in their superior interpersonal sensibilities. The younger girls wear this compliment as a badge of pride—they announce to their parents that they have superior interpersonal sensibilities—until they realize that it's something he says to everyone, sometimes whole classes at a time.

But what he doesn't understand about girls, Dixie Doyle thinks, is that they do *not* in fact have superior interpersonal sensibilities. Instead, they emerge from every single social situation feeling at least a little bit bad—and most of the time not knowing why. What girls know is that everything good, honest, or true has a price, the payment of which—whether actual or anticipated—takes all pleasure away from goodness, honesty, and truth.

Boys do not function in this way. She has observed them interacting with each other. They shrug and grunt and seem pleased to talk in a vulgar way about vulgar things. She admires how organic it all is, and simple. They talk to each other as though there is nothing in the world to figure out. She assumes they must be quite content.

She wants to explain this to Mr. Binhammer, who has recently been paying a lot of attention—for reasons she can't imagine—to Liz Warren.

"Really, Dixie," he says to her now, pleadingly, "I have to go. The day's over. Don't you have somewhere to be?"

"But Mr. Binhammer," she says, giving a convincing waver to her voice—she'll cry if she has to—"*It's not fair.*"

These are the words that always work with Binhammer. He cannot resist the squeaks of injustice from the leashed throats of little girls. Perhaps he has some sense that any claim on the scales of justice is a valid one. Perhaps he does not want to appear blind to the victims of unknown crimes. Perhaps he simply cannot abide a girl in high-pitched distress.

"What's not fair?"

The room is empty. Dixie has remained in her seat. Through the windows, they can see the light growing weaker. First he looks at it, then she looks at it. In the hall outside, they can hear the sound of the janitor wheeling his mop bucket, starting his evening rounds.

She turns to him again, but seems to change her mind about something.

"Have you ever been to Paris?"

He sighs. "I haven't."

"*C'est belle.* You should go."

"Okay."

"No, I mean it. You should go. You would like it."

"Okay, I'll go."

"My parents took me there last summer. One night I walked all over the Rive Gauche. All night. All by myself. Rive Gauche—that's the Left Bank."

"I know what the Rive Gauche is."

"It's very pretty. There are a lot of artists. And little cafés. Did you know French boys walk around in groups, like girls do here? And they touch each other more. Like hugging each other and stuff like that."

He looks at her.

"It's not that they're gay or anything. The men there are just more comfortable showing affection to each other. I think it's sweet."

The door opens, and the janitor comes in. He nods to Binhammer, and Binhammer nods back. Taking the small waste-paper basket from the corner of the room, the janitor turns it upside down over the larger trash can he's carting around. Then he looks as though he might start straightening desks—but he glances again at Binhammer and shrugs. When he leaves, the door shuts behind him with a weak shiver.

"I mean," Dixie continues, "the thing about Paris is—"

"Dixie," Binhammer interrupts, leaning forward and folding his hands across the desk. He's now staring at the girl eye to eye, their gazes locked and curiously confidential. Her leg, which has been nervously pistoning up and down under the desk, stops altogether. For the moment, she looks like a painting done by a cruel artist. "Dixie, let me ask you a question, okay?"

"Sure, Mr.—"

"Dixie, what are your plans?"

"You mean for college? I'm going to Europe for the summer, and then—"

"I don't mean just for college. I mean for after. Your life. What do you picture yourself doing?"

It isn't a rhetorical question. And not one of those pointed questions that adults ask to get teenagers to think about the important things in life. There is a sincerity in his voice—as though he really wants to know. As though this issue has been bothering him for a while, and he wants to get to the bottom of it.

"Well," she begins. "For a while I thought I might be a fashion designer. But Andie's the one who knows how to draw. Whenever I try to draw anything, the legs come out too long and crooked. Like they're mangled or something."

"That's not what I—"

"I guess I know what you meant." She glares at him for a moment, pouting. She folds her arms and juts out her chin. "What do you want to know for? Why does everyone always want to think about these things?"

"Okay," he says. "Never mind."

They sit there for a solid minute looking out the window. Then she says:

"I suppose . . . I mean, I guess if I *had* to think about it . . .

I guess I picture myself like my mom." She shrugs and shakes her head.

Then: "I guess every girl does. You know."

She shakes her head again and humphs—as though she has been forced into confessing something. She is a witness on a stand, talked into testifying against herself.

"It's not what they *want* to be," she explains further. "Not what they *dream* about being. That's something different. But what *we're* talking about—what they really *think* they'll be like. Everyone figures that's how they'll be. Like their mom."

"And what's that like?"

"You mean *my* mom?"

"Yes. Your mom."

"I don't know." She sits up straight in the chair, pulls the hem of her skirt down, and folds her hands in her lap. She looks like she's posing for a portrait. "She's always looking somewhere else, you know? Like when she's talking to my dad, she's always looking at the salad she's eating. Or she's looking at the signs going by if we're in the car. And it's funny, because if she's on the phone, she'll look at her nails—but if she's getting her nails done, she'll look at a magazine."

She hugs herself.

"My dad used to make a joke about it. He would make faces at her when they were talking, but she would never notice because she wasn't looking, and I would laugh and she would wonder what I was laughing at. But when she asked me, she would be looking up at the sky." She laughs a little now—an aborted little chuckle that stumbles over itself and falls askew across a landscape of sudden silence. "Anyway. It seemed funny then."

He smiles. This girl sitting across from him is a banged-up brass vase—dented and discolored but still holding its form.

"I wonder," he says, "what she's looking at, your mother."

She shakes herself, snaps the usual coy little smirk back on her face. "*Je ne sais pas,*" she says. "Who cares? The woman's crazy."

Then Dixie stands up and stretches. The talk is over. She

has other things to do. She runs a hand through her hair and twirls one strand around her forefinger. The look on her face says that she hates her hair right now.

Binhammer follows her to the door of the classroom, but before she opens it, she spins around so that he's almost on top of her. He takes a step back and runs a palm over his eyes. He sighs.

"You know what I hate?" she says.

"What do you hate, Dixie?"

"I hate people who think they're smart just because they go around not saying things. Me, I can't stop talking. But anyone can not say things and sound smart."

There is something surprisingly lovely about this girl—the kind of sincere beauty that sneaks up on you from behind the pigtails, the strawberry lipstick, the ridiculously crooked expression she gets on her face when she doesn't understand something. Every now and then you could look at her and see her as some boy's girlfriend, hiding her face in his chest and saying nothing for a long time.

"I mean," she continues, "just because you found a new way to be unhappy, that doesn't mean anything. Big deal."

Binhammer wonders if he is attracted to her. He wants to think about it objectively. He has, of course, pictured her naked—just as he has pictured all of his students naked at one time or another, usually from the back of the room while they are giving a presentation in the front, droning on and on about some self-evident aspect of the book (usually to receive an A-minus anyway, since more often than not he doesn't hear a word of it and cannot critique it if pressed). This is the great secret of all the teachers at Carmine-Casey and, Binhammer is sure, all the other high schools, public or private, in the world: there is a massive naked cocktail party going on in the head of every high school teacher. Everyone thinks that teachers are like doctors, immune to the sexual charms of their clientele. But teachers are not like doctors. No one is like doctors. In fact, Binhammer would be willing to bet that doctors are not like doctors.

So, yes, he has pictured her naked. But what's happening right now is different. It's the desire to take her home and feed her soup, to sit down sententiously on the edge of her bed and have a talk, to defend her against something. His stomach realizes it first, dropping away like the floor of an elevator, and then it comes to him: Oh god, he feels, for the moment at least, *paternal*.

No good can come of this. He has to get out of there.

"Listen, Dixie—"

"And you know what else I hate?" She's standing in front of the door, her breasts pointing at him like aggressive udders. All he wants to do is rock her like a baby in his arms. "I hate Liz Warren."

"I know you do, Dixie," he says, trying to hammer out all the fatherly affection in his voice but obviously failing because she looks at him strangely. "I know you do."

chapter 19

After his conversation with Dixie Doyle, Binhammer begins to suspect something awful about himself. How long has he been entirely blind to the fact that he has no control whatsoever over the women in his life? Has he, in fact, *ever* had any control? At what point in his charmingly precocious, Frank Sinatra, disarmingly bold, hopelessly male life had the women snuck around the back and settled in at the rusty knobs and levers that dictated all his movements? He can feel their long fingers, nails either bitten cute-short or painted the colors of gumballs, plunged into a hidden hole in his back—like a ventriloquist's dummy—and tinkering around with the clockwork of his organs.

How long has this been going on?

He has memories—real memories, surely, true and accurate ones—of himself in the center of circles of women, playing them like Christmas bells, tapping each one with his winning smile and harmonizing their particular feminine tones. Their voices were like one long medley of "Carol of the Bells," played furiously with the panicked delight of a shopping mall during the holidays. That was him. Wasn't it? Now he's not so sure.

He realizes, then, that he's been trying to regain control of things by coveting his secrecy. That's one thing he has: secrets. How many things does he know that no one else knows? If knowledge is power, how full, how positively brimming, is his arsenal of information! From his wife, the Lady Sarah Lewis, he keeps the secret of his camaraderie with Ted Hughes. From Ted

Hughes, rising star of Carmine-Casey, he keeps the secret of his wife. From both he keeps the secret of Sibyl, her greenhouse of an apartment, those afternoons of coming dangerously close to something. From Sibyl he keeps everything except a generous contempt. From Dixie Doyle he keeps his own childish heart, pitifully and achingly akin to her own.

So there. If he tries, he can imagine himself as a kind of puppeteer himself, pulling strings and making everyone around him dance. Until, of course, the strings get tangled and the whole damn show collapses around its cardboard proscenium. But not yet. Not yet.

The first real occasion on which he needs to exercise his powers of concealment has to do with the Carmine-Casey annual dinner—a fund-raiser for parents who feel that their tens of thousands spent each year in tuition is so paltry that they seek opportunities to give the school even more cash. The teachers are not only invited but paraded around—guest on arm, whether spouse, lover, or relative—so that everyone can congratulate themselves on what a fine faculty they have assembled. Normally he would go with his wife, but that's out of the question now that Ted Hughes is going to be there.

"We can go if you really want to," Binhammer says to her one evening. He is pretending to read the paper. He casually thumbs through a few pages as though looking for something.

It is one of those moments. He is always a dizzy inch away from telling Sarah everything—about Ted Hughes, about Sibyl—because he does not know what to do with the world unless he parades it before her every day. He supposes this is what is meant by love—the compulsive need to entangle someone else into every knotted, thorny mess you manage to produce in any given day.

Look at what I've done, he thinks, wanting to show her. Can you believe what I've done now?

"You don't want to go?" she asks.

"Not really. Aren't you tired of it? The same every year. You might get stuck next to Walter's wife again."

"You don't have to convince me. I was only going because I thought you liked to go."

"Me? Ha." It's outrageous, his tone of voice claims. What an outrageous thought.

"So we won't go."

"Great." He pretends to become engrossed in an article, ticking down the seconds in his head. The timing has to be perfect. The silence has to be fully cultivated but not overripe. He watches it grow like one of those time-lapse movies of a budding plant they show in science class.

She gets up and goes into the kitchen. He can hear her rinsing off the small plate on which she has just eaten an English muffin. Behind the sound of the water running in the sink, he hears the occasional chord of a tune she's humming. That's good. That works.

He folds the paper and slaps it down on the coffee table. Then he follows her into the kitchen and walks behind her to the refrigerator. Opening the door, he leans down and peers at the shelves of food.

"Of course," he says, squinting his eyes and moving the carton of milk aside, "*I* may still have to go."

She shuts off the sink and looks at him.

"Mrs. Mayhew likes to put me on a leash like a pet dog and walk me around all the tables."

She's drying her hands on a dish towel.

"But you," he continues, "you don't have to go."

Click, click, click—snap. Like a cat burglar picking a lock. All the pins fall into place and the lock pops loose.

"Are you sure it's okay if I don't go?" she says.

So that's that. Of course, the easier way would have been not to go at all. But he doesn't relish the idea of Ted Hughes being there and soaking up all the attention himself.

It is a black-tie affair, and the combination of tuxedos and the constant feed of alcohol frequently results in the women teachers pawing at his chest as though they were kittens making biscuits. They say things like, "Can I tell you a secret?" and "You know, I once dated someone like you," and "Do you think she's pretty? What about that one, do you think she's pretty?" And every now and then they will get an abstracted look to them, gazing into the flicker of the candles in the table centerpiece and pursing their lips. At which point they will shake their heads and say, barely audibly, "I don't know. I don't know." That's the moment when he offers a comforting hand (his palm flat against the warm skin of the back between the shoulder blades, feeling the heart beating beneath the strapless evening gown—god! women, there's so much to them, so many crevices!), prompting the woman in question to smile that inviting smile and place her head on his shoulder, using one of the linen napkins to blot her eyes. "Am I drunk? You'd tell me if I was drunk, right?"

He wouldn't miss that for anything. And he has a feeling that Ted Hughes might be equally if not more talented in the confidence and comfort department, so Binhammer has to show up just to box his own corner.

A week before the event, Ted Hughes confronts Binhammer in the mail room, a small closetlike niche off the administrative office with a honeycomb of boxes on one wall.

"So am I finally going to meet Mrs. Binhammer?" he asks.

There is a xeroxed reminder about the annual dinner in each slot, and he holds one up to show Binhammer.

Fortunately there's no one like Walter around to interject, "Mrs. Binhammer? You mean Dr. Lewis. Binhammer married up, ha ha." Then it would be out. That would be the end of it. That would be the whole show.

"Unfortunately," Binhammer says, "she's going to be out of town. Her sister's birthday."

"So when am I going to meet this woman?"

"Soon enough. She's excited to meet you."

Ted Hughes comes forward and puts his arm around Binhammer's shoulders. "You know," he says, lowering his voice to a confidential whisper, "I can be less charming, if that's what you're worried about."

Binhammer elbows the other man playfully in the stomach and wriggles out from under his arm. "No, Hughes—I don't think you could be any less charming."

They smile at each other, their eyes shining.

"But seriously," Ted Hughes says. "We should have dinner some time. Just the three of us. We'll lavish her with attention. Every woman's fantasy."

"All right," Binhammer says. "That would be nice." And some part of him really means it.

Then Sibyl comes into the little mail room and looks back and forth quickly between the two men before determining her opening gambit and addressing Ted Hughes.

"So, Mr. Hughes, are you going to be my date for the annual dinner? I'm wearing something strappy."

Binhammer wants to drop her a devastating look, a look that could level cities and rip the leaves off trees, but she refuses to meet his eyes.

"Well, Ms. Lockhart," Ted Hughes says, "that sounds like an invitation I'd be crazy to pass up. But somehow I've gotten roped into taking this girl, a friend of a friend, I don't know how it happened. She doesn't hold a candle to you, of course—but, well, she's fond of these upscale things. So she's my Cinderella for the night. But let's say right here and now that it's you and me for next year. What do you say? Pick you up in a year?"

"Sure," she says, disappointed but trying hard to hide it. The scene is certainly not playing itself out as she has planned it. She goes to her box and takes out a stack of papers and pretends to become absorbed in the process of turning them all right side up. She might be defusing a bomb for all the concerned attention she gives these papers.

Then, as she's about to leave, Ted Hughes comes up with an idea:

"Wait, how about this: our boy Binhammer here is going to be a bachelor that night. His wife, lady of mystery, has other things to do. I'm sure he'd love to be your date."

She doesn't even wait for the shock wave of awkwardness

to strike her. She sees the first hint of red coming into Binhammer's cheeks and simply laughs on her way out the door, as though it were the funniest joke in the world.

The last thing she can hear as she walks down the hall is Ted Hughes's confused voice, saying, "But I was serious."

Sibyl does a little calculation in her head. Lonnie will bring her husband George. Pepper will bring, as she usually does, one or another of the perplexed bearded men she seems to like—who always try, unsuccessfully, to seed a conversation about politics or Hunter S. Thompson. Even Mrs. Mayhew will bring Mr. Mayhew, the small Chihuahua-like man who just sits at the table all night, hands in his lap, gazing demurely into his water glass.

Sibyl will be the only woman there without a date. She doesn't like the looks of that. Maybe she can give it a twist—give it a touch of the femme fatale. But no, she still doesn't like those numbers. She considers not going at all, but now she wants to know who this friend of a friend is, the one who's going to be on Ted Hughes's arm.

She wants to see this woman. Then again, she doesn't want to see this woman.

And of course there's Binhammer. She doesn't understand how things got so complicated so quickly.

When it finally arrives, the night of the annual dinner brings with it the season's first snow in the city. It begins early in the morning as the girls of Carmine-Casey wake up to hear the stippling of flakes on their windows; pulling up their blinds and leaning their elbows on the sill, they press their noses to the pane and feel the coldness seeping in, as coldness does. Their breath, still warm from sleep, leaves a cloud on the window, and they have to decide whether or not to draw a face in the cloud with the tips of their fingers. This decision seems like an important one—but by now the girls have gone, stumbling into the bathroom, where they brush their teeth and put clips in their hair to keep it out of their eyes while they eat cereal.

Some of them are going to the dinner, those girls who are on the Service Squad and are tasked to help seat guests, those girls in the chamber chorus who are giving a special performance during dinner, and those girls who simply like to be involved in everything and have managed to procure some job or another for the evening. Liz Warren and Dixie Doyle, if nothing else, have this in common: they both shun participation in such events—the former because there would be too many eyes on her, the latter because there would be too few. And whether she calls the dinner "asinine" or "*très gauche*," each of the girls feels superior to the event in her own unique way. Neither of them will be in attendance.

The dinner is held in a fancy hotel downtown, and the girls who are present tend to dress either as bridesmaids, in big architectural gowns, or as wealthy divorcées out on the town, in slinky black and maroon numbers with velvet sleeves and teardrop pearl necklaces that you can barely see against their pale, bony chests. Early in the evening, two of these girls greet Lonnie and George Abramson, the first among the English department faculty to arrive. The young duo stand with their hands folded behind their backs, their chins pushed forward, and they point with open hands toward the coat check and the ballroom where the guests can find their table numbers. They are miniature adults, these girls, little worldly-wise sophisticates. After the Abramsons are gone, they debate whether George is going to get lucky tonight.

"Do you think they've ever done it in the kitchen?" asks one.

"Why not?" says the other, whose stepfather is a marriage counselor. "It's good to keep relations fresh."

"I bet she wore special underpants just for tonight."

Mr. and Mrs. Mayhew are the next to show up, looking chastened and severe, respectively. Then Pepper Carmichael with a red-bearded man who seems entirely benign and even a little afraid to touch her. Sibyl Lockhart arrives so quickly that no one has a chance to register it—rushing past the girls, who only catch a glimpse of her behind the parents who are brushing the snow off their coats. She makes her way quickly into the bathroom, where she positions herself in front of the mirror to collect herself and make adjustments to her sleeveless black dress.

Meanwhile, the girls of Carmine-Casey are doing their best to glide like starlets across the open spaces of the hotel. They are scattered all over the couches in the lobby, putting makeup on each other and puckering at reflections of themselves in pocket mirrors. There is no difference, each girl imagines, between me and *women*.

When Binhammer arrives, it's from the wrong direction. He comes in from a side street, by accident, and has to make his way through a crowded bar—a rather masculine woman stepping on his foot with the heel of her pump—before he finds the lobby. He is very grateful to the two girls who tell him where to go from there, and they blush and look away from each other after he has gone.

It is another half hour, however, before Ted Hughes shows up with a woman on his arm. She's pretty in a degenerate sort of way, with a wide red mouth and a pile of hair on her head, and her name is Paulette.

Sibyl is the first one to see her. Paulette is wearing a bright red dress, the same color and even the same satiny texture as her lips. Sibyl, who has been worried that her exposed shoulders and fitted bodice will draw too much attention, now worries that no one will notice her at all. She actually deflates a little—you can see it—and that's when everybody else, Binhammer, the Abramsons, Pepper and her red-bearded boyfriend, all turn around to gaze upon the woman who's just walked in with Ted Hughes.

"Oh my god."

To Sibyl, the woman gives the impression of having been roughed up by life. She is still young, maybe twenty-nine, but it is a youth that has been damaged—a cracked kind of girlishness that might sell for ten dollars at a flea market. And her smile, when you see it, seems degraded—a smile that might have long ago known something about innocence, purity, and clean-sheeted childhood. She keeps digging cigarettes out of her small purse and placing them between her lips before remembering that she's not allowed to smoke inside the hotel. Men, Sibyl supposes, cannot help being attracted to her because she seems to invite depravity—and they find themselves wanting to stick their tongues between those thick red lips of hers, wanting to sink themselves into that crooked, smeared chasm smelling of wine dregs and cigarette butts.

About Paulette, women think, "I could be dirty like that, too, if I wanted to." But: "That's not really what men want. They only *think* they want it. It's rather sad, actually." And then they look haughtily in the other direction.

"Can you get me some zinfandel, Teddy?" Paulette says as they come through the doors of the ballroom. "I'm in a zinfandel mood."

Sibyl wonders where Ted Hughes found this woman, and she conjures up a history for Paulette: cocktail waitress—now retired, after her uncle, who had made some semblance of a fortune investing in questionable Florida real estate, died and left her buckets of money. She spends her time reading magazines about posh living and trying to picture herself in those rooms decorated to look like seaside resort hotels, in those clothes that seem superior to sex, that seem to roll their eyes at sex.

Ted Hughes spots his colleagues and brings her over. He does not seem at all embarrassed to be introducing her—perhaps because he is not paying much attention to her at all. As soon as the introductions are made, he runs his hand through his hair and tells everyone to sit tight, he's going to get a drink from the bar.

"Don't forget my zinfandel, Teddy," Paulette calls after him, then turns back to the others. "Hey, this is some swank party."

"Yes, it's nice, isn't it?" Lonnie says, as someone else who can appreciate the finer things in life.

"You said it. We never had anything like this when I went to school. All I remember is fish sticks." She grimaces with great

authenticity, as though she has just eaten a steaming platter full
of subpar fish sticks. But then she brushes it off with a sound like
a cat clearing its throat and pivots on her heel to take everyone
in. "So you're all English teachers, huh?"

"That's right," Binhammer says smilingly to her. He leans
in close and adds, confidentially, "The soul of the school."

Sibyl can see he is already enamored of her. The cute trashy
little thing. So predictable. For the first time in many months,
she feels like she wants to be alone with the other women, Lonnie and Pepper, to talk about this grubby little interloper. She
assures herself that it will only be a matter of minutes before
Binhammer gets bored of her. And Ted Hughes—well, Ted
Hughes must be performing some philanthropic act.

"Teddy and I only met three months ago," Paulette is saying. "It was at an art gallery. I like to invest in art, you know?"
She winks at Binhammer. "The colors. Anyway, there was this
professor there giving a lecture that seemed like it was going on
for—"

"You know," Sibyl interrupts, unable to help herself, "Binhammer's wife is a professor. You should meet her. She would
adore you."

But, Sibyl should have known, Paulette is not the type to
be immobilized by wives.

"Is she really?" Paulette says, giving Binhammer, who is
now looking nervously toward the bar, a playful slap on the arm.
"I bet she's smart as a firecracker, isn't she?"

Dinner is about to be served, so they all go to sit down at a
big round table, the English department table in the middle of the
room. Sibyl can't bear sitting down with these people yet and excuses herself. She walks over to the small bar set up in the corner
of the ballroom, where the boy serving drinks gives her a wink
and she blushes like an idiot. She leaves before he has a chance
to call her "ma'am." When she returns to the table Ted Hughes
is back, Paulette has two glasses of zinfandel in front of her, and
there is a conversation in motion—though she can't figure out
what it's about, so she just looks from face to face for a while.

When she sees her opportunity, she leans over and whispers to Ted Hughes, who is sitting next to her:

"Are you trying to make a point?"

"What do you mean?"

"The girl." She juts her chin in the direction of Paulette.

Ted Hughes looks at Paulette and then back at Sibyl.

"I don't get it," he says, puzzled. "A point?"

Then she gets up again and wanders out to the lobby, which is mostly empty by now. She goes back into the ballroom, where she stands with her back against the wall for a few minutes, watching little satellites of girls circling the table where Binhammer and Ted Hughes are sitting, oblivious. The girls make quick fly-bys, looking at the men out of the corners of their eyes, pretending to be on important missions while making their way to the other side of the room.

While she's watching, two of these girls decide to talk to Sibyl.

"Ms. Lockhart, what do you think of Mr. Binhammer in a tuxedo?" one of them asks.

"Very nice."

"What about Mr. Hughes?" the other girl says. "I can't decide if I like the white tie or the black tie better."

"They both look nice."

The two girls look at each other and giggle. Then one of them, smiling furtively at Sibyl as though the teacher were just another student sharing gossip, says, "Ms. Lockhart, do you know who that woman is sitting next to Mr. Hughes?"

"Is that his date?" the other asks.

"She's pretty."

"Do you like her dress?"

Sibyl takes all of these questions in and answers them as a set:

"Her name is Paulette. Yes, I do. Why don't you go talk to her?"

But the girls indicate that this would be impossible and go back to their stealthy rounds of reconnaissance.

Sibyl heads back to the table, where Paulette is dipping her fingertips in her wine and sucking on them as she talks. Fifteen minutes later, she's drunk.

"So what do you think of Hughes's girl?" Binhammer says to Sibyl when nobody else is listening. There is a hint of cruelty in his voice.

"I like her," Sibyl says, making her face as blank as she can.

"You do?"

She nods. "Very pretty, don't you think?"

Binhammer looks at her suspiciously. "I guess so."

Meanwhile, on the other side of the table, Paulette is laughing raucously at Ted Hughes and exclaiming to Lonnie Abramson: "Isn't he just a riot? It's like he doesn't even know how to be a man! You know what I mean—in a good way." She snorts a little when she laughs, and waves her napkin around as though it were a flag of surrender.

"Still . . . it's kind of sad, isn't it?" Sibyl continues to Binhammer.

"What is?"

"Well, she's a little needy, isn't she?"

"Needy? Is she?" This seems to astonish him. He looks at Sibyl and then at Paulette, who now seems to be flirting with the busboy. "She doesn't look needy."

"Yes, she puts on a good show, doesn't she? But you can see right through it." She dislikes herself for saying these things, but she can't seem to find the middle ground between victim and attacker. "She thinks it'll fool you and Hughes—but you two are woman savvy."

"Well . . ."

"Still, it's nice of you both to pay attention to her. It seems to make her feel good. I just feel sorry for her—it's going to be hard when Hughes gets bored of her."

Binhammer considers this. She watches his face as he gazes across the table at Paulette, who is now talking about bras with Pepper, pushing her breasts around as though they were tokens in a board game. Finally, he begins to nod slowly. A look of concerned pity sweeps across his brow, and he says, "Yes. It *is* sad."

The rest of the evening unravels in much the same way. Paulette is a big hit. Sibyl is not surprised. Everyone wants to be around the woman—driven by the same impulse, no doubt, that causes one to write one's name on a grimy car window. The desire to be around something that was once clean but is now a little spoiled. They disengage themselves from anxious conversations with parents, administration, other faculty members— conversations that make them feel like actors who have failed to be convincing in their roles—and they encounter Paulette with great billowing sighs of relief. "Paulette, are you having fun?" "Paulette, can I bring you a drink?" "So, Paulette, what do you think about all this ridiculousness?" It is not necessary to put on any performances around Paulette. She has the integrity of coarseness—an empathetic candor derived from the belief that every person in the world, on some level, is just as vulgar as she is.

The word most associated with Paulette this evening, spilling from the lips of sagely nodding faculty members, is *refreshing*.

At one point, nearing the dying fall of the evening, Binhammer finds Ted Hughes looking silent and pensive, turning an empty wineglass around and around by its stem. Paulette is next to him, talking to the husband of one of the math teachers. Everyone else at the table has either gone home or is mingling elsewhere.

Binhammer goes over and takes the empty seat next to Ted Hughes. The two men look at each other for a while without saying anything. Instead, they just smile and nod—as though in tacit agreement on the condition of the universe.

"I like her," Binhammer says quietly.

"Hmm?"

Binhammer gestures toward Paulette, who is talking animatedly on the other side of Hughes.

"Oh, her. Sure. She's my cousin's friend. She doesn't really fit here. But I like her."

"She's nice."

Hughes shrugs and nods. Then he says:

"I was just thinking about women. In general, I mean."

"What about them?"

"Everything." He waves his hand as though it is impossible to encapsulate his thoughts. Binhammer smiles and nods again. There is something sad about Ted Hughes, and, at this moment, he wishes there were a way to reach out and clasp the man's shoulder. If there were a way, he would.

Instead, they just go on talking quietly, enclosed by the lilting white noise around them, like two boys strategizing in a fort made of packed snow or couch cushions. They lean in toward each other until their knees are almost touching. They are trying to figure out something—nothing concrete or of great importance, but rather just an impression, the shadow of a puzzle. Whatever it is, they turn it over in their hands, they hand it back and forth, they set it on the table and take turns tapping at it. They hold it up between them and gaze at it together—and that's what they are looking at when it seems like they are looking at each other.

Then, some time later, they look around and realize that Paulette is missing.

"Oh no."

When they find her, she's sitting at a table with three girls from the junior class—all Ted Hughes's students. It was originally a parent table, but all these parents have gone home, and Paulette is picking at a pile of mashed potatoes on one of their abandoned plates. As she talks, she scoops a finger into the potatoes and punctuates her sentences by putting her finger in her mouth and making a popping sound with her lips as she swallows. Through all this, she does a little swaying dance in her chair.

What she's saying is:

"Come on now—let's be serious. You must all have crushes on him."

The girls smile and nod. This seems to be the place where it's okay to admit you have a crush on your teacher. One of the girls finds on the table a quarter glass of red wine that has somebody else's lipstick on it and drains it furtively while Paulette is between thoughts.

"I tell you," Paulette continues, "if I had him as a teacher when I was in school . . ." She rolls her eyes as if the rest goes without saying. "Well, let's just say I'd never uncross my legs, if you know what I mean."

She cackles, sucks some more potatoes from the end of her fingertip—and realizes that, no, the girls don't know what she means.

"Aw, fuck," she says. "I guess I shouldn't be saying these things to you. Boundary issues, that's what I've got. Hey, don't listen to me. I don't know what the hell I'm saying. What do I know about teenagers? Just—I don't know—just don't get into trouble, I guess."

That's when Ted Hughes and Binhammer find her and take her by the arms back to their own table, where they cajole her into drinking some coffee.

She rubs her eyes and says, "I'm not embarrassing you, am I? Am I an embarrassment?"

"No," Ted Hughes says. "You're beautiful. You're Paulette."

The two men take turns complimenting her while she smiles abstractedly into the bouquet of flowers at the center of the table. Some of the flowers already look dead.

"My teeth are crooked," she says. "I should get them fixed."

Half an hour later, the annual dinner has just about run its course, and Sibyl walks across the almost empty ballroom to say good-bye to the Abramsons and Pepper Carmichael. She embraces them. It is easy to be warm to people at the end of a party—the solidarity of the last ones still standing. Then she goes into the big restroom in the lobby outside and stands in front of the mirror, thinking about what will happen next. She will go home. She will undress, hanging up her clothes with delicacy. She will turn off the light and make her way in the pitch-black to her bed. She has done it many, many times now.

The evening has numbed her. She is not in love with Binhammer; her attraction to him is jumpy and ill-fitting. She is unhappy these days, what with her divorce, and sometimes her unhappiness coincides with his. And that coincidence leads to physical flutterings that are stopped almost as soon as they are started. She understands that. At times like these, gazing into mirrors in women's restrooms, the whole thing looks silly and harmless.

And Ted Hughes is fascinating—but Ted Hughes is a shiny thing, passed around from one person to another. Anyone could see that.

Behind her, one of the stall doors opens and Paulette emerges. Her eyes are bloodshot, and her face is streaked with lines of mascara that make her look either clownish or tribal. She has been crying.

"Oh, hi," Paulette says. "Are you still here?"

"I was just getting ready to go."

"Us too," Paulette says, approaching the mirror. "Oh god, look at me. I'm a mess."

She begins wiping the mascara off her face with a wet paper towel, but it smears into a greasy gray stain. So she scrubs harder until her cheeks are pink. She says:

"I embarrassed him. These fucking men, huh? How are you supposed to know what they want all the time?"

The two women gaze at each other in the mirror. Bathroom intimacy. To turn their heads more and look at each other directly—that would be too much.

"I can't keep up. I guess you smart girls know how to deal with it better," Paulette says.

Smart girls. Sibyl the smart girl. She thinks of the hallway of her apartment, Binhammer edging toward the door, her own little-girl desire to keep him. And those men, Binhammer, Hughes, all of them, feasting on Paulette, feasting on Sibyl herself, having no idea what goes on in the blighted tile bathrooms of fancy hotels.

She can't think about it anymore.

She suddenly feels nauseated.

Paulette goes on: "I'm not such a smart girl."

Even though she feels like she's going to throw up, Sibyl rushes out of the bathroom, through the diminishing crowd in the lobby and out the revolving doors to the street. She wants to be among strangers; she wants to be lost in a crowd somewhere. She wants to be in a place where no one expects her to say anything and where no one can tell her apart from anybody else. Anonymity—perfect, pure blankness. She thinks about suicide—not about doing it herself, but she thinks this is what people must be looking for who kill themselves. Like Sylvia Plath. The chaste white oblivion following that electric jolt. Emptiness and quiet. No name. No character. No expectations. Just a place to sit down and be exhausted in private for a while, and maybe forever.

It has stopped snowing.

She decides to walk home, even though it's late and the walk will take almost an hour. What she's looking for is the foreignness of the city after dark—the beautiful estrangement of swarms of city dwellers brushing past each other with civil indifference.

She decides to walk home, because right now she hates everyone she knows.

chapter 20

Every time Mrs. Mayhew wants to see Binhammer in her office, he anxiously revisits all the events of the previous week to determine if there's anything he's done wrong. He thinks about the papers he hasn't returned to students and classes he has shown up late for. He thinks about students he has yelled at and low grades he has given. He thinks about the things he's said to other faculty members and whether those things might have been overheard. He thinks about things he's said in class that might be considered inappropriate for a girls' prep school. Then—walking down the crowded halls toward the office and ignoring all the girl voices calling out to him, "Mr. Binhammer! Mr. Binhammer!"—he strategizes his response. "I never said that," he mutters to himself. "Besides, it's nothing worse than what they would hear on prime-time TV." Or: "The only reason I was talking about women masturbating in the first place is because they brought it up. One girl asked what Janey was doing beneath the pear tree in *Their Eyes Were Watching God*. Was I supposed to lie?"

So when Binhammer gets a note in his mailbox the day after the annual dinner that reads simply, "See me. Mayhew," the process begins again, and he promises himself that he will be more careful in the future.

But Mrs. Mayhew does not scold him. Instead, when she sees him deferentially edging his way into her office, she barks out:

"Absecon Day."

"What?"

"It's a day school in New Jersey. Outside of Atlantic City."

"Oh."

"They have just split into two separate campuses, one for boys and one for girls—and they're hiring new liberal arts faculty for the girls' school. They have asked for our help, and we're going to give it to them."

The administration of Absecon Day, she explains, is modeling their girls' division on Carmine-Casey, one of the oldest and most successful girls' schools on the East Coast. So Carmine-Casey wants to send two faculty members to help the administrators look through their applicant pool and educate them about constructing an effective faculty.

"I was thinking about you and Sibyl." Mrs. Mayhew looks sideways out of her eyes. She always gives the impression of being able to see into your soul. Binhammer wonders how much she could possibly know about his relationship with Sibyl. Nothing. Really, nothing. Still, he dries up under her gaze. He swallows. Twice.

"Well—"

But he can't think of anything to say next.

Then, eventually: "I think Sibyl . . . I think she might not be up to it."

Mrs. Mayhew squints at him. She is made of brass. He feels her stare like a collar around his neck.

"You mean the divorce," she says.

"Yes, the divorce. And everything."

Finally, the woman relents. "Maybe you're right." She taps her pen on her desk blotter. "Then how about Hughes? Show off our latest acquisition. Show support for the new man. What do you say?" Another hard look. "How do you two get along?"

Oh, god. Well . . .

He imagines it: the Atlantic City boardwalk, he and Hughes like characters out of a black-and-white movie in seersucker suits, a screwball heroine wearing a hat with a broken feather in it, fistfights with cigar-chewing pit bosses, ducking underneath punches, narrow escapes.

The whole thing is absurd and embarrassing, and it makes him grin.

When he tells his wife about the trip later that night, she gives him a mocking laugh.

"So it's going to be the boys out on the town, is it? Are you going to get drunk and flirt with strippers?"

One of the things Sarah knows about her husband is that he holds an automatic grudge against all men for not being women. The idea of spending time with other men rankles him. He dislikes football. And beer. And fraternal high spirits. He mistrusts men and is embarrassed around them. It is, she thinks, one of his most charming qualities.

Women, on the other hand, are all right. He likes women. He's not just attracted to them—he *likes* them. Which is, in her estimation, rarer in most men than she would like to say.

Carmine-Casey, of course, is the perfect place for him. Women to the left of him, women to the right of him. Like Alfred, Lord Tennyson in a sorority house. That is, until the new teacher came along.

"I think it's sweet," she says, teasing him.

"Stop it."

"Aw, come on. It's nice that you have a buddy."

"You think it's funny? We *could* go see some strippers. You think we can't?"

"I'll give you fifty dollars if you do. All in singles."

She laughs, and he turns pink with embarrassment.

So, a week later, it's Binhammer and Hughes on the town in Atlantic City. There is an absurd quality to the whole thing, a madcap boondoggle. Except this one is full of sweat and deception—full of foul and secret things. There is some part of Binhammer that relishes it, the vertiginous masochism of getting as close as possible to the edge of the precipice, the romance of an intimacy with your enemy. He feels as though he is doing something, dangerous or not—as though suffocating on life were the same thing as living fully.

The ride down to Atlantic City is mostly a quiet one. Binhammer drives the rental car. Ted Hughes stares out the window. They stop once because Binhammer has to go to the bathroom. Ted Hughes doesn't go to the bathroom. Binhammer has never seen him go to the bathroom.

They are not sure how to fill up two and a half hours in the tight confines of the car.

"I've never been to Atlantic City," says Ted Hughes at one point.

"Never? How can you have never been to Atlantic City?"

"I don't know. I've never been."

Then they settle back into the silence, as though it were the very upholstery of the car. Binhammer wishes they were smoking men. He likes to think of Ted Hughes offering him a cigarette from a pack, him plucking it out and perching it between his lips, the smoke being sucked out the cracked windows in long ribbonlike streams, the two of them flicking the butts out the window and seeing them hit the pavement in the rearview mirror—just a momentary rain of red ash. That would be all right. If they were smoking men, then Binhammer would know what to do.

When they finally get to the hotel, Binhammer says, "Here we are."

"Here we are," says Ted Hughes.

They are staying in Atlantic City itself, on the boardwalk, a move engineered by Binhammer, who explained to Mrs. Mayhew that the rates would be cheaper than in Absecon, and only twenty minutes from the school itself. They share a room with two double beds and a view that looks out over the ocean. From the window, Binhammer spots two people walking hand in hand on the beach despite the cold. The sky is filled with a murky soup of clouds, and there are no shadows anywhere on the ground.

They don't have to be in Absecon until the next morning.

"I'm going down to the tables," Binhammer says. "Do you want to do some gambling?"

"I'm not much of a gambler," Ted Hughes says. "I have

trouble paying attention to the cards. I think I'll just stroll the boards."

"Suit yourself."

Binhammer, relieved to be alone for the moment, takes the elevator to the casino floor, and the doors open on a panic of lights. It seems to him that there is never any place to focus your eyes in a casino. There are no dimensions—just one flat surface of sound and color. Walking between the rows of slot machines feels like walking across the painted canvas of some modern artist.

He finds a blackjack table and sits down between two old women. He takes out ten twenties and lays them on the table and watches the dealer count them out and set a stack of chips before him. While he plays, Binhammer is silent. The other people at the table are more amicable—joking with the dealer, congratulating each other on winning hands, jovially cursing their luck. But Binhammer looks either bored or uncomfortable—like he's killing time waiting for somebody who is already an hour late. He barely moves his arm, either tapping on the table to hit or making a slight horizontal gesture with his fingers to stay. When the shoe is finished and the dealer shuffles, Binhammer uses the interim to lean back and look down the aisle of tables. There's nothing he's looking for.

For a while he is up fifty dollars, then he loses a hundred and decides to switch to a different table, where he loses a hundred more. He's down to his last two twenty-five-dollar chips when Ted Hughes shows up.

"How are you doing?" asks Ted Hughes.

"I'm losing."

"Really?" His response seems compulsory. "Listen, you should see this Old West casino down the boardwalk. They have a talking buzzard and everything. It's awful and beautiful. It's incredible."

"I've seen it."

"Do you like funnel cake? I found the best place to get funnel cake."

Binhammer tosses a chip in and waits for the dealer to bust, but instead the dealer gets a five and a jack and takes his chip.

Ted Hughes looks around, as though he is eager to move on to the next thing. Then he looks down at the table.

"Is that your last chip?" he asks.

"Yes."

"Oh." Then, "Here, wait, play a hand for me," and he pulls two twenties and a ten from his pocket and hands them to Binhammer.

"You might lose it," Binhammer warns.

"If I lose it I lose it."

Binhammer gives the dealer the cash and gets two chips and puts them both in. When the dealer sweeps the cards across the table, Binhammer gets an eight and a queen and the dealer has a six showing. He hits and looks at Ted Hughes to see if the man can tell that you shouldn't hit on an eighteen—not ever, and especially not if the dealer has a six showing. But Ted Hughes is looking at the table with only the most abstracted curiosity, like a child watching a processional of ants.

Binhammer realizes then that he wants to see Ted Hughes lose. He would gamble away all of Ted Hughes's money if he let him.

But the card he gets is a three.

"What happened?" Ted Hughes asks when Binhammer hands him the chips.

"You won."

"How much?"

"Fifty."

He stuffs the chips carelessly into his pocket and says, "Great, I'll buy you dinner. Listen, I hear they have this building down the shore that's shaped like an elephant. It's called Lucy the Elephant. We have *got* to see that."

They exit the casino together and pause at the entrance. Ted Hughes wants to walk down to the water, but Binhammer tells him the beach closed at ten.

"How can you close a beach?"

Binhammer follows behind the man as they walk down the boardwalk, looking at him look at things. Ted Hughes romanticizes the city in a curious way, and Binhammer wonders what he sees in these plastic and neon facades. He would like to feel what Ted Hughes is feeling—he tries to see the splendor where Ted Hughes points it out, but all he can see is decay. And the tired masks that are hung loosely over that decay.

Later, as they're walking back to their hotel, Ted Hughes starts talking in a broadly gestured way about a woman he once met in Las Vegas. Her name was Carolina, like the states, and she was a showgirl, and he met her in a bar where she said she liked his glasses. He bought her a drink, and she told him about what it was like to be a showgirl and how when she first came to Vegas she couldn't imagine showing her boobs to everyone every night but that it really wasn't so bad, and if you thought about it you might as well show your boobs to people while they still want to see them because one day they won't and wouldn't that be a sad day. And Ted Hughes supposes he fell in love with her a little because there was something wonderfully childish about her, like a little girl pretending to be a woman, and how that was what he liked about Las Vegas itself and now Atlantic City too. He pictures them—the cities—as little girls who put on their mothers' makeup and sequined dresses that drag along the floor behind them as they strut back and forth in front of the full-length closet mirror, wobbling precariously in high heels that hang off the backs of their feet like slippers. Oh god that Carolina with her coarse little smile and her bad teeth! And her saying that if he wanted to see her boobs he would have to come to the show—but then giving a corruptly seductive giggle and saying he could see them before if he wanted to—and the whole time him trying to figure out what he's going to do with her, but after a while it's all moot because she seems to lose interest and drift into the arm of the next guy who buys her a drink. And Ted Hughes is left behind there at the bar, watching her go, still a little in love with her and wondering what to do with that miniature dollhouse love—maybe just put it in the corner where you put other things you can't bear to throw out. And then dust it off when you find yourself on a boardwalk in a town of dissolute virginities—

Finally Binhammer stops him. He has to stand in front of Ted Hughes and take him by both shoulders before the man even notices him. But then their eyes meet.

"What are you talking about?" Binhammer says.

Ted Hughes is still lost somewhere. Gone, moving forward on the impetus of his own imagination. Like an attack. Like epilepsy.

"Take it easy," Binhammer says calmingly. "Take it easy. These things don't mean anything."

"No," Ted Hughes says, looking embarrassed. "They don't mean anything."

They continue to walk back to the hotel. When they get to their room, Ted Hughes takes everything from his pockets, including the four twenty-five-dollar chips from the blackjack game, and tosses it all carelessly on the bedside table. One of the chips nearly rolls off the table but remains teetered on the edge.

In the morning Binhammer counts the chips while Ted Hughes is in the shower, to make sure none of them have fallen between the table and the bed. But all four are there, and he stacks them in a neat little column. He doesn't think Ted Hughes will notice, and Ted Hughes doesn't.

"Look," Binhammer says when Ted Hughes comes out of the bathroom, a towel wrapped around his waist, "I'm going to take you back to the tables tonight. We're going to parlay your winnings."

"I don't think so," Ted Hughes says.

"Come on, you're ripe with beginner's luck. Now's the time. What else are you going to do with those chips?"

"Cash them in."

"That's no fun. Where's your sense of peril? You could win big."

Ted Hughes shrugs and begins going through his luggage, looking for something to wear.

It's then that Binhammer notices something: for him it has become essential to their time here that Ted Hughes gamble away those four green chips.

"You're doing it," he says. He is surprised at the angry insistence in his voice. Slightly embarrassed, he walks to the window and looks out over the shore. He says it again but in a different voice, to try to modulate the moment. "You're doing it."

"What's the matter with you? I'm not interested."

"You shouldn't have won that hand."

"What?"

"Last night," Binhammer says. "You shouldn't have won that hand. Nobody hits on an eighteen."

"I didn't do that, *you* did it."

"You're playing those chips."

"You play them if you want to so bad," Hughes says. "Go ahead."

"No, they're yours—you're playing them."

"Forget it. I don't want to play them."

"You afraid you might lose? You can't win all the time, you know. You can't win everything."

"What?"

Binhammer can feel the hysteria pulsing in his voice, but he can't seem to control it.

"You're gonna lose those goddamn chips. You're gonna play them, and you're gonna lose them."

"You want me to lose them? Fine, I'll lose them." Hughes raises his voice to meet the fever of Binhammer's own. He takes the little stack of chips and opens the door and pitches them out into the hallway, letting the door slam shut behind them. "There, are you happy now? They're lost. What the hell is the matter with you?"

"Jesus," Binhammer says. "Forget it. Just forget it."

He tells Ted Hughes to meet him at the car when he's ready to go. He waits in the parking structure, listening to the echo of strangers' footsteps until Ted Hughes shows up.

On the drive to the school, they say nothing to each other

at first. But the tension between them is so strange and baseless that it cannot hold. It shivers away like a mirage, leaving them with common humor.

"I saw a bunch of jellyfish yesterday," Ted Hughes says, "while you were in the casino."

"Did you?"

"They were washed up on the beach. At first I didn't know what they were. They looked like round sacks of clear jelly. Like silicone breast implants."

"Is that right?"

"It was a whole beachful of counterfeit breasts."

They both look thoughtfully out the windshield of the car, skewered by the image.

They get to Absecon Day by eight thirty, and they are finished by four. On the way back to the hotel, they stop to see Lucy, the building shaped like an elephant. They stand at the base of it and gaze up. It looks like an elephant, except it has windows.

"It's great, isn't it?" Binhammer says to Ted Hughes, by way of apology for his outburst that morning.

But also because it *is* great, authentically great, that gray pachyderm with its toenails painted red.

chapter 21

"You know what your problem is?" Binhammer says. "You don't know how to indulge. Nobody ever taught you how to indulge."

"Is that my problem?" Ted Hughes responds.

"Yeah. That's your problem." Binhammer has to admit he's beginning to enjoy the man's company. The anger of the morning has transformed itself into something else—a staticky frisson.

It's the evening of their second day in Atlantic City, and the two men sit across from each other at a wide table positioned around the perimeter of the massive frescoed hall that is Caesar's Palace Buffet. The place is made up to look like the patio of an Italian villa: whitewashed arbors with plastic grapevines climbing in arches overhead, the faux finish on the walls giving the studied impression of age and dust and even painted in areas to look like the plaster has fallen away to reveal the ancient brick beneath. It is a masterpiece of trompe l'oeil, and Binhammer has to resist the urge to gaze up at the pinprick stars in the ceiling above and look for constellations.

Places like this always make him feel a bit foolish because, in moments of genuine honesty, he suspects himself of being susceptible to their seductions.

"Take a look at this, for example," Binhammer continues, pointing to the plate in front of Ted Hughes. "A little salad, a few baby potatoes, two green beans. *Two* green beans. Are you serious about that? Because from where I'm sitting it doesn't look like you're serious about those green beans. And look—you've got everything in separate little piles."

"I'm not hungry."

"Everybody's hungry."

"What does that mean?"

"Look around you. This is a buffet. You have to think in terms of shovels and troughs, not teaspoons and salad forks." He points to the Vesuvius of food on his own plate. "Look!"

"Ugh," Ted Hughes says. "You're going to make yourself sick."

"The throes of love," says Binhammer. "Sometimes they're painful, Hughes. When will you look it in the face?"

Ted Hughes picks up one of his two green beans and throws it at Binhammer's chest, where it leaves a small oily snail mark on his shirt.

"Now you're getting into the spirit of things," Binhammer says, casually scrubbing his shirt with his napkin.

The two men smile at each other. A shared smile full of boyish clamor.

Ted Hughes toys delicately with the few items of food before him while Binhammer wonders if there is something wrong with him because he is so hungry.

After a while Binhammer pushes his plate back and lets out a low moan. "I'm going to get a bucket of cheesecake. And when I come back, we're going to get to the bottom of this need you have to compartmentalize everything."

"Not *everything*."

"So you say."

Binhammer gets up and makes his way through the middle-aged patrons of the restaurant, trying to read the words on all the T-shirts, which seem to be particularly declarative this evening.

"Take a bowlful of this cheesecake," Binhammer says when he returns. Ted Hughes moves to comply. "That's my boy."

"Oh my god," says a voice behind them. The two men turn around to see a young black-haired woman, maybe twenty years old, in a green military jacket, a camera slung around her neck. She's pointing to the table—and with good reason. The waitress seems to have lost track of them on her rotation, and all of their plates—mostly Binhammer's—are stacked in precarious, bloated piles everywhere. It looks like the detritus of a bar mitzvah compacted onto a single table between two speechless men looking suddenly bewildered.

Before they can say anything, she's taking pictures of them and the mess over which they are sitting like two dull-witted players of chess.

"You don't mind, do you?" she asks, not waiting for a response. "It's for my Atlantic City Garbage series."

"Your what?"

Her name, it turns out, is Dora, and she is going to be a photographer some day. Right now she's building her portfolio with pictures of authentic Atlantic City trash. The two men see something in her that reminds them of the girls who sit in the corners of their classrooms, a certain ironic toughness—the old jean, dirty hair kind of self-dispossession of smart girls who have given over to the embarrassment of everything. Something in her voice gives the impression that she's sick of herself.

"Join us, Dora," Binhammer says. He is happy to be talking to her.

"Yes," Ted Hughes adds. "We know our trash. Wait while we finish our coffee, and we'll all go nosing around for garbage together. We've been looking for an adventure, haven't we, Binhammer?"

"Dora's a nice name," Binhammer says as she sits down at the table.

"Sure." She rolls her eyes. "Get this, my parents named me after one of Sigmund Freud's patients. They think it's hilarious. You should hear them cackle about it. I think it's gross."

She changes the film in her camera as they watch, telling them how she spent most of the afternoon crawling around under the boardwalk. She is fearless, but they are used to dealing with fearless girls.

"You two aren't coming with me, though," she says in warning.

"Suit yourself." Binhammer sips his coffee.

"But you should know," Ted Hughes says, "that my friend here produces garbage by the pound. He leaves trails of it wherever he goes."

"Look!" Binhammer says, pointing again to the table.

Dora smirks. It's the smart girl's smile, and they know they've got her.

So the two men go with her, one on either side, out to the boardwalk. They like this turn of events. They realize that this is what they've been missing on the trip so far—someone to watch them. An audience. When she's not looking, they smile at each other with big, excitable backstage smiles.

"So what do you guys do for a living anyway?"

"We're teachers," Binhammer says with the conviction of someone who believes that people will be impressed by that.

"Come on."

"Binhammer, I don't think she believes us."

"Why wouldn't she believe us?"

"Maybe she finds us threatening."

"We *are* sinister," Binhammer concedes with fake regret.

"Okay, okay," Dora says. "If you want to be teachers, be teachers. So what is it you teach."

"Girls," Binhammer says. "A lot of girls. And we teach them English."

Dora laughs. "Both of you? You're both supposed to be English teachers? At a girls' school? I don't get it. What's the joke?"

"Look," Ted Hughes says, "Binhammer here'll say something to prove it."

"Season of mists and mellow fruitfulness—close bosom-friend of the maturing sun, conspiring with him how to load and bless with fruit the vines that round the thatch-eaves run."

"See?" Hughes says.

"Big deal," Dora says. "My boyfriend picked me up in a

bar with Wordsworth. Anyone can memorize a few lines of poetry."

She refuses to believe that they are what they say they are,
perhaps because they say it with the glee of schoolboys telling
made-up stories about their summer vacations. She rolls her eyes
at them. She does this numerous times, and they begin to understand it as a gesture of affectionate intimacy—as though she
needs to defuse her own sparking vulnerability. Soon, whenever
she rolls her eyes, the two men look at each other and smile.

The night grows colder, and they walk back and forth
on the boardwalk, from New Jersey Avenue to Montpelier,
looking for trash that she can photograph. They find a sleepy
young boy sitting on a wrought iron chair outside the doors of
a casino. His parents are nowhere in sight, and he is holding a
rainbow lollipop the size of his head, which he has apparently
dropped on the beach because one side of it is caked with sand.
While Dora photographs him, he sits there looking dour and
drawing his tongue in long, canine lapping motions up the
clean side.

At another point, soon after midnight, Dora becomes
gloomy, staring out in the direction of the ocean, even though
it's too dark to see.

"This is such a waste of time. Atlantic City Garbage. Jesus.
I can't believe I thought this was a good idea." She looks like she
would like to get up and walk out on herself. "It's *so* pretentious.
I mean, seriously. All of this—it's just *trash*."

"Oh, now." The two men console her.

"Trash is trash," she says. "There's nothing clever about it."

She falls quiet, and they take turns offering suggestions.

"You just need a break," Binhammer says.

"That's right," Ted Hughes agrees. "Nothing looks good if
you look at it for too long."

"Or just give it up entirely."

"That might work too."

"What else are you good at?"

"Can you crochet?"

"Well, maybe not crochet."

"Maybe not. The industry is dead."

"How about painting?"

"Painting might work. Then again . . ."

"What?"

"Painting may be too close to photography."

"Oh, right. And she's not very good at that."

"No."

"Well, there's always dog-walking."

"Ha ha," she says, interrupting the banter sourly and rolling her eyes. "Yeah. You guys are teachers. Sure."

They stop at a pub just off the boardwalk and order three Cosmopolitans, and that's when they find out she's actually twenty-three. Sometimes while they're talking, she'll playfully slap one of them on the arm or shake a little belligerent fist at the other. When the bill comes, they declare that they are paying— and she simply shrugs and lets them.

"Thanks," she says and puts on her coat.

For the next hour and a half, they continue walking the boardwalk and stopping for drinks in casino bars. Dora no longer seems like she's in the mood to take pictures, so the camera dangles forgotten from her thin wrist. When she goes to the bathroom, Binhammer and Ted Hughes wait for her, standing with their backs to the casino wall like two escorts of a debutante.

Around two in the morning, they walk her back to her hotel to discover that her room has been given to someone else because she had only made the reservation for one night. The three stand in the lobby of the big casino, all of them a little drunk and looking back and forth at each other.

"What did you think you were doing?" Ted Hughes asks, paternal with drink and weariness.

"I was supposed to meet up with this other girl," Dora says. "She never showed."

"Now what?" Binhammer says. "You'll have to get another room."

"Sure, whatever," she says and walks toward the exit.

"What is she doing?" Binhammer asks.

"I don't know."

"Hey, what are you doing?"

She stops and turns toward them. "I don't have any money. It's okay. I'll just hang out in the casino. The night's halfway finished anyway." She sways a little as she talks.

"Forget it," Binhammer says, taking her by the elbow. "You're staying with us."

She rolls her eyes, and they take her back to their room and lay her out on the bed, mostly asleep already. Ted Hughes takes off her shoes, and Binhammer folds the bedspread over her. "I think our girl's out for the night." Then they sit in two chairs in front of the large window and look out over the lights to the immense darkness of the Atlantic. Binhammer twirls the glass ashtray on the table between them, wishing again that he knew how to smoke.

Only once does Dora stir, sitting up and rubbing her eyes. They look at her, and she looks at them.

"I guess I should be worried," she mumbles. Then she shoos it all away with a wave of her hand. "Eh. You two don't even like girls anyway." And with that she readjusts her pillow and falls asleep again.

"What was that?" Binhammer says. "What did she say?"

"Did she say we don't like girls?"

"I like girls."

"So do I."

"What did she mean?"

"Is that what she said?"

"I think so."

"What did she mean?"

"I don't know. Wake her up and ask her."

Ted Hughes goes over to the bed and shakes her by the shoulder.

"Hey," he says. "Hey, Dora. What did you just say?"

But her body just curls itself away from his hand, and her breathing becomes wheezy with the sleep of the immobile.

"Well, forget it," Ted Hughes says, sitting back down.

"I guess. She didn't even believe we were teachers."

Neither of them knows how to discuss the logistics of going to sleep with a witty artist girl in one of their beds, and so neither of them does. Instead, they talk about other things, leaning back in their chairs and glancing at the sleeping girl every now and then. When they get thirsty, Binhammer goes down the hall to the vending machine and buys cans of soda and bags of chips.

"She's cute," Ted Hughes says.

"Yeah, she's cute." Binhammer nods. Then he says, "I never went out with anyone like her."

"No?"

"I never knew how to talk to girls like that. And now that I've figured it out, they're all twenty years younger than I am."

"But they love you. Fifteen-year-olds love you."

"No, they love *you*."

Later Ted Hughes says, "What do you think of Sibyl?"

Binhammer shrugs noncommittally. Then later Ted Hughes says it again:

"So what do you think of Sibyl?"

"Compared to what?"

"I don't know compared to what. What do you mean?"

They both turn and look at the girl sleeping behind them, as though she were Sibyl herself. What Binhammer wants is for Ted Hughes to talk about Sibyl, because he knows the man must see something in her that he himself doesn't. What he wants is to catch a glimpse of the Ted Hughes version of Sibyl, that jittery figment of language and bright eyes like a receding dream. He would like to take a look at that Sibyl. That's a Sibyl he might be able to fall in love with. They could weave that Sibyl here between them, like the two fates, forever—with no one around to cut the thread.

Instead, Ted Hughes says, "Did you ever read Lawrence Durrell? He says something in one of his books. What was it?" He leans forward and looks out the window, as though Lawrence Durrell himself were floating out there in the night sky. "It was something like, 'She was no longer a woman. Now she had become a situation.' "

Binhammer watches the man's hands, which seem to build something invisible and impossibly complex. He feels like he wants to know what that thing is—the thing that Ted Hughes holds square between his artisan fingers.

"That's what I feel like," Ted Hughes continues. "I don't know any women. I only know situations."

He is quiet again for a long time. Then he starts talking about a woman he once knew—a woman who wasn't anything like Sibyl. He describes the way she sat, the way she crossed her legs and looked at him as though there were nothing in the world that he could get away with. He describes a windowsill, like this one here, where they sat and looked out and saw a group of children playing hopscotch outside on the sidewalk—except they were playing it wrong and she wanted to go outside and explain to them how to do it, and he wanted to see her do it too but she didn't.

Then he laughs and brushes it off, but he's still looking down at his hands, shaping the clay of memory, when he nods and says, "She was a situation. She was a whole gorgeous situation." The way he says it makes Binhammer think that the woman he is describing is probably his wife.

And Ted Hughes, too, Binhammer realizes, has become a situation. Where Binhammer should feel jealous, he only feels sympathy. Where he should be angry, he only feels grateful. Ted Hughes, the center of so much feminine attention. Binhammer realizes, embarrassed, that what he wants most is to beat those women and girls at their own game, to be dynamic enough to hold the gaze of Ted Hughes. To be the center of attention of the center of attention. That would be something.

Good lord, he thinks. What now? Where do you go from here? Perverse, the idea of wanting to befriend your wife's lover behind her back. It would be so much easier if he could hate the man—and hasn't he tried?

Binhammer gets up from the chair, suddenly awake. Outside, finally, the darkness coming out from over the sea is tinged with color. On the boardwalk below two men emerge drunkenly from the doors of a casino to greet the sunrise. They support each other for a while, loping from side to side and declaiming to the sky in big gestures like ancient Greek stage actors. Then something happens and they become belligerent, pushing each other until one of them loses his balance and sits down on the boardwalk with a heavy thud. The other begins to walk away, but turns around before he's gotten twenty feet and says something to the sitting man, who is now holding his head in his hands. The sitting man nods and the other one nods and they say some more things and then they both nod. After which the one offers the other a hand and raises him up, and they punch each other playfully on the shoulders and walk toward the beach again, laughing heartily.

"Should we wake up our girl?" Binhammer asks.

"Let's go get something to eat first."

"Okay. We'll bring her back something."

"Sure. And then we'll kick her out."

"Do you have your door key?"

"Yes."

"So I don't need mine?"

"No."

"Listen," Binhammer says as they shut the door behind them and wait for the elevator in the hall. He feels generous, magnanimous. "You and Sibyl. It's not such a bad idea."

"You think so?"

"I think she could use someone like you."

Ted Hughes nods, as if considering an algebraic proof—and then, as they step into the elevator, something seems to occur to him and he smiles boyishly at Binhammer, as though the two of them have reached some kind of final accord after hours of debate. The elevator doors close and the two of them ride down to the lobby, watching the floor numbers tick by.

chapter 22

During the days that Binhammer is out of town, Liz Warren finds herself sitting in the back of the class staring at the substitute with a face as close to porcelain still as she can get it—trying not to react in any way to the inane exchanges between Dixie Doyle and her ridiculous cadre of confidantes. She considered not going to class at all, but she's getting something out of this exercise: a study in military stillness. She gazes at the lumpy shape of the substitute, who has not even made an attempt to teach but instead sits at the front desk, casually turning the pages of her magazine and looking up once in a while to make sure that nothing untoward is occurring.

Can she even see me? Liz Warren wonders. I am invisible. I have willed myself invisible. The invisible girl. I will find out what people really think of me.

She remains still as death even as she overhears Dixie Doyle relating the ridiculous story of her weekend.

"So my mother made me go talk to this girl in the hospital. Her leg got run over by a truck. Can you believe it? A truck! It was so awkward. What am I supposed to say? 'Hi, I'm Dixie, how's your leg?' 'Crushed, thanks. How's yours?'"

"How did her leg get run over, Dixie?"

"She was crossing the street against the light. Someone tried to pull her back, but they didn't in time and her leg still got crushed. Can you believe it? I mean, what do you say to someone like that?"

"How come you had to go see her, Dixie?"

"Well, apparently she's my cousin."

"Your *cousin*?"

"I know. That's what I said."

Despite her extraordinary control up to this point Liz Warren flinches, and, just as she thought, with that slightest movement her invisibility pops off. Now Dixie is looking at her from
four rows ahead.

"So, Liz," she calls. "I hear tonight's the big night. You
better be careful—Jeremy's a little pushy, if you know what I
mean. At least he was with me. He might be more *gentlemanly*
with you."

"Shut up, Dixie," Liz says, swinging her book bag over her
shoulder and heading toward the door. The bell starts ringing by
the time she gets there, and she's the first one out of the room.

Earlier in the week, when Jeremy Notion asked her out, she
said yes without thinking—that autonomic function of girlhood
that makes her embarrassed now. Does she really want to go out
with him? There is a part of her that wishes she could simply be
asked out by boys, accept, and have it recorded in her journal
without ever having to go on the dates themselves. The worst
part about the date, it seems, is the date. Would she feel differ-
ently if it were someone else? She tries to imagine different boys,
but she soon feels ridiculous—like one of those girls in frilly
socks pining over pictures of movie stars in magazines.

Let's be practical about this.

How does Dixie do it? The performance—how does she
pull it off? How is she able to say the things she says?

During a Bardolph/Carmine-Casey canned food drive last
year, one of the boys started talking to Liz while boxing up the
cans. At first she was flattered by the attention. But then she began to suspect that there was something behind it. In her head, a
scenario played itself out in which: he liked her from a distance;
but when he started talking to her, he lost interest because all she
could talk about was how much homework she had, and nobody
wanted to hear about that; and then he wanted to be rid of her
but couldn't because he felt sorry for her and was a pretty decent

guy and so went out of his way to continue talking to her even though he didn't really want to.

She felt in her bones that this was the case. She wanted to let him off the hook since he was at least nice enough to talk to her in the first place, so she kept telling him, "You know, you don't have to talk to me if you don't feel like it," and "You don't have to walk me home. I have some work to do anyway," and, regarding their one date, "You can go see the movie with someone else if you want to. I know you said we would go, but you shouldn't feel obligated."

And she was right, because eventually he took her up on her offer and stopped walking her home and stopped talking to her altogether. So far, that is the closest Liz Warren has come to having a boyfriend, and she supposes that it's rather pathetic if you look at it for too long.

It doesn't help her mood that when she gets home that evening her mother stands in the doorway of her room, wanting to help her get dressed.

"What are you going to wear, Lizzie?"

"I don't know. I haven't thought about it." She says it as though it would be the very summit of absurdity to even consider the question. She can hear the way she talks to her mother, but she doesn't know how to stop herself.

"You haven't thought about it? But, honey, isn't he going to be here in an hour?"

"He's not coming here. I'm meeting him."

"Oh." Mrs. Warren frowns and picks a thread from the front of her blouse.

"I have to finish reading this chapter, Mom."

"I think you should wear—"

"It's Tolstoy, in case you were interested. *The Death of Ivan Ilyich*."

"I think you should wear your green skirt. Green always makes you look so *sophisticated*. Against the color of your hair. A lot of women wish they had your hair."

"They can have it. I'm not wearing a skirt."

"Oh, I really wish you would consider it. You don't have to wear those jeans all the time. Sometimes it's nice to dress up. What if he gets dressed up? You don't want him to think you don't care. Boys like skirts."

"Can we just—" says Liz, who has been flinching throughout her mother's speech. "I'm not going to wear a skirt."

"I don't know why you have to be so difficult about it."

"*Mother*—"

"Uh-oh. I know I'm in trouble when you start calling me Mother. Okay, okay. I'm going."

When her mother has gone, Liz calls her friend Monica Vargas to complain that her mother won't leave her alone about Jeremy Notion. Monica Vargas explains, with the preternatural wisdom of a child of divorce, that mothers are the broken reflections of their daughters, deeply flawed and shimmering at you full-length from the closet door. "They're just like anyone else," Monica says. "They like to look forward to things. But really they just don't know what to do."

Talking with Monica about mothers and fathers is like seeking the counsel of a Tibetan monk. While all the other girls are whining about how unfairly they have been treated at the hands of their parents, Monica sits cross-legged on her bed and utters koans that bend your mind back upon itself. And suddenly, before you know it, you feel like you want to make your parents breakfast in bed.

Then Monica asks, "So what are you going to do on this date of yours?" She does not approve of Jeremy Notion, and neither, to be honest, does Liz. So whenever they talk about it, it's as if they're discussing a scientific experiment.

"I don't know. I think he's taking me to dinner."

"Where? I'll put twenty bucks on Italian."

Italian food is the only way teenage boys know how to be romantic.

After she hangs up with Monica Vargas, Liz looks up to find her mother pretending to walk nonchalantly by her door.

"Oh," she says, as though it has just occurred to her in pass-

ing, "by the way, you can borrow these earrings if you want."
She holds out two green teardrops in her palm. "But they're
emerald—you may want to wear something that goes with
them. Just an idea."

"Okay," Liz says, trying to be sympathetic. "But I think I'll
just wear the ones I have on."

Her mother takes this as an invitation to come into the
room and examine Liz's ears—whereupon Liz makes a face and
uses her thumbnail to scratch the side of her nose. She pulls herself away from her mother's groping hands and sits with her back
against the pillows of her bed.

"You know," her mother says, "I was really hoping to meet
him. Will you bring him around next time?"

"We'll see."

"Tell me," her mother says, brightening suddenly, "what
does he look like? Is he cute?"

"Oh my god."

"Do you want to know about a boy I dated when I was
your age? He had a big mop of curly hair. It was adorable."

Liz cringes and pulls her knees up to her chest. "Listen,"
she says, trying to be nice, "I have to go pretty soon. Can we
talk about this later?"

"You know, Lizzie, this is a big time in a mother's life, too.
I mean, I've loved going to all your award dinners and everything. I couldn't be more proud. But this . . . You know, for a
mother, her daughter's first real date—"

"Can we just please stop talking about this? Please?"

"Okay, okay," her mother says, holding up her palms in
retreat as she exits the room.

Before leaving to meet Jeremy, Liz closes her door and tries
on the green skirt that her mother wants her to wear. Standing
before the mirror, she thinks it makes her look okay. But then
she thinks about him thinking about why she would wear the
green skirt. So uncharacteristic of her. He'll see it as a pathetic
attempt to impress him. So she takes the thing off and tosses it
aside and puts her jeans back on.

She doesn't want him thinking that she takes this whole thing too seriously.

They meet at the fountain in Central Park—his idea. When she gets there, he hasn't arrived yet, so she walks in a wide circle along the winding paths, and by the time she comes back there he is, leaning against the concrete edge of the fountain with his ankles crossed like some kind of larval James Dean.

"Hey," he says and reaches to hug her—but she's not prepared and doesn't get her arms uncrossed in time, and so he ends up embracing her awkwardly with her arms pressed between their chests.

"Okay," she says, whatever that means.

"You smell nice," he says. "What is it?"

"I don't know," because she really doesn't. "Just my shampoo, I guess."

She wonders if she smiles too much—or not enough. The thought bothers her, and she decides to keep a tally. On the left side of her brain she'll count the number of times she smiles, and on the right side she'll count the number of times Jeremy does.

"Are you ready to go?" He smiles.

She smiles.

Then she begins to suspect that she's not actually smiling when she thinks she's smiling—that what feels like a smile on her face just looks like a thin-lipped nonexpression to everyone else. When they get to the restaurant, she'll go into the bathroom and check in the mirror.

While she's thinking about the concordance of her smiles, Jeremy begins talking about the weekend he spent swimming in the lake at his uncle's house upstate. By the time they reach the restaurant she discovers that she only has to listen to about ten percent of what he says to respond appropriately.

After they're seated, he asks if they should try to get a bottle of wine. "I look pretty old. Sometimes I can get away with it."

But she shakes her head.

They order, and the waiter brings their food, and while Jeremy Notion is twirling his fettuccini around his fork, he becomes philosophical and says, "Yeah. I don't know what happened with Dixie. I'm not sure why I was going out with her in the first place."

"Well, she's very sophisticated, *n'est pas?*"

"I guess she was sophisticated—oh, I get it. You were joking."

She's embarrassed. How did she get so petty? So mean? She gives herself a brutal pinch on the thigh as punishment, hard enough to make her eyes water.

"I guess it was just nice to think she wanted to go out with me. You know. The way she is."

The way she is.

Throughout the evening Liz has the feeling of being watched, the uncomfortable sense that her actions are being monitored by a note-taking critic. She has frequently felt this in circumstances that require social grace, but tonight she can actually name the critic gazing at her from the wings: Dixie Doyle. That's right. No matter how much she tries to lose herself in the soft, blue, innocuous puddles of Jeremy's eyes, she cannot get past the feeling that she is actually on a date with Dixie herself. Dixie Doyle by proxy—the inane, grinning, pigtail-wearing, lollipop-licking incarnation of plastic-doll girlhood. Sure, on some level she feels an obligation to impress Jeremy—the *boy* in the matter (she thinks of romantic espionage, of Graham Greene)—but overriding that feeling is the obligation to impress Dixie.

Dixie, she realizes with a sickening twist of her stomach, would have wanted her to wear the green skirt.

Liz drops her fork onto her plate with a clatter and leans back. She can't eat anything else.

"What's the matter?" Jeremy asks worriedly.

"Nothing. Nothing's the matter. I'm just full."

"Oh. Okay. I just thought . . . I mean, that's okay. You don't have to eat any more. . . . You know, I really like your play. The play you wrote. It's really good."

After dinner he walks her home, and when they get to the corner of her building he stops and stands in front of her and looks at her deeply for a second, like a party magician trying to hypnotize someone. They are standing in front of a newsstand, and the fat oily man behind the counter is smoking a cigar and staring at them. She notices that one of his ears looks like it's been chewed away, and she wonders what it would be like to be attacked by a dog.

Then Jeremy leans down and kisses her. First once, tentatively, and when she doesn't do anything he readjusts his whole body and sinks himself into her face again, for longer this time.

She thinks she should put a hand somewhere on him, on his shoulder or his hip or something, but she can't quite focus on what's happening.

The newspaperman with the chewed ear watches them solemnly and scratches himself.

At any minute she expects Dixie Doyle to pop out from behind the newsstand, laughing and pointing, pointing and laughing—shrieking in that preposterous bubblegum voice of hers, that voice that seems to trick people into melting over it, the voice that rings out clearer through the halls than any bell at Carmine-Casey.

chapter 23

During the winter, the courtyard of Carmine-Casey is barren and miserable and inspires thoughts of death in the minds of the students who sit staring out the windows, deaf to their history lectures and their French recitations. Gazing at the leafless branches of the sugar maple (they look like the pictures of ganglia in their biology textbooks—exactly like frozen ganglia) and the rutted, hardened mud, each girl imagines that she knows the best way to die—the most dramatic, the most meaningful. And each can picture the parades of mourners weeping loudly, regretting the things they had done or not done to her.

Ganglia, they whisper to themselves, as though the word were magic—and a little sinister smile creeps onto their lips.

But the winter also brings the semester's drama performance, which is without question the faculty's favorite school function. The teachers, standing proudly at the back of the auditorium, like to smile and comment upon the marvelous individual talent there is to be found among their girls. They even go so far as to snicker modestly to each other, "Don't you wish you could take credit for that brilliance up there?"—when, in fact, they do privately take credit for it, each teacher swallowing warmly the thick, molasses-sweet belief that he or she is the secret inspiration behind the performance onstage.

As the sun begins to go down sooner and sooner each day, this semester's dramatic offering, *Salmonburger*, written and directed by Liz Warren, patterned after the *Oresteia*, starring Dixie Doyle in the role of Clarissa, is in final rehearsals that go so late into the evenings that some of the girls who live outside the city have to sleep over at the homes of other girls who live closer to the school. Arrangements are made over the phone with parents who are beginning to recognize that their protective function has become, somewhere along the line, a casual formality—and the girls order sandwiches, without mayonnaise, from the deli around the corner.

And one evening, even after all the other performers and stage crew have gone home, there are three figures left in the cavernous auditorium, their voices echoing off each other against the tangle of lighting overhead. Two of these figures are standing together onstage, and one of them sits far back, almost against the rear wall, watching the action.

"I can't hear you," calls the figure at the back. "Remember, we're not using mics. Be louder. But still intimate. Don't lose the intimacy."

This is Liz Warren. She wears jeans and sneakers and a T-shirt that advertises some product that hasn't existed in thirty years. Her hair is pulled up away from her face and held with a simple silver clip, and she wears round tortoise-framed glasses that, if you look closely, reveal fingerprints resulting from her habit of removing them and using them to point at things.

Everything about Liz Warren is designed to call attention to the absurdity of everything around her. The impression one gets when speaking to her is that of constant embarrassment—not for herself, or not always for herself, but more for the inane circumstances into which we have managed to stumble. Look around you, she seems to say with her eyes. Can you believe this? Don't think *I* had anything to do with it.

Her teachers respond to this in one of two ways. They either shrink from her, calling her arrogant and lamenting the fact that she is among the top students at the school ("And she certainly knows it!"), or they find her self-consciousness intriguing, believing that embarrassment is a sign of intelligence, since only fools are honestly comfortable with themselves. The latter reaction can be found more frequently in her male teachers, who like to believe that their conversations with her are enriched by the subtext of her crush on them—a subtext that they further believe she is playing like a coy game of chess. Clever thing!

But the fact is that, with the exception of Mr. Hughes, who sometimes looks at her *hard* and makes her chest feel warm, Liz Warren rarely thinks about her teachers in intimate terms. Even when Mr. Binhammer approached her in the hall earlier that day with a rather personal remark, she thought that he must be criticizing her work.

"I met—Mr. Hughes and I met someone in Atlantic City who reminded me of you."

He was reticent—more like a high school boy than a grown man—and almost apologetic, as though he were waving a white flag in truce. But she could not figure out what battle he could possibly be conceding, so she determined that he must be feeling guilty and trying to criticize her without hurting her feelings.

"Was she a bad writer?"

"No, no. She was a photographer."

"A bad photographer?"

This is Liz Warren. And now she sits hunched over on a chair with a script on her knees, biting her nails and watching her two actors sweat under the stage lights. It's only two days after her date with Jeremy Notion, and now he is up there with Dixie Doyle licking his lips nervously because he knows what's coming next.

"There's the whistle," Dixie says. "Get on the train, Ivan."

"Come with me, Clarissa."

"No."

"Will you be here when I come back?"

"I don't know."

"We got along. For a while."

"Did we?"

"You couldn't stand to be without me."

"And now you're the last person in the world I want to be with."

"Look around you, you pretty little fool. I *am* the last person in the world."

Dixie stops and unrolls the script to examine it.

"Now what?" she says, looking into the back of the auditorium and shading her eyes with one saluting hand.

"Read the script," Liz says from the darkness. "Now you kiss him."

"We don't have to rehearse that," Dixie says with a superior glance at Jeremy. "We know how to kiss."

"This is a certain kind of kiss," Liz asserts.

"All kisses are the same," Dixie says knowingly. "But whatever you say. You're the boss. If you want me to kiss your—" She cuts herself short and waves it off.

Liz is thankful for her discretion—her whole body would have cringed, shrunk up like a tightened fist, if Dixie had used the word "boyfriend." In truth, she is unbothered by the idea of Dixie kissing the boy that she herself has kissed. Instead of jealousy, she feels something like malevolent curiosity. The two of them forced to kiss each other at her command—the idea is almost delightful to her.

So they reread the scene. Jeremy says, "I *am* the last person in the world," and Dixie leans over and kisses him sardonically.

"No," Liz says. "You like him, but you don't like him. That kind of kiss. Try it again."

They reread the scene.

"I *am* the last person in the world."

She kisses him, sneeringly.

"Try not to sneer. And don't roll your eyes. You're not just irritated by him. You hate him—and you love him."

They do the scene again and again. Sometimes, during the kiss, they can hear the groaning of some machinery behind the walls of the school.

"I *am* the last person in the world."

She kisses him, aggressively this time, like she's trying to beat him up with her mouth. He touches his lips after, as though they are tender and bruised.

"No. Too rough. The hate is good, but you lost the love. Think about this—think about being exhausted. You love him and you hate him, but you're too exhausted to tell the difference. Exhausted."

She herself feels exhausted and taut as she says this, perched on the edge of her seat. Now she stands and begins to walk slowly toward the stage.

By this point Dixie has lost all her humor and simply looks embarrassed and ravaged. She and Jeremy don't look at each other at all, and she chews on her lower lip when they're not acting.

They do it again and again. They do it until Liz is standing at the edge of the stage, leaning over it—until there is no acting left in the two actors.

Once more: "I *am* the last person in the world." They *are* the last people in the world. And this time the kiss is different. It has a quality. There is something in it that makes all three stop dead. For a few seconds the only sound is fatigued breathing and the low rumbling in the school walls.

"That's it," Liz says finally, and all at once everything hits her—a lead ball dropping in her chest. What she sees in Dixie Doyle is everything she has put there, the authenticity, the exhaustion, the girlishness; the simple, unaffected loneliness; the honest, brutal truth of everything, the blinding horrible truth—everything that she herself has collected in a little tin box inside her own aching chest. "That's it."

She feels like crying, but she won't let herself. Instead she says:

"Do it again."

"Again?"

"Again. Just the kiss."

They kiss.

"Do it again."

They kiss again.

"Again!"

At this moment, opposite the auditorium where Dixie Doyle and Jeremy Notion are kissing by order of Liz Warren, Mr. Doran, the chemistry teacher, opens the heavy wooden doors and enters the quiet marbled lobby of the Carmine-Casey School for Girls.

Everyone knows Mr. Doran, the chemistry teacher who speaks very quietly like a mouse and has front teeth like a mouse and wears round glasses that make his eyes look like a mouse's eyes. He scuttles around the chemistry lab and is associated in the girls' minds with the tap-tapping of a rack of test tubes being carried about. Also known to the girls is the fact that Mr. Doran's wife spends many weekends away on business trips, which they firmly believe are really an alibi for an affair she is having with another man. This makes the girls feel protective of Mr. Doran because they like him, even though you can't really talk to him about anything but the way sodium will explode if you add water to it.

As it turns out, his wife is currently out of town for four days, and tonight Mr. Doran, who lives in Westchester, has stayed in the city after school to see a foreign movie that he once saw long ago in college. Coming out of the theater, he remembers the first time he saw it, the vibrant tautness of his life back then—the thundering forward motion of things, like a train on a track that can go as fast as it wants because there's only one direction to go: the inevitable and always receding horizon. He thinks about this and wrinkles his mousy little nose. It is only then that he realizes he has left his briefcase at school and, looking at his watch and thinking about the empty house awaiting him, determines that it's not too late to go fetch it.

Back at Carmine-Casey, he greets the security guard in the lobby and takes the elevator to the lonely lab on the third floor. The girls tell him it smells like chemicals, but he must be used to it because the room doesn't smell any particular way to him.

It is on his way out that he hears the voices coming from the auditorium around the corner. He looks around and readjusts his round spectacles, and then opens the door a crack to discover Liz Warren, a student of his from last year, standing at the foot of the stage and calling out loudly to Dixie Doyle and some boy who are kissing each other repeatedly.

"Again! Again! Kiss her again! Again!"

Mr. Doran lets the door shut quietly and stands looking at the wood grain, thinking about what he's just seen. He thinks about it while sitting in the back of the taxi that takes him to the train station, and he thinks about it during his forty-five-minute train ride. And he thinks about it some more as he gets into his car, parked in the commuter lot, and makes the slow but short drive, coming to a full stop at all the stop signs, back to his home, where he has to grope down the hallway to find the light switch and where he stands at one end of the living room listening to the sound of the ticking clock with its big brassy chime— the only thing to listen to in the empty house.

He gets a glass of water from the kitchen sink and notices that it's leaking again. The house leaks. It leaks water from the taps, air from the windows, sound from the walls. He wishes he knew how to stop them.

Unlocking the kitchen back door, he takes his water out to the little worn deck and looks at the suburban rooftops over the fence that circles his backyard. Sweeping some of the snow off the edge of the deck with his foot, he shivers—but he likes the look of his breath against the crisp dark night.

He and his wife have lived in this house for seventeen years. She is not having an affair with another man. She is a very successful financial consultant.

He thinks about youth and its rhapsodic tenacity—like an animal with a locking jaw that winds its way around your heart and squeezes. A persistent and beautiful parasite. Those girls he saw tonight, they come from a different place. They remind him of something, and he wants to try to nail it down in memory.

Fairy-tale little girls in blue puffy dresses . . . young street-wise girls with eyes like hard rubber beads. Biting their nails and rubbing their palms on the knees of their jeans. The teenage boys who bumble around and knock things over and push each other into walls. The noise of the young—the great lost roaring ardor of the young.

They burn. He thinks about them burning like embers in the still houses around him, behind the masonry walls within their own hot little wildernesses of plastic confusion—their posters and their poetry and all their hidden things.

chapter 24

She remembers him the way he used to be, the way he is still sometimes when the mood takes him, when the wind blows just right and his eyes begin to dance like the curtains that blow inward weightlessly. Those bright amazing moments. She can remember them.

The crush of fabric against her skin when they were leaning over the edge of a ferry railing and he took her arm. Sitting on the hard bench in the airport and finding him in the crowd coming through the gate, the way he actually picked her up and she thought for a second that his being gone might have been worth it—might have been worth it for this moment. The sounds of his waking in the morning, an hour after she had gotten up to work in her office, the bedroom door opening and the creak of the wood floor beneath his feet, the yawn and the sniffle and the sleepy grunt when she called out good morning.

And not just before they were married. For a long time afterward too. Until the conference, her indiscretion with the man who had the impossible name. That changed things. Just a little, like a picture hung crooked—the skew unnoticeable at first glance but now she can't stop looking at it, dismayed by her inability to tap everything back into alignment.

It was the way he looked at her sometimes in those years before. His gaze would fall on her with sudden intensity like a private wink that made it the two of them against everyone else. He was the kind of man—she knew them—who put on a show for anyone who might be watching. His performance for the world, and sometimes his world was only her. All of this in a little room with dingy walls, just the two of them, he talking his magic talk and she holding her feet and rocking back with delight.

He would be sitting up on the bed, leaning his back against the wall, and he would say, "Tell me a joke."

And she, "I don't know any."

"Come on. Everybody knows at least one joke."

"I don't. Besides, I'm a bad joke teller."

"Why are you holding out on me? I know you've got one."

"Okay, but it's really not funny."

"That's all right. I laugh at everything. It's a policy."

Then she would tell her only joke. He would watch her hands as she did it. He always said that her hands got to places twenty minutes before the rest of her.

Then his stare. "You're right," he would say. "That's a terrible joke."

"I told you."

"You shouldn't tell jokes."

"I *told* you."

"Really. I'm being serious now. Don't let me talk you into it again."

And then she would clobber him and he would laugh, deflecting her blows the way he would shoo away gnats. There was nothing that could take that smile off his face.

When he got the job at Carmine-Casey, he was nervous. He couldn't sleep the night before school started, and she remembers having never seen him that way before. But she knew he would do well. He was a man who adored women, and those girls would feel that, feel it in their armpits and behind their knees the way she herself had, feeling it in the very levers of her body. It was the perfect job for him. She liked to think of him— still does like to think of him—surrounded by all those little girls with their glistening eyes and their fluttering voices, dashing in circles around him, their hearts like tiny engines keeping them moving in quick blurs lighter than air. There they are, when she occasionally meets up with him after school, a blushing chaos of feathery girlhood around him.

"Is that your wife, Mr. Binhammer? Is that your wife?"

Like hummingbirds, he once said. Well, then, she thought, so am I a hummingbird—older and slower and more skeptical, but my little engine of a heart the same as a girl's, uncontrollable, easily won by men with funny names and magic speeches who touch my fingers or smile in just that way that separates me from everyone else in the world.

That's what she remembers.

And now, as she folds her clothes into neat squares and layers them into her suitcase, she thinks, This is what it would look like if I were leaving for good. These same gestures, the same clothes, the same suitcase, the same sound of the refrigerator humming from the kitchen. But she's not leaving for good. She's only packing for another weekend conference, this one in Milwaukee.

And yet she would almost rather be leaving one last time than have to endure another of those awkward farewells, the two of them standing in the hallway, she with her coat on, her scarf wrapped tight around her neck like a noose, both of them saying things and meaning something else.

"Be careful," he says, but what he means is, Promise me you'll be good.

"Don't worry, I will," she says, meaning, I promise. I promise.

Because he's too good to say anything. Too generous to say it in words. And she wants desperately to hear him talk about it, to hear his opinions, to hear his incantatory words cut through the situation like sudden sunlight—but she also understands that her desire is selfish. She is not in a position to ask for things.

Because what is even worse—what is almost too unbearable to think about—is that maybe he means something else entirely. He says, "Be careful, huh? Take care of yourself," and she suspects sometimes that what he means is, Find what you want. Even if it's not me. Find what you want, because I don't like to see you unhappy.

And that possibility, the weight of it hanging like chains

around her lungs, is too much to think about. She will never leave him. She will stay with him no matter what. He is a lovely cracked thing. She cannot leave him.

It surprises her, when she thinks about it, just how binding a thing damage is. Bones mending rough and calcified—or scarred skin, thick and knotted. Yes, they are sewn up together in the scars of their marriage.

She takes a deep breath and looks around her as if surprised by her surroundings. She realizes she's been standing in front of the suitcase for many minutes now, clutching a black sweater against her chest. She shakes her head and makes a mental list of all the things she needs to take with her to Milwaukee.

Later, after the good-bye in the hallway, when he seems different—distracted and even a little sweet—she's in line at airport security and watching a young couple say good-bye to each other. She has become a great connoisseur of good-byes. An expert witness available for depositions on the flavor and bouquet of good-byes.

The young man adores the woman, that much is clear. But she is holding back a little—a tinge of playfulness masking distance. He believes it's because she's embarrassed by the public display of affection, but he's wrong. She is thinking about something else, waiting to be alone finally so that she can shut her eyes and shift things around in her head to where they make sense again. That's what the young woman wants. Quiet and darkness. For once.

After the plane takes off and she feels herself pressed into the seat like a flower in a book, she thinks about the young woman and decides to close her eyes herself and look at what shapes might form on the inside of her brain. But she can't get the shapes to hold and gazes instead out the window, where the city lights are beginning to be obscured by clouds. Pretty soon there is nothing to see because the deep black of the night becomes reflective as obsidian. She squints her eyes and tries to see stars, but no matter how she moves her head or how close she brings her nose to the pane, all she can see is herself.

chapter 25

It is a bitter cold Friday night the second week in December, right before the Carmine-Casey School for Girls lets out for Christmas, when Ted Hughes and Sibyl Lockhart can be found (if, in fact, anyone were looking for them) ducking into a small dark restaurant fifteen blocks south of the school. The restaurant is long and narrow with an exposed brick wall on one side and large murals on the other depicting the canals and row houses of some small Eastern European village. They have come directly from school, and because they are the only patrons so early in the evening—it is just dark outside—their waiter spends most of his time gazing at them from the back of the restaurant.

"I was a waitress once," Sibyl says. "I wasn't any good at it. I have no balance."

This is the fourth time they have seen each other outside of school like this, Ted Hughes leaning across the table toward her, she wondering if this is what it is like to be the object of his distraction rather than the passive audience of it. Is this what it is like to be looked at by the eyes that go everywhere?

They talk about things from the past to create a surrogate history to anchor themselves in this place, in this restaurant, with that waiter standing in the back, watching them. She tells him about Bruce, her ex-husband, about how nice he seemed at first when she was still a waitress and he would be waiting for her outside when she finished her shift because he was too poor to eat at the restaurant where she worked.

"And then I married him," she says.

Ted Hughes nods.

"Don't you want to know why?" she asks.

"Why you married him?"

"Most people ask. If you're separated and you talk about your ex, most people ask why you got together in the first place. Like it was obviously destined to fail from the beginning."

"Oh."

"Anyway, I'm going to tell you why I married him. Do you want to know why? It's because he told me I wasn't a very good waitress. Nobody else told me that. He just said it like it was a fact, the same way he would say that this tablecloth needs ironing. And I knew it was true, and I liked that he said it because it made me think I could trust him. I thought it meant that he was honest."

"And was he?"

"Mostly. It wasn't dishonesty that split us up."

"What was it?"

"Other things."

Ted Hughes nods and waits. Instead of continuing, she grabs her purse from under the table and begins to dig through it. She brings up handfuls of things—little jeweled pill cases, plastic tubes with writing on the sides, slips of paper that look like receipts, single earrings that have lost their mates—until she finds what she is looking for, a pink cylinder of lipstick and a pocket mirror that she unfolds in front of him. She twists up the lipstick and uses her pinkie to pick off a bit of lint stuck to the end, then dashes it in quick strokes across her lips. She glances up from the mirror and says, "You don't mind, do you?"

He seems enthralled by the process, just the hint of a smile on his lips. "You know what's good about you?" he responds. "You know those backstage musicals they used to make? The ones where you see everything happening behind the scenes and you never see the performance itself? That's what you're like. You're all behind the scenes. Between the acts."

"Is that good?"

"Of course it's good. Couldn't be better. Every man wants to know what goes on backstage. The best thing about the show is thinking about what's going on in the wings. It's magic."

She drops her lipstick and mirror back in her bag along with the other items and lets it fall to the floor with a glassy thud. "Sure," she says, wryly. "But then, once you see it, the magic's gone. You want to know a secret? Women aren't supposed to run out of surprises too quickly."

He laughs. "Then I'll tell you another secret. Men aren't too smart. They're easy to surprise, even if they've seen the same trick a hundred times."

The two sit there, looking at each other out of the corners of their eyes—as though tugging playfully at opposite ends of an invisible cat's cradle strung between them.

"So why," he says, "did you and your husband split up?"

"Oh, *that*." She shoos away the topic. "It's not even tragic. It's just dull. You know those men who live their whole lives as though they think someone is making a documentary about them? Those men, when they realize it's not a movie anyone would pay good money to see . . . well . . ."

When it becomes clear that she doesn't want to talk about her ex-husband anymore, he begins to tell her about how in his college days he once met a man on a train between New York and Chicago, a man who seemed to take an almost paternal interest in him and asked him all about the classes he was taking, the literature he was reading.

"T. S. Eliot!" the man commented reverently. "Ha!" Whenever Ted Hughes mentioned an author he recognized, the man would say "Ha!" as though it were an old friend and he was pleased by the sudden reacquaintance.

"John Donne. Ha!"

He was a salesman—sold industrial planers—but he remembered his school days, how reading was his favorite subject and how he had a picture in his head of how each of the authors looked. In his mind Jonathan Swift was tall and thin and nimble, and Tennyson was a big round man like Santa Claus. Jane Austen was a proper lady, like the old southern woman who lived down the street from him when he was growing up.

And then he talked about how he always hoped his two sons would go to college and read books and get together with other people to talk about those books. But they didn't seem to take to literature and didn't make very good marks in high school, so college wasn't really in the cards for them. But they were good boys, and they knew to do the right things in life. And he was just happy he had done well enough in the selling game to help them out with buying their houses and having their kids—and that maybe he could use his money to send some of his grandchildren to college some day.

"Let me ask you a question," he said then to Ted Hughes. "Your father. Was he a—was he an educated man?"

No. In fact, Ted Hughes's father had dropped out of high school to work as a grocery clerk.

"And you did it anyway!" the man said, laughing warmly to himself and shaking his head. "You went to college anyway. You made good, kid. You made good."

Then the man was quiet for a while, looking at the window, smiling and shaking his head every now and then. When they were five minutes from Chicago he turned to Ted Hughes and explained that he was a betting man and that he would bet him a hundred dollars, cash on the nail, that he, Ted Hughes, couldn't name ten Shakespeare plays.

A hundred dollars was a lot of money, but Ted Hughes knew that he could easily win and began to recite the names.

"*King Lear. Macbeth. Romeo and Juliet. Hamlet. Julius Caesar* . . ."

After the name of each play, the man would nod and his eyes would glisten fondly as though he were a child listening to his favorite bedtime story for the hundredth time.

"*The Merchant of Venice. Titus Andronicus. A Winter's Tale* . . ."

Until he had named ten.

"And I bet you could keep going, too, couldn't you?" the

man said, seeming pleased. Then he took his wallet from his jacket pocket and counted five twenties into Ted Hughes's hand. "Well earned, my boy."

When they got off the train, they got separated in the crowd, and when Ted Hughes saw the man again he was twenty yards down the platform. The man nodded his head and waved, and that was the last he ever saw of him.

"He wanted you to have that money," Sibyl says, looking into the candle between them. "He wanted to give you the money."

Ted Hughes nods. More people have come into the restaurant by now, and there is a lot of movement around them. Outside the streets are lit up by the dingy glow of streetlights reflecting off the dirty snow in the gutters.

"Tell me another story," Sibyl says. "I just like the way you talk."

After dinner, they walk a winding route through the streets of the city until they end up at Sibyl's apartment.

"I'm a mess," she says, standing one step above him on the stoop so that their eyes are at the same level. "I'm a divorcée with a penchant for men who dislike women. Just to warn you."

"You know," he says, drawing her hair out of her eyes with a finger, as if pulling aside a curtain, "you're the second woman this month to tell me I don't like women."

"I didn't mean—"

"I know what you didn't mean."

And then, upstairs, she flutters nervously about the apartment plucking dead leaves from her plants. She's not sure what to do, how to behave. She excuses herself and goes into the bathroom and looks at herself in the mirror, reapplying her lipstick and fixing her hair. "A mess," she says in a whisper to herself. "I'm a mess." When she comes out of the bathroom, there he is sitting on the couch, smiling thoughtfully at her as though she were a semi-interesting piece of art hanging on the wall of a museum. Not a masterpiece, mind you—just something to fill out an exhibition.

"I like your apartment," he says. "I like the plants."

She can't help it, she begins walking around nervously again. She moves back and forth from kitchen to living room to bedroom, back and forth, until he stops her—putting an arm out in front of her as she passes by and taking her, hands on her hips, and shifting her body to face him where he's sitting at the edge of the couch. He looks up at her for a second, not saying anything. And he draws her down to him. . . .

Then they are lying together in the dark of the bedroom— a city kind of dark, which is never really that dark. There is incandescence everywhere in the streets. It seeps in through the cracks—it creeps in under the door and between the blinds.

She is lying on her side, looking at his face in profile. He is lying on his back with his arms crossed behind his head. He's concentrating on the ceiling, as though he were trying to read it. The secret language of ceilings, the messages they give. If anyone could comprehend their fractured poetry, he could.

"I'm thirsty," she says. "Do you want a glass of water?"

"Sure."

She gets out of the bed and crosses the room—conscious of her body, pale and ghostly in the shadows of the dim, stale apartment. She returns, and he hasn't moved. Putting a glass next to him on the bedside table, she goes around to the other side and climbs back into the bed—sitting up and leaning her back against the wall. Then she looks down and is unhappy with the way her breasts and stomach look, so she draws the sheet up over herself.

Next to her, Ted Hughes turns over and raises himself onto his elbows.

"What do you think Leo would say if he knew?" she says.

"Binhammer?" He smiles into the darkness as though picturing the scene. "You know what one of my students told me yesterday? She said that he has an unofficial fan club—this group of girls who go around calling each other Mrs. Binhammer."

"No!"

"Can you picture it? For some reason I imagine them having

tea. 'Pass the sugar, would you, Mrs. Binhammer?' 'Of course, Mrs. Binhammer.' 'Lovely day, isn't it, Mrs. Binhammer?' 'No doubt about it, Mrs. Binhammer.' "

"Did you tell him?" She giggles. "He would be in raptures."

"Not yet. I'm going to."

"They adore him."

"They sure do."

"Those girls just adore him."

He nods. He rubs his face in his hands. Then they look at each other, and their smiles fade—the talk of Binhammer having made them feel suddenly self-conscious, as though he were the ghost in the machine of their interaction.

"I have to go," he says. "Unless you think—"

"No," she says, nodding her head. "It's okay."

She watches him dress, and then she gets up and puts on a shirt. When she flips the light switch, they both close their eyes against the sudden light. The mundanities of the bright world come tumbling back. They are now like two colleagues again, and she wants to ask him if he's finished writing his semester final yet, but she reconsiders.

"Oh god," she says, looking at herself in the mirror above her dresser. I'm a mess, she thinks, but she doesn't say it because she's already said it out loud too many times tonight.

In the hallway, as he's putting on his scarf by the door while she leans against the wall, he chuckles and says, "You know something? For a while I got the impression that Binhammer didn't like me. The first few weeks I was here. He would give me these looks like I was trespassing on his territory."

She smiles. "You were. You are."

"But I'm no threat at all. Those girls—you've seen them—they would die for him. They're loyal as Nazis. Little love Nazis."

She shrugs. "Well, maybe it's just that you're a man. He always says he doesn't know how to get along with other men."

He nods thoughtfully. "Yeah," he says. "I can see that. I'm like that too."

And that's when she finds herself laughing.

"What's so funny?"

"Nothing. I just like the way you talk. Nothing you say ever seems quite true—but I believe it anyway."

chapter 26

Once Ted Hughes is gone, Sibyl turns to face her empty apartment. Nothing moves in the place unless she moves it. She imagines it sitting silent as a grave while she's gone all day at school. Still leaning against the wall, she closes her eyes and listens to the rumble of the refrigerator, the hissing of the radiator, the muffled voice of a television coming through the wall from next door. Down the hall she hears a door open and then close again. Two voices descend the stairwell, laughing. She imagines the apartment those two voices have left behind. It would look like her apartment, except without her in it.

She looks at the clock. It's just after midnight. Suddenly decisive, she gets dressed again and reapplies her makeup in the bathroom.

Shutting off all the lights, she locks the apartment door behind her and takes the stairs down to the street, where she hails a cab and gives the driver an address. Ten minutes later, she's knocking at the door of an apartment.

"Who is it?"

"It's me, open the door."

The door opens, and Binhammer is standing there in his underwear.

"What are you—"

"I know Sarah's out of town. I wouldn't have come otherwise." She pushes her way past him into the apartment, and he closes the door behind her.

He puts a hand through his hair. "But that doesn't mean—"

"We have to talk."

"Listen, I don't think . . . I don't know if it's a good idea for you to—"

They are standing in the dimly lit hallway. The only light in the apartment is coming from the bedroom.

"Were you sleeping?" she says, as though that were the only indiscretion of note.

"Not yet."

"It's stuffy. You need to open a window."

"What?"

"A window. Aren't you choking in here?"

"No, I don't know what you're—"

She goes across the living room to the window and pulls it up a few inches. She takes a deep breath of the icy city night outside and turns to face him again. He turns on some lights, and the glass of the window becomes a mirror.

"It's like this whenever she goes out of town," she says. "You don't know how to take care of yourself."

"I was in bed. I—"

She shakes her head. "Oh, listen, I don't care about any of this. I just came to tell you something."

"What is it?"

At first she doesn't say anything. Then she says:

"I'm getting to like your friend Ted Hughes. I'm getting to like him a lot."

Binhammer takes a few steps back until he hits the couch, and then he sits down hard.

"That bothers you, I know it does. But you're not the hero of every story, you know. Sometimes you're just a minor character in someone else's story. Jesus, you men are like dandelions. One puff of air, and you're blown all to pieces. Anyway, I just thought I should tell you."

He takes a deep breath and looks straight ahead—right past her to something in the dark beyond.

"Hey, listen." She goes over to him, more sympathetic now, and stands before him. She takes his head between her hands and makes him look at her. "It has nothing to do with you. I mean, it's not something you should feel bad about."

He doesn't say anything. He doesn't look angry. He just looks gone.

Her previous strength is diminishing. She feels herself shriveling up.

"Look," she says. "I don't know what to do. What do you want me to do? Continue my campaign to make you unfaithful to your wife? It's over. You won. I'm vanquished."

"It's your choice," he says finally. Even his voice isn't angry. Is it that she does not possess the power to affect him?

"What do you mean? What's my choice? What choice?"

"I mean—" He squeezes his eyes with his thumb and fore-finger. "I just mean do what you want. It's up to you."

She sits down, not on the couch but on the floor in front of him. Now she is looking up at him and he seems powerless, which makes her feel powerless too for some reason.

"It's up to you," he says again.

"What if I don't want it to be up to me? What then?"

"But it is. It's up to you."

"Wait, wait. Just a second. Just stop for a second. I don't know—the thing is . . ."

She gets up on her knees in front of where he's sitting, now looking levelly at him. But his face is like a deep black well—there's no expression, and it's hard to focus on. Her first impulse, in a panic now, is to kiss away the remoteness, and she leans forward to do it, but his lips are immobile and his eyes have all the paralysis of a face on a coin.

After she pulls away, he says, "Goddamnit." He says it low and quiet, somewhere between helpless and cruel. "Goddamnit. He gets everything he wants. He got you too."

She stands up again, folding her arms. Her fist clenches in-advertently. She would like to knock something out of him.

"For Christ's sake, Binhammer. Do you even notice when there's someone else in the room? I hope you're not like this with your wife."

"What does that mean?"

"I mean, do I have to spend all my time listening to him talk about you and then come over here and listen to you talking about him?"

He looks at her, mystified. She has made him see her, at least. For the moment. Then, not wanting to look backward for fear of seeing them clearly, she wonders what lines she has crossed.

"I'm sorry," she says. "I didn't mean to . . . What do you want me to do?" she says.

"Nothing," he says. "I don't want you to do anything."

The hall light is on, and one small lamp by the couch. The brutality of the moment strains like the glare of the sun when you come outside for the first time. It is two thirty in the morning.

"To hell with you then," she says, moving toward the door. "To hell with you."

"You were the one who did this. You were the one who came here."

"I didn't start anything. I don't know how to start things. It was your wife. Your picture-perfect wife with her picture-perfect affair. I'm taking up smoking again."

He doesn't say anything. He looks at her, silently raging. She is trying to unlock the door, but she doesn't know which deadbolts are engaged or which way to turn them.

"Your wife—the tragic heroine in a fucking Russian novel."

"Get out," his voice quivers. "Get out now. I don't want you here."

"Your wife with her outré affairs and her tragic martyrdom. I need a cigarette."

"Go." His face is pinched and red, and he puts the heels of his hands into his eyes. "Please."

"Your wife." She turns the deadbolt knobs and pulls at the door, but it won't budge. "What the hell is the combination to this thing?"

The door finally comes open, throwing her a little off balance. She braces herself against a table in the hall, toppling a stack of books to the floor. Now she's on the threshold of something, even if it's just the space outside the apartment, quiet carpeted halls with their humming fluorescents, the lines of doorways just like this one—indistinguishable stacked cubicles of hope and lethargy. Each one its own little inferno of sleeplessness. Things brimming over the tops of other things. Bubbling up.

"Don't talk about her," he says. Measured now—he has regained himself. Though his arms are held out in a pose of paralysis, itching to move, to act, but without vector or purpose. "You don't talk about her. What has she got to do with this?"

"No, of course. I wouldn't want to sully her. Let's not bring her down into the dirt with the rest of us. And how about this—whenever you feel pissed off at her, why don't you just be pissed off with me instead."

"You don't—" He flinches.

"If we work together on this, I think we can keep her out of the muck. What do you say?"

She waits for him to say something, but he refuses to look at her. The way he's standing there, poised—the whole scene looks like a drama in a cheap hotel.

"Jesus," she says finally. "You're just looking for someone to be mad at."

She turns and walks through the door. Out in the hall, she is three paces toward the steps when he appears in the doorway behind her.

"And what are you looking for, huh?" This is what he says. "What is it exactly that you are looking for?" She can still hear him as she walks away. "What are you looking for?"

Out in the street the cold air feels nice against her skin. She looks at her watch; it's almost three in the morning. The city lies dormant—a cab rattles by and slows down to see if she wants a ride. She shakes her head and it moves away, its taillights making the hardened drifts of snow on the sidewalks glow red. These are the insomniac hours of night. If she were in the backseat of that cab, she would hear the rattling of the car, the groan of the artificial leather seat under her, the driver sucking his teeth, and nothing else. An oasis of sound in a desert of wintry billowing steam from under the streets.

She turns a corner and goes into a twenty-four-hour bodega. A man behind the counter is watching a small black-and-white television showing a sitcom that was canceled ten years ago.

"Yes," he says. "What does the lady want?"

"Cigarettes," she says, pulling some bills from her coat pocket. "Marlboro 100s, Ultra-Light."

"Yes. Cigarettes for the lady." He pushes a box of cigarettes across the counter. "Matches?"

"Yes, matches."

Outside there is no wind, so she stands on the sidewalk and lights her cigarette and watches the match burn down almost to her fingers before she shakes it out and walks to the corner to put it in a trash bin.

The smoke curls into her lungs along with a bracing jolt of raw icy air. It has been seven years since she gave up smoking. She smokes that one down to nothing where she stands and presses it out against the rim of the trash bin. Then she lights another one and begins to walk west along the deserted streets. She walks until she gets to the edge of Central Park and then keeps on going.

The park isn't a place she should be at night—the sprawling emptiness of shadows and corners and echoes. People are mugged in the park all the time. People are killed. Reckless people, like the ones who have just taken up smoking again after seven years.

She follows the winding paths in no particular direction. She has gotten lost in the park before—getting turned around and trying to use the tips of the buildings above the trees as a compass. Now she just walks.

She passes a young couple, walking arm in arm, looking as they would if it were the middle of the day and children were running and playing all around them. A few minutes later she sees a group of teenagers at a distance. Boys and girls, the age of her students. Their voices, crude and unselfconscious, make her feel voyeuristic. They hoot shrilly and laugh, the timbre of their cries modulating from the guttural and animalistic to the poetic and almost musical. Like infants discovering the power of their own throats. Always loud. Always loud. They disappear in the opposite direction.

She wonders if she can walk until dawn, until the faint glow of morning rises in the city. And now she pictures the city as a hot coal, an ember on an empty beach, its burning glow tinting the night around it with a smoky orange.

"Shit," a voice says, startling her. "Look at this." The path is narrow, and three young men suddenly appear before her, presenting a wall of oversize coats and yellow eyes. The one who spoke has a toothpick dangling from his lip. He shakes his head at the other two. They are looking up and down her body.

This is it, she thinks. This is it for me. Everything is over. The end of the whole show.

She's watching this as though it were a play being acted out on a stage before her, as if the only thing she has to do is just wait for the curtain to drop so she can stop thinking about it all.

"Woman, what do you think you're doing?"

She doesn't know whether he wants her to answer or not.

"Do you know what time it is? This is a bad fucking place to be at this time of night."

"Bad," one of the others says.

"A lot of mean motherfuckers around here. Rip you up."

He shakes his head, as if to say it's a shame. And he looks truly regretful.

"You know some girl got herself killed last week? Is that what you're trying to do? You trying to get yourself killed? Huh? How come? You unhappy?"

"Yeah," she says quietly, looking down at her feet and the frozen path under them. "I'm unhappy."

When she looks back up, he is staring at her in a different way. He seems embarrassed and rolls the toothpick with his tongue to the other corner of his mouth.

"Well, you're lucky is all I'm saying." His voice is softer now. "Lucky that we aren't the bad guys. Isn't she lucky?" He turns again to his friends, whose eyes are still focused on her breasts, her legs. "Okay, motherfuckers, cut it out. The woman don't need you feeling her up in your nasty porn-brains."

He laughs apologetically. "See?" he says to her. "This is what I'm talking about."

She stands there. Nothing is going to happen.

"Why don't you go home now."

Nothing is going to happen.

And here she is, still in her body, unmurdered. Another day unmurdered. It's a funny thing to think. She wants to laugh, but it's cold and she shivers instead.

"Go on home now," he says again. "You know where you're going? You want us to walk you? I promise I can keep these motherfuckers in line."

"No," she says. "No thank you."

"Okay, lady. You take it easy now, all right? Don't be doing this anymore. You just stay at home if you feel bad. Okay?"

Nothing is going to happen. There is no danger in the world except from the brightly lit bedrooms of charming men.

chapter 27

It is said now among the girls of Carmine-Casey that Ms. Lockhart, the English teacher who always seemed to resent her students for not being boys, is not long for this job. Her divorce has wrecked her, they say. She has turned into an unhappy old spinster. And strange. In the past few days she has been seen by the senior girls (the ones who have permission to leave the building during their free periods) standing outside smoking cigarettes, one after another.

And when one of the girls inquired about it, saying, "I didn't know you smoked, Ms. Lockhart," the woman's response was taut and sneering: "Don't you have anything better to do? Shoo."

She actually said "Shoo"—it has been confirmed.

In addition to the sudden smoking, Ms. Lockhart has also taken to making snide and groundless remarks in class about other faculty members—mostly the men, which further supports the speculation that she is an embittered divorcée whose only option now may be to become a lesbian and live communally with other lesbian man-haters.

On a recent day, when she overheard some of the girls talking in animated tones about Mr. Binhammer, she called across the classroom, "All I hear about is Mr. Binhammer. He must be some teacher. The great educator of his time. And when was the last time he handed back a paper to you?"

On another occasion, the girls were reading *The Great Gatsby* and trying to decide, between Mr. Binhammer and Mr. Hughes, which was Jay Gatsby and which was Nick Carraway.

"You know," Ms. Lockhart interjected, "most critics see something deeply homoerotic in the relationship between Gatsby and Nick. Did you know that? You better reread that book."

She pretended not to have heard the context of the girls' conversation, but the Higgins sisters, Sally and Patty, both of whom were there, agreed that there was something nasty in the way she said it. And after she said it there was no more fun in imagining their two teachers as Gatsby and Nick anymore— which the girls blamed and resented Ms. Lockhart for.

"She's become *objectionable*," says Samantha Cowley, who is known for her Victorian way of speaking.

And some of the girls now tell of a rumor that Ms. Lockhart was spotted walking by herself in the park at four in the morning. But, as a rumor, that one is quickly put aside by other buzzing inquiries that strike closer to home: What girls were in the park to see her? What were they doing there at that time of night? Were there boys involved?

For her part, Liz Warren does not take any pleasure in the circulating gossip. She was taught by Ms. Lockhart only as a freshman and has always resented the woman's drama-tinged personality as a subtle way to derail the class from actually learning anything. In fact, the problem seems to be common to the English teachers. If it weren't for Mr. Hughes, Liz Warren may have left the school convinced that the entire department was narcissistic and dilettantish. But the girl's dislike of this particular teacher goes beyond her general impatience for the department: the woman is a panderer. She panders to men. Liz has seen her in the halls flirting with the male faculty, using the same pathetic ploys that the girls use except with a shinier veneer of authenticity—and she suspects that Ms. Lockhart, who has so little patience for the girls in her class, would do anything in her power to gain the attention of a man.

It's not that Liz Warren considers herself a feminist, loyal to the sisterhood of woman, or anything so papier-mâché idealistic as that—it's just that she can't bear to look on the *weakness* of the woman, that embarrassing fawning that Liz tries so hard to drive out of her own eyes every night in the bathroom mirror. It's a puppy-dog femininity: panting and yelping and eager. It makes her want to slink away unnoticed. The mothers of our race. The pretty pretty dresses. The eyes like drops of moisture on a varnished surface, failing to sink in.

She would much rather read Ernest Hemingway. At least in literature the pathetic are rendered beautiful; you can imagine them as cracked sculptures, or portraits effaced by time and mishandling.

Magnificent blemishes.

On the other hand there is something about Ms. Lockhart, when Liz comes out of the building after school one day and finds her smoking against the black wrought iron fencing at the edge of the sidewalk, that makes the girl stop and look more closely.

She looks defeated. Wrecked. But also *advanced*, as though she has come through the other side of a long tunnel.

Liz watches her for a while, unseen, watches the thin specter of a woman gazing upon the girls walking by without noticing her. And she feels bad. It's that sickly, gnawing self-swallowing feeling that you get when you wait for your adversaries to fall and they do and you want to feel triumphant but you don't.

There is very little left of her, Liz thinks. She is rebuilding from scratch.

So when Ms. Lockhart looks up and sees her standing on the steps above her, Liz feels her features dissolve into a perceptible half smile.

And in response the woman gives a pinched, self-deprecating smile of her own—and a nod.

"This is it, girl," the nod says. "This is where all the pretty fluttering gets you."

And Liz nods back, because she knows this to be true. Even though this doesn't mean she and the teacher are now fast friends. And even though whatever truths Liz knows are derived from fictions and realities much reduced—like Jeremy Notion, with whom she has her third date tonight.

That nod stays with her as she walks home, and stays with

her through the rest of the afternoon and on into the evening while her mother is warning her that she better get ready for her date. She doesn't want that nice Jeremy boy to think she's un-eager, does she? Leaning wearily over the top of her bureau and gazing into the mirror, Liz tries to replicate that Lockhart smile and nod. She thinks she would like to see it in a movie—and then she wonders if she already has. It reminds her of a Fellini film (she has been renting Italian films since Mr. Hughes men-tioned in class that they were "devastatingly gorgeous," watch-ing them secretively after her parents go to bed, illicit intellect), Ms. Lockhart with the silent nod, wearied experienced laid bare and tacit, like a housewife snapping up a sheet and letting it bil-low softly down onto the mattress, that sigh of wrinkled fabric.

Later, when she sees Jeremy Notion waiting for her on the street corner outside the movie theater, trying to brood as he leans against a signpost, she has even less patience for him than usual.

"I just got here," is the first thing he says.

She looks at her watch. She's fifteen minutes late. "Sorry I'm late."

"No problem," he says. "Because, you know, I just got here too."

He leans over and plants a kiss on the side of her mouth, which leaves a little trail of wetness. She thinks of snails. She has to wait for him to look at the show times above the ticket booth before she can reach up quickly and wipe it off.

"So what's the movie we're seeing again?" he asks. "How come they don't have regular movies here? I've never heard of these. *Sister Moon*, is that the one?"

She nods. "It's French."

"Oh," he says. "Do you take French? I take Spanish. Señor Lopez kicks ass."

The theater is only half full, and for the first part of the movie she has to contend with Jeremy tossing popcorn into his mouth and, every now and then, brushing the kernels off his lap when he realizes how much he has dropped. Once the popcorn is gone, she can see him out of the corner of her eye checking the time on the glowing face of his digital watch.

Then, suddenly, he lunges at her, his lips like two thick rubber bands on her neck.

"What are you doing?" she says, recoiling from him. In any other situation she might try to hide her revulsion more carefully, but she has discovered that Jeremy's perceptiveness is not so finely tuned. She can be broad as a television sitcom in her responses, and still he looks at her through squinted eyes, trying to read the subtlety in her expressions.

"I'm kissing you," he says.

"Now?"

"What's the matter?"

She points to the screen as though it should be obvious to him. But he just stares back at her mutely, so she has to articulate it. "This is a movie about *incest.*"

He looks back at the screen like a moping child. "Okay, okay."

After the movie, they walk together on the sidewalk, the hardened chips of ice crunching beneath their shoes.

"That was a good movie," he says unconvincingly. "If my sister were that hot, I think maybe I would—"

"Oh my god."

"Come on. Lighten up. It was just a joke. Jeez. How come you're always so serious all the time?"

She looks at him suspiciously. "I'm not serious all the time."

"Okay. It's no big deal. Let's forget about it."

They walk the next block in silence.

"Listen," he says at the next corner. "My parents are out of town. Do you want to come up and see my room?"

She knows what this means, and the prospect is not appealing to her, but she is also chafing under the accusation of being too serious. She's not too serious. She knows how to have fun when she wants to. Maybe even more than other girls, since she doesn't suffer the limitations of nonsensical convention. She is liberated. She is progressive.

"Okay," she says. "But just for a little while. I have to get home."

His parents are in textiles, and the apartment is lushly decorated in deep earth tones with a sort of Arabian feel to the woodwork. But when they turn the corner from the hall into his room, it's as though they step through a portal into teenage suburbia. There are posters of sports figures tacked to the walls, and the detritus of boyhood—clothes, scratched CDs, magazines creased open to pages with swimsuit models, balls of various sizes and colors—is settled into the corners against the baseboards as though someone had spun the room like a top and let centrifugal force take over.

He makes a big production about sweeping aside some of his dirty clothes from the bed—as though he were dusting off a throne for the arrival of a queen.

One thing she likes about Jeremy Notion: he is almost entirely unselfconscious. Which means that there aren't any awkward, bungling attempts at conversation or those pitiful little seductions that teenage boys perform as though they were following instructions step by step in a manual. No, Jeremy is a lunger. Which may be bad in the context of a French film about incest, but is rather a relief when it comes to moments such as this one.

He leans over to kiss her, and for a few minutes they are sitting side by side on the edge of the bed, craning their necks to reach each other. He puts an arm around her shoulder, but she doesn't know what to do with her hands, so she just leaves them in her lap. With his other hand, he reaches across to her arm, as if in embrace, but then draws back slowly until it is on her breast. He leaves it there for a second, as if awaiting reprisal, but when he gets none, the hand begins to squeeze and knead her breast as though it were Play-Doh.

She can feel her left foot falling asleep, so she shifts the angle of her body—an act that he seems to take as an invitation to lean over and leverage her backward onto the bed. Now he's half on top of her and her left leg is dangling off the edge of the bed, the foot tingling now that the circulation is returning to it.

She tries to comply with his kisses as much as possible, but his lips and tongue are everywhere, and she begins to think it's like playing tennis with a maniac—you can never tell where the ball is going to go.

Finally she gets the courage to put one of her hands on his back. His hands are all over her, so she figures that's an appropriate response.

At one point she becomes aware that a hand on her left knee is beginning a slow but resolute ascension up the inside of her thigh.

"Wait," she says, pressing both palms against his chest and pushing him to the side. "Wait a second."

"What? What's the matter?"

"Nothing," she says, sitting up and straightening her hair. "Nothing's the matter. I just want to know—"

"What? My parents aren't going to be home until tomorrow night."

"It's not that." She turns away from him as he sits up next to her. She can feel herself flushed, and she doesn't want him to see. "I just want to know what all this *means*."

"Oh, come on. It doesn't have to be such a big deal."

"I know that. I know it doesn't have to be a big deal. But I just want to know *whether* it's a big deal or not. That's all."

He gazes at her, nonplussed. Those poor dewy eyes. He thinks it's some kind of test—that he has to give her the right answers before she'll let him touch her—and in the duress of the situation, his mind seems to have shut down altogether.

"I mean," she continues, "I'm not unwilling. I just want to know what it signifies. You know, where this puts us."

"Not *unwilling*? What it *signifies*?" he says. She cringes at her own words repeated back to her. There is no more exquisite torture than having to listen to herself. "What's the matter with you? Why do you have to think about everything so much?"

"I don't—"

"Why can you just *do* things? Everything has to have subtitles with you."

That's a surprisingly elegant way of putting it, and it throws her for a second. She turns to look at him and tries to discern whether or not his artfulness was intentional. But he's just sitting there with his arms crossed over his chest, huffing and shaking his head.

It's time for her to go.

"I think I'm going to go," she says, standing up.

"Good," he says. "Just go already."

Good-bye, Jeremy Notion. Good-bye, you poor baby.

She makes her way down the dark hall and trips over a long-legged side table, knocking over some carved ivory figurines on top.

"Don't break anything on your way out," his voice calls from behind her.

Then she's in the elevator of the building, riding down and feeling inexplicably pleased with herself—the strange, half-disappointed lightness of spirit that she experienced last year when the schoolwide poetry reading was canceled and she didn't have to get up in front of the student body and read her poem about the achingly gaudy brilliance of an abandoned fairground. That airy relief when something is going to happen and you don't know whether to dread it or be excited about it but then it doesn't happen and it doesn't matter and you can just put away all those feelings that you had about it in the first place. Just put them away somewhere and cover them over with a sheet.

That's how she feels.

Good-bye Jeremy Notion! You little shiny thing! Good-bye, you glinting pebble, you water-softened stone.

The numbers on the elevator panel count down, each one with a barely audible tick. She has heard that they do that on purpose, that tick, for blind people, so they know what floor they're on by counting the ticks.

That's nice, she thinks. That's a good thing to do for blind people.

She closes her eyes and listens to the ticks go by. But her

mind wanders back to Jeremy Notion and then to the character of Ivan from her play and then to Ms. Lockhart standing outside the school against the wrought iron fence and then to Mr. Hughes her English teacher, and she loses track of the ticks.

Blind people must have very good concentration, she determines.

When she reaches the ground floor, she walks quickly across the marble-tiled lobby and through the rotating door to the street, where the cold night air strikes her hard like broken glass—and she wonders if that's what it's like to be thrown through a window.

chapter 28

"Seventy-five years ago—" Mrs. Mayhew begins and then waits for the auditorium to quiet down. She stands like a furnace, her smoldering gaze blasting heat out in the direction of any girls who are still whispering behind their hands or adjusting their skirts.

"Seventy-five years ago the Carmine-Casey School for Girls celebrated its first Christmas. Under the guidance of Charlotte Casey-McCallum, our founder, a woman of tremendous industry, compassion, and vision, this school opened its doors to a first-year class of only thirty-seven girls. The building has grown since that time, of course, to accommodate the more than four hundred students that we have here today, but whenever I consider those thirty-seven young women carrying their books through these halls when the marble was still new and the smell of wood shavings from the carved banisters was still lingering in the air—whenever I consider those young women, I imagine what it must have been like to embark upon something brand-new, something unique. A flagship of girls' education. A touchstone the country over for progress, ingenuity, and the independence of women."

The Carmine-Casey Christmas assembly always begins with an address by one of the three headmistresses on a rotating schedule. This year it's Mrs. Mayhew's turn, and because she is also chair of the English department, there is an expectation that the speech will be full of spirit and poetry. Unlike Mrs. Landry, a former calculus teacher, whose speeches are all business, very purposeful and direct, as though she were drawing lines on the blackboard—as though she were holding a ruler beneath her voice.

Standing up on the stage at the front of the crowded, girl-smelling auditorium, broad, powerful Mrs. Mayhew possesses vigor. It chugs out of her like steam from an engine, her large bust projecting aggressively against the rivetlike buttons of her blouse.

"Seventy-five years. It may not surprise some of you that I have been here in this place for almost half of that time, first as a teacher of English, barely beyond girlhood myself, then as an administrator and headmistress, and I can tell you that this is a different school from the one through whose doors I once walked as a bright-eyed girl with a passion for Plato and Aeschylus and Sophocles. In fact, it is a different world from the one I knew then. I remember with great piercing clarity the values that were important to me as a young woman, the values that I carried around with me and that used to give my world alignment: honor, charity, self-reliance, and, most significant, integrity. . . ."

"*Quel* boring," Dixie Doyle whispers to Andie next to her. "Why does she always have to talk like an old movie?" Andie shrugs but doesn't have to time to respond because Mr. Pratt shushes them from the aisle, where he's standing at attention with his hands clenched behind his back.

No, Dixie thinks. Not exactly an old movie. More like those superhero comics that Jeremy Notion had stacked in the corner of his bedroom. When he saw her looking at them while visiting one day, he said they were collector's items—that he didn't actually *read* them. They were filled with the same kind of big speeches, in bold, black lettering—all about *justice* and *honor* and *truth*. What do you do with those things other than declare them? And how do you really declare things anyway? Maybe it's a skill that some people have, like juggling or crocheting, but it's hard to get her mind around it. She wonders if she can do it, if there is any declaration in her waiting to get out. Maybe she should try declaring something in front of the mirror when she gets home.

Once, in one of those specialty Asian zen fabric and plant stores, she saw a bowlful of truth and love and passion and hope and trust. The words were carved by laser into polished stones that cost three dollars and fifty cents each. She didn't understand their purpose then. But now, looking back, she thinks maybe they weren't such a bad idea after all. At least they were things you could actually carry around with you—or skip across the surface of a pond in the park.

She looks around and finds Liz Warren in the very back row shaking her head with displeasure. If Liz Warren doesn't like the speech either, then Dixie must be on the right track. Liz is a smart girl. Dixie would never tell Liz, but she wishes that she could write a play herself and invent crazy people like Clarissa and Ivan and have them do things to each other. It must feel good to have that kind of power over things.

Though from what she's been hearing in the halls recently, Liz and Jeremy Notion have called it quits. So maybe it's not so easy for the smart girls either. Still, it's all silliness. Kid stuff—

Then she sees him, Mr. Binhammer, down in front leaning against the wall. Twirling one strand of hair around her finger, she thinks that she would like to write a play about herself and her favorite teacher:

"You know we can't, Dixie. It would be too dangerous." Reaching out to her but pulling back his hand at the last minute. "People wouldn't like it."

"Why do you care about people all of a sudden?"

"Maybe you're right. How is it that you see things so clearly?"

She shifts in her seat and decides she would go to bed with him if he asked. She wonders what he would do if he knew it were that easy. All he has to do is ask. And she would lie there smiling politely and acquiescing. He could move her all around like a rag doll.

She bites on the edge of her thumb.

Mrs. Mayhew is chugging forward, saying something important, leaning over the podium in her paisley blouse with sweat stains under the arms.

". . . Integrity. We like to think of it as a philanthropic quality, a moral stance akin to empathy and generosity. Why cherish integrity? So that we do not give ourselves an unfair advantage over others. So that we do not take advantage of the good faith of our fellow men and women. We do not cheat, for example, because it makes the playing field unfair, and others will suffer. But this is only half the story. All too often we forget the other, infinitely greater value of integrity: the impact upon ourselves. Why ought we not cheat on an exam? Why ought we not plagiarize an essay? Because of the subtle and insidious damage it does to ourselves. It is a luxury to think that our moral crimes only impact our fellow students, our community. We discover too late, only when we are older and we look back and see pieces of ourselves strewn on the road behind us—irretrievable crumbs of our identities—only then do we discover that it is a luxury we cannot afford. . . ."

What do they want from me now? Binhammer thinks. What are they asking of me now?

The girl, Dixie Doyle, is staring at him. He sees her out of the corner of his eye, sitting there in the middle of that undulating sea of girlhood. Biting on her thumb. Orally fixated. That used to be the joke when he was in high school. He wonders if it still is now. She has her hair up in pigtails, a T-shirt pulled taut over those big breasts of hers. Somebody in the teachers' lounge was talking about an article, something about the hormones in the milk we drink, new in the last twenty years. As a result the girls develop sooner. Develop bigger.

At least Dixie, buxom, silly Dixie, is better than that Liz Warren with her constant scowling. He has given up on her, having decided that he will never be able to win her over. There she is now in the back row—always in the back row—looking miserable.

These little girls like screaming merry-go-rounds—that hot, high-tempo calliope. These little girls like panicked birds.

Then he spots Sibyl Lockhart, giving him a stare like a hypodermic injection. There is no going back there either. He remembers his stomach like a bagful of acid—bent over double after she left that night—wanting to throw up. Thinking, She's right, she's right, she's right.

He hears she has been talking about him to the students. But that doesn't bother him. The girls are fiercely loyal to men, he's found. Plus, he feels sorry for her. She is not the center of anything. Instead, she is herself the fallout from larger relationships—the dust kicked up in a yelling match. The dust that gets in your throat and makes you cough. And down she settles, pale and ugly and nothing left of her to speak of.

But she has things to say—and when she says them, she is usually right.

Mrs. Mayhew has stopped for a dramatic pause. She gazes down over the faces of students and faculty alike. She is more listened to for her silences than her words. What is the woman talking about? Binhammer thinks.

In the opposite corner of the auditorium, Ted Hughes leans back against the wall and gazes up at the tangle of light fixtures on the ceiling. The man with the impossible name. A snake charmer. His slow movements hypnotic and seductive to all the smart girls of the school. A magician on the stage, drawing your attention to one minor prestidigitation while there are always some other machinations taking place behind his back. No. No. He is not so much of a performer. Not so crass and artificial. No, Ted Hughes is just a man who people pay attention to. A guy with uncommon charm.

The things that Ted Hughes has stolen from him. His perfect wife. His angry near-mistress. His position in the all-woman Carmine-Casey English department. His reputation as a favorite among the students.

Binhammer gives up. The man can have whatever he wants.

Then he sees Ted Hughes letting his gaze fall tiredly from the ceiling of the auditorium and dance with overwhelming disinterest across the mass of faces between them—until he spots Binhammer and, eyes locking, gives him a wide, eloquent grin, as though the two of them know something that no one else in the world can understand.

Binhammer grins back. The man can have whatever he wants.

"A quarter of a century ago," Mrs. Mayhew continues, drilling her voice into the ears of the girls nodding off before her, "integrity was something we talked about quite a bit here at Carmine-Casey. Founded on a tradition of palpable truths, we knew how concrete goodness and decency could be. That was before such notions became abstract—before we conceded to the prevarication of the age. Ralph Waldo Emerson once wrote that our age is retrospective, constructing itself on the sepulchers of our fathers. He then went on to ask why it seemed impossible to enjoy our own original relationship to the universe. Well, Emerson had the luxury of blind anticipation. As it turns out, the sepulchers of our fathers were not so bad after all. . . ."

Sibyl Lockhart feels like she's watching a game of chess. In fact, she frequently feels that way—watching the people around her move pieces forward and back, advancing and retreating with their eyes, seizing with their words, creating boundaries that cannot be crossed and pockets of opportunity that seem to invite danger or at least confrontation. And every now and then she feels herself being picked up and placed on the board among all the other pieces.

Look at Binhammer and Hughes, grinning at each other like two little kids who don't know their mother is watching. All these girls—the entire auditorium full of the glowing bodies of ridiculous virgins—and the two of them gazing at each other as though they are playing marbles, the click-clack of little glass baubles being shot and ricocheted elsewhere until there's nothing left between them but an empty chalk circle.

What is it she wants? To be a part of that gaze? To be a member of that secret inner circle of grinners?

There are men who want her. Men who would love to take her home and lavish her with the attention of their eyes, their hands, their voices. How did she end up with these two? They really believe sometimes, she can tell, that they are interested in her.

And then there's Bruce, her ex-husband. She does not hate him. She has never hated him as much as she feels she should. A long time she waited for the vitriol to rise in her throat. She waited, closing her eyes and feeling around inside herself for some seed of resentment that might nurture itself into full-blown wrath. But she never found anything like that. Just twangs of regret for a hundred different things that didn't mean anything.

There were nice times. Moments collected like matchbooks. A bright sun coming through the blinds and tying up his sleeping form in cords of light. Him sitting on the kitchen counter watching her attempt some complicated recipe. Putting up a picture, his voice muffled by the nails he's holding between his lips. The pressure of his thigh against hers, sitting next to each other on a subway train.

The recognition, at distinct moments—moments like framed pictures—that she is happy.

And then she stops herself. Embarrassed by the petty dramas of her own heart. She chuckles softly and looks around as though to see if everyone else is in on the joke.

To shake herself out of this, she thinks about what she needs to do. She needs to stop by the grocery store. She needs to get her watch battery replaced. She needs to change her sheets and do the laundry. She needs to go through her shoeboxes of photographs and put them into albums. She needs to finish grading last week's papers.

She scans the audience of girls. There, in the back row next to her friend Monica Vargas, is that Liz Warren girl. She hasn't taught her since the ninth grade, but everybody knows about

Liz Warren. The jewel in the crown of Carmine-Casey's senior class. The favorite daughter.

She found Liz staring at her the other day—out in front of the school. Sibyl was smoking a cigarette and turned to find the girl standing at the top of the steps gazing down purposefully at her. She looked as though she were going to say something, her mouth opened then closed. As though Sibyl were a mathematical equation that needed solving. Sibyl could see the girl's mind working, the machinery of that fevered little brain chugging overtime, adding and subtracting and shifting numbers from one side to the other until $x =$ Sibyl Lockhart.

And, damn it all, wouldn't Sibyl like to know what that x is?

So she smiled at the girl and the girl smiled back, but the moment was over and Liz, seemingly satisfied with her solution, hefted her massive backpack over her shoulder and loped away leaning sideways.

Mrs. Mayhew finally seems to be winding down her sermon. Integrity. It's the kind of speech Mrs. Mayhew excels at. She seems to be fluent in the secret language of universal values—and listening to her, you begin to wonder what it's like in that foreign land where the language is native. Maybe you'll visit there one day.

"As Christmas quickly approaches, do not forget what the holiday stands for. Whether you are Christian or not, whether you are religious or not, Christmas is a time for kindness, generosity, and the strength of character to forget about your own problems for a while. And with that, on behalf of the administration and faculty of the school, I want to wish you all a very merry Christmas."

There is a light smattering of applause, which becomes louder as the faculty see that they need to fill in the empty spaces by clapping themselves. Some of the girls who have been sitting with their heads on their arms, leaning against the seat in front of them, now look up, squinting against the light.

"And now," Mrs. Mayhew says, waiting a few moments for the sudden chatter to die down again. "And now it is my pleasure to present the Carmine-Casey Choir."

The curtain behind her rises to reveal thirty-two girls standing in escalated rows and wearing gold robes. Mrs. Clarkson, the music teacher, stands before them and raises her hands.

O holy night, the stars are brightly shining;
It is the night of the dear Savior's birth!
Long lay the world in sin and error pining,
Till He appeared and the soul felt its worth.

This hymn. The first music ever broadcast over radio. Liz Warren heard that once. She imagines the hymn coming through all that static. It must have seemed miraculous. Like the gates of heaven opening up, the light coming down in sharp beams between the clouds the way it always does on the covers of those pamphlets advertising God. She herself does not believe in God—but she can appreciate the aesthetics of it all. Those huge, arching cathedrals. The candlelight and the chalices. The music of voices breaking through the grinding static of the very first radio.

It is her secret that she is susceptible to such clichéd forms of beauty. When she feels her throat clenching—"Fall on your knees, O hear the angel voices! O night divine . . ."—she swallows down her emotions with a sneer. It's not that she's embarrassed. It's just that . . . it's just that there are some things better enjoyed privately and not as part of some big, aching, weeping audience of stupid teenage girls.

Behold your King; before Him lowly bend!
Behold your King; before Him lowly bend!

Music like that is designed to grab you, designed to take you by the neck and throttle you until you see God. It's times like this when she begins to think about what she has instead of God—times like this when she could almost be convinced of a whole assortment of sentimentalities. Even from the back row, where the auditorium is nothing but a mass of jaunty hairstyles, she could almost look kindly on Dixie Doyle, Beth Barber, and the other members of the Carmine-Casey Kit-Kat Klub. Now that things with Jeremy Notion have been aborted (the universe clicking itself back into proper realignment, is how she thinks about it), she wouldn't begrudge Dixie anything. After all, the girl knows how to do things Liz herself could never do. Dixie has, Liz is happy to admit, little firecrackers of wisdom popping off in her head every now and then.

> Truly He taught us to love one another;
> His law is love and His Gospel is peace.
> Chains shall He break for the slave is our brother,
> And in His Name all oppression shall cease.

The damn song. She wishes she could stop thinking of Christmases in the 1930s—children gathered around radios, hymns breaking through static, unlikely Depression-era joy and peace. Ugh. She has to stop before she feels the desire to braid friendship bracelets to distribute to everyone on graduation day.

Next to her, Monica Vargas seems to be doing calculations in her head. So instead she turns and focuses all her attention on Mr. Hughes, who is standing like a statue in the aisle, looking casually up at the ceiling as though God himself were sitting up in the rafters, dangling his sandaled feet. Mr. Hughes, so mildly bearing the fascination that all the girls have for him—entirely oblivious to the fact that he is so different from everything else in their lives. Like a paper-doll cutout stood in front of a painting, casting its shadow on the figures behind it and making it all look painfully two-dimensional.

It is true that he is something beautiful. She could stare at him and do nothing else and be quite content. She is aware—

how can she put this?—she is aware of how aware she is of him.

After the first week of school when Binhammer mentioned, with implicit criticism, that Mr. Hughes shared his name with a famous poet, she went to the library and read everything she could find by Ted Hughes and then by Sylvia Plath—hating how everything about them was perfectly dramatic and perfectly beautiful and perfectly artistic and perfectly impossible. What she wanted was to be able somehow to see her way into this chaos of artistic tragedy. But tragic heroines have sharp, steely names like Sylvia Plath—a scalpel of a name. Not slurring, muddy puddles like Liz Warren.

Still, what she did find, in a poem that Hughes wrote about Sylvia, and which Liz copied out in tiny script on a scrap of paper and folded up to keep inconspicuously on her desk in her bedroom, was this:

> There is no better way to know us
> Than as two wolves, come separately to a wood.
> Now neither's able to sleep—even at a distance
> Distracted by the soft competing pulse
> Of the other. . . .

What Liz feels for Mr. Hughes isn't anything so ordinary as love or lust. Instead, it's the feeling of him standing behind her when she's writing something, or his voice speaking the words as she's reading the hypnotically long and filigreed lines of Virginia Woolf. Catching a glimpse of him at the other end of the school hallway and feeling her spine go taut, instant erasure of all those other bodies between her and him. She imagines she can hear him breathing even above the screeching voices of all her "peers." Not love. And certainly not the diminished form of the word that people like to use when they're talking about teenagers: the crush. Not love, but just awareness. His presence always in the back of her mind, thudding away like a headache.

She knows though, that he is not so aware of her. She suffers no such girlish delusions. Though on one occasion, after having turned in a story about an aristocratic southern gentleman and a prostitute in a hotel room in Georgia (she was proud of her title, "Our Year of Moving Slowly"), she caught him staring at her in the back row of the room, could feel his gaze as she straightened her hair with her fingers. And then, when he handed back the stories at the end of class, hers was at the bottom of the stack—which is where teachers put your paper if they want to talk to you about it—and he stopped her as she was slinging her bag over her shoulder to leave.

"Your story was phenomenal."

"Thanks." She could feel herself rolling her eyes. She has been told that she doesn't know how to take compliments.

"I don't know how you do it," he said, his eyes, all that weight, crushing her—the increased gravity of intimacy that brings you to your knees. "You write like someone twice your age. A lot of moxie. Like an ex-stripper."

So she writes like an ex-stripper. She has never received a better compliment. Honestly, she doesn't think she would ever like to be a stripper, but she wouldn't mind being an ex-stripper. The bells of tragedy ringing all around. The fallen honor. The smoky voice of experience. She covets that compliment, writes it down on the same piece of folded paper where she has inscribed the Ted Hughes poem.

And for a few days afterward, she thinks she can feel his awareness of her—two wolves come to a wood—him distracted by her pulse in the back row of the class.

> *Fall on your knees, O hear the angel voices!*
> *O night divine, O night when Christ was born!*
> *O night, O holy night, O night divine!*

The voices of the choir reverberate to a finish, and she is woken from her reverie. She straightens her hair and presses her palms into her eyes. She is supposed to have been learning about integrity. Those human values lost and regained. But she hasn't been listening very closely, and she feels bad because she doesn't want to be just another one of those fidgeting girls who can't sit through a twenty-minute speech.

She glances over to where Mr. Hughes was standing, but he's already gone. And as the girls begin to file out of the auditorium, she thinks maybe next time she'll write a story about an old radio and things you can hear on it beneath all the static.

chapter 29

It is the last day of school before Christmas vacation when things come undone.

The Carmine-Casey faculty holiday party is an annual event organized by the members of the faculty council and held in the auditorium at seven o'clock in the evening on a day when all after-school extracurricular activities have been canceled to make sure that every last student is expunged from the building before the teachers start drinking. This year the sky is clear and cold and someone has decided to wrap the leafless sugar maple in lights—even though you would only catch a glimpse of it through the windows on your way to the auditorium.

The halls of the school take on a whole different quality at night. The windows that normally give students endless things to gaze at are now only rectangles of reflective black. Everything is inverted upon itself—as though blankets have been pulled up over the whole building—and the fluorescent lights in the empty halls buzz steadily with their pale, diffuse glow.

At seven o'clock exactly the last of the girls are being escorted out of the building. They have made excuses—art projects that needed to be completed before vacation—but now, with faculty spouses arriving, the girls cannot be allowed to stay and fawn.

As one of the faculty council members moves them slowly but steadily in the direction of the front doors with outstretched arms, these last three girls spot Mr. Binhammer leaning against the far wall and call out to him.

"Mr. Binhammer, are you going to the party?"

"Mr. Binhammer, is your wife coming?"

"What is she going to wear?"

"Does she like coming to these parties?"

"Is she pretty?"

And, finally, "Okay, okay, we're going," as they are driven forward through the doors and out onto the street.

Binhammer is, in fact, waiting for his wife to arrive—this being the one faculty function since the beginning of the year that he has determined she can safely attend without disrupting the delicate balance of lies and elisions that he has constructed around himself.

Earlier in the week, sitting on opposite couches in the teachers' lounge, Ted Hughes looked over the top of his newspaper at Binhammer. For someone just coming into the room, the two of them might have looked like Greek statues positioned in opposition across a long corridor. But this is one of the things the men have grown accustomed to with each other—the mutual speculative stare just prior to a quick, machine-gunning exchange, as though the air between them is being primed for their waltzing words.

So Ted Hughes gazed at Binhammer over the top of his newspaper, and Binhammer gazed back. Then Ted Hughes asked:

"Are you going to the Christmas party?"

"Probably. Why?"

"I'm not."

"Because—?"

"I'm going away."

"Where?"

"Connecticut."

"What for?"

"My sister's having a party."

"I didn't know you had a sister."

"Everybody has a sister."

"Fair enough."

They shared a hint of a smile, as though, having wandered off in different directions, they had both arrived at the same place.

Then Binhammer, who was aware that his wife's absence at these functions was becoming suspicious, had an idea.

"It's too bad. Sarah's going to be there."

"Sarah your wife?"

"That's right."

"Oh, no," he says, looking truly disappointed.

"And she was looking forward to meeting you."

"She was?"

"All she's been saying is, 'So I finally get to meet this Ted Hughes character.' "

Perverse, the way he makes these situations flirt with each other—like too many kites in the air, daring them to collide. He wants to get to the bottom of it all. To figure it out. And while constantly risking the apocalyptic volatility of actual contact between Ted Hughes, Sibyl, and his wife, he believes that there is some secret, personal and profound, to be discovered somewhere in the permutations. If he gets the right combination, if he lines them up in exactly the right way—like the eerie symmetry of an eclipse—something will click into place, and the whole thing will make sense.

Ted Hughes was silent. Then he said, "Can we go out to dinner after Christmas? Just the three of us?"

"Sure. Absolutely. She would love it."

"I'm serious. It's getting embarrassing."

"I'm serious too."

So now Binhammer waits in the lobby for his wife, who will be able to appease both his colleagues ("We missed you at the annual dinner") and his own miserly sense of insecurity with regard to Sibyl Lockhart, who will not dare to approach them.

When Sarah arrives, he can see her through the glass-paned doors of the lobby. Before she opens them, she puts her face up to the glass, shielding out the glare with two hands held across her brow. He is in love with her for doing that—the gesture that he interprets as wanting to be assured of his presence even before she opens the door. It is a tiny thing that makes his skin crackle. If twenty-four hours a day he could be on the other side of glass panes that she had her beautiful nose pressed up against, then everything would be okay.

She is wearing a skirt and a blouse and has her hair tied up in some kind of complicated knot, and when they walk arm in arm into the auditorium the other teachers begin to crowd around them, telling him how beautiful a wife he has and joking that Binhammer must be secretly wealthy, otherwise why would she ever marry him.

He looks around for Sibyl, but she hasn't arrived yet. He takes Sarah over to the stage where they have set up a makeshift bar, and he knows to order her a gin and tonic, which he likes to do because it makes him feel like he's married a real sophisticate. For him, just a glass of red wine.

Then Pepper Carmichael and Lonnie Abramson sneak up on him from behind. He knows something is coming because he can read the expression in Sarah's eyes as she gazes just past his shoulder. She looks bemused.

"Darling, it's been ages since we saw you," Lonnie says to Sarah, leaning into her for a kiss on the cheek. He can see Lonnie's big bust pressing against his wife's chest, and he wonders how Sarah feels about that. "You must be keeping yourself busy. You'll have to tell me all about it."

"Hi, Sarah," Pepper puts in meekly.

"But I don't want you to worry," Lonnie continues. "We're all keeping an eye on the boy here. Making sure he does his work and stays out of trouble and gets enough to eat."

"Oh, Lonnie," Pepper scolds, slightly embarrassed.

"Well, okay. Honestly, though, he's such a sweetheart to have around. Such a lovely person. I can't even tell you. All the times that I've wanted to bring my husband George to school with me, just to tell him, 'Now you just follow this man around and watch what he does and take notes because there's going to be a quiz afterward.' Ha ha ha. Really, though, I've thought about it. I really have. But George wouldn't even come here with me tonight. He's a stinker, isn't he?"

Sarah smiles politely. Binhammer tries to change the subject because he knows his wife, and he knows that, for some complicated reason he has forgotten, she interprets compliments about him from other women as aggressive.

When Sibyl finally arrives, he catches a glimpse of her out of the corner of his eye. She stops just inside the auditorium to survey the situation. Spotting the four of them standing there, he with the three women, she pretends to make her way slowly and casually toward the bar. But then, halfway across the floor, her resolve seems to shift and she sets a dead-eye course in their direction.

But she will not do anything. She will not say anything. She is smart. She does not have a secure enough homeland retreat to scorch the earth behind her. Also, it gives her something to admire in herself—discretion beyond the call of duty. Being the better man.

"And here's Sibyl," Lonnie narrates.

"Merry Christmas," Sibyl says.

"Merry Christmas," Sarah replies with a business smile.

For the next hour Binhammer sits back in nodding approval of the situation in which he has found himself. He hasn't felt this satisfied in a long time. He isn't sure what he has created here— these delicate intricacies that pull themselves taut between the various people in his life—but for the time being it, whatever it is, seems to be holding itself stable.

He enjoys watching these women talk to each other. The way they sometimes reach out and touch each other's forearms. The way they stand together in a circle as though stirring up some boiling brew in a cauldron between them. And then they bring him in, linking his arms in theirs, and he is suddenly privy to the secret lives of women—the floral gaudiness of it all, the grinning insecurity, the questions of clothes and what parts of the body are showing and what parts are hidden.

And he watches Sarah his wife, who, though she does not

like to participate in the traditional girl talk, always knows the right things to say. She always antes up in any social situation, even if she folds early and rarely bets.

He likes the way she looks tonight. Watching her interact with other people, she has a distance like a museum piece. The pointillistic painting that blurs into bright color when you stand with your nose to it but resolves into sharp focus as you take ten paces back. She looks good that way. The enchanting witchery of remoteness. Her face pressed up against the glass of the door, searching. Her small form enclosed in a covey of other women, lighting itself up for him like a little pale beacon. He studies her, the way she holds her drink with both hands, the way she forms her words with smiling surety, staking her claim firmly, sometimes like Fortinbras in *Hamlet* on a patch of land that nobody wants. There she waves her flag. And other people are convinced—they *are*—that they should have gotten there first. And she smiles on and on.

There is no question of his love for her. Times like these there is no question. It's in his fingers wanting to graze her hand or the back of her neck.

He is happy. Calm. And the evening proceeds with his colleagues coming over to wish him happy holidays while he shakes hands and gazes at his wife over their shoulders.

"Have a great holiday, Binhammer! See you in the new year!"

It is not until almost ten o'clock, while Sarah is in the ladies' room upstairs just prior to their good-byes, five minutes before they would have been gone, in a cab on their way back home, five minutes away from her leaning her head against his shoulder in the backseat of a taxi and the two of them making jokes about the people they've encountered, like spies pooling their data at the end of a mission—this is marriage, ultimately, the partnership of spies in a hostile world—not until almost ten o'clock that Binhammer looks over at the auditorium entrance and sees Ted Hughes stamping the snow from his shoes and saluting him broadly as though reuniting with an old, old friend.

Oh no.

"Binhammer!" he calls, coming over and taking him by the hand. "My kid sister's had a baby. Eight pounds even. The party's canceled. I'm an uncle. The traffic was terrible. Where's your wife? What's the matter with you, you don't look so good."

He can feel his pulse all over his body. There is something pressing against his chest. "I have to——"

But it's no good. He can see her coming across the floor toward them. Both smiling, her from a distance, beautiful, perfect, coded with secret affection, and him up close, bold, mischievous, like a friendly, lonely Lucifer.

"You have to what? Come on, where's this Sarah I've been hearing so much about? I'm dying to——"

When they see each other, there is an impetus in the situation that carries forward even though everything has stopped dead.

His wife's face has for a moment that worried laughing expression of someone who suddenly realizes a joke is being played but is not sure what the joke is or who is the butt of it. Then she seems to register something, and her eyes drop with anger and humiliation. She looks frantic.

"What are you——" she stammers. "What's going—what is this, Leo? Leo, answer me. I don't understand."

They look back and forth between each other and Binhammer. Ted Hughes cannot take his eyes off her. As though their reunion were accidental and as uncomplicated as a bouquet of flowers. Then there is the confusion of the little boy who is about to be told that it was all just a performance, a test he has failed.

"New teacher," Binhammer mutters. "He works here."

And then she must see something recognizable in his downturned face, because she starts saying, "You knew? I don't understand. You knew?"

"What the hell . . ." Ted Hughes begins but falters.

Oh god. All the things we do without thinking. Everything tumbled down in a second. What did he expect? So precarious, that house of cards. He feels sick in his gut, the wrongness of it all knotting up inside him.

"Why, Leo?" Sarah says, her eyes gone suddenly red and wet. He did this to her. Not Hughes. He, Binhammer. He hurt his wife. "I thought this was over."

It is impossible for Binhammer to stay here, in the middle of this. They have to understand. It's just impossible. He rushes out and down the hall through the lobby doors to the street and finally stops himself by holding on to the frozen wrought iron bars of the fence in front of the building.

What did I do? he thinks. And for a while, that's all he can think over and over as though short-circuited on that single thought. What did I do? What did I do?

For a long time there he had the illusion that he could maintain the delicate balance forever. A master architect, constructing gorgeously intricate structures of human interaction. But now this is what it all comes to. A pathetic clunk. As much as he likes to imagine it sometimes, his story is no modern curative to the clichés of the past. He is no dramatic character to be discussed among girlvoices in classrooms. Instead he is inconsequential, like an aluminum chair being pushed over. That's what he feels like, a little boy who, in the middle of a wedding, pushes a chair over—which makes a noise just loud enough for people to stop dancing and turn their heads to find him standing there, sullen. Why would the boy do such a thing? What is it that he wants?

Yes, it's true, on some level this is what he has been waiting for: his grand moment of perfect justice. And the moment is not dramatic at all—it's just small and petty and childish. What has he accomplished? Nothing has changed. All he has done is hurt them.

It is a quiet night. A cab rolls by and slows to see if he wants a ride, but when he doesn't respond it continues on looking for a fare. Farther down the street there is a plastic bag caught on a low gate, billowing full with wind and then settling and then billowing full again. Like breathing. Sometimes, even in the middle of the city, there is no one around and everything is quite clear.

After a while he goes back in but can't find them anywhere in the auditorium. Then he discovers Ted Hughes sitting on the stairs outside in the hall. He doesn't look angry, just confused.

"Where did she go?" Binhammer asks.

"Binhammer, why did you do it?"

"I don't know. There are things . . . I don't know. It doesn't matter. It's not something to talk about."

Ted Hughes tries to look at him, but his eyes keep slipping away sideways.

"Where is she?" Binhammer asks.

"I think she went out back," he says, pointing to the courtyard where the sugar maple is rearing up against the night with its strings of icy lights.

He finds her out there, hugging herself against the cold, looking up into the leafless branches of the tree. The lights reflect back in her moist eyes.

He would like to say something to her—would like to do something for her. Pull in the raw, exposed night, glistening like a fresh wound. Pull it in and fold it up like a blanket and set it down on the frozen grass for her to sit on. The breath coming from between her lips condenses in weak puffs that dissipate almost instantly. He would like to break all the windows and take the shards of glass and use them against the night to make mirrors to reflect her from a thousand different angles at once. Surround her with the shimmering mosaic of herself. Or rip through the fabric of the moment and join by force the past and the future, a muscleman linking together two hook-ended chains that hold the weight of memory and anticipation. And stand proud, arms akimbo, before the taut shackle for her to see. The rend in the night would look like the lights on the tree, radiance with torn edges.

He would like to do these things.

And he would like to say other things. Say he's sorry perhaps. Or that he didn't mean it. And that what he really meant was . . . Or that the way he felt about things—and while he intended one thing at first except what happened was—

But then, rather suddenly, he feels calm. There will be time to say these things. They do not need to be said right now. There will be time.

What he says, finally, is this:

"You shouldn't be out here. I mean, without your coat."

"It's okay," she shivers, rubbing her upper arms. "It feels good."

And they stand there, side by side, not looking at each other, gazing up through the branches of the luminescent tree as though it were an altar and they meager supplicants.

chapter 30

When they were first married, she recalls, she had her own trajectory, and he had his. It wasn't until later that they became so knotted up with each other.

In their first year of marriage, they went to Mexico, the Yucatán. Those viny ruins at Kohunlich, the two of them lost to the foreignness of the place, bracing themselves against the screech of howler monkeys in the cohune palms. It was hot, their shirts soaked through with sweat.

"Ms. Lewis, where have you taken us?"

"It was your idea, Mr. Binhammer."

"We are out of our element."

They stood before five stone masks that represented the sun god Kinich Ahau. She looked at him looking at those masks. She liked the way he considered them with great seriousness, as though he were measuring them for his own wearing.

And then he slipped and fell on the moss-covered stone steps and had to hop, wincing, on one foot back to the car.

It was a sprained ankle, and the doctor wrapped it in a tight bandage and said he should not put pressure on it.

"I'm crippled," he said.

"You're a beautiful cripple," she said.

Their hotel room had a ceiling fan, and they slept underneath it on top of the sheets until the light crept in through the shutters.

"How are you feeling?" she asked in the morning.

"It's important, Ms. Lewis, that one forges ahead in spite

of complications that may arise along the way." And he reached over and put a hand on her breast.

They had sex, being careful of his ankle, until their bodies were slippery with sweat. She remembers that, years later, the way their bodies were so oiled with perspiration that they would not adhere to each other. She remembers that on the winter nights in the city when her skin is rough and goose-pimpled.

She held him up all the way around Mexico, the weight of his body new and strange to her. She could not anticipate his movements. She wondered, Who is this man I've married? and she was not afraid of the answer. Their lives were supposed to be different, and now it was their mission to lock themselves together, to discover or invent all the possible nodes of complementarity.

Now, eight years later, sitting by herself at a table in the farthest back corner of a small café, she wonders if maybe they've done their intertwining too well—if maybe the knots are too taut.

She looks at her watch. It is five minutes to two o'clock.

Why did he do it? Why did he keep the secret of Ted Hughes? The answer, obviously, has something to do with her own indiscretion—her own affair with Ted Hughes that she did *not* keep a secret. It has something to do with the fact that by telling him the truth about the affair two years ago, she had set it down between them as something to share. They had gone through it together. Like his sprained ankle in Mexico. She had taken a thing of contention and turned it into a thing of confederation.

Still, she can't quite bring into focus his intentions, and she doesn't dare ask him. Now there is a stately quiet around the apartment shot through with angles and ends and crooked things. She is not sure if he is angry at her or if she is angry at him. Or even if simple anger enters into it at all.

The fact is that eight years ago, this all would have seemed different—the swollen and aching adjustment of two people pointing in different directions, trying to reconcile their proximities.

Now it's something else. Larger or smaller, she cannot tell. But the chamber of their lives is wider now, and so the deed echoes of both past and future. It never exists simply in the moment.

She looks at her watch again. Two o'clock.

I'm tired, she thinks. There must be a way to purge the history of things, to squeeze down memory into a thimble and put it away so that it's possible to look at things with fresh eyes.

"Those eyes gone distant," says a voice above her. It's Ted Hughes. "I remember you looking like that. I have a picture of it in my head."

She says hello, stands to greet him. But she's not sure what kind of greeting is called for, so they just gaze at each other for a moment—poised in suspended nonreaction. Then they sit. She wants to thank him for meeting her, but that would sound too businesslike. Instead, she says:

"You manage to cause a stir everywhere you go, don't you?"

He smiles at this. "Well, who would have thought that I would end up teaching at the same school as your husband?"

"It's definitely a coincidence."

"Downright Dickensian is what it is."

She remembers him, two years ago in San Diego, leaning in toward her, as though he didn't want to miss a single utterance from her mouth.

"It's good to see you," she says.

"Is it?"

"I don't know. I think so, yes."

"I kept thinking I would run into you," he says. "Here in New York. On the street somewhere. I pictured how it might happen. What kind of poses I might strike. Silly. But that's the best part of the brief affair, isn't it? The flustered encounter afterward. All your senses lit up with static. But it never happened."

"Until now."

"Right. Until now."

There is a pause—all lit up with static.

"So," she continues, "I hear you're a very good teacher."

"Some of the girls like me. But I'm no Binhammer. That man inspires loyalty."

The comment hangs there a moment before either recognizes the irony of it. Then it drops and settles for another moment before either recognizes the deep truth of it.

"God," she says. "This is ridiculous. I don't know why I wanted to meet with you. It just seemed like something to do. After everything."

"How are things? Between you two?"

She shrugs. "Elliptical. How about the two of you?"

"Adumbrated."

"It's not a simple thing, is it?"

"No, it isn't."

They talk more, speculating, briefly, about what her husband might have intended in keeping the secret for so long. They wonder about what went on in his head. She is surprised to see that Ted Hughes has gotten to know him very well over the past few months. And she suspects, as she has on more than a few occasions in her life, that men must have a language of their own by which to link their thick muscled hearts.

What she wants from him, she supposes, is some foundation on which to build her response to the whole thing—someone to point in the direction of what she should be feeling, whether anger or guilt or frustration. But she doesn't get this today. Instead, sitting in front of her is a charming man who two years ago traced his fingers along her spine and made her shiver down to her toes.

"What about the big question?" he says at one point. "Do you regret it? Do you regret what we did?"

"No," she says demonstratively, and her response surprises her.

"Would you do it again?"

He smiles, leaning forward. Those hands. The two of them are on the cusp of something together. That's what it felt like before, too. Teetering precariously, gorgeously. The wind buffets you up there at those heights. It gets in your hair.

"Do you mean if I had to do it over again? Or do you mean . . ."

The vertigo of the moment. The seizure in the legs, to be hoisted up in the air, and, for a terrific second, to feel as though you are flying.

And then they back away. Both of them. Back onto solid ground, laughing nervously. Something has been decided.

"So what do we do now?" she asks.

"Well, I don't know about you," he says, "but I could go for a milkshake."

"That sounds good."

"And then, I suppose," he adds, smiling, arch, "we go back to marching along in life's wicked parade."

"That sounds good too."

"Oh, one more thing, and then we'll never talk about it again."

"All right." She girds herself. The man is a constant revelation. He announces rather than suggests. The heroic declarative. "What is it?"

"I still think you're wrong about Nathalie Sarraute."

chapter 31

Over the two weeks of Christmas vacation, the Carmine-Casey School for Girls is a hollow, silent edifice watched over, on shortened hours, by Mr. Cuthbert the maintenance man. When Mrs. Mayhew comes through the doors the Tuesday after Christmas to get some work done in the peace and quiet of her office, she finds him leaning back in an old desk chair in the lobby, his feet propped up, with an old plastic radio, bent wire hanger winding upward like a vine for increased reception, perched on the radiator beside him.

"Happy holidays, Mr. Cuthbert."

"Happy holidays to you, Mrs. Mayhew."

On the radio the sounds of a football game in progress.

"Everything under control?"

"Quiet as a tomb, Mrs. Mayhew. Just the way I like it."

She nods approvingly and takes the elevator to the top floor. She has her key in the lock of the administrative offices when she stops and looks behind her down the long vacant corridor. The overhead phosphorescents are shut off, but the daylight bleeds in through the frost-crusted windows far enough to give the entire place a look of dusky abandonment. The mote-filled air reminds her of the summerhouses of her childhood, her mother covering all the furniture with sheets, those irregular white forms like a parade of lost, blind ghosts.

She leaves her key ring dangling from the door and walks slowly down the corridor, her hands folded behind her back as though she were making her regular morning rounds, nodding to the girls and saying "Good morning" in the short, clipped tones appropriate to her role in the school. One of the classroom doors is ajar, and she pushes it wide and walks in. The desks have all been lined up neatly, one of the final duties of the maintenance crew before the holiday, along with the wiping down of the chalkboards, the polishing of the floor, the cleaning of the bathrooms. Walking between them, she finds one desk at almost the exact center of the configuration and sits down at it.

Somewhere in the building a window rattles in its frame. There is a distant sound of water rushing through the pipes as the radiators click into function and begin knocking, hissing, spitting.

The chairs are now all cold, their plastic rigid where it is normally humid and pliant under the ruddy organic bodies of the students. If you step into a room while there is a lesson in progress, you can feel the pulse of the class—the accumulated rhythm of all those little hearts beating in time with the timpani of the teacher's voice. The musicality of the glances between teacher and student, student and student, the itching throats of girls on the verge of contributing something to the conversation, staking their claims in the common corpus of sticky intellect.

It has been a long time since Mrs. Mayhew has been simply a teacher, a long time since her days were filled with the easy, riotous pleasure of students. In those days, things in her life tumbled into position rather than being scheduled hour by hour.

On the desk before her is written, in ballpoint pen, the motto:

> *My heart is an engine—*
> *My sex is a gaudy circus.*

Her eyes narrow a bit, but you would not be able to read any other reaction on her face. You might just assume she has simply felt a shift in the breeze, or a fly buzzing past her ear.

She seems to be waiting for something—waiting for the class to begin. Settling back in the seat, she sets her head on a tilt and focuses her attention on the blackboard, where to all appearances she is reading the invisible palimpsest of all the classes ever taught in this room.

Then she closes her eyes and seems to be listening to something—and for the first time in quite a while the slight pursed edgings of a smile can be seen to soften the features of her face.

The radiators clack on like the lungs of valve-operated bovines through the halls of the school, and when they settle down again, their thermostats satisfied for the time being, there is nothing to upset the thick hush that suffocates the rooms.

It is two hours later that Mr. Cuthbert, who buys his lunch from the deli on the corner, takes the elevator to the top floor to ask Mrs. Mayhew if he can treat her to anything (she has always been kind to him, despite what people say about her) and finds her keys hanging like a stopped pendulum from the door of the office. He nods sadly and utters aloud the words "Oh lordy" and turns down the corridor toward the door at the end that stands open in mid-yawn.

"A good woman," he says, standing in the doorway. "Oh lordy, a good woman."

When school is under way again the following week, the mood of the classes is buzzing yet somber—as though death itself were suddenly made part of the curriculum. Some of the girls burst into spontaneous sobbing during class and have to be sent to the nurse to lie down. Others seem uncomfortable—as though attending a party where they don't know the guest of honor—and these are the ones who want to get straight back into the work of the day. Mrs. Landry and Dr. Harrison, the two other headmistresses, lead an assembly in honor of Mrs. Mayhew and ask for volunteers among the student body to write short memories of the matriarch to be bound together and given to the Mayhew family.

At the beginning of the following week, however, the school settles back into its accustomed rounds. The school play, *Salmonburger* by Liz Warren, having been in production for many months, finally has its premiere. The culmination of many late nights at the school for its writer/director and its stars, all leading to this, three day performances for the students and two night performances for parents. It receives a generally positive response. Dixie Doyle is lauded for the way her voice resonates to every corner of the auditorium. The round of applause for Liz Warren is all the more enthusiastic for the fumbling embarrassment with which she takes her bow. On the other hand, some of the viewers come away mystified. "Liz Warren is so smart," one girl says, "that I don't really understand what they're talking about." Some of the fathers fall asleep, and Liz's mother compliments her daughter profusely and asks with a wink if her next play is going to feature a leading man as cute as Jeremy Notion.

Ultimately, though, the cast and crew of the production go home feeling a keen sense of anticlimax—as though they have invested hours of time and energy in the service of what has turned out to be just another day, nearly indistinguishable from the rest. Nothing has changed, nothing is different in their lives. The world, they realize, does not hold its breath for such trifles.

After Christmas an unseasonal warm front pushes through the city, melting all the ice collected in gray mounds in the gutters. For three days the sidewalks are striated by veined cross-cuttings of melted ice—rivulets that darken the pavement and fill the cracks.

In the teachers' lounge of Carmine-Casey, the teachers stand at the window and gaze out contemplatively through the curtain of dripping water from the once-frozen eaves above. Each asks politely what the others have done over the holiday. The Abramsons had a lovely Christmas at home for once in their lives. Pepper Carmichael spent the holiday upstate in a cabin with some friends. She learned how to build a fire. Binhammer and his wife flew to Florida to see her cousin, who took them sailing up and down the coastline in his boat.

Things are quieter than usual in the teachers' lounge. For a while Mrs. Mayhew's death overshadows everything in the building. Nobody wants to be the first to resume lightness. But then there are hints of other discord unrelated to Mrs. Mayhew. Binhammer and Ted Hughes, for example, are normally to be found sitting on opposite couches in the lounge, sparring at each other playfully and boisterously and engaging anyone who passes in whatever absurdity they might be discussing. But since Christmas some teachers have noticed that when Binhammer comes into the room, Ted Hughes leaves. Once, Lonnie Abramson observes from a distance a strange interaction between them. Ted Hughes saying something to Binhammer, using gestures that have some pleading in them. But, as she continues watching from down the hall, Binhammer just shaking his head in response, looking pained by what the other man is saying, and walking away.

"Uh-oh," Lonnie says to herself. "The boys are fighting."

But when she tries to ask Binhammer about it, he smiles brightly, says there is nothing wrong at all, and derails her by asking about her daughter and her husband.

"Well," she finds herself saying, "you wouldn't believe what George said to me the other day. I do wish you could talk some sense into that man."

The month of January passes by with the thudding regularity of a funeral march. Mrs. Mayhew's death gives way to a sense of death abstract. There is a creeping feeling of lowering things into the ground and covering them over with mats of grass turf that have been carefully removed the hour before. Lowering them down into holes cut specifically for them. The neat walls of earth and clay, the cold mealy soil. The dizziness of standing at the edge and imagining yourself within.

When February comes, everyone is tired of the cold. The girls sit stubbornly in overheated rooms sweating with their winter coats wrapped around them in some backward protest—not against the administration that makes them dress in scanty uniforms all through the frigid winter, but rather against Mother Nature herself, who seems unfair and inflexible about this whole cold thing. Does it have to be cold *every* day? *Quel* boring.

So there they sit, bulky in their jackets, wiping sweat from their foreheads with their palms and looking aggressive, as though daring the teacher to teach them something. Not thinking too hard about the nature of their resentment. Waiting with little clenched fists for whatever might be coming next.

chapter 32

For Dixie Doyle, death is a flavorless topic of conversation. It is one of those subjects she has never managed to navigate correctly, frequently earning disapproving looks and tsk-tsks from her audience. It seems that Dixie Doyle cannot be Dixie Doyle when the dead are in question, and as a result, she has banned Mrs. Mayhew from the discussion amongst the group of girls who stand in a small huddled circle out in front after school.

"Did I tell you who we had staying in our house for Christmas?" Dixie opens today. Her hair is in pigtails for the first time since she was cast in the school play, during which time she wore her hair down for the sake of drama.

"Who, Dix?" Caroline asks.

But Caroline's attention alone is not sufficient, so Dixie says again, "Did I tell you?"

When the other two girls, Andie and Beth, shake their heads, Dixie consents to continue.

"Uncle Peter the drunk," she says. "He flew in from Houston."

"Oh no," Beth says, her face already curled into a sympathetic sneer. Though it is not difficult to get Beth to sneer.

"*Quel dommage!*" Caroline says.

"Ugh," says Dixie. "French. Madame Millet-Johnson gave me a D on my last quiz. I'm never speaking French again. I don't even like cheese anyway."

Caroline looks chastened. But only for a moment, and then

she discovers a scab on her knee that requires attention. She lifts her leg to set her foot on the concrete pediment and in doing so exposes her underwear to the street.

Andie quickly shoves Caroline's leg down and scolds her for being so indiscreet.

"You don't care who looks up your skirt."

Caroline just shrugs.

"Anyway," Dixie continues. "Uncle Peter the drunk stayed with us for four days."

"Wasn't he the one that liked to give you pony rides on his knee?"

"Yeah. Until I was like thirteen—and then my dad had to tell him to stop it."

"Ick."

"No kidding. And he's got this big Adam's apple. It's gross. Like he swallowed a pair of scissors or something."

The other girls cringe.

"So on Christmas Eve we had a big dinner and Uncle Peter the drunk got drunk of course. They couldn't stop him because it was Christmas Eve and everything. Even after I went to bed I could hear them arguing with him in the living room. And then in the middle of the night I wake up and guess what."

"Oh no."

"He's standing there in my room. Right over my bed. And he's kind of swaying back and forth like this." Dixie mimics the motion; she looks like someone on the deck of a small boat.

"What did you do, Dixie?"

"Well, he's just an old drunk. I wasn't afraid of him. I knew he wouldn't *do* anything. So I just said, 'What do you want, Uncle Peter?' And do you know what he said? He said, 'I want my life back.' "

"What does that mean?" Caroline asks.

"That's sad," Andie says under her breath, but none of the other girls pay attention to her.

"So what did you say, Dixie?" Beth says.

"Well, I just told him that I didn't have his life and I didn't know where it was and I didn't know who took it. And then I told him he better go back to his own room before my dad found him there."

"And then what?"

"And then nothing. He just called me a name and left. Well, he did do one more thing. On his way out he picked up Sizemore, my stuffed pig, and threw it at me. But it was just a stuffed animal, so it didn't hurt."

"That's kind of scary, Dixie," Beth says, with a face like she just drank sour milk.

"He's just a drunk."

"But he's so *old*."

Dixie looks toward the windows of Carmine-Casey—the third row up, about where the teachers' lounge is. "It's not about *age*," she says. "He's not *old* old."

"Whatever," Beth says.

Dixie continues gazing upward, her eyes narrowed in thought. The girls kick at the concrete and begin looking up and down the street. Finally Dixie emerges from her reverie and looks around as if surprised that the others are still there.

"What are we doing?" she asks. "What are we waiting for, anyway?"

"Aren't we waiting for Jeremy?" Caroline asks. "That's what you told us."

"That's right," Andie confirms with a raised eyebrow. "Your boyfriend."

"He's not my boyfriend," Dixie says.

"Then what is he?"

Dixie doesn't answer. Caroline goes back to picking at her scab, but bends over this time instead of raising her leg. Andie leans back to make sure she isn't exposing her underpants again.

Finally Beth spots Jeremy Notion coming down the block. "There he is."

He's wearing pants that are spattered with something like paint and a polo shirt two sizes too big for him. His hair and face look like he's been bobbing for apples in vegetable oil. The closer he gets, the wider Dixie's frown spreads across her face.

"You're ugly as a dog," she says to him.

"Hey," he says, taking exception. "I thought we were friends again."

"I don't have any friends that dress like that."

"Jesus. Why do you have to be sour all the time?" For a second it looks like he's going, but then he seems to decide against it. He's going to stick it out.

At that moment, the big glass doors of the building open and Dixie spots Liz Warren and Monica Vargas emerging, pale and unimpressed, into the stark afternoon light. They are debating something, and their gestures, Dixie notices, are magnificently theatrical. Dixie wonders what they could be talking about with such passion. What topic would she herself argue about with such bodily vigor?

"There they are," Beth says, directing everyone's attention to the two girls. "Mr. and Mrs. Warren-Vargas."

When Liz notices the cadre of girls at the bottom of the steps, she stops talking in mid-sentence and her arm, arcing with a large sweeping gesture, drops out of the air like a shot bird and falls limply at her side. The look she gives to Dixie and Jeremy is one of complete antipathy and condescension—as though it hurts her even to have the two of them populating the same city as she. What a shame, Dixie imagines her thinking. What a sad, pathetic, stupid little shame.

"Look at that look she just gave you," Beth says, grabbing Dixie's arm. "Did you see that look, Dixie?"

"I saw it."

"Are you going to let her give you a look like that?"

Dixie thinks that she would like to see those magnificent Liz Warren hand gestures again. She does a little version of one with her hand at her side. What words could she say to accompany a gesture like that? What words would be big enough to justify it?

Then she realizes that Beth and Caroline are looking at her, waiting for her to do something. She gathers herself up.

"Hey, Liz," she calls for the sake of appearances, even though her heart's not in it, "what's the matter? Are you scared of boys now?"

"Shut up, Dixie," Liz says as the two get to the bottom of the steps and begin walking quickly in the other direction.

"He told me how you couldn't do it. He told me, Liz."

Everyone stops. Jeremy sits down on the pediment with a deflated thud. All the girls have stopped breathing. Dixie suddenly finds herself in the middle of a void, falling directionless, like a dream, unable to get herself back upright. She hears herself saying these things, but they have no meaning. She's thinking about those hands of Liz's—but when she opens her mouth strange words come out.

Liz stops and looks back. "Your boyfriend is an imbecile, Dixie. And I think you know it." Then she shakes her head poignantly, and she and Monica begin to walk away again.

"Well," Dixie calls after her, "if you're so smart, why don't you go find a bank president to fuck."

Now Jeremy is up on his feet. He didn't like that imbecile comment, so he's yelling after Liz too. "Yeah," is all he can muster, "a bank president."

But the two girls don't turn around again.

"Oh, shut up, Jeremy," Dixie says, disgusted. "Sit down."

Liz and Monica reach the corner a few moments later and turn out of sight. Dixie, emerging from the rabbit hole into which she had stumbled, wonders if she managed to hurt Liz. Is she hurt by anything? If so, where does she hide her scars?

Suddenly, like tripping over your own feet, it occurs to Dixie that she doesn't actually hate Liz Warren. The fact is surprising to her, and she turns it over in her mind like a child's toy puppet—something that's cute and scary at the same time.

She thinks about Liz's world, what it must be like. A world where everything *means* something. A world where big hand gestures aren't just play but are actually necessary to unlock se-cret truths that other people don't even know are there. Like she has magic sunglasses or something. Everything Liz sees is right and relates to the big world that, truthfully, frightens Dixie a little bit.

It would be all right to be Liz Warren, Dixie decides. It must be a thing like being rich or beautiful—but possibly even better.

She looks over at Jeremy, who looks defeated, though un-sure of how it happened.

"You're an imbecile," Dixie Doyle tells him. "And you're ugly as a dog."

chapter 33

Liz Warren looks askance at Mr. Binhammer's choice of Hemingway for the Women in Literature class. Not because *The Sun Also Rises* is written by a man, but because everything in the book seems contingent on the rise and fall of *maleness*.

Other girls in the class dislike Hemingway for different reasons.

"I don't get this book, Mr. Binhammer," says Marilyn Lepke, whose father has connections to the mob. "All they do is drink Pernod and ride in taxis."

Liz wishes Mr. Binhammer wouldn't pander to students like Marilyn Lepke and Dixie Doyle. But instead he seems to possess a fond affection for them—and that's disappointing. If that is the kind of girl who impresses Mr. Binhammer, then there is no place for herself in this classroom.

But every now and then, she has to admit, he will say something that sticks and turns like a blade in her gut.

"But isn't it romantic?" he says in response to Marilyn Lepke's observation.

"Romantic?"

"Sure. Isn't it romantic how much Jake loves Lady Bret Ashley?"

"If he loves her so much," Dixie Doyle asks, "then why isn't he with her?"

"He can't be with her."

"How come?" Dixie says. "Oh, you mean because of his penis problem?"

Liz is embarrassed for her, and the other girls in the class chuckle—but her question is a sincere one.

"No," Mr. Binhammer says. "Well, sure, but it's more than that. He can't be with her—because she's not real."

Liz sits up. This is something new. And he says it in a way that intrigues her, as if he were discovering the meaning of the thing for the first time.

"What do you mean?" Dixie asks. "You mean like she's a ghost or something?"

"No," he says. He leans against the desk and looks down at his hand as though he's trying to solve an invisible puzzle with his fingers. "It's—it's like—haven't you ever been in love with— no, wait, forget about love. Haven't you ever been fascinated by someone? I don't mean liking them, it doesn't even have to do with liking or hating. I mean fascination—like everything they do seems to be a secret key to something important. You want to follow them everywhere because even . . . even what they order on their sandwich at the deli could be a clue to some treasure. You know what I mean?"

There is silence in the room. Liz's imagination begins to bubble and pop.

"Except," Mr. Binhammer says, and she has already figured out what's coming next, "except that as hard as you try, you can't seem to get any closer—it's like a mirage, or a horizon. Because the person you're really looking for isn't in there. The person you're looking for is someone you made up in your head."

The room is quiet like after a church service. School can be like this sometimes, at its best. So monastic that the still air wouldn't make a candle flicker.

"That's sad," says Caroline Cox.

"Maybe," Mr. Binhammer says. "Or maybe it just means we're our own secrets."

Liz wonders about the people around her. Who has she invented in her own head? Mr. Hughes? What about Dixie Doyle—that ideal fluffy pink arch nemesis? How does one tell the reality from the invention? She imagines Carmine-Casey as one big masquerade, everyone wearing the masks other people have put on them. And she wonders this, too: Of whose mind is she herself the invention? Who here makes her more than she is?

Binhammer himself has gotten lost in contemplation. He's thinking about glowing, flowering incarnations—and about the poor fragile things crouching behind them.

The clock on the wall says it's fifteen minutes before the end of the period. Time to give up.

He says, "Let's call it a day."

He sits and holds his head in his hands while everyone files out. He can hear their shuffling feet, the zippers on their bags, the tittering voices that seem lethargic at the end of the day. The last class. Time to go home. He presses the heels of his hands against his eyes and hears the door close behind the last of them.

Except when he looks up there's one left. Dixie Doyle, sitting there in the front row. Smiling at him.

"It's me," she says.

It's a funny thing to say. As though she were identifying herself on the phone or behind a door.

"Hello, Dixie."

"Can we talk about something?"

This is the second time today someone has wanted to have a talk with him. Earlier it was Ted Hughes, coming up behind him in the hall and grabbing his elbow. It was late in the morning, and Binhammer was pacing the empty halls during one of his free periods when Ted Hughes found him.

"Follow me," Ted Hughes said, pointing up and away as though they were embarking on an expedition.

"Where?"

"Up. And don't tell me you're busy. I know your schedule. You're not teaching again for an hour."

They rode the elevator to the top floor, and then Ted Hughes led him to the stairwell, where they climbed one more flight and opened a door onto the roof. The black tar was flat and seamed and had metal blocks and pipes sticking up here and there like settlements in a desert.

"I didn't know you could come up here," Binhammer said.

"This is where the girls come to smoke," Ted Hughes explained, pointing to the cigarette butts collected in the corners where three-foot parapets edged the roof.

"How did you know that?"

Ted Hughes shrugged off the question. "Listen," he said. "We're going to talk. Whether you like it or not."

Binhammer walked to the parapet and looked onto Fifth Avenue below, the front of the building where he could see a group of girls sitting on the steps. For a second he felt an attack of vertigo looking at the tops of their heads, and he had to pull himself back.

"What is it you want?" Ted Hughes asked, raising his arms against the low horizon, the rooftops beyond. "A showdown? A face-off? Pistols at dawn? There aren't going to be any fisticuffs, are there? Come on."

So this was what Ted Hughes wanted. To get it over with. Well, Binhammer wasn't going to give him the satisfaction, despite his own curiosity, despite his own desire to hammer everything back into shape. Forget it. Despite his wanting to put the man on the spot with questions. It would be petty of him. Beneath him. No, he wasn't going to give—

"How many times did you sleep with her?" he finds himself asking suddenly.

"Three. No, four."

"Who ended it?"

"She did."

"Why did you do it?"

Ted Hughes, having taken two steps toward Binhammer and braced himself, set to answer any question posed, opened his mouth to respond but then said nothing.

"Never mind," Binhammer said. "Forget that last one."

Ted Hughes scratched his head. He paced back and forth for a minute and then stopped, looking down at the tarred roof.

When he spoke, his voice took on a different quality altogether.

"This is some job, isn't it, Binhammer? Can you feel it? Six floors of girls beneath our feet, waiting to be read to. They come in tired, exhausted by their chemistry classes, their calculus classes. They open a book to a page, and all they see are stupid little black ants marching across—until you begin to talk about it, and then you can hear the bombs going off in their heads. You make that writing dance. And their eyes get all lit up with burning."

Binhammer thought about their burning eyes.

"Listen," Ted Hughes said, his voice palliative, "this isn't about me. I don't care about me. But the two of you . . ."

"You're very generous," he said wryly.

"Progressive."

"Yes, very progressive."

"Sophisticated." Ted Hughes's smile spreading across his face like dough rising.

"Indeed."

Binhammer looked down again to the street below. He marveled at the turn of events, realizing, embarrassed, that he was spending just as much time thinking about Ted Hughes as he was thinking about his wife. It wasn't supposed to be this way. He was supposed to despise this man.

"Okay," Ted Hughes starts in again. "So now what? You want to tear off our shirts and wrestle? Will you feel better if you bloody me up some? How about we shoot pool for the prize of her honor? Or draw for the high card?" He walked over and stood by Binhammer, shaking his head in affectionate pity. "Look, you jackass. You already won."

From below Binhammer heard the sounds of girls' voices.

"It's great being a teacher," Binhammer said. "You're right about that." He walked toward the door leading back down into the building. Turning back once more, he said, "I don't think I'm ready for this."

"For what?"

"For this," he repeated, motioning to the space between them. "For this conversation."

"Okay," Ted Hughes conceded. "But let me tell you something." The smile disappeared from his face. "You're not interested in punishing her. So you better figure out what you did all this for."

Binhammer left him there and went down into the halls, where he had to squint to see because his eyes had become accustomed to the bright winter sunlight outside. He didn't see Ted Hughes for the rest of the day, but he thought about the burning eyes of the girls he taught, and how sometimes they just smoldered slowly.

And now Dixie Doyle sits before him expectantly.

"I really can't stick around, Dixie."

"I know. You don't have to stick around. I just wanted to ask you something."

"About Liz Warren?"

"No!" she says, looking a little outraged. Then she smooths out her skirt. "But since you brought it up . . . do you like her more than you like me? It's okay if you do, I just want to know."

"Dixie. . . ."

"You know, she doesn't do the reading for this class."

He looks at her questioningly, and she lowers her head, chastened.

"Well, I don't know that for sure. I guess she probably does. But if you found out she didn't, would you stop thinking she was so great?"

He notices the way she has her arms folded across her chest now and the crease in her forehead, as though she has him under an exposed bulb and is interrogating him. He would put his hand on her cheek if he could. He leans back in the chair and gazes at her across the desk.

"You have to stop doing this to yourself," he says. "There's no competition between the two of you. You don't even belong in the same sentence."

"Whatever that means."

"Look," he says lightly, hoping to bring this to an end, "how could I like anyone more than I like you?"

This seems to satisfy her. She unfolds her arms and leans forward. "Okay. You're just joking, but okay."

She shifts in her seat, and he thinks she might be getting up, but really she's just shifting. She has more she wants to say.

"How come you never had kids?"

"Kids? I don't know. I guess I don't really like them."

"Yeah, that makes sense. I don't either."

She waits. Then:

"You know what my father does?"

"What?"

"He makes floss. You know, dental floss. Isn't that stupid? He got rich on dental floss. He has a factory where all you see are huge spools of floss. Which he sells to companies. They all get their floss from the same place. Did you know that? No matter what the brand is, they all get their floss from my father."

"Hmm."

"But I guess it worked out okay for me." She flashes him a wide smile to show off her teeth. They are perfectly straight and white. "We floss twice a day. Most people only floss once."

"Interesting."

"No, it's not. You don't have to say it is."

"I'm one of those people who only flosses once a day," he says apologetically.

She rolls her eyes. "*Anyway*," she goes on. "My father always talks about his tenth-grade history teacher. My mother hates it when he does, because all he says is how beautiful this teacher was and how she really knew how to teach about the French Revolution. She would make fists and everything while she was lecturing. My father imitates her. And then he says how he fell in love with her and she was all he could think about for his tenth-grade year and part of his eleventh."

"Uh-huh." He doesn't like the direction this is going. It feels like they are on the precipice of a declaration. Yet there's no way he can stop this. How can you stop a girl from telling you she loves you? It's an inhuman proposition. Ted Hughes would understand.

"And he always said that if he had it to do all over again, he would have told her. He says, 'That kiss is the only one I regret not getting.'"

"Is that right?"

"That's what he says." She waits. "So what do you think about that?"

He leans forward across the top of his desk and folds his hands together as though he has something difficult to say. "Dixie—"

"I know, I know. You don't have to say it. But the truth is that I'm getting pretty tired of everyone around here, and you're one of the only people I still don't hate. Doesn't that sound stupid?"

"It's not stupid." Suddenly he feels like he wants to save her. He thinks about the messes he has made elsewhere. About the damage he has done while believing he was acting noble and true and modern. Maybe a little childish romanticism is the key after all. This Dixie Doyle—maybe she is one he can save.

He would like to offer her something. She deserves to have something.

"You know what?" he says, and his words are a gift wrapped in curling ribbons. "If things were a little different. If I weren't married. Then there's nothing that could hold me back."

And the second after he says this, he regrets it. She lights up from the inside like a brand-new jack-o'-lantern.

"Really?" she says.

"Oh, Jesus. I shouldn't have said that. I'm sorry. That was inappropriate."

"Yeah, it was, kind of. But I don't mind. I think you really meant it too."

"Dixie, can you not tell anyone about this?"

"Come on, who would I tell?"

"Oh god." It all plays out in his head. The call over the

loudspeaker from Mrs. Mayhew. No, not Mrs. Mayhew. The other one. (Poor Mrs. Mayhew!) The conversation in hushed, acerbic tones. The sneer of disgust. How could you? Sibyl and her brutal, smoky laugh. Ted Hughes shaking his head at him in the hall. Really, Binhammer? Little girls? I thought you were the one with self-control. The other girls, steering themselves away from him in the halls—out of reach of the pervert who molested Dixie Doyle. His wife driven into a panicked evaluation of her own complicity in his degenerate decadences—tearful calls to her mother, a woman on her own third marriage. You never know what kind of monster you're going to get.

It's all right there, just behind his eyes like a movie run at high speed.

Dixie is now up, reenergized, and heading toward the door.

"I think I'm going to walk home. It's not too cold—it's perfect walking weather. Have a great night, okay, Mr. Binhammer? I'll see you tomorrow."

And when he looks up again, all he can see is the little flip of her pleated skirt as she bounces through the doorway and off to the land of teenage girlhood where secrets are currency and Dixie has just become a very wealthy girl.

chapter 34

In the works of Thomas Hart Benton, Liz Warren always sees distorted grandeur—that is, things distorted into grandeur and not the other way around. Here is one such painting. In the corner a group of musicians, their legs wavy with reverberation like the strings they are strumming, the background a wheat field that is serving them up as though on the end of a giant tongue. In the center a farmer with a scythe looking rugged and noble but with eyes that have nothing in them. He is captured in mid-swing. Here, every little action looks like ecstasy. Cartoonish. The sublime and the ridiculous brought together. All our noble deeds, all our silly little gestures . . .

That just about sums things up, Liz imagines.

She is surrounded by Thomas Hart Benton. The whole room is Thomas Hart Benton, part of an exhibit called *America: The Epic of Diminishment*. She came by herself, this Saturday morning, her mother calling out after her as she closed the door behind her, "Are you going to meet your friend there?" Her mother is under the impression that she and Jeremy Notion are still dating. She doesn't know how to tell her otherwise, and she resents having to think about it.

Meanwhile Dixie Doyle is telling her to fuck a bank president—by which she means, presumably, someone as dull, crusty, and barnacled as Liz herself. Silly Dixie and her lapdog Jeremy Notion leaning against the gate. That's all the boy ever does—lean against things.

So maybe she should fuck a banker. She looks around at

the men in the room—many of them gray-haired, some of them wearing sport jackets. As long as he didn't smell like her grandfather, the tinge of the grave always on his breath. One man, standing next to her, is wearing a bow tie. Dixie would approve.

Yes, maybe she should fuck a banker. There are worse ways to lose your virginity. And suddenly her virginity seems to her like a painting by Thomas Hart Benton—colorful and absurd, a stormy sky and a landscape that recedes forever, something blown up out of proportion by the buckled mirror of a fish-eye lens. Spectacular and ridiculous.

You only think about your virginity until you lose it. And then it's like a child getting a shot at the doctor's office, the pain forgotten by dinnertime. That's where she would like to be, sitting at dinner, unvirgined, not even thinking about it enough to quaintly reminisce. Just like a child with a little soreness in the behind that's gone by morning.

She looks around again. The crowds of people, like birds, standing in little chirping flocks in front of the paintings.

Then she spots someone she recognizes. It's Mr. Hughes, her English teacher, standing in a corner pointing to a painting. He is talking to two slender women about her mother's age—except they're different somehow. These women seem dressed too nicely for looking at art in a museum. They keep touching their hair and laughing gaily at everything Mr. Hughes says. At first, she wonders if he's giving them a tour—something about the way he points to sections of the painting and then folds his hands in front of him when the women ask questions. But then she sees him trying to edge away and realizes the two women have him trapped there in the corner.

She wonders if he likes to be around those women. She wonders, if he were given a choice of looking at Thomas Hart Benton with two full-grown women or one teenage girl, which he would pick.

He is not a banker, but maybe this is what Dixie Doyle meant after all. The two of them, Mr. Hughes and Liz, are above convention, aren't they? He is not married. (She wonders why.)

She is not a beautiful girl, she knows, but her skin is smooth where the skin of these women is wrinkled.

How do single men decide what girls to seduce? Do they think about it for a long time first, turning it over and over in their heads as they sit in their spartan apartments buttering their toast and gazing out the window? Or does it all happen on the spur of the moment, a light switch going on in their heads and suddenly they're trying to kiss you?

She approaches the trio of adults slowly, pretending to look at the pictures and watching him out of the corner of her eye. She is almost right next to them before Mr. Hughes notices her.

"Liz?"

"Oh, Mr. Hughes. I didn't see you. What are you doing here?"

"I'm here to see the exhibit."

"Sure, right. That makes sense. I mean, why else would you be here?" She can hear the words tumbling out of her mouth. She can't stop them.

"Oh," one of the women says, "is this one of your students, Ted? She's adorable!"

The two women lean back and smile at her as though they are admiring a baby in a bassinet.

While they gape, Mr. Hughes presses between them, moving closer to Liz and looking relieved.

"Adorable? She's more than that. This is Liz Warren. The legend of Carmine-Casey Academy for Sagacious Young Women. She has the merit badge for precociousness."

Liz doesn't know whether she likes that or not. Precocious is what they call smart people before they are old enough to be taken seriously. She is embarrassed.

He moves closer beside her so that it's the two of them facing the women.

"Liz," he says, "Bessie was just saying . . . I'm sorry, Bessie, was it?"

"Betty," reminds the one with the gray streak. "And this is Violet."

"Right. Betty and Violet were just telling me that they find Benton's work to be indulgent. What do you think, Liz? Do you think Thomas Hart Benton is indulgent?"

"Well," Betty says, "of course we're not connoisseurs. We're just a couple of girls who like to look at pictures." They nod at each other and dissemble. Their opinions, they suggest, are modest.

Liz stands still, glad no one is expecting her to answer the question posed. But she comes up with an answer anyway in case she should have to deliver one later.

While the two women are giggling to each other, reaching out to squeeze Mr. Hughes's forearm, he leans down and whispers to her, "Stay close. These two are scorpions."

And it's true. They keep trying to sidle up to Mr. Hughes, pushing Liz out of the way. The one called Betty gives her dirty looks when Mr. Hughes isn't looking. And once, when she has Liz to herself in a corner, she says, "I bet you have a crush on your teacher. Well, I think that's sweet. But he's a grown-up, you know."

Finally, Mr. Hughes and Liz leave the two women behind at the top of the front steps, waving and calling, "It was so nice to meet you, Ted, and your lovely student too!"

Liz cringes, as she has every time they referred to her as his student.

"Where are you headed?" Mr. Hughes asks as they make their escape.

"Across the park."

"Me too. I'll walk with you a little ways."

"Okay." She shrugs. His coat is unzipped because the sun is shining, and he is wearing a plain brown sweater underneath. And jeans and tennis shoes. She is not used to seeing him this way. He looks younger dressed like this. If she fixes her face, if she tries to appear casual and experienced, then the two of them might look no more than ten years apart, walking together through the park.

"Were those your friends?" she asks.

"Betty and Veronica?"

"Violet."

"No. They weren't my friends. They're urban predators. They prowl museums, ballets, and poetry readings."

"They didn't seem so bad." She feels obligated to say it. But she likes the description, likes being next to him while he excludes others—as though she has passed a test. As though if they sat down on one of these park benches, he could exclude the whole world, one by one, until it's just the two of them remaining.

"Not to you. But single men are like guppies to them. They have nets, and they take men home and put them into glass bowls."

She laughs at this, and he looks at her, appearing to enjoy her laughter. She wants to be careful. It's like she's walking across a floor of glass. Any thoughtless step could send her crashing down.

"So," he resumes, "what about you? Do you always go to the museum by yourself? Couldn't get any of your friends interested in Thomas Hart Benton?"

"I don't know," she says. "Monica—you know Monica Vargas?—she's with her father this weekend. But I don't really like to go to museums with other people. I hate waiting for them to catch up—or for them to wait for me. It never seems like I'm moving at the right speed."

He nods and looks into the distance. Then she wonders if she has made a faux pas.

"I mean," she corrects herself, "it wasn't like that with you."

He still doesn't say anything.

"I like Thomas Hart Benton a lot," she continues. "I read a book about him. Did you know he designed movie sets? Wouldn't you love to see those movies? I tried to rent some, but I couldn't find them."

This makes him smile. He says, "Can you picture him as a set designer? Him wheeling in this massive tortured landscape and the director shaking his head and saying, 'All we needed was a simple cornfield.' "

They walk some more, and when they come to the edge of a lake they realize they have gotten distracted and lost track of their destination. They turn around and follow a winding trail leading back through some thick undergrowth.

When they are sure they are walking west again, she decides to ask him a question.

"Can I ask you something? You don't have to answer it if you don't want to. I mean, it's really none of my business. But I was just wondering . . . why you never got married."

He gives her some perfunctory answer, one that she might have written for him if he were a minor character in a play—the kind of character that beautifies the background scenery of a heroine. And the answer might have made her feel elided, snipped off at the base, if it weren't for the fact that right before he says it, he gives her a look—a look that keeps coming back as he speaks, first about why he never got married and then about the number of dogs and strollers in the park.

She even sees that same curious, knitted expression when he doesn't think she can see him looking at her, when she stops at a bench to tie her shoe.

I am aware of you. I think I know what you are doing. Do I know what you are doing? That's what the expression says. Just the edge of a question. Enough hesitation to make her feel impressive somehow.

But then she is embarrassed again and folds her arms across her chest. It is possible that he sees her as cute and harmless—that he recognizes her words for the trembling, pathetic offerings that they are and that he is only humoring her. If that's true, then she is prepared to hate him. She will go home and write about how much she despises him.

Her stomach begins to hurt at this and, standing at the crest of a footbridge, she stops and stretches. She pictures her nerves as little parasites, all mouth, eating away at her insides.

He stops a few paces ahead of her and turns to wait. "You

know what?" he says, evaluating the brief entirety of her short life with his eyes, "I'm glad you like Thomas Hart Benton."

He nods his head as if deciding something. "Yes," he continues, "that seems perfect to me. Let's say that Thomas Hart Benton is yours and nobody else's."

He can see into her. He knows of the wild turbulences that pass like weather systems through her mind. He can see the people who reside inside her heart, the tangles of men and women dancing, their limbs sweat-locked and organic, like vines trellising up around her lungs, squeezing her so hard she can feel it whenever something beautiful happens. Little girl. Her father's voice, always echoing in her bones, that low deep-down rumbling. Oh that she could move the earth in such a way! Little girl, come and look at this. Squatting next to her father in her sunflower dress, looking at what he has in his hand. A crawling thing in his cupped palm. Like her. Writhing like the musicians in the painting. Thomas Hart Benton and his westward expansion beating like a tribal blood in her ears. Those feral Americans! Those grounded angels, twisting upward as though they knew what religion was—the machines of their bodies, the oily gears of their toil. And Ted Hughes can see it all. He can see right through her. She, a walking vivisection. All skin. All skin.

They walk a little farther, neither saying anything for a few minutes. When he sees her looking at her watch, he says, "You should get home."

"I know, it's okay. Look, there's the street."

"I should be going too."

They have almost reached the other side of the park. But to get to it they have to walk down a slope to an underpass that is shadowed from the sun. Sometimes violinists play here because the sound is cavernous and rises up through the park like the music of the tarmac itself.

There are no musicians playing here now, however, and as they walk through it toward the bright half circle at the other end, their footfalls are gravelly and resonant, as though they have discovered each other in the warm wet gullet of a beast.

chapter 35

It is a widely acknowledged fact that the girls who live farther away and whose commutes depend upon the sched-
ules of hourly trains generally arrive at school earlier than
girls who live around the corner and feel no great fear about
oversleeping. Indeed, some of the Carmine-Casey girls travel
from as far away as Connecticut. Each morning, they land
in front of the building having traveled on commuter trains
and then in taxicabs from Grand Central, weary and serious
as gray-eyed investment bankers, nodding hello to the security guard and to the maintenance men sweeping the lobby.
They arrive before the teachers and before the administrators.
Theirs are the first echoing footfalls down the halls between
the darkened doorways of the classrooms. Sometimes they
nap before the others arrive, curled on top of their own jackets, their hands prayer-wise between their knees, their book
bags acting as pillows.

It is one of these girls, Darcy Kimmel, a sophomore, who
on Tuesday morning finds the words spray-painted across the
third-floor lockers. Portrait-sized and red, the letters span fifteen
lockers, hers one of them. She stands before them with the quiet
satisfaction of a discoverer, taking in the whole meanness of the
scrawled message:

DIXIE DOYLE ♥S COCK

Her mouth shapes the words in silence. She sniffs and scratches her nose. She knows she should tell someone, but she doesn't want to leave her post lest someone else get credit for the discovery. Instead, she touches her fingertips to the K, and they come back red. Later she will be found in the office, holding her two red fingers up and offering herself to the administration as evidence in the investigation. "It was still wet," she will say. "I must've just crossed paths with the perpetrator."

Before second period is over, Carl the maintenance man has already scrubbed the words away with a chemical solvent that leaves behind an odor so acrid that he has to open the windows to let the cold winter air purify the space once again.

But by that time, everyone has already seen the message. The girls themselves are stirred into a frenzy of delight and speculation. Who might have committed such an act? The Bardolph boys have penises, and they are the first ones suspected of breaking into the building and spraying their boyishness all over the lockers. That would make sense, too, since Dixie Doyle has been known to flirt shamelessly with those boys and probably deserves whatever she gets. The boys are evoked in dramatic ways, pictured sneaking through the empty hallways with their khaki pants and their parted hair.

Some of the girls, the kind who always look for clever reversals in life, suspect Dixie Doyle herself of writing the words as a way to get attention and sympathy—or perhaps because she really does love cock and can't help herself from scrawling her desire on the walls of the school.

Other girls don't speculate at all. Many are discomposed by the grammar of the word *cock*: having only recently gotten used to the prospect of reckoning with a single cock, or maybe even a series of cocks over the course of their near future, they are arrested in contemplation of cock as an abstract quantity like tungsten or foliage. What is it that Dixie Doyle loves? Not *a* cock or *many* cocks, but rather the general quantity of cock as it exists in all the pants of the world.

Chins resting on fists in their first-period classes, they measure their own reactions in secret: On the issue of cock, taken altogether, where do I stand?

The faculty, for the most part, remain silent with regard to the vandalism. Ms. Carmichael merely shakes her head. Mrs. Landry is sullen and serious, and the girls know to stay out of her way when she is like that. "We'll have to write a letter to the parent body," she says to her assistant. Ms. Lockhart is overheard giving a sharp, cynical chuckle when she sees the graffiti, mumbling mysteriously to herself, "Men are magic, girls. They do cast spells."

Even Mr. Binhammer, normally so eager to discuss any and all controversy at the school, is unusually tight-lipped on the matter—even nervous, which leads some girls to speculate that he may have done it himself. But why? Well, say a few, it's obvious, isn't it? It's a lover's quarrel.

Which is exactly what Binhammer himself is worried everyone thinks. The timing. It seems impossible to him that it could be simply a coincidence. Four days after his grotesque declaration to Dixie Doyle, and now this. He can picture the information traveling, becoming sullied and strained as it moves from ear to outraged ear. Until it gets to someone who has a grudge against Dixie and wants to see her abomination with the teacher writ large. Surely everyone knows. He tries to read it in their faces, the shadow of his sin. He feels sick.

In the teachers' lounge, too, the subject is bandied about enthusiastically. Except for Walter, who shakes his head sadly at the vulgarity of girls these days and recalls a time when a girl wouldn't know a cock from a rooster, everyone seems pleased to have something to discuss apart from grading semester finals.

"The real clue to the culprit," Ted Hughes says to Lonnie Abramson and Pepper Carmichael, who sit side by side on the couch gazing up at him, "is the S."

"The S?"

"Just consider it. Who would add the S after the heart? Think about our girls. You've read their papers. You've seen the things they scrawl in the margins of their notes. How many of them would take the care to conjugate a heart symbol?"

Lonnie nods.

"It's true," Pepper says. "They would take the S as implied."

"What do you think, Binhammer?" Ted Hughes asks.

Binhammer shrugs, feeling his throat tightening. There are some things you cannot come back from, he thinks. There are such things as permanencies. He sees clearly his demise at the school, his humiliation and embarrassment, the end of his marriage, his inability to find a position teaching elsewhere, his relocation to one of those states in the middle of the country. Nebraska or Arkansas. A job at the post office, or as a short-order cook, a one-room apartment overlooking a parking lot. The life of a pariah. There are some doors that close and lock for good.

How does he talk to these people, knowing that as soon as the story comes out they will refuse to speak to him? He anticipates their outrage, their disdain, and a little ball of wretchedness burns in his belly. He clutches the edge of the table and puts a hand to his stomach.

"Are you all right?" Lonnie says.

"I'm fine, fine," he says. "Just a little nausea. It'll pass, it's nothing."

"I can cover your classes for you, if you need to go home."

"Thanks, but don't worry about it. I'll be fine."

He pictures her kindness melting away with the discovery of his crimes. How did it happen so quickly? Where was the moment—did he miss it?—the moment when he stepped foot outside society and became a monster? He has unleashed something. Not just the witchy, incantatory graffiti. Not just the moment with Dixie Doyle on Friday. Not just that. It happened before. Years ago. A seed was planted. He bore inside him the black organic blossom of a man who could say disgusting things to girls.

He would give anything to return to Friday and redo it—to edit out just that one sentence, slice it away like a cancerous cell before it has a chance to infect everything. But for all the tangles in his life that slip easily around each other and refuse to catch or knot, there are such things as permanencies.

All around him, the building contracts like a muscle spasm. Binhammer can feel it, everyone can feel it. Like nerves in the knees. Something has *happened*. Everything becomes a clue to a mystery not yet defined. Every little thing has significance. On the chrome spout of the water fountain on the fifth floor, Miranda Siebold discovers a smear of lipstick, the color of which she is sure is not worn by any of the girls in the school. Zoe Cathcart, no matter how hard she looks, cannot find her compact mirror in the shape of a cat's head that she always keeps in the exact same zipper pocket of her bag. Freshman Lucy Polchak, whose locker was one of the vandalized, develops a rash on the inside of her thigh in exactly the same spot where—and she has never told anyone this—she let Lenore Spitzer kiss her when they were both in the third grade. Emmeline Davis and her best friend Emily Douglas get into a fight over a magnet in the shape of a chocolate bar, even though they had both agreed at the beginning of the year never to let their friendship be threatened by petty things.

Soon it becomes too much to bear, all these signs and portents, and a small group of three girls takes refuge from the fuss outside in the courtyard, despite the cold, underneath the sugar maple. They sit atop the picnic table, and their breath condenses in clouds when they speak.

After a while a fourth girl in pigtails joins them. She has just come from the fourth-floor office, where Mrs. Landry, the headmistress, has subjected her to a confusing series of questions, the purpose of which—to comfort or to accuse—the girl can't figure out.

"How are you doing, Dix?" Caroline asks.

"I miss Mrs. Mayhew," Dixie Doyle says. "Mrs. Landry smells like chalk and paper and dust and splinters. Every time I'm in her office, I feel like I want to put lotion all over myself."

They talk for a while about dry old Mrs. Landry and assure each other that they will have all died terribly romantic deaths before their skin becomes like that.

Then Dixie says, "I don't think it's fair. I don't heart cock."

"We know, Dixie," says Caroline.

"I mean, I don't have anything against it. But I don't heart it. At least I don't think I do. I've never even seen one up close."

"You haven't?" Beth Barber asks.

"Well, I've played around with them. Who hasn't? But I never got around to *studying* one. It's always dark, and they're always moving."

Beth nods.

"So I don't think it's fair to claim I heart them."

"Are we supposed to not heart them?" Andie Abramson says. She isn't making a proclamation. This is a real question, and the girls ponder it silently.

"That's the other thing I don't like about this," Dixie says. "It's one of those catch-33s."

"Twenty-twos," Andie says.

"I always heard it as thirty-three," Dixie says. "I'm pretty sure you're wrong. But anyway, it's like one of those. If you say you do heart cock, people make fun of you. And if you say you don't heart cock, people make fun of you."

"Who do you think wrote it, Dixie?" Caroline asks.

Dixie shrugs. "I don't know," she says. "I have enemies everywhere. Anyway, I'm tired of the whole thing. I wish the school year was over. Maybe if we close our eyes together it'll be June when we open them. Let's try it. Keep them closed until I say."

All four girls close their eyes tight. But Dixie opens hers early and leans back on her hands, looking up through the branches of the sugar maple into the flat gray sky. She wishes she had wings like an angel to fly over the rooftops of the city—then people would admire her as she has admired so many people. She would make them feel longing, and then they would know what it was like on the inside of her mind.

"Okay," she says eventually. "You can open your eyes. I think it's too cold out for magic."

chapter 36

The following week, on Monday, the summons that Binhammer is expecting from Mrs. Landry finally comes, after ten days of the event burning in his stomach like a stubborn coal. *If I weren't married, nothing could hold me back.* Those were his words. Put out there for everyone to hear, as though they were scrawled across a billboard. And why did he have to say "If I weren't married"? Isn't the more significant barrier the fact that he is her teacher? The fact that he is an educator entrusted by the parents of the community not to molest their children, even if those children *ask* to be molested? Why didn't he say that instead: If I weren't your teacher . . . Or, better yet, nothing at all.

The summons, when it comes, comes over the loudspeaker. "Mr. Binhammer, please call extension 4762. Mr. Binhammer, extension 4762." He leaps up from the couch in the teachers' lounge, his fingers itching to get it over with. "Mrs. Landry wants to see you," the secretary says when he dials. "She says it's important. Can you come up now?"

On his way up in the elevator he goes over the script in his head. The look of mild interest, as though nothing in the world could be wrong. Oh, really? What did she say I said? The laughter, waving his hand at the absurdity. Well, I think she may have misunderstood a little. If I weren't married? No—why would I say that? She asked me why I never had kids, and I was talking about my wife. I can't imagine how . . . I think at one point I said that if I weren't married I would be so miserable I would spend all my time giving homework. How that got twisted around in her mind, I can't imagine. She's a great kid. I like her a lot. I hope you don't have the wrong impression of her because of this. I think she's just overwrought—the vandalism and all. She's going to miss her friends when she goes off to college. I'll be happy to talk with her about it if you think I should. Or just let it drop if you think that's best.

Walking into the office, he presses his palm against his gut where the coal burns white-hot. Mrs. Landry is a tough woman, cut from the same cloth—no, hammered in the same foundry as Mrs. Mayhew had been. She has a face like the skeleton of a skyscraper, all rivets and seams. And when Binhammer comes into her office, she barks out, "Shut the door behind you."

The inquisition begins.

"I am sure you understand," Mrs. Landry begins, punctuating certain words with pauses in which her eyes staple him to his chair, "that Carmine-Casey has always been deadly serious about keeping its girls safe. There is no use educating them if at the same time we are also exposing them to . . . negative influences. Mrs. Mayhew believed it. Dr. Harrison believes it. I believe it."

"Of course." He is harrowed by this. He hoped that the talk would evolve along a different line—some questioning before getting to the bottom of things—but it seems to have jumped directly to the accusation. He must play dumb. He must stick to the script. "Absolutely."

"It used to be easier," she laments. "You made sure a girl dressed modestly, you made sure she had the fear of god in her with regard to boys, you made sure she got on the bus at the end of the day, and if you did those things, you were doing your job. Now things are different. It's the parents. The new status symbol is the degree of liberality with which you raise your children. Do you want to know something? I got a call from a parent just two weeks ago giving her ninth-grade daughter permission to leave school when her boyfriend, who is a freshman in college, came to pick her up in his car."

She shakes her head. He wants to say something—voice his sympathetic outrage—but he doesn't know what exactly she knows.

"In any case, that's neither here nor there. I may not be able to keep my girls safe after they leave this school, but I consider it my duty to keep them safe while they are within these walls. And"—hinging her head around slowly to stare into his soul—"in the hands of any representative of this institution."

Oh god.

She draws herself up again and takes a deep breath that sounds like the billows of a great steam engine. She folds her hands on her desk and leans forward, her bulky bosom dropping like a counterweight on the blotter.

"We have a problem."

"What's the, uh—what's the problem?"

"It has come to my attention that a serious faculty-student . . . indiscretion has taken place."

Just get it over with. He swallows hard. He begins thinking what his life will look like from now on. The fall, the humiliation. He feels dizzy. He wants to chew on his fingers.

"It's about Mr. Hughes. I may need you to take over some of his classes for a while."

"Mr. Hughes?" Like a dream in which you are running over a cliff but, miraculously, you don't fall.

She takes another deep breath. The mighty billows.

"It seems he spent the night with a student."

Everything adrift. A weightless moment. Looking down on the earth from miles above—and not recognizing a thing. Ted Hughes, the exalted and merry . . .

"But he wouldn't—I don't—"

"I'm only telling you this because you'll hear rumors. And I know you two have gotten close. The girl was seen coming out of his apartment building at two o'clock in the morning—the parents didn't even know until we spoke to them. The student was Liz Warren. You might as well know. It'll be no use trying to keep this from anyone."

Liz Warren. Ted Hughes and Liz Warren. Inconceivable. Binhammer could never even get her to unscowl.

Mrs. Landry pauses. His hands unclench, and he looks at them—a pale pink translucence with white underneath. Ghostly and pathetic.

"We talked to the girl, and she denied it. She obviously feels loyal to him. But when we spoke to him, he admitted to it. We asked for his resignation. He gave it."

He has shaken the hand of Ted Hughes, and he remembers it being a strong hand, but also long and cool. The hand of an artist. A hand that in touching things pushes them into the perspective of distance rather than drawing them into unfocused nearness.

"I see," he says.

"In any case, I have a list of his classes that don't conflict with yours. I've gotten the others to cover the other sections. I hope you won't mind helping out."

"Of course. Of course I don't mind."

On his way out, she says, "Oh, and one more thing. You may see him around. He's gathering his things. But I asked him to leave before the rumors take hold."

In the elevator back down to the teachers' lounge, he thinks once more about his own indiscretion and holds it up to Ted Hughes's. He feels not relief but instead a sense of being shown up again. Not that he would rather be in Ted Hughes's shoes now, but he has to admit, in the smallest, meanest places of his heart, there is some measure of rankling envy when he thinks about the man spending the night with his student. Setting her down on the bed and unbuttoning her top, like some diminished Henry Miller with his miniature Anaïs Nin. Hughes has done it again. Whatever weak gesture Binhammer may make in the direction of life, Hughes has already made it, sooner and larger.

He finds Ted Hughes in the classroom where he first saw him many months ago—when he went from room to room looking for him, peering at him through the narrow window in the door. Binhammer stood alone in the empty hall then, and he watched Ted Hughes speaking words like regurgitated nourishment to the upturned throats of nested featherless baby birds. Now everything has shifted, and Binhammer himself stands among the gawky bodies of students in the hall—and Ted Hughes sits alone at the front of an empty classroom. Ted Hughes, once so grandiose, now seems lonesome and small.

When he opens the door, Ted Hughes lights up like an electrical appliance after replacing a fuse it has blown. That moment of relief when everything suddenly works again. Except relief isn't what Binhammer feels.

"Binhammer! I've been looking for you."

"Goddamn you," Binhammer says. He can feel his own body, rigid, furiously aflame. His fingers could strangle, his feet could kick, his teeth could rip. "Goddamn you. You fucking disgusting pig—"

"Take it easy. What are you so upset about?"

"What am I—? Goddamn you. You fucked that girl. You fucked her." Binhammer moves toward him, and Ted Hughes backs up between the rows of desks. "And it's not cute and it's not charming—it's just perverse and vulgar. You're garbage."

"Wait, hold on—you don't get it."

"What don't I get?" Binhammer stops, inches from Ted Hughes, his fists clenched at his sides, his heartbeat loud in his ears, almost deafening.

"You don't get it, but you of all people should."

Afterward, Binhammer remembers only a few things. The weight of his arm, feeling like a slug of concrete, a feeling of the wind being knocked out of him, as though he were the one being punched instead of doing the actual punching, the clatter of the desks as Ted Hughes is driven back against them, toppling over onto the floor. And this, too: the immediate sense of remorse, a sickliness in his legs, the desire to sit down right there on the floor and never move again. Except that he is already out the door, pushing aside a few girls who, drawn by the noise, rush in to aid their fallen teacher.

chapter 37

The look on her face when she hears: a million little calamities in her eyes and her whole life tipped sideways.

"I can't listen," she says. "Don't tell me, I can't hear it."

"But—"

"You don't understand. Jesus, how could you understand? I feel . . ."

"What? What do you feel?"

"Diminished."

He says nothing.

"The two of you," she goes on. "You're beginning to look the same to me."

He wants to tell her—he wants something from her, though he does not know what. Explanation, maybe. Approval. Comfort, like a child. But she seems broken, more upset than he is himself. And when he finds himself beginning to defend Ted Hughes, he stops short.

They argue, she puts her face in her hands and does not allow him to come near her. He sits, seized by a curious paralysis. He can see things dissipating before his eyes. Everything turning to cloud and mote.

Eventually they sleep, but in the morning she is packing for a trip. She has been planning to go to Philadelphia to do some research. She was going to go in the spring, but she's decided to go now. She doesn't know for how long. She is sorry. She is culpable. She is implicated in the ugliness, and she cannot be around it right now. Not Ted Hughes, not Binhammer, none of it. She'll be all right. She'll call.

At school, he teaches by rote, letting most of his classes out early and not even bothering to show up to some. Cutting classes, like a sullen teenager. No one notices, as there are larger concerns.

He keeps expecting to turn the corner and find Ted Hughes standing there smiling—expansive and jolly. But even if it were to happen, Binhammer doesn't know what he would do. His hands ache, and it feels like all his guts and brains are in the joints of his knuckles. Lately all he seems to be able to do is wind his hands around each other.

"Binhammer," Pepper Carmichael says in the teachers' lounge, "what's the matter with you?"

"He misses his little friend," Sibyl says, her voice arrow-straight.

I would kill you if I knew how, he thinks. I would kill you if my hands would let me.

Liz Warren is out of school for a week. Later he hears she is not coming back, she is going to be graduated early. Mrs. Landry calls him to the office again to tell him. She thanks him again for covering Ted Hughes's classes temporarily and tells him she's interviewing for a replacement. But in the meantime, he should know about Liz Warren, and if there was any information he wanted to pass along to her, it should go through Mrs. Landry. In addition, would he mind letting his colleagues know about Liz's early graduation?

Outside the office, he is faced with a rushing fulmination of bodies—short and screeching, ruddy and soft. There are girls everywhere, and he is carried out into the current.

The slick and the faithful, Ted Hughes once said, referring to the student population, *the meek and the blighted*.

The rush of feather and claws around him, of nails and paint.

And suddenly he realizes that he despises them with an infantile rage. These girls with their accidental sexuality. Luxuriating in their irresponsibility. They are not to be held accountable—they have risen above accountability. *Did he kiss you?* They are always talking about some boy or another. *What else did he do? Do you think he's going to do it again?* As though they were speculating about an artist carving a piece of wood. Trying to figure out what shape this girl might take when he's finished with her. Giving like balsa in his hands.

Little fleshy protrusions so densely packed in the hallway that it's impossible not to brush against them. Somewhere behind him he hears them talking.

"I think this shirt makes my boobs look too big."

"I don't think so."

"You don't?"

"Why don't you ask Mr. Binhammer about it? He's right there."

"Stop it! Oh my god. I can't believe you said that!"

He, pretending not to hear. The voices retreating, giggling coarsely down the hall. These rafters are filled with femininity, like an infestation of bats crawling upside down inside his skull. Sometimes they drop sleeping to the ground with a pathetic plop, and then they struggle to right themselves. You reach out a hand to help and those teeth, like slivers of broken glass, sink into your skin.

Everywhere he looks, the arrogant pinkness of womanhood. The hive is abuzz. Cicadas in the bushes. So many locusts that they blacken the sky. He can feel their eyes burning into his back.

He had been wondering, upstairs, how to tell the others about Liz Warren—how to tell Sibyl and Lonnie and Pepper that the girl is gone for good. But when he opens the door to the teachers' lounge and finds them standing there in a furtive whispering circle, when they look up at him and hush themselves and metamorphose their expressions with great practiced smoothness into disapproving half smiles (*they were close, the two of them—he's just as bad as the other*), when he realizes that he can no longer tell the difference between their eyes and those of the vespine creatures in the hall—that's when he realizes he doesn't have to worry about how to tell them because they already know. They already know.

chapter 38

Adulthood feels like empty rooms with clocks ticking. It feels like being at home alone and suddenly becoming aware of the refrigerator when the motor shuts off. It feels like staring at the ceiling or straightening pictures or listening for the mailman.

When Liz Warren has had enough of conjuring up metaphors for adulthood, she puts on her coat and goes out. She has not been outside for three days, and the cold is surprising to her. She feels the icy air in her lungs and on her skin like tiny frozen clips biting at her all over.

Adulthood is like winter mosquitoes.

Sometimes she is tired of herself. So sick of herself that she would be happy to think of anything else in the world.

She enters the park in the dimming light of the late afternoon and walks the paths past the joggers until she comes to one of the playgrounds. There she stops and puts her fingers through the chain-link fence and watches a mother pushing her yellow-bundled baby on a swing. The woman makes faces at the baby at first, but after a while her mind wanders to other things and her gaze goes blank.

Walking in the direction of Carmine-Casey, Liz goes past the boat pond where a thin layer of ice grays the surface of the water, and then up to the concrete dais where the large bronze sculpture of Alice in Wonderland sits atop a mushroom—a kind of metal Dixie Doyle, surrounded by a company of men: the March Hare, the Mad Hatter, the Dormouse, the Cheshire Cat.

And that's when she sees Mr. Binhammer sitting on one of the benches, something gone wrong with his eyes, as though they have been emptied out and filled back up with sculpted mud.

She is about to turn and leave when he sees her.

"Liz?"

"Hi, Mr. Binhammer."

"I was just . . . looking at the sculpture."

"Me too."

"Do you want to sit down?"

"Okay."

She has never been able to talk to this man—even under the best of circumstances—and now it seems impossible. What do they have to talk about? She is gone from the school—and she is sure he has heard the reason. She should be embarrassed, she supposes, but recently her mortification has been so great that it has numbed her.

She waits out the silence with him. They sit next to each other and say nothing, and they say nothing for such a long time that it becomes comfortable, sitting there and saying nothing with Mr. Binhammer.

After a long time, Mr. Binhammer speaks, and it is as though they have been conversing all along.

"Did you ever read *Alice in Wonderland*?"

"Once. I didn't like it."

"How come?"

"I don't know. I guess because there were no rules. It seemed like anything could happen. When anything can happen, nothing that does happens means anything."

He nods.

"I never read it myself," he says. "Isn't that funny? An English teacher who's never read *Alice in Wonderland*."

She does not know the response to this, so she keeps quiet.

"You want to know something else?" he asks. They are at the edge of the park, and he jerks his thumb in the direction of the school. "I have a class right now. I'm missing it."

"They'll be okay," she says, though she's not sure he wants reassurance.

"What about you, just wandering?"

"I'm supposed to meet my parents at the school. Later, when nobody's around. We have to have one more meeting with Mrs. Landry. But it's not for another two hours."

"Oh."

Again they say nothing for a long time. Her ears fill up with wind and cold as she discovers something: she likes being silent with Mr. Binhammer much more than she ever liked speaking to him.

Eventually, he says:

"Liz, listen—I want you to know that I'm sorry for what happened to you."

"You don't have to be sorry."

"I mean, I wish it hadn't happened."

"You don't have to wish that. It's all right."

She wants to tell him something, to explain something, but she's not sure what it is. It has something to do with her own lack of nervousness at this moment. And it has something to do with the way Mr. Hughes looked the last time she saw him. And it has something to do with a new feeling in her gut that she is someone other than simply Liz Warren, the sullen straight-A student.

The way things happened was this:

It was Sunday, the day of the Thomas Hart Benton exhibit. They walked on the paths in the park to the tunnel, and it was there that he kissed her. He took her and pushed her against the wall and the space between them was nothing—and she didn't have to worry about what to do or how she might be doing it wrong because he kissed as he lectured, overwhelmingly, until your mind went bare with brilliance. She closed her eyes and felt the cold hard stone through the back of her jacket. He held her face, his hands warm and unyielding, as though giving her no option for awkwardness or fear. He would take her and position her like a puppet. He would pose her beautifully, powerfully, as he did with characters in literature. And she could look upon herself and see something she hadn't seen before.

Then he stopped and she waited for him to do it again, but instead he pulled away and apologized.

"I'm sorry," he said. "I shouldn't have done that."

She wanted to tell him it was okay, but she thought the apology might just be an excuse for his disappointment in her. And besides, she didn't know how to reassure someone like Mr. Hughes. So she said nothing.

And then he was gone.

Afterward she looked inside of herself to see how she felt, and what she discovered there was loathing. She hated herself for not being natural like other girls who could just kiss boys and not think about it and not have them run away afterward as though they had been bitten by a snake. She hated herself and she hated girls like Dixie Doyle who managed somehow to turn their silliness into seduction. She had watched Dixie flirt with Mr. Binhammer, for example, parading her ridiculousness before him like a peacock, and Liz invariably thought Mr. Binhammer would see through it, would see Dixie for the twee cartoon character that she was. But instead he always seemed charmed by her—and she hated him for being charmed by her and hated her for knowing he would be charmed.

No doubt if Dixie were to be pushed up against a wall by Mr. Binhammer, she would know how to keep him from running away.

That was Sunday. The Monday and Tuesday after that she spent her time hating all the other girls in the school. In her mind, Liz added up all the things in the world she wanted but couldn't have. It was an impressive list, and she could feel each item in her stomach. Mired in embarrassment, she hid in the bathroom during Mr. Hughes's class so she wouldn't have to see him. She was afraid he would be kind to her—and the kindness would certainly be of an uninterpretable variety, laced with strands of pity and disappointment and fear of what she would do, who she would tell.

But she would tell no one. Why couldn't he understand that she would tell no one?

On Wednesday he found her in the hall and asked her to follow him to one of the empty classrooms.

When they were alone, he said, "I'm sorry."

"Okay."

"You haven't been in class."

"I've been sick."

"No, you haven't."

She shrugged and crossed her arms across her chest to keep him from seeing her trembling hands.

"Listen," he said. "I'm sorry."

"Stop saying that. Why do you keep saying that?"

He looked at her in a new way.

"You don't want me to be sorry?"

"I get it," she said. "You're not attracted to me. I understand."

"Is that what you think?"

"You don't have to worry. I'm not going to tell anyone."

He laughed, and she felt, as she did frequently, that she had misjudged something important.

"All right, Madame Bovary," he said.

He was going to say something else, but then the bell rang and students started coming in. For the next two days, she went to his class and sat in her seat and watched him teach and thought, I have kissed that man, I have kissed him on the lips and felt him like a leaning timber pinning me to a stone wall. And when his glance landed on her it was not disappointment or fear that she felt coming from those eyes.

On Friday she lingered in the lobby after school and pretended to be leaving just as he emerged from the elevator with his coat over his arm.

Outside on the steps, he said in a low voice, "Do you want to talk?"

"Okay. Where?"

"It can't be where someone could see us. Here."

He wrote something down on a torn half sheet of paper and handed it to her. It was an address.

"I'll meet you there," he said, "in an hour."

Yes, she thought. Something is happening. Something is finally happening. And when she arrived at his apartment he showed her his books, lined up neatly on the shelves, and offered her a glass of orange juice and told her how sometimes he could hear the people in the apartment above arguing in a foreign language. Then he sat next to her on the couch and explained that he was sorry if he had made her uncomfortable that day in the park but that he was not sorry he had kissed her.

"I've had boyfriends before," she said, by way of explaining her credentials. The plural was a stretch, but before Jeremy Notion there had been a boy in the third grade who labeled her his girlfriend for the duration of a week—so it was true in the strictest sense.

He smiled as if there were nothing she could say that would surprise him.

"I'm not sorry either," she said. "I mean about—about the park."

He smelled nice when he leaned in to kiss her again, different from the Bardolph boys who smelled mostly of sweat and acne cream. She closed her eyes and tried to mimic the motions of his mouth and tongue. She felt it was important to get things right, and she wondered whether her lips were too dry or whether she should take her glasses off or if that would ruin the moment. But then he put one hand around the back of her neck and tilted her face up to him so it was impossible to do anything but kiss him.

He stopped, once, and looked at her.

"We can't be boyfriend and girlfriend," he said. "You know that, right?"

"I know." She wasn't at all sure what she knew, but she didn't want to be someone who needed things explained to her.

He kissed her again and then stopped and got up and went to the window and looked out.

"It's getting dark," he said. "Your parents will wonder where you are."

"They're out of town," she said. In fact, they were at a dinner party on the West Side, but the lie was an easy one. She pointed to the shelf next to the television set. "You have a lot of movies."

"Do you want to watch one?"

So he ordered Chinese food and they watched *The Third Man*, and she didn't tell him she'd already seen it because he seemed excited to introduce her to it.

Afterward, he said, "What do you want to do now?" and she shrugged.

In the other room his phone rang and he went to answer it. For a few minutes, she listened to his half of the conversation. The words were light and meaningless and she didn't like how they excluded her. So she walked down the hall and found him sitting on the edge of the bed, the phone to his ear. She stopped in the doorway, leaning against the jamb. They looked at each other through the thin veil of his conversation. He smiled at her. Then she went and sat by him on the bed and leaned back, supporting herself on her palms. When he hung up the phone, she looked at him, and she made her eyes tell him it was okay. He could. It was okay. She lay back for him. And now her mind was going like mad, and she wondered if her breath smelled like General Tso's chicken, and she wondered if she should go to the bathroom first, and she wondered if she would bleed like Sylvia Plath did in *The Bell Jar*, though she also knew not to be disappointed because many girls didn't bleed at all, she heard. She wondered if he would do everything, or if there were things she would be expected to do, like unbutton his shirt for him or put her hands on his back. She didn't want to be a little girl about any of it, and she was proud that she didn't feel like crying at all, not even a little, because that was such a cliché. And then her clothes were off and his were off, and he moved her around on the bed, which was good because she didn't want to figure out where to go, and then she felt something against her thigh and she thought, Something is happening, yes, something is really and truly happening, and this moment can run on and on and wrap itself in thinking all it likes because this is a physical thing, an organic thing, a thing of carbon and blood and physics, and there's nothing that will stop it now, not even my calamitous brain. And she waited for it in the dark, and then she felt it, like a pressure between her thighs—it was inside her, *inside her,* and it was happening, and she was thinking of a million things, of ambulances below on the street, of James Joyce and John Donne, of Orson Welles and that whistling tune from *The Third Man,* of her fingernails and how she should stop biting them, of cartoon characters and world wars and calculus exams and music that made her chest heavy. And then there was something that replaced the thinking, like a drain had opened in her head and all the million words and images swirled away, because she was aware of her stomach and her legs and her toes, and the way her hands gripped the shoulders of this man, this man, and the way her nipples felt when his chest brushed against them, and everything else went away except her ankles and her spine and her belly and her teeth and—

Afterward, she went to the bathroom and turned on the light and looked at herself in the mirror. There was no hurry in her gut now. Just a peacefulness.

"Not a virgin," she whispered.

She wondered why she couldn't think of a word that meant "not a virgin," and then she thought maybe being a virgin was like being French: there was no word for not being French. And she breathed in deep and breathed out and examined her eyes very carefully in the mirror and was pleased to find that she was still the same except for the parts of her mind and body that weren't.

She felt restful and good, and she went and lay down next to him in the bed.

He asked if she was all right, and she said she was fine.

She told herself that she would only stay a little while longer, looking up at the dark ceiling and making sense of a few things.

There was no need for clamor or spite. It had been revealed to her that everyone on earth was gorgeously fallible. Men she had equated with gods or industries fell asleep, apparently, with their heads on their arms. She had seen it now. She knew.

She had finally done something. And the gaze of the world seemed all of a sudden more benign.

But she fell asleep and someone saw her coming out of the building at two o'clock in the morning, and Mrs. Landry called her into the office on Monday, and things had gone desperately wrong for Mr. Hughes after that, and she stayed at home for a week thinking how she ruined the life of a man whom she respected and admired above all others.

And now she sits on a bench next to another teacher who keeps apologizing to her as though she were the victim.

"You don't have to be sorry," she says.

"I mean, I wish it hadn't happened."

"You don't have to wish that. It's all right."

She wants to explain it to him. But she doesn't have the words.

"The thing is," she tries, "you go through life feeling towered over by things. Giants and skyscrapers and mountains. But then you get up close to them, and you realize they're tiny. They fit in your hand. Everything that seems big is actually small. That's the joke. I didn't get it before."

He looks confused for a moment, but then a smile spreads across his face and he chuckles as though something has been decided—and they gaze together at the bronze sculpture of Alice in her frozen Wonderland.

"It's because you're getting older," he says. "And that's funny, because me?—I feel like I've been kicked in the stomach for my lunch money."

She would like to tell him something else, since she may not see him again. Something about how she liked being in his class even though it didn't always look like it.

So she tries, and she doesn't have the words exactly, but the ones she does have, they do all right.

chapter 39

A t the end of the day, the school empties its students all at once—dumps them out through the lobby doors where they linger on the sidewalk in clots. Teachers heading home press through the tight knots, though it is too loud for any of the girls to hear them say, "Excuse me." Instead, it is acceptable practice for the adults to apply a little pressure to the backpacks suspended from the girls' shoulders—physical force without bodily contact.

Recently, the teachers can sense in the girls an even greater reluctance than normal to disperse immediately after school. The school has become a place of secrets and violence and ghosts—like a church except not as many angels. Things are happening in this place of stolid book learning. Scandals have the potential to spread exponentially in the five-minute gaps between classes, so that in the course of a school day, the entire population shares a common account. Even accurate, more or less. The girls have a great intolerance for misinformation. They do not want to be forced to revise the scenarios they conjure up in their heads.

But after a while when no news is brought down from behind the closed doors of the headmistresses' offices where confidential summits are taking place, the girls lose interest and drift off—until there is only one girl left over, looking up at the windows of the school, her pigtailed head arched back and gazing longingly as though she were the one remaining mother waiting on the platform for her soldier son who did not arrive on the last train of the day. She has a lollipop poking out of her mouth, and every now and then she gives it an absent suck.

"*Bon soir*, Dixie," says Madame Millet-Johnson as she comes out through the doors and down the steps to the street.

"Good night," she replies. She and the French language are like summer camp friends—once inseparable but now unable to withstand the practical realities of the nonidyllic everyday life of young womanhood.

Alone, Dixie Doyle looks both directions up and down the street, her hands stuffed in the pockets of her favorite coat, which has a white furry collar that used to be sparkly before the sparkles rubbed off on her hair and cheeks. With her tongue, she shifts the lollipop from one side of her mouth to the other. Then she turns around and looks back up at the windows.

She crosses the street and sits on a stoop and leans her head against an ironwork gate. She doesn't know what she is waiting for, but she is not ready to go home. And sometimes looking at the empty building calms her. She hums a tune for which she only knows some of the words:

> *Frère Jacques, Frère Jacques,*
> *Dormez-vous? Dormez-vous?*

Then she sees something. A girl coming from the direction of the park, walking without haste and gazing straight ahead, climbs the steps of Carmine-Casey and goes in through the doors. It is Liz Warren. Dixie hasn't seen her since the day before the news trickled down about her and Mr. Hughes. Some say Liz has been expelled. Others say she's had a nervous breakdown.

Dixie gives her lollipop a suck.

"Huh," she says.

Another five minutes go by, and then she seems to decide something. She looks up and down the street and crosses over and again leans back through the doors into the lobby of the school. Then up in the elevator to the fourth floor where the administrative offices are. Peering in through the window in the office door, she can see through the secretarial vestibule to the headmistresses' offices at the back. All the doors are still closed. These are classified meetings—parents, teachers, students. Liz Warren is probably in there somewhere. In one of those rooms. Surrounded by tall figures of authority who are tiptoeing around the questions they really want to ask.

They are ridiculous, Dixie knows. You don't have to tiptoe around Liz Warren. She's tougher than all of them. If she wants to talk about it, she'll talk about it. She's no victim. And you're not going to convince her she is.

Dixie sighs and turns back slowly toward the elevators. But then, through a slit window in one of the classroom doors, her eye catches the girl sitting by herself. On top of a desk, dangling her feet and leaning back on her palms. Staring at the ceiling as though bored. Liz Warren herself.

Dixie checks to confirm that Liz is alone in the room and then opens the door and steps in.

"What do you want?" Liz asks. Her voice sounds aggressive, but her heart's not in it.

"How come you're in here?" The door closes behind Dixie.

"I'm waiting."

"They told you to wait in here?"

"Do you want something?"

"No." Dixie considers her lollipop briefly and grimaces. She tosses it into the trashcan and marches straight over to Liz, pulls away the desk directly in front of the girl, and sits down on top of it, facing her. She leans back on her palms, and for a moment the girls look like two mirrored statues at the entrance of an Egyptian tomb. But then, seemingly aware of this, Liz folds up her legs and leans forward.

"You know what I hate?" Dixie says. "I hate those kids who cheat on the SAT. I mean, isn't that pathetic? Why can't they just take the test like everyone else?"

Liz stares at her. Dixie's words are apropos of nothing, but she is trying to reach out to Liz, and she knows Liz likes to criticize things. She thinks maybe they could criticize something together. And cheating seems like something in particular that Liz would like to criticize.

"You know, I had the chance to cheat on the SAT. My Uncle Peter the drunk knows this girl who takes the exam for you if you pay her five hundred dollars. But she must owe him a favor because she was going to do it for me for only two hundred. He's probably her drug dealer, if you want to know the truth. Anyway, they were going to set it all up, but I said no way. I take my own tests. I may be of average intelligence, but I'm not *tacky*."

"Dixie," Liz says, putting a hand to her forehead, "can you just leave me alone?"

"I'm just trying to be nice. We did that whole play together, and everyone said we did a great job with it. And now since you're in trouble, I thought—"

"Oh god. Why do you think you can talk to me about this?"

"I'm just trying to—"

"Well, don't. Don't try."

Dixie straightens her back and leans in, pointing her finger at Liz's chest. She has had enough. "You can be a real bitch, you know that? I know what you think. You think I spend all my time being mean to people and that you're some kind of moral superhero swooping down to make people feel better. But you don't make anyone feel better. You just make them feel worse in a different way."

"Shut your mouth," Liz says, her voice trembling with quiet outrage.

"No. Why don't you shut *your* mouth for once. And now you think that just because you fucked a teacher even your stupid teenage angst is better than everyone else's. Big deal. You think you're the only one who's ever fucked her teacher? You're not even the only one in this room. Well, almost."

The door opens suddenly, and Dixie sees Mrs. Landry filling up the doorway. The headmistress seems surprised to find Dixie there.

"Oh, hello Dixie." Then, turning her attention to Liz and speaking in tones of implied gravity. "Liz, your parents are still in with Dr. Harrison. I'm sorry this is taking so long. We should be ready for you in about five minutes." The woman gives Dixie one more hesitant glance before retreating and letting the door close behind her.

Liz stares down at the floor. Her arms are crossed over her stomach.

Dixie doesn't like to see her like this. She is surprised to discover how much she misses the Liz Warren from a few days ago. The sulky, nasty, clever Liz Warren.

"I'm sorry," Dixie says. "I didn't mean to—"

"That's okay. Forget it. I didn't mean anything either."

Dixie nods. The other girl still won't look at her, so she rises from the desk and smoothes the front of her skirt. Then she reaffixes the ponytails in her hair and heads toward the door. She's almost out of the room when Liz stops her.

"You too, huh?"

"What?"

"You too? With who? What teacher?"

"Oh. That. You can't tell anyone."

"*Dixie.*" She makes a wide shrugging gesture to everything around her—the absurdity of Dixie's admonition.

Dixie sits back down on the desk in front of Liz, and the two girls lean forward conspiratorially.

"Well, everyone knows I have a crush on Mr. Binhammer."

Liz nods, and Dixie checks herself.

"You're in that class. Don't you think he's stunning?"

"Stunning." Liz smiles. "Sure."

Liz laughs a little, but not in a mean way. If Dixie had an older sister named Liz Doyle, that's how she imagines Liz Doyle might laugh at her. And even though Dixie would put on a performance of being insulted, secretly she would do things to entertain Liz Doyle and make her laugh like that.

"Can I ask you a question? What was it like? With Mr. Hughes, I mean."

"I don't know. It was something I just decided to do. That's what they don't get." Gesturing with a thumb back toward the administrative offices. "They think I'm suffering posttraumatic stress disorder. But it was a decision I made. And so I wasn't surprised. The next day, when it was all over, all I could think was 'This is the man who understands Emma Bovary, the man who can tell you what Elizabeth Bennet is thinking. This is the man who talks about Tess of the d'Urbervilles as though he used to be in love with her. So what does he want with me?' Isn't that funny?"

Dixie looks confused, smiling and screwing up her eyes as though she's trying hard to picture what Liz feels.

"And," Liz adds, confidingly, "his skin smelled like chalk."

Dixie lights up with this information. She crinkles her nose and can't figure out if she likes this detail or not. The dry, dusty chalk clouds of teachers. She imagines Mr. Binhammer's palm enclosing her cheek, his own smell of chalk.

"What about you?" Liz says then. "You and Binhammer."

"Oh. Well, we never did anything. I mean, we almost did. We talked about it. We discussed it. But we decided it was best not to give in to temptation. You're lucky Mr. Hughes is single. Mr. Binhammer said if he wasn't married, nothing could hold him back."

"He said that?"

"Uh-huh."

"Isn't it funny?" Liz says, looking wistful. "Isn't it funny? These men?"

"Yeah," Dixie agrees, though she isn't entirely sure what Liz means.

"You think you're going to get a look at something new. You think that the adult world is going to be like Oz—once you're through the door everything is suddenly going to be in color. You find someone to take you there, and it's like going to a different country. But when you land on the other side you realize you haven't gone anywhere at all. You're back where you started. There aren't any new colors."

"Yeah," Dixie says again. Despite the fact that she feels she *has* gotten a glimpse of a new world. She *has* seen new colors.

Things look different to her now. Don't they? But maybe that's the difference between having sex with a teacher and *almost* having sex with a teacher. Maybe for her the cycle never completed itself. Maybe her new world is just the old one in a good disguise.

Liz is a smart girl. Dixie trusts her judgment.

"Dixie, listen," Liz says. "The graffiti . . ."

"I don't heart cock, you know."

"I know. It wasn't nice. I'm sorry."

"It's okay," Dixie says, embarrassed. "I'm sure it was just someone who—"

"Dixie, listen to me. *I'm sorry.*"

For a moment she doesn't understand. And then she does.

"You?" she says. The image of Liz doing such a thing, when she tries to form it in her head, keeps snapping in half. It doesn't seem right. The circuit shorts itself. "But—you?"

Liz nods.

"Why?"

"I was confused. It was while everything was happening with Mr. Hughes. I mean, before it happened but after it started happening. I thought he didn't like me. He kissed me in the park, but then . . . never mind, it's stupid. I was jealous of you."

"Jealous?"

"You and Mr. Binhammer. The way you two are with each other."

Hearing this makes Dixie immeasurably happy.

Just then Mrs. Landry comes in again and tells Liz they are ready for her.

"I'm coming," Liz says. "I'll be there in a second."

Only Liz can get away with talking like that to Mrs. Landry. The headmistress looks as though she might say something more but decides against it and heads back across the hall.

Yes, Liz knows the colors of the world.

"Look at us," she says. "Liz Warren and Dixie Doyle. Civil."

"Civil," Dixie nods.

Liz gathers herself up.

"Dixie Doyle," she says again in a singsong way, chuckling under her breath as she walks toward the door.

"I know it's a silly name," Dixie says. "They were the only kind of cups I was allowed to use when I was a little girl. 'A Dixie for Dixie.' My aunt lived with us when I was growing up and we were both named Elizabeth, so they started to call me Dixie after the cups."

"You're kidding. Your name is Elizabeth?"

Dixie nods.

"I can't believe it."

"What?"

"Our name."

"Hey, we're two Elizabeths!"

"What do you know."

This fact seems to please Dixie as much as anything else, and Liz leaves her nodding and smiling up into the air as though projecting onto the ceiling all of the implications of their new-found kinship.

Liz sits through the meeting with her parents and those two wrinkled engines of industry, Mrs. Landry and Dr. Harrison. She remains impenetrable without being belligerent. The four adults seem to dance a waltz of words around her, swaying back and forth between oblique apology and stubborn defensiveness. None of this has anything at all to do with Liz.

Afterward her parents drive her home and her mother tries to talk to her about a crush she once had on her high school teacher, and how, honestly, she would almost rather have Liz be with someone like that cute Mr. Hughes who seemed respon-sible and urbane about matters of sexuality rather than some dopey boy who might forget about protection because—

At which point Liz asks her mother if she can please shut up, and they ride the rest of the way home in silence.

That night, when Liz pulls her bedcovers up to her chin in a tight fist, sleep comes before she can even recognize it. As though her dreams and her waking life are only a blurred tran-sition apart, the absurd and the sensible merely two different languages in which to express the same thing. At one point she wakes suddenly and thinks she sees Mr. Hughes lying in the bed next to her. Except that he is shrunken to the size of a child, and by the way his hands are folded over his chest she infers that he is dead. She feels sorry for him, this puny dead child with purpled eye sockets. To know how little she can do for him. It makes her want to cry.

She turns away and feels her body convulse in something like a sob, but she's already floating away from her own sadness. And in the morning when her alarm goes off she rises eagerly and without hesitation—feeling as though she has been drained of everything in the night, emptied, restored to nothing, and now must go out to find something else to fill herself up with.

chapter 40

"Binhammer!" Ted Hughes says happily on the other end of the line. "I didn't think you would call. The last time I saw you, you were clobbering me in the hallowed halls of education. My shoulder hasn't been right since."

"I spoke with Liz Warren," Binhammer says. He is on the phone in the teachers' lounge. It is the early afternoon, and the room is empty at the moment.

The voice on the other end grows serious. "I was never cut out for teaching, Binhammer. You need apathy. I never had the apathy. Liz—how is she these days?"

He says this as if asking about an old acquaintance.

"Actually she's fine."

"God, I've never seen a mind like hers. You can't plot it on a map."

"I want to talk to you. In person."

"Sure thing. Hey, listen, I'll meet you on the roof of the building in an hour."

"You can't come back here."

"They'll never see me. I can make myself invisible. Besides, I want to see the place one last time."

An hour later, Binhammer makes his way through the hallway and up the stairwell to the roof. There he finds two girls who spin around guiltily when they are discovered. He thinks: There are girls everywhere.

"Mr. Johansen told us to come up here," one of the girls says. "He wants us to draw the horizon."

But they don't seem to have any implements for drawing. And even though it's the middle of winter, they aren't even wearing their regulation blazers. One of the girls shivers, and Binhammer notices that her nipples are evident through the taut ribbed fabric of her turtleneck. Goddamnit. Pink puckered flesh under the fabric of everything. He's tired of it. Made sick by his own weakness.

He looks at them, disgusted. "Is that your cigarette?" He points to a burning butt at the feet of the two girls.

"No," says the one.

"No," says the other.

He gives a casting-off gesture with his head—barely noticeable, the situation isn't worth more—and the two of them scurry back down the stairs.

A few minutes later the door opens again and Ted Hughes bounds through, looking happy and unshackled.

"Here I am, Binhammer. Ready to pay the piper. But be careful, I'm reckless. Haven't you heard? I'm a loose cannon. I would just as soon teach a sonnet as kiss your daughter behind the barn."

"Or my wife."

The smiling mask melts away. Binhammer suddenly thinks of his father. A man of dire strength. A man with a voice like burning when he was angry, when he was tested. And oh how Binhammer liked to test him. He would climb up on the kitchen counters or neglect to wipe off the soles of his shoes before he came in from the rain, just so he could feel that warm, lashing strength of his father's voice. That heat, that fury wrapped around him like a blanket. And then, when he was a teenager, the day that his father broke. Binhammer's coming home at two in the morning, his father slumped in his chair in the dim living room lit ghostly by the screen of the television. *I've been out. That's all, just out. What are you going to do about it?* And his father leaning forward slowly to rise, a great creaking brass colossus—then seeming to change his mind, something heavy pressing him back down, defeating him. *Do what you want. You'll do it anyway*. His strength sapped, tested in too many ways. Like Superman asked to leap a tall building one too many times. And Binhammer's self-loathing. He had made weak that which he thought would always be strong.

This is what he knows: sometimes you battle against things hoping never to be victorious.

And now he sees his father's face in Ted Hughes. The mention of his wife. It was too much.

"I'm sorry," Ted Hughes says, folding up as though he were made of tin. "The truth is, I don't know how to do things right."

"Forget about it," Binhammer says, conciliatory.

"No, really. I never thought I was this kind of man. You picture yourself as something—and then it turns out—"

Then they talk of other things. Of the cigarette butts accumulated up here on the roof. Of the trees in the park, which from this height look like bony monuments of the dead. Of the winter and how long it is.

"So what are you going to do now?" Binhammer asks.

"I'll find something. It won't be hard. I got a glowing recommendation from Mrs. Landry. They want to keep it quiet. It would be bad for business if it got out." He pauses. "Maybe I'll take the rest of the year off. I'd like to go to Egypt. Have you ever been to Egypt? I wouldn't mind seeing those pyramids. Big. Unassailable. What do you think?"

"Sure. Why not."

"Those Nubian—" He stops short and looks at Binhammer sideways. "You know, it seemed okay. The girl, I mean. I don't know what they're saying—"

"I know. You don't have to—"

"It really felt—I don't know. It felt like everything was contained in that moment. As though whatever was going to happen was just going to be sealed up in a jar and put on a shelf in the basement. And that was going to be it. Sealed off. And things would just go on."

"I understand." And he does. His own moment with Dixie Doyle. The impossible, ephemeral perfection of it.

"I guess it couldn't have been that way. Just another delusion, I suppose. If you're going to build a pyramid, people are going to come visit it."

"You've built other things too."

"Do you think so?" He looks hopeful.

"She liked you. The girl. She never liked me. I could never get through to her."

"Well, you have your own fans."

Ted Hughes stretches and leans back against the low parapet overlooking the street. He shuffles his feet against the pebbly tarmac of the roof.

"So do you think you can handle this place without me?"

"I'll do all right, I think," Binhammer smiles. "I never really liked you anyway."

"Likewise. You were a pain in the ass from the beginning."

The two look out over the rooftops into some common distance. It is impossible to tell what they are looking at because what they are looking at converges at the horizon like railroad tracks, and then it doubles back around and winds between them, tying them up in clumsy knots and making them feel embarrassed.

"Well," Ted Hughes says finally, "I better get out of here before they call the FBI. Will you walk behind me and make sure I don't kiss any of the girls on my way out?" He chuckles humbly and heads toward the stairs.

"I guess I forgive you," Binhammer says quickly.

"What?"

"I said I guess I forgive you. About Sarah."

"Oh."

"She's gone. She left."

"Oh my god."

"No, it's okay. She says she'll be back. I think she wants to be done with me for a while. And with you."

Ted Hughes nods. "She'll come back," he reassures Binhammer.

"She'll come back," Binhammer reassures back. "But I think you were right. I wasn't punishing her."

"Then what?"

"I don't know." The wind comes hard for a moment, and he finds himself shivering. He imagines Ted Hughes walking down those stairs, pictures him going out large rather than sneaking away, getting lost among all that girlflesh, waving farewell as he's carried away by those feminine currents, and then through the lobby and out the front door, finding, somewhere in the city, some other outlet for his curious distractible energy, some other person to act as receptacle for his wildly inspired and quickly perishing glances. Romantic. This idea of him. Carried like a muse on the winds of mythology to the next paralytic.

Yes, romantic.

"I wasn't punishing her," Binhammer says.

"Then what?"

"I don't know. See what she saw? Be part of it?"

"But you didn't do anything. You could have had an affair of your own."

"No. That's not what I mean."

"Oh," he says. "Right. Men are funny, aren't they?"

"A riot."

He follows Ted Hughes down the back stairs, through the room where the recycling bins are stacked on top of each other, to the side door leading out onto the sidewalk. There he stops and watches the man continue through the door.

"I'll see you later, Binhammer."

"Yeah. See you later."

The door closes, and Binhammer stands still for a moment. He turns, then stops and turns again toward the door and stops once more. It's true, there are such things as permanencies. Making up his mind, he climbs back up the steps and walks through the corridors flush with students.

In the teachers' lounge he goes directly to the window and gazes down at the street. Ted Hughes still stands in front the building. He hesitates on the sidewalk, looking back and forth—

as though unsure about which direction to go, as though it matters very little which direction he goes. Then he makes up his mind and walks away.

"What are you looking at?"

Walter is the only other person in the lounge. He looks up from his stack of quizzes on the American Revolution and watches Binhammer suspiciously. His grizzled features are emphasized by gray wiry hairs that seem to sprout in unlikely places. He coughs loudly and wipes his mouth with a handkerchief.

"Nothing," Binhammer says. He goes over to his book bag and shuffles through it. He must look busy. He doesn't want to talk to Walter. He flips casually through one pocket and opens another, pretending to look for something. In the next zippered section of his bag he finds a collection of objects that he recognizes. This is where he puts the things he has picked up around the school, like a child's cache of treasures kept in an old cigar box. There are the obscene pink dice he confiscated at the beginning of the year. And the green dial he broke off the copy machine. And a love note from one anonymous girl to another that he found under a desk. These things, charged like the batteries that run the school.

"No, really," Walter says. "You were looking at something. What was it?"

"Ted Hughes," Binhammer retaliates. "He just left."

"Hughes? What the hell is he doing here? I thought they got rid of that pervert." He puts down his stack of papers in preparation for one of his lectures. "I could tell that guy was trouble from the beginning."

"Walter—"

"It's the direction of education nowadays. The sensitive teacher. The teacher who lets students call him by his first name. Your grown-up pal at the front of the class. It's the same with the subject matter. It used to be you could *teach* history. You could tell them what actually happened. You had history in one class and fiction in another. Now it's all *interpretation*." An expression of distaste, as though he has just sipped an inadequate wine.

"No, when I started teaching, teachers were teachers and students were students. And you could tell the difference. Now you go out for a walk, and you find them strolling together. Next thing you know they'll be going steady."

Binhammer doesn't stay to hear any more. He throws open the door and hurries out into the hall. He presses the button for the elevator, but when it doesn't come immediately he decides to take the stairs instead. In the lobby he cries out "Excuse me!" to break up a group of girls standing in front of the doors. Then he's on the street heading quickly in the direction he saw Ted Hughes go.

The world is a Ted Hughes world. Those kids playing on the stoop there. They are Ted Hughes kids. Filled with a filigreed art nouveau beauty, intricate and dense. That bus passing, the shampoo ad pasted on its side. There are layers of meaning to be found there. Onionskin you can flake off with your inquisitive fingertips. The cracked, dirty ice on the sidewalk frozen around leaves of garbage. How can you have the patience to look at everything? How could you not be distracted? To maintain focus, to look straight ahead, is to limit yourself—to feel safe within the ignorance of your own chosen territory. Those women—women everywhere, each one a tropical island with hidden estuaries. How *not* to be a pirate in this extravagance?

He finds Ted Hughes three blocks away, balancing on his toes on the curb—waiting for the light to change.

"Binhammer! What are you doing—"

"You're a great teacher," Binhammer says, catching his breath.

It's something to say, and he says it. It's not exactly what he wants to say—but then, he doesn't know exactly what he wants to say. And when he hears the words come out of his mouth, they sound like a bag of groceries set down wrong on a counter and left to topple over.

It's not exactly right. But it will have to do.

"I just wanted to tell you," he repeats, leaning against the lamppost and smiling at this man—his brother, his usurper, his dark double. "You're the greatest teacher I know."

chapter 41

When Binhammer leaves school at the end of the day, he is one of the first out the lobby doors after the final bell rings. He doesn't want to get caught up in the clumpy mire of girls who will inevitably be milling around outside, looking into the eyes of every teacher who walks by in order to divine, like craggy witches, the contours of the privacy into which he now heads.

He is already down the street when he hears the first high-pitched girlvoices emerging from the doors behind him.

Once around the corner he is safe. He slows his pace and lifts his head.

"Hey, mister."

It's his wife, Sarah, standing before a newsstand, her hands in her pockets. She knows the route he takes home. He's so startled he doesn't know what to say at first. He waits for some clue about what she wants to hear—worried that if he says the wrong thing, she will disappear again into the crowds.

But she says nothing. Eventually he speaks:

"You're back."

"I'm walking home with you," she says, taking his arm with great deliberateness. "And we're stopping at the market. We need some groceries for dinner."

Since the Christmas party at Carmine-Casey over a month ago, neither of them has mentioned what happened. For a while their marriage looked much as it did before. That fraternal affection that comes with endurance over time. The laughter. Sometimes he would reach out and touch her face, and she would tilt her head into his hand. Not unhappy. Supremely not unhappy.

He had wondered how long they could go on this way. Could it be possible to go on indefinitely without talking about things? How long before the silence became a corrosive virus like in some kind of Edward Albee play? But maybe they were superior to the travails of other couples. Maybe they would just keep on going, steamrolling over all convention—invulnerable to the thousand unsettling tremors that upset the foundations of more provincial homes.

Maybe discussion is a medium for the poorer of spirit.

"Ted Hughes is gone," he says, looking straight ahead as they walk.

"For good?"

"I said good-bye to him today."

"Did he say anything about the girl?"

"Not much."

He watches closely for her reaction, but she either doesn't have one or is hiding it too well. She simply nods and squints her eyes into the distance.

"So what are you going to do now?" she asks.

"What do you mean?"

"Will you miss him?"

"This isn't about me."

She laughs. "Sure." She is infuriating. She is the most beautiful person he knows. "Then who is it about, darling?"

They go to the market, which is crowded with people in suits on their way home from work. The men's ties are crooked and undone, as though at some point their necks had expanded to hulkish size, burst the collar, and then shrunk back down again.

He follows her down the fruit and vegetable aisle while she prods at the produce, puts it to her nose, and places it carefully in the basket he's carrying.

"Do you want melon?" she asks.

"Sure."

"Or strawberries?"

"Sure. Either one. I don't care."

"I don't care either."

"Melon."

"Really? I would have thought you would have said strawberries."

"So get strawberries."

"No, I don't care. I just thought . . ." She shrugs and puts a cantaloupe into the basket.

"Are you angry at me?" he says.

"Angry at you? Why would I be?"

"I don't know. You just seem a little mad. Not a lot mad, just a little mad."

"Well, I'm not."

"Okay."

"Should I be?"

"No. . . . I just thought—we never talked about—since I never told you I knew about you and him, I mean . . ."

She shakes her head. Leans up and kisses him on the cheek. "Forget it."

They stop in front of the herbs, and she looks carefully to pick out the cilantro from the parsley and the mint.

"You know," she says, "I really *wanted* to be mad at you. For keeping it a secret. I wanted to be mad."

"But?"

"Well, I'm not in the best position to make judgments."

"That wouldn't stop some people."

"It stopped me."

"The consummate rationalist."

"Besides, it's not like you were the one who compromised the fidelity of the marriage."

"That's true." And he means it. His desire for Sibyl never compromised anything, and now she—and that—feels a long way away.

"Anyway," she continues, "I'm glad you did it. Now there are two reprobates in this marriage instead of just one."

"That's why I did it. It was all for you, sweetheart."

Then she says, "You know what?"

"What?"

"I think we've spent too much time on him. It's almost like he's our son."

He nods. "So we're finished with him, huh?"

"Maybe not forever. But just for the time being. Do you want to be?"

"Okay, let's be finished."

And they are for a few weeks. Then one day an airmail envelope arrives with a postmark from Madrid. It's addressed to Binhammer and has the initials T. H. in the corner where the return address should be. He finds it on the coffee table when he comes home from school.

"Your boyfriend wrote you a letter," Sarah calls out from the other room. "I left it there for you."

He opens it. A single sheet of thin paper, the kind they used to use for typing. It reads:

> I never made it to Egypt. Got to Spain and found plenty to keep me entertained here. No pyramids, but did you know they have the most incredible ruins up in the mountains? Ancient monasteries with collapsed roofs. And if you stay the night you can see the ghosts of monks floating in and out of the doorways. It's the truth. I met an old man who lives by a railroad and he says he's going to be my guide and take me to a little village where the ghosts have come down from the mountains and live side by side with the living. They have mortgages and everything.
>
> That's just the thing about being dead, isn't it? You never really are.
>
> Here's something else. Just before I left I got a letter taped to my mailbox (she came to where I lived!) from that diabolical Lolita in spectacles. You know, the one responsible for my ruin. Anyway, I've been carrying the let-

ter around in my suitcase and I take it out every now and then and reread it over an Orujo at the bar. You'd never guess it was written by a teenage girl. It's about what you would expect of a middle-aged woman who flaunts the conventions of romance and goes to see foreign films by herself. It breaks my heart how perfect they are, these girls, sometimes. But she included a piece of a poem by my namesake, and it occurs to me that you might be able to make some sense of it.

> There is no better way to know us
> Than as two wolves, come separately to a wood.
> Now neither's able to sleep—even at a distance
> Distracted by the soft competing pulse
> Of the other. . . .

I'm off. There are ghosts to discover. I'm telling you, they are beautiful—they seem to be lit by fireflies.

Good luck, my lupine brother. Keep that wilderness alive while I'm gone. Don't let those little scurrying foxes outpace you!

T. H.

Six weeks after Ted Hughes leaves Carmine-Casey, the administration brings in his replacement. She's a quiet, deferential young woman who has just finished a degree in education and seems to cower like a mouse whenever she's around students. Her name is Ms. Prentiss, and she wears clips in her short hair that make her look even younger than she is, so some of the girls take pity on her and protect her, forming an almost maternal shield among them.

Binhammer is assigned to be her mentor and get her settled, and on her second day of teaching she comes into the teachers' lounge looking pale and rent.

"I think the students miss their old teacher," she says to Binhammer.

It seems some of the girls have gotten through the shield and have been testing her tenderness with their teeth.

"Maybe, but they'll forget about him. They have short memories."

Ms. Prentiss nods. "He must have been some teacher."

Binhammer smiles. "His name was Ted Hughes."

He leans forward and waits for her reaction, but there is none.

"Like the poet," he continues. "You know, Sylvia Plath's husband?"

"Oh, I guess I should have known that. I have a lot of catching up to do in my reading."

Binhammer shrugs and leans back again. "It's not important."

"Was he a really good teacher?" She looks at the clock anxiously in anticipation of her next class. "I bet he was."

"Actually," Binhammer replies, "I never really saw him teach." Just that one time. Through the window. His eyes lit up as though by fireflies. "But, yes, the girls really liked him. They were . . . upset when he left. Heartbroken, even. They really were."

acknowledgments

I owe a deep debt of gratitude to Josh Getzler for his faith, persistence, savvy, and sincerity; and to Sally Kim for making this—every single page—a better book. I also want to thank Simon Lipskar for his incisive reading of the manuscript and his support throughout the entire process. And, most of all, thanks to Megan Abbott, who taught me everything I know about teenage girls and grown men.

about the author

Joshua Gaylord teaches high school in Manhattan. He is married to author Megan Abbott and received his Ph.D. in literature from New York University.